BARGAINED

FOR

EXCHANGE

*

James Macomber

James Macomber

Scorpion Books

This book is a work of fiction. Names, characters, places, and
incidents are the products of the author's imagination and/or are
used fictionally. Any resemblance to actual events, locales, or
persons, living or dead, is coincidental.

Scorpion Books, a division of Scorpion, Inc.
PO Box 20127, Bradenton, FL 32404-0127.

Library of Congress Control Number 2001116823

Macomber, James,
   Bargained for Exchange / James Macomber
      p. cm.

ISBN 0-9709538-0-1

First Edition

10 9 8 7 6 5 4 3 2 1

Printed in the United States of America

Innumerable dedications have been made in which the sentiment
is expressed that the book wouldn't have been possible without
a certain person.
I had no idea how true that could be.
This book is dedicated to

Sandy

Who suggested, prompted, encouraged, supported, edited and
occasionally criticized (ever so gently) at every step of the way.
She has become – and is - my *sine qua non. A*nd not just with
regard to this book.

Chapter One

Despite the campus obsession with security, the Parker Quadrangle was almost totally dark at 10:00 PM on the night of September 8. For some unfathomable reason, no outside lighting of any kind had ever been installed and the only sources of illumination came from the overflow from the interiors of the buildings which formed the four boundaries of the quad. On this night in particular, there was no light spilling from the Gold Recreational Complex which formed the eastern boundary of the quad. And neither was there any light emanating from the classroom buildings on the north and south edges of the area.

In the office building which formed the west side of the Parker Quadrangle, John Cann, Visiting Professor of Law, was sitting at his desk, the only illumination in the room provided by the green shaded floor lamp which stood by the door on the opposite wall. With its sixty watt bulb, it made no discernible contribution to the lighting of the Quad.

Cann wasn't actually sitting at his desk. He was behind it but turned with his back to it, his large imitation tufted leather chair - really brown vinyl - tilted back and his feet up on the painted pale green metal cover that sat atop a radiator which would allegedly heat the room if and when needed. He did his best thinking this way - just staring out the window into space and letting his

1

thought processes take him where they would. It had stood him in good stead in the past and he found it relaxing.

He was in his office, Room 215 of the Page Building, at 10:00PM the night before the first day of classes because he figured that he should be preparing some kind of outline for the Contracts class he would be teaching for the first time tomorrow. The original plan had been for Cann to stick with his specialty of International Law which would have been fine with him. But just two days ago his friend - and the Dean of the Law School - had announced that he - Dean Roger Walder - was in a bind and would John mind taking over a couple of first year contracts classes.

As with most fields of endeavor, academic preparation - while vital to what follows - demands a different viewpoint from the actual practice. So, although John Cann had been involved in numerous contract negotiations involving transactions in amounts up to the billions of dollars and trillions of other currencies - indeed precisely because he had been involved in such transactions - he agreed that he needed to ratchet down his perspective and get back to the basics. As Dean Walder had said, he needed to "come down from the macro to the micro."

And so he had come to sit and stare and do what he could to free his mind of the excess intellectual weight that had accumulated over the years which would interfere with communicating the elementary concepts of contract law. In first year law school, one learns the basics of what goes into making a contract - as well as what goes into making an enforceable contract. They were not one and the same.

Later, one spends years finding and learning - and learning to find - the exceptions and modifications to the basics. It was discovering a methodology of re-simplifying the concepts for himself so that he could pass them on to the students that was giving him some difficulty.

Then the light came on.

Not in his mind, but from the Rec Center across the Quad.

Because of the almost total darkness, the sudden illumination was striking and startling. Cann leaned forward in his chair and peered the forty or so yards across the Quad at the source of the light and saw that someone had entered one of the dance rooms on the quad side of the Gold rec center. Because of the light, he could see clearly into the room which was mirrored along the entire length of the inner wall. The end walls weren't mirrored but had rails along them for the numerous exercises that Cann used to know the names of - or some of them at least. The outer wall of the room which was the west wall of the building and looked out on the quad was entirely glass from floor to ceiling with motorized curtains that could be used to completely close off the view to the outside.

The person who had come into the dance room was a young women who was apparently a student at the university. She appeared to be too young to be an instructor. But Cann had begun to notice that as he progressed through his forties, the identifiable ranges of ages among groups were becoming more and more blurred. In any case, because he could see so clearly - since the room was the only source of light around and all the glass magnified it - he still would be very surprised to learn that this particular young lady was more than a freshman or sophomore.

He wondered briefly what anyone would be doing there at 10:00 PM on a Sunday and then wondered how this young woman would even have gotten into the building. Notwithstanding the lighting situation in the Quad, security was such that there was no way it would have been left unlocked. Of course, it certainly wasn't unheard of for one of the professors or instructors or even day attendants to allow a particularly promising student to have access to the facilities at will - even after hours. Cann didn't pursue the thought any further but continued to look over at the lighted room.

Then, as he watched, the young lady began to undress. Not provocatively - nor with extraneous movement of any kind - not even watching herself in the mirror. She was removing her clothing in a totally matter of fact manner with complete unconcern as if she were at home in the privacy of her room. It occurred to Cann from her movements and demeanor that she was acting as if she didn't know she could be seen.

But then why would she know that? From inside the room, with the pitch blackness outside and the bright lights inside, the outer wall would act as a mirror - and if she didn't already know it was a window, she wouldn't be able to tell from inside.

Cann was no prude and he didn't find it intrinsically evil for him to appreciate the sight of the nude body of a woman about half his age - or less. He watched as the young woman pulled the blue tank top over her head and as she let the white shorts slide down to her feet before stepping out of them. Then, still entirely without self-consciousness, she reached behind her back, unhooked her bra, and slid it forward over her arms before letting it slide through her fingers to floor. Without any pause or hesitation, she then removed the white string panties she had on and dropped them into the small heap of clothing to her right.

Only then did the young lady look at herself in the mirror. Again, not in any kind of provocative or prurient way but simply with the casual interest of an observer glancing at an object looking for imperfections.

As far as Cann could see, she wasn't going to find any. She looked to be about five foot four with a body that was not slender but neither did it have any excess about it. Her breasts were of the shape that was almost perfectly round with no acknowledgement of the existence of gravity. And her bottom was of similar contour curving almost suddenly at the top of slender athletically muscled legs.

Then she began to move. It appeared she was doing warm-ups starting with stretching exercises. The total simplicity of her movements combined with her lack of self-consciousness - and clothing - turned the essentially antiseptic activity into an erotic ballet.

But Cann's libido, which was enjoying the scene, had begun to hear an opposing viewpoint. He had no daughter of his own and in fact had never had any children at all - "that he knew of" as the old joke went. But, like most reasonably decent men of good will, he had a latent paternalism that had started to make its presence known.

To Cann, there was nothing wrong with what the girl was doing. If she knew her surroundings and knew that people were or might be watching and she didn't mind, then that was okay. But what if, as Cann strongly suspected, she wasn't aware that she could be seen.

He turned and reached into the lower right hand drawer of his desk for the campus telephone directory. He looked back at the dance room where the young lady was still exercising but he could see no phone. It was unlikely that there was one there anyway. It was also unlikely that there were any phones in the building other than in the offices or perhaps a couple of public phones which wouldn't be listed in the campus directory anyway.

Then Cann thought, "What would I tell her, anyway? 'Do you know you can be seen and you're being watched'?" That would really help the situation, wouldn't it. If she already knew, she wouldn't care. If she didn't know she'd be embarrassed. "But at least she could stop if she wanted to," thought Cann.

Then Cann thought about going over to the building himself but rejected that idea immediately. He pictured himself walking across the Quad and then peering up against the window as he rapped on it to get the young lady's attention.

"Just as a campus cop comes along," he said aloud as he rejected the thought. "That's all I'd need." The possibility made him hesitate - made him second guess his own thoughts of involving himself - and he resented the fact that it did.

It was something that always bothered Cann - what he called 'villainization'. Decent people automatically having the worst motives ascribed to their actions for no other reason than that a lack of villains might create a void in someone's agenda. He resented the idea that he - and others - might find themselves basing their actions or inaction on a reluctance to expose themselves to phony indignation and false accusations. Like all decent men, he wanted to think that he would stand up to injustice despite the cost. "What's that quote?" he thought.

"Something like, 'for evil to triumph, all that is necessary is for good men to do nothing'."

But then Cann's dilemma was resolved for him. Through the pathway that ran along the north side of the rec center, he saw the blue lights of a campus patrol's Isuzu Trooper. Then he noticed three campus security personnel - two males and a female - walking quickly down the path toward the Quad. They reached the northeast corner of the center and turned and walked along the outside of the glass wall all the while looking into the dance room at the oblivious young lady who was just finishing her nude exercises and was beginning to practice dance movements. The campus cops disappeared from view as they went into the rec center but almost immediately reappeared when they entered the lighted dance room.

Any doubts Cann had about whether or not the dancer knew she could be seen - or cared - were erased when the first of the two males walked into the dance room. The young dancer had her back to the door as the cop came through but turned immediately when he walked in. Her eyes went wide open and she seemed to cross the room in one leap to where her clothes were lying in a pile. In what seemed like one movement, she picked up her shorts and shirt and tried to hold each - ineffectively as it turned out - in front of her to cover her own top and bottom.

The second male cop followed the first into the room and the two of them stepped aside as the third officer - the female - came in. The two males never took their eyes off the young girl who held her clothes between herself and them but who continued to expose her rear view to the mirrored wall opposite the windowed wall. The way she was standing her face was also visible to Cann and he could see that her expression had by this time changed from one of fear to one of bewilderment with a touch of anger. At that point, it appeared that the the female campus cop told the young lady about the glass wall because her head snapped almost violently to the left and her eyes got wider than ever as did her mouth. To her credit, the young dancer seemed to regain her composure quite quickly and said something to the female cop who in turn spoke to the male cops, who then turned their backs. It appeared to Cann however, that at least one of them had positioned himself so that he could continue to watch through the mirror.

As soon as the two males turned away, the girl straightened noticeably and adopted a posture of exaggerated proudness as she dropped the shorts and top and put on her underwear and then the shorts and top. When she was fully dressed, the two males came over and each took her by an arm to lead her out. Cann expected that she would be sent on her way when they came out of the rec center and was surprised when, instead of simply releasing her, the campus police continued to escort her, rather forcefully Cann thought, along the side of the rec center, and around the corner and, it appeared, back to their vehicle.

Part of campus security's job was to escort students back to their dorms or apartments at night on request. That was commendable. But the way they were treating this young lady seemed to indicate that she was in custody - and rather than escorting her home, it seemed clear that they were taking her to campus police headquarters. That seemed odd.

Chapter Two

Cann wheeled the 87 Corvette into the faculty parking lot and into his assigned slot. Even though he had bought the car new almost ten years earlier, it only had about thirteen thousand miles on it. For the greater part of the intervening period, it had spent far more time in storage than on the road thanks to his frequent absences. For the next ten months or so, Cann figured that the car would get pretty regular use.

As he turned off the ignition, it was eleven minutes to eight - Monday AM. With that many minutes to spare before the contracts class with the first year law students, he headed at a half-run for his office to pick up his copy of the text to be used in the contracts class - "Cases on Contracts".

"A nice creative title," he thought. Of course, he should have taken the book with him when he left the Page building the previous night but he had just plain forgotten it. After witnessing the events in the rec center of the night before, he had simply turned back toward his desk and mulled it over for a while and then just got up, turned off the light and left.

He also hadn't formulated any lesson plan for this first class of his. Ultimately, he had decided that twenty years of experience counted for something even in academia and he would just wing it. He took his role and responsibility to the students seriously but at the same time knew that he was dealing with first year law students with little or no idea of what awaited them - and he had a few ideas.

He unlocked the door to his office and went straight to the desk where the book lay just where he knew he had left it. As he picked it up and turned to head out the door and up to the classroom on the third floor, he noticed the pink message slip on the floor where it had apparently been slipped under his door.

"See me. Two messages for you." It was signed "Roger."

*   *   *   *

It had been barely three months earlier that Cann had agreed to the suggestion that he take a sabbatical from the Washington DC law firm of Loring, Matsen, & Gould where he had been for nine years, the last four as Senior Associate. In reality, the sabbatical was more than a suggestion. The reaction in some circles - the center of one very high circle to be precise - to his genuinely principled refusal to accept an assignment for the first time in his career had been considered by many to be unduly harsh and out of proportion to the perceived affront. But that's how things were. It was only the friendship - and backbone - of Senior Partner Arthur Matsen that had made Cann's exile a temporary one.

So on a warm June day, he had called Roger Walder, his law school friend and drinking buddy of considerable skills who, in their law school days, had become a legend for his capacity to consume at the weekly "bar review" held in the Moot Court room on most Fridays.

Walder, despite the number of brain cells that had to have expired each weekend had made quite a success of himself. Actually, Cann thought that he'd just read somewhere that the death of brain cells by alcohol was no longer a truism? Like eggs being bad for you and Catholics going to hell for eating meat on Fridays.

In any case, after a relatively brief stint with the Justice Department, Walder had returned to teach at the Jefferson Law

Center of prestigious Charlestown University in Charleston, South Carolina. And there he had found his calling.

As it turned out, he was an excellent teacher and, it was quickly discovered, an administrator of no small consequence as well. Before his seventh year at Jefferson was complete, he found himself the Dean of the Law School at the Jefferson Law Center.

Cann and Walder shared many fond memories of law school - those that they could remember, anyway - and had kept in touch after graduation. They had developed a close friendship during those three very significant years in their lives partly because they were both a bit older than most of the rest of the students in their law school class. They also shared the distinction of having been two of the top students in the class which came as a great surprise to most of their classmates. Given their public image of "party animals," most of the other law students had no idea of their academic accomplishments until the moment their Juris Doctor degrees were awarded to them. Both often recalled with amusement the consternation of their fellow graduates when Walder's "cum laude" and Cann's "magna cum laude" were announced at graduation. One young woman on whom Walder had focused attention on several occasions to no avail came up to him after the ceremony and just stood before him in silence. Finally she muttered, "I had no idea," and took his hand, not letting go and making it it very clear that then and there he was now held in sufficient esteem to be eligible for her favors. Being a contrary sort, Walder had simply said, "I guess you really can't judge a book by its cover, hmmm?" And walked away.

And even though that was twenty years ago, Walder's and Cann's paths had crossed enough during the years that followed that they were always at least vaguely aware of the others whereabouts or station. And they kept in touch.

So it was no huge surprise and a stroke of luck for both when Cann called advising Walder of his forced leave of absence and suggesting they get together. And it was with genuine excitement and pleasure that Walder noted to his friend that the Johnson Chair for Visiting Legal Scholars was open and that, given Cann's credentials, combined with Walder's considerable influence, Walder was sure that Board would award him the chair for the ensuing academic year.

"I have to warn you, though, John, the world has changed in at least one very significant aspect here in legal academia." He paused dramatically even as Cann, equally dramatically, failed to rise to the bait. "There are no 'bar reviews' anymore", he announced solemnly. He was referring to the school sponsored keg of beer that was made available every Friday evening in the Moot Court Room for the students.

Cann no longer consumed the quantities of beer he once had but the reference brought back fond memories - some more blurred than others - and he asked why.

"Because we teach our students too well." Walder explained. "On three separate occasions, some students were arrested for DUI after attending the bar review. - And guess what? "

Cann half-chuckled although he didn't find it funny. "They sued the school for letting them drink on the premises, right?" It wasn't even a guess.

"You got it, my friend," Walder rued, "and we lost each time. So, we stopped the bar reviews. The rest of the students of course loved that and cold-shouldered the students who sued. So - guess what, again?"

"What?"

"We got sued again by one of the same DUI students on the basis that our action in canceling the bar reviews was the cause of their social 'ostracization?'" At opposite ends of the phone line, unseen to each other, both men shook their heads in unison. "But at least we won that one." Walder made a 'whew' sound of not entirely mocking relief. "Still like to take a shot at the chair?"

"Sure, why not. I assume it pays enough to cover my bar bill, anyway. Right?" Cann continued deliberately. "Of course I'll need other benefits to make up for the loss of the 'bar review'?"

"Like what?" Walder waited. He was pretty sure that his long friendship with Cann would preclude any outrageous demands but still Cann was very well know for being a difficult negotiator.

"Dinner - your treat - weekly."

Relief. "You got it." Walder got a little more serious. "But you know, John, This chair really does have a lot of prestige to it in legal circles. It'll look good on your CV. And you'll get your fifteen minutes of fame - sort of - at the reception for new faculty. You'll be introduced with no small fanfare to your alleged peers."

Cann tightened his lips across his face. "Any way I can pass on that, Roger."

"Well, I can't put a gun to your head but it is traditional to the point of near mandatory. It would be awkward for me to explain why the Johnson Chair wasn't there. You really should do it, John."

Enough said. "Okay, I'll be there," Cann conceded. "By the way, who's the Johnson in the name of the chair?"

"Well, some people say Arte," Walder deadpanned, "but it actually refers to Lyndon. Any problem with that?"

"No." Cann paused when he got the sense that to Walder that was a serious question. "Why would I have a problem with who the chair is named after, Roger."

"John, my boy, let me give you part one of your orientation. There are people on the faculty here who refuse to enter certain buildings because they're named after someone who's politically incorrect. You've spent the last eighteen or so years in the real world of business and realpolitik." He paused. "At least in most ways it's more real than this." Then he got more serious. "I, on the other hand, have spent the same period in an environment where form rules mightily supreme over substance. Do almost anything you want as long as you say the right things. Say the wrong thing - as defined subjectively a thousand different ways depending on whose listening - and somebody takes offense. Hell, almost everybody takes offense at something at least twice a day and more often than not, its not even real offense. It's like pretend offense - monopoly money - a way to keep score and pile up points to be held on account and used when needed."

"So explain to me how that differs from Washington?" Cann expected Walder to chuckle but he didn't.

"I don't know. Maybe it doesn't. All I know of your world since we graduated is the public part. I only know some of what you've been doing. I know who Loring Matsen mostly represents and I know you play in a very tough league. But don't underestimate the politics of academia. The stakes may be different - maybe not - and the violence is intellectual - usually. But within the context of what's considered important here, these people play hardball."

Then Walder lightened somewhat. "But, I'll look out for you, John. Don't worry. Uncle Roger won't let you down."

"Thanks unk."

"See you in September, as the old song goes."

"Careful, Roger, you're showing your age."

*　*　*　*

Cann reached the amphitheatre-like classroom with about a minute to spare. Even so, except for one student sitting in the first row directly in front of the dais, he was the first to enter the classroom. "Nothing ever changes," he thought. "Never enter a classroom until the last minute."

He went to the front of the room and stepped up onto the raised dais which held a desk and chair in front of a blackboard. He put down the casebook he had gotten from his office and parked himself on a corner of the desk and waited for the students to file in.

The classroom could seat about 400 students arranged in center, right, and left sections of curving rows of chairs that sloped up and away from him toward the back of the room. The center section was twenty rows across and ten deep - the side sections ten across and ten deep. As the students filed in at what seemed to be one second before eight AM, Cann noted with amusement and no surprise that the first seats filled were in rear center rows. Only after those seats were taken did the remaining students spill over into the next row down and then the next and then the next. It reminded Cann of one of those pyramids of champagne glasses one sees at wedding receptions where the lower glasses are filled by the overflow of the one above. As their numbers grew, the students found themselves coming ever closer and closer to the front of the classroom - and the dreaded professor. By the time the flow of students had ceased, the center sections was filled except for the first two rows and both side sections remained empty. Cann wondered if the three students who had taken seats in that front row - and had done so even while other seats to the rear were still empty - would be the stars or the butt kissers of the class.

In any case, he faced 183 faces - some eager, some bored, some appearing to be actually frightened. 183 total strangers that Cann was supposed to lead, prod, coerce, cajole, and, perhaps, intimidate for the coming academic year.

But at the moment, he had a more practical concern.

"God," he thought to himself, "Am I really going to know all these people by name before the year is out?"

And he would be teaching three other classes each day as well. But truth be told, he would probably have all of the names down within the week.

* * * *

Notwithstanding the events of the night before, Janie Reston had actually slept rather well. That was partly because of the stresses she had experienced and partly because, after all was said and done, she had not gotten back to her room until almost two AM - and she was now rising at six AM.

But the main reason that Janie had slept was that she was a person who just didn't lose sleep. Although she often laughingly told herself and others that she was "but a mere child," she had a stability that belied her youth.

As she entered her first year at Charlestown, she was only seventeen. She wouldn't be eighteen until October of that year. Even so, she was starting her college career as a second semester freshman having taken - and excelled at - several college level equivalency tests for which she had been awarded college credits before she ever set foot on the campus. While she was not committed to any particular time-table, she quietly and confidently expected that she would graduate from college before she was twenty-one.

She wasn't usually an early riser and didn't particularly care for being up at six AM. Indeed, she had structured her own schedule so that her first class was never earlier than ten AM. But in another exhibition of wisdom beyond her years, she knew when to take advice. And Dean Walder, who had been called to campus security at eleven PM the night before had given her some advice that required her to rise at this hour.

She had experienced some apprehension - even real fear - when the campus security people didn't appear to be taking her back to her room the night before. That was tempered somewhat by her knowledge that she didn't know the campus all that well yet and maybe they were just going a different way. But then she thought that she didn't even know for sure that they were campus security and was relieved when they pulled up outside what she recognized as campus security headquarters. But she was also confused.

"Why am I here?" she asked. "How come you didn't just take me back to the dorm?"

The female officer answered. "We need to take a report, Jenny. It shouldn't take too long."

"Its Janie," she noted evenly. "But why do you need to take a report. I didn't hurt anyone - except myself maybe."

"Because there's been a formal complaint filed. And when that happens, we have to take a report for the record."

"Oh great," Janie snorted, "so now you're telling me that not only does the world have to know how dumb I am but that somebody saw me and they're going to make an issue of it."

"That's about it, Jenny - Janie, sorry."

"Who filed the complaint?" Janie asked.

"We're not at liberty to say."

"What?"

"That's confidential information - its private."

"Yeah, and I thought what I was doing was, too. How come my privacy doesn't count?"

The campus security officer saw that she was being outmaneuvered and got down to business. "We need you to write down your version of events. When you're done, we'll give you a ride back to your dorm."

This was becoming too much. Janie concentrated for a moment.

"If I remember the University handbook, you have to do that anyway." Janie closed her eyes and in her mind read more of the handbook as it pertained to disciplinary action.

"Correct me if I'm wrong, but when a complaint is filed against a student, they have to appear before some sort of board, right?"

The female officer was trying to be friendly and cordial.

"I don't really know how it works after we're done here, Janie. I think you're right. But why won't you...?"

"And you call the dean, right?"

"A dean. The dean on call. Right."

"So where's the dean?"

Janie wasn't sure if it would be to her advantage to make them get a dean in at this time of night, but her instincts told her that she needed to get some degree of control.

The female officer sighed and got up. "I'll phone the dean on call. You just wait here."

And as luck would have it, the dean on call that night was Roger Walder, Dean of the Law School. Janie was impressed - with the title at least - and hoped she'd made the right decision.

It wasn't long before she was pretty sure she had.

Dean Roger Walder sat silently as the female officer recounted the events of the evening. When she was done, Walder sat for several moments staring blankly at the officer. Finally he spoke.

"And?"

The female officer stared blankly back. After a moment, she said, "And what? That's what happened."

"That's it?" Walder's eyes were wide and his brows almost touched his hairline. "This young woman didn't realize she could be seen. By your own version of the facts, there wasn't exactly a crowd gathered out side the rec center, and now she's facing charges on the first day of class?"

"Give us a break, Dean, I think its an overreaction on someone's part too but we can't pick and choose the rules to follow. We didn't write the policy."

"Yeah, I know. Nothing personal." Walder thought for a moment. " But I'll tell you what. The rules you're following also entitle Ms. Reston to be represented during the disciplinary process and I am interpreting that to mean that such representation, in order to be meaningful, should occur before she commits her thoughts in writing and only after she knows what she is being charged with. As the Dean of the Law School and the dean on call, I would be inclined to think that I should not be that representative but she is entitled to representation nonetheless. I would suggest to you that you can fulfill your obligation to file a report by writing down your version of the events as you know them and adding that Ms. Reston elected to confer with her representative prior to responding to the complaint."

The campus security officer was cowed.

"Jeez, Dean, how am I supposed to debate the rules with the Dean of the Law School?" She looked imploringly. "Will you please at least tell my chief that I tried?"

Walder was sympathetic. "I'll do better than that. I'll put it in writing." He gestured for the security officer to give him a pen and paper and as he wrote, he spoke to Janie.

"And Ms. Reston, if you wish, I can give you a ride back to your dorm and the name of someone you might wish to talk to."

Chapter Three

"Jesus Christ, Arthur! A fax in a golf cart?"

The ringing of the facsimile machine in Arthur Matsen's cart had begun just as Carlton Bishop was beginning his backswing on the first tee of the Congressional Country Club at precisely 7:06 AM that Monday morning. Fortunately for Bishop, the unwelcome noise had come early enough in his swing for him to stop himself. He took a breath, composed his thoughts, and re-set himself to begin again. When - finally - he was ready, he took the three wood slowly back away from the ball, reached the top of his backswing while at the same time mentally checking to see if the clubhead and the alignment of his left arm from his elbow to his shoulder were precisely pointed down his target line. At that point, he knew that his focus should have been on nothing except striking the golf ball solidly at the bottom of the swing but in reality his mind was completely absorbed in a chaotic jumble of trying to think of forty different components of a golf swing all at the same time - and make sure they were all correct and properly adjusted. This, of course, could not be done. So, as always, he found himself thinking about none of them and instead was concentrating on trying to concentrate as he brought the club down and toward the ball. As if that were not bad enough, at the precise instant before the club was to arrive at the spot where the little white ball had been sitting patiently awaiting its arrival, the fax transmission finished, emitting the abrasive drawn out beep familiar to office workers everywhere.

Bishop didn't miss the ball completely but the arc of the swing at the bottom came up just prematurely enough so that the bottom edge of the club hit about three-quarters of the way up the backside of the ball starting it out on a downward trajectory but with tremendous topspin on it much like a "follow" shot in pool. The ball slammed into the ground not six inches in front of where Bishop's tee used to be - it was now shattered and scattered in several different locations around him. The golf ball gouged out a mark down and through the turf's surface until its dimpled texture found a grip in the soft clay underneath the grass causing the force on the forward spin of the ball to propel it up and forward, rolling and bouncing about fifty yards or so before it came to a stop in the middle of what would be fairway if the ball had traveled far enough to reach it.

In his mind and heart, Bishop knew that it was unlikely he would have struck the ball solidly in any case. He seldom did. But it is far less unpleasant to blame an external force than it is to accept the consequences of one's own inabilities. So almost immediately at the point of impact and before the ball had even cleared the front of the tee, Bishop had turned to glare again at Arthur Matsen who was being kind enough to suppress the smile that was aching to come out.

"Goddamn it, Arthur! I'm taking another one."

"Okay, Carl. Just reload. Mulligan's on the first tee anyway."

"No way, Arthur, this doesn't even count as a mulligan because of that damn high-tech vehicle you call a golf cart. I still have my mulligan."

Matsen finally felt able to release the smile. "Of course, Carl. You've still got your mulligan."

Bishop stepped up to the ball, went all the way through his ritual once again, and swung. This time, the ball went almost straight up in the air but at least it was straight. As Bishop stood on the tee searching down the fairway for the ball, it continued to climb. Finally, he turned back to Matsen and asked, "Did you see where it went?" just about the time that it finally plopped down no more than ten feet from the first one. Matsen, still laughing on the inside, calmly observed, "Sure glad you didn't waste a mulligan, Carl."

Too angry to return to the cart, Bishop walked forward off the front of the tee muttering, "It wasn't a mulligan. I'm playing the first one, anyway."

Matsen stayed where he was with the cart. Bishop's ball was not far enough down the fairway for Matsen to bother pulling the cart forward to it so he remained by the tee. He knew that Bishop would use the three wood again anyway so he didn't need another club. And Matsen knew that his friend's slow burn would extinguish fairly quickly - unless he topped the next shot, too - which he did.

Matsen took a deep breath, mostly in empathy to his friend and reached down to retrieve the fax. As with most of the faxes he received, it was on the letterhead of Loring, Matsen, & Gould which, in addition to the three name partners, contained the names of the thirty or so associates at the firm, the jurisdictions some or all were licensed in, and the phones, faxes, and telex numbers of the various office locations around the world. The information at the top took up almost a third of the entire sheet. In addition, almost the entire bottom third was taken up by the standard - and unenforceable - facsimile disclaimer whereby notice is given to a recipient that, if they should receive the fax in error and dare to read it, all sorts of dire but unspecified ills will befall them. It left little room for a message.

But this message was short. "Wagner PIR. Need DH - AAA or better. Second and three."

Arthur Matsen groaned over the use of the sports references instead of plain english in the message. Once thought to be cooly cryptic, it was now a mere affectation, thankfully rarely used, that was a throwback to the World War II device of asking potential infiltrators a baseball question to check their American-ness.

That was not surprising considering the background of the founder of the firm, Gordon Loring who, unlike many of his

World War II OSS colleagues, had not moved on into the newly formed CIA after World War II. He had taken his discharge and his GI Bill and gone on to college and then the University of Virginia Law School before returning to Washington to form the firm in 1952.

To be sure, the relationships formed in wartime were enduring and as soon as Loring passed the bar and hung out his shingle, his former colleagues saw to it that his firm did not lack for clients, some of whom seemed to spring into life as needed and where needed and just as quickly disappear. But they paid the bills - and well.

In some circles, it was thought that the Law Office of Gordon Loring, later Loring & Matsen, and still later Loring, Matsen, & Gould was not a real law firm - that it was some sort of a cover. But it was a real law firm. Of course the opposite impression was not harmed in the least by the firms close associations with the intelligence community nor by the affectations of the intelligence community which developed in the Loring Matsen culture.

It seemed that everybody had to be an expert in something that had nothing to do with their job. Preferably the less macho the better. Loring, like the legendary James Angleton, had been something of an amateur horticulturist. Instead of orchids, he had developed an extraordinary knowledge of hibiscus and its unlimited potential for hybrid coloration. While summer in Washington was ideal for hibiscus, the unpredictability and variability of the weather the rest of the year caused Loring to eventually spend a fortune on an artificial climate in a section of his large home so that he could indulge his passion year round. He had eschewed the bow tie, however.

Matsen thought of other members of the firm. Berk had his photography. Cunningham arguably could quote more Shakespeare from memory than that guy on Pantomime Quiz years ago - what was his name? Hans Conreid. Wagner had his rare wines and Boulier - what was Boulier's obsession? Oh yes - chess master - perhaps grandmaster by now.

Being the contrarian that he was, Matsen didn't have one single obsession. He, like Cann, thought of himself as a generalist. Both of them wanted to know more about everything that there was the slightest reason to know anything at all about.

And neither of them ever used the vapid sports metaphors. Matsen was surprised that a serious professional like Brian Iverson had. Of course, it was more likely that whomever had relayed the message through the Frankfurt office had added the references. The more senior people in the firm were aware of Matsen's antipathy to the device and avoided it. The newer people soon learned that lesson as well. But Matsen hadn't banned it outright. When he had once mentioned doing so, it had been suggested that it was "important to the troops." "These things are part of the identity, Arthur," he had been told. "Like badges of honor." Or "tartans to the Scots, if you will." To Matsen, however, they were more like the secret coonskin cap tail waggings of the Loyal Order of Racoons or something.

If the medium was frivolous, however, this message was not. As much as he disliked the terms, he understood them. PIR was 'permanent injured reserve' - that meant dead. The message said that Wagner was dead and needed to be replaced. That would be a real problem under the circumstances - more difficult than usual. Cann should have been there in the first place, anyway. But then, he might be dead instead of Wagner.

No. Probably not. Regardless of the circumstances of Wagner's death, John would have been immeasurably harder to kill.

But over and above the irritating use of the sports codes, the brevity of the message was also a problem. Exactly what had happened was unclear. The message gave only the most skeletal information .

The first part was unambiguous - Wagner was dead.

The second part of the message was superfluous. As senior partner of the firm, but also case manager on this file, Matsen certainly didn't need to be told that a replacement was necessary or that the replacement needed to be an advanced player. Major league only or, in a pinch, someone ready for the big time.

The last reference was to the urgency of the situation. Matsen noted that the first reference was to baseball while the second referred to American football. The mixing of references within a single message also bothered Matsen. Not because he was a grammatical purist - which he was - but because it created unnecessary problems. Some people in the field thought that switching about among frames of reference showed cleverness and creativity on their part. Not Matsen. It merely allowed for ambiguity and ambiguity could be deadly.

In this case, however, it wasn't critical. "No harm, no foul, I guess," Matsen thought with a conscious sense of irony. Since he was fully informed on the matter Wagner was involved in - had been involved in - he knew the analysis to be in line with his own opinion. Second and three - no great urgency.

Matsen looked at the top of the faxed page to read the where and when of the transmission. Across the top it read in very small print: 011-34-567-0938   Frankfurt Am Main - Loring Matsen - 12:24CET.

Matsen then looked at the signature line at the end of the message and saw no initials there indicating that the message was composed by a staff member. Matsen would have been surprised indeed to see a "BI" on that line - Brian Iverson was the manager of the Frankfurt office and not one to engage in what Matsen had come to think of as the juvenile code shenanigans.

Even though Wagner had been working primarily out of the Geneva office, Matsen wasn't surprised that the fax had come from the Frankfurt office. He was aware that Wagner had planned to drive his restored Austin-Healey 3000 from Geneva to Frankfurt for the Monday meeting on the IMF loan to the new Palestinian Authority. When Wagner had first been given the assignment, he had accepted it in an appropriately business-like manner. But since it would mean he would be detailed to Geneva for as long as six months, he knew he would finally get the chance to do something he had wanted to do for as long as he could remember. Open it up on the Autobahn.

Like many of the Loring Matsen associates, and in addition to his wine hobby, he was a sports car enthusiast. It was unclear whether the high number of automotive aficionados at Loring Matsen was because people with like interests were drawn to the same profession or location, or whether they absorbed the fascination from each other. But it was almost a rite of passage for those with the taste for it to want to take their restored whatever out on the autobahn and let it out, at least on those stretches of the autobahn where there was still no speed limit. While the assignment placed Wagner in Switzerland - Geneva to be precise - there would be ample opportunity for him to head north and live his dream.

"Or die trying," Matsen thought. Since the faxed message to Matsen came from Frankfurt, it seemed safe to assume that Wagner's demise had occurred near the end of his trip. But at that point, that was all Matsen knew and he needed to know the details of what had happened before he made any decisions. He picked up the cell phone on the cart and pressed the #1 speed dial number.

*   *   *   *

Even at just past 7:00 AM, the huge chest-high solid mahogany reception desk in the foyer of the Washington DC office of Loring, Matsen, & Gould was staffed. Unlike most other law firms, there was someone there twenty-four hours a day - seven days a week. Loring Matsen's clientele, its world-wide scope, and its line of work required that it be so.

The chief paralegal and Matsen's right hand was already in the office at that early hour and saw on the computer screen who was calling. She punched the incoming button on the keyboard even before the night receptionist was able to get to it.

"Good morning, Mr. Matsen. What can I do for you?"

"Good morning, Milly. Been there long?"

"Not too. Have you seen the fax from Frankfurt."

"I just read it. You forwarded it here, I presume?"

24

"Yes sir, it was already here when I arrived. I knew you'd want to see it right away. I have a call placed into Frankfurt right now to get you some follow up with Iverson."

Mattsen wasn't even surprised. All of the people who worked at Loring Matsen were absolutely top of the line and rarely if ever needed direction. Everyone knew what needed to be done and did it. Even apparent beginners were not beginners. It was often said - inside and outside the firm - that there were no entry level positions at Loring Matsen. You had to know your job before you walked in the door.

"Thanks, Milly. Please forward him to this phone as soon as he gets back to you. And, Milly, once we have confirmation, please send the firm's condolences to Carrie Wagner. The usual, please."

Milly didn't need to be told that either but she simply said, "Of course, Mr. Matsen." She had already entered a tickler into the computer to remind the firm to send out the standard benefits information in one week. The widow Wagner would learn that Loring Matsen was a very generous firm indeed.

Matsen then hesitated. He was not one to make promises but once made, it was a matter of honor to him that they be kept. Thus, he had to quite literally force himself to give Milly this last order.

"And, Milly, find John Cann for me."

*　　*　　*　　*

Sembach - a picture-postcard German village, population about three hundred, sat just off Highway N40 about 15 miles north of Kaiserslautern in the region of Southwest Germany called the Rheinland Palatinate. It was not actually accurate to describe the village of Sembach as off N40. It was right on it. The rear of the buildings which formed its western boundary actually backed directly on N40 and the street which ran in front of those buildings ran almost straight and directly off N40 at almost no angle at all. Except for the fact that it was reduced from the two lanes of N40 to the single lane of the village, the main street -

Hauptstrasse - of Sembach village seemed almost to be an extension of the federal highway - just a right hand fork in the road. Because Hauptstrasse and N40 split as they did, the southernmost end of the building which divided the fork of the two roads was exceedingly narrow and came almost to a point. The building widened as it extended north and away from the fork and overall was shaped like a wedge of cheese.

It was into the point of that wedge that Ted Wagner had driven the 1964 Austin-Healey 3000 at high speed earlier that morning. A check of the auto's papers which were found in the remarkably intact glove box revealed to the Stadt Polizei Wachmeister that Wagner was attached to the Geneva office of Matsen, Loring, Gould. It seemed fortunate to the frugal sergeant that he also noted the various branch offices and phone numbers of Matsen Loring including the Frankfurt office and decided, in a happy marriage of parsimony and practicality, that it would be better to contact the office in Frankfurt rather than going through a separate country entirely.

The message slip from the Sembach police regarding Wagner's accident was on Brian Iverson's desk when he came into the Frankfort office of Loring Matsen at about 8:45 AM Central European Time. Immediately upon reading the message, Iverson instructed his secretary to place the return call and clear his schedule. It had not looked to be a particularly busy day but, even if that had not been the case, Iverson would have responded as he did. Matsen Loring did not take the death of associates and other employees lightly and there was a standing order that such an occurrence took precedence over anything but the most critical emergency. No delegation of authority either. Such matters were to be handled by the office manager or the highest level associate available. Careers at Matsen Loring had ended for failing to abide by the set procedures in cases like this.

Having been given the precise location of the accident by the Sembach Police officer - one of the two which comprised the entire force - Iverson had called the motor pool and directed that one of the stand-by rentals be brought to the front of the building at once. "No, it doesn't matter which one," he snapped.

He placed a call to Gunther Abel of the Federal German agency called the BundesSicherheitsKraft and asked him to please make a call to the Sembach Polizei and direct that nothing - nothing be touched at the scene.

"Aber naturlich, mein freund," Abel had answered, "and my sympathies. I will see that nothing is touched. And that the local polizei will be informed that you will take charge of the body and the automobile. If you need anything else, you will call, ja?"

"Ja, danke, Gunther."

"Do you know why he was in Sembach, Brian?"

"No. But we should be able to trace his whereabouts since he left Geneva Friday evening. Maybe that will tell us something. Right now, I just assume that he wanted to drive smaller roads off the autobahn. It's still on the way to Frankfurt."

"Yes, of course, but six hundred kilometers is not such a long way. If he left Geneva on Friday evening, he certainly took his time or stopped along the way."

"Not unheard of in the annals of European travel, Gunther." Iverson blew some air through his nose in what was all he could muster to pass for a laugh.

"Ja, ich annehme. I suppose so. Viel gluck, mein freund." The BSK colonel said in parting.

*   *   *   *

Staring down at the wreck, in one of those vacuous sorts of rationalizations with which people try to comfort themselves, Iverson had thought - quite genuinely - that it was better that Wagner had not lived to see what he had done to the car. While Iverson was not quite as obsessed with cars as some of the others, he knew of the love affair between the man and his machine. The chrome front bumper of the Austin - clearly inadequate by today's standards of safety - had been simply folded into an angle more acute than a vee. The two ends were virtually parallel and just about touching and the center of the bumper was now the joint of the vee which had pierced the radiator and penetrated the engine block. The sweeping hood of the restored classic had buckled on impact and then popped loose off its hinges and flown up and over the back of the body of the automobile and still lay in the street - part of it in N40 and part of it on Hauptstrasse.

The cockpit of the car - the passenger compartment - had remained more or less intact. At least, the shape of what had been the opening with the instrument panel, and steering wheel, and seats was reasonably recognizable. Under the sheet of white plastic in the drivers seat, Wagner was also quite recognizable - from the shoulders up. What had killed Wagner was the result of simple physics. The highly movable force of the Austin-Healey had met the immovable object of the four hundred year old building and, as the saying went - something had to give.

What gave were the engine mounts. The front end of the car hit the point. The bumper buckled and assumed the shape it now had. The continued forward movement of the Austin caused the bumper to go through the radiator and on into the engine block itself.

Of course, the bumper was much too fragile to push the block off its mounts and if - somehow - the Austin's momentum could have dissipated in that instant, Wagner would now be preparing for the afternoon meeting in Frankfurt.

But again physics.

The energy that the Austin had when it initially made contact with the building was nowhere near spent. The mass of the building simply bent the bumper, folded it over, and pushed it back toward the engine. Continuing on, the engine made very solid and very forceful contact with the wedge of hard cheese. That was the impact that pushed the engine block and the entire drive train - as one piece - straight to the rear. Under the pressure, the drive shaft passed under the car and pushed the rear axle and wheels out from their appointed place so that when it was over, they formed a tee jutting straight out from the back of the car. At the other end of the drive train, the oil pan cover had been torn off and the crankshaft ended up under the driver's seat still attached by the connecting rods to the pistons inside the engine which rested inside Wagner's chest. The thoracic region had been crushed instantly and totally. Presumably Wagner had felt only a fraction of a second of enormous pressure - not really even pain - before he lost consciousness. At least that's the usual presumption. The human body is capable of extraordinary things which are often chronicled as miracles when they result in the saving of a life or some other perceived benefit. In this case, Iverson could only hope that no anti-miracle had occurred which would have let Wagner know what had happened to him - and what would soon be of him.

Iverson conferred briefly with the Sembach polizei to confirm that the officer heard from Gunther Abel. He had, he was duly intimidated, and he left Iverson to examine the scene without interference.

Iverson would not disturb anything. He would wait for the crew from forensics at the Weisbaden Air Base to come and make their preliminary inspection, remove the body, and take custody of the vehicle.

The body would be taken to the hospital in Weisbaden and examined and autopsied to determine the cause of death which certainly seemed obvious at the moment - but you never know.

The car would be taken to the secured investigative forensics area in the motor pool at Rhein Main Air Base. It too would be autopsied to determine if there had been a mechanical failure or if human error was the culprit.

The only thing for Iverson to do at this point, other than make sure nothing was disturbed, was to get the locater carried by every Matsen Loring associate on assignment. That would involve retrieving the wristwatch from Wagner's arm.

Iverson was not squeamish but one didn't have to be squeamish to not want to reach into a colleague's mangled remains and come out with a handful of - something. Iverson gingerly lifted the side of the plastic covering that draped Wagner's body and lifted it out from between Wagner and the driver's side door which appeared to have sustained only a horizontal dent about eighteen inches long bordered top and bottom by parallel scratches.

Fortunately for Iverson, Wagner's arms - or the left one at least - Iverson was not about to completely undrape the body so he couldn't be sure of the condition of the right arm - had not been between the engine and his chest when Wagner was killed. The arm was in fact surprisingly intact and still attached and was lying on the arm rest on the inside of the door with the dual SU carburetors on the left side of the engine almost touching the thumb. As a result, Iverson was able to ease the wristwatch off the wrist and over the hand without disturbing anything else in the car. He replaced the covering over Wagner and looked over at the local police officer who was not about to question the act of such an apparently important person - so he made what he hoped would be taken as small talk.

"It appears that he either strayed off the N40 or was attempting to swerve into the village and missed the road," the police officer said. "It has happened before - several times."

"I can see where it might, Officer. Where does the road through the village go?"

"After passing through the village, it splits off into two branches. The left branch just curves back to the N40 and the right branch continues on up the hill to the former American Air Base that was closed in the mid-eighties."

"Is the base used for anything now?" Iverson asked.

"There are plans for it to become a regional airport and industrial center," the policeman replied, "but for the moment, it's mostly empty except for some squatters in the old barracks."

There was an awkward silence as the two men stood there with no intention of discussing the matter before them.

Finally, Iverson spoke. "I need to call my office and have them send a fax to the US. Do you have a cellular in your police car. The one in mine isn't working."

The officer flinched inside knowing the frugality of his sergeant. But he had been told to offer "complete cooperation", had he not?

"Yes sir. Please feel free."

Chapter Four

"Welcome to the Jefferson Law Center, Charlestown University, and, of course, welcome to Contracts 101. My name is John Cann, Visiting Johnson Scholar, and I will be leading you into the morass of contract law." He winced at his own words. "Maybe not quite so melodramatic," he cautioned himself.

"I've been told somewhat pointedly by several other professors that I am one of the few law professors who didn't assign summer reading to the incoming students." He smiled. "Don't read anything into that. I'm new at this and didn't even know I'd be here until earlier this summer. I'll get it right next time."

He'd intended it to be a little joke - a tension breaker but what little response there was to it couldn't really be called laughter or even chuckling. It was more like barely audible and nervous smiles. Cann continued, feeling a little of the awkwardness that a stand-up comedian must feel when a joke bombs.

"The truth is," - he thought about saying, 'But seriously folks,' but rejected the idea - , "what you will get most out of law school will not be found in the books that come right out and tell you, 'This is the law.' We use the Socratic method which means that together we will search for and deduce the principles and points of the law by way of discussion and give and take. We'll not only teach you the law but we'll teach you how to think like a lawyer." He paused briefly and said, "And notwithstanding what you have heard ad nauseum, that is a good thing."

He glanced briefly up as the rear left side door opened and a straggler skulked into the classroom and hesitated faced with the choice of walking down to the front of the classroom or sitting in the end seat of the left section at the rear of the room. She chose the latter and slid as far down in the seat as she could.

Cann went on with his introduction. "You've already seen that the book we will use in this class is called, 'Cases on Contracts.' That, ladies and gentlemen is exactly what it is. Truth in packaging personified. It contains actual cases from actual courts, frequently appellate opinions, many by the greatest legal minds in the history of the country. Some not so great. You have a syllabus in front of you that assigns cases to be read for each class. We will discuss those cases and will elicit the points of law that each case illustrates. And don't read ahead, believe it or not. The cases follow a particular sequence and one is based on the others that precede it. You will only complicate and perhaps confuse yourselves if you outrun our discussions."

Here Cann paused for emphasis.

"But let me stress again, this is not high school. This is not even college. You will not simply be told what the law is. We will find it together and rest assured that a large portion of your grade will depend on your participation in the search."

Cann walked around the dais and spoke from behind the lectern.

"One other thing. As I've said, we use casebooks but some of you may already know that another kind of law book exists called a hornbook."

He noted a number of odd looks and anticipated the question. "No, I have no idea why they are called that. I probably should - but I don't."

"The point is that hornbooks are more like the textbooks that you're used to. They come right out and tell you what the point is or what the law is. But, ladies and gentlemen, please - do yourselves another favor and don't use them. Not in first year anyway. You will do yourself a disservice and not get what you need to get out of first year which is the analytical ability that will be your stock in trade."

Of course, Cann knew that some would go straight from this first class to the book store and buy the books but he also knew - unless law students had changed even more than he thought from when he was in school - that most wouldn't. The speech he had just given was essentially the same as one his Real Property professor had given on the first day of his legal education and he had listened and saw the benefit. He hoped most in his classes would also.

"Now, once again, welcome to law school. Let's begin"

There was a rumbling and shuffling of papers as every student in the room shifted position as if gearing up for what was to follow.

Cann began. "A few years from now, many of you - not all - will be attorneys. And you will be called upon to represent clients. This is a contracts class and therefore we will address this as it relates to contracts. Before you can undertake to represent a client with regard to a contract they either want to enforce or deny, I think we will agree that we must determine what makes up a contract."

Cann moved to the side of the dais and picked up a yellow legal pad. He reached up and patted his shirt pocket. Not finding any pen, he proceeded to pat his other pockets and feel around the rest of his body apparently searching everywhere but without finding what he was looking for.

He smiled what he hoped was a slightly sheepish smile and walked over to where one of the front row students sat holding a fat and very expensive looking fountain pen.

"May I?" Cann asked holding out his hand for the pen.

The student handed it over to the professor without hesitation and bent over to his side and rummaged through his brand new attache case for a substitute.

Cann stepped back to the dais and stood in front of it examining the pen.

"This is a very nice pen, Mr........?"

"Cawley, sir."

""Oh, by the way," Cann advised the class as a whole, "for the immediate future - or at least until I get your names down - I would appreciate it if you would give me your name before you respond."

"Now, Mr. Cawley, as I said, this is a nice pen. A very nice pen indeed."

Cawley smiled.

"In fact, this pen is so nice, Mr. Cawley, that I think I'll keep it."

Cawley's smile faded.

Cann reached into his pants pocket and took out a coin. "Here Mr. Cawley, here's a nickel. I just bought your pen."

Cann was gratified to see that he had gotten the entire class' attention.

* * * *

In the rear of the classroom, Janie Reston was fascinated but a little apprehensive. She knew - as all students know instinctively - that by seating herself apart from the main body of students, she heightened the risk of being called upon. If she were called upon, she would have to give her name. And if Professor Cann checked his list, he would find that she was not registered in his class. She didn't imagine any great harm would come of it but it would be embarrassing - and she'd had quite enough of that in the last day or so, thank you.

She was happy to see that the class was participating voluntarily and vigorously in the ongoing discussion so that Professor Cann hadn't had to call on any students. So far so good. As long as that continued, there didn't appear to be any danger to Janie. She also found both the discussion and the method fascinating.

"This is cool," she thought. She'd always found the usual lecture style of teaching to be a total bore and most of the time she had been several steps ahead of the teacher anyway but this...this give and take was exciting. Even before starting college, she'd begun to give serious consideration to a legal career. And yet, of course, she was a "mere child" and had plenty of time to make that decision.

Watching John Cann lead the discussion, she was impressed. As a woman, albeit a relative beginner, she examined him physically. Six feet, about 180 pounds, no apparent excess. Salt and pepper hair and dark eyes. She placed him at somewhere in his thirties or forties and attractive for his age she supposed. But at seventeen, an older man to her was twenty-one and her examination had little of the sexual about it. In that regard, someone Cann's age was just there. He was what he was and she could appreciate him as cool and smart and attractive - for his age - but the rest was irrelevant at this point.

What she was most interested in was whether she felt he could help her and whether she could trust him. The first question had already been answered to her satisfaction after watching him work with the law students for a few minutes. He seemed to know his stuff and wouldn't let go of a point until he was sure the students had grasped it. At the same time, she noted importantly, he seemed to go out of his way to be gentle to them even in confrontation and not harsh the way she had heard most law professors were with their students. It indicated to her a kindness that she felt she had with others and was something she wanted in an ally. As for the trust part, her initial impulse was favorable but only time would tell. As her representative in the upcoming hearing, she was comfortable that he would do.

*   *   *   *

Cann had continued to insist to the hapless Mr. Cawley that he, Cann, now owned the fountain pen in question because he had paid Cawley for it. He opened the discussion up to the rest of the students in the class who - to a person - felt that Cann was wrong. They just couldn't say why.

Ms. Liggett in the row half way back expressed the opinion that this was not a valid contract because it wasn't fair.

"So you feel that fairness is a pre-requisite to an enforceable contract. Is that correct, Ms. Liggett?"

"Yes. I...well, at least I think it should be."

"Ah, but what should be and what is may be very different things under the law, Ms. Liggett."

The young law student started to squirm a bit and Cann smiled in an attempt to keep her from becoming too uncomfortable.

"Let me pose this question to you then, Ms. Ligget. You wish to purchase a new house in a subdivision. You visit the model and talk to the sales people and purchase a home. Are you with me on this?"

"Yes I am."

"But several months after you move in, the developer has only four houses left - all of them identical to yours in every way. And he wants to conclude this project and move on to the next one. So he sells those four houses - just like yours - for ten thousand dollars less than you paid for yours. Is that fair?

"No."

"I agree but is it grounds, do you think, for you to be able to give your house back and get your money back. Or better still - to get a rebate of ten thousand dollars to make the prices equal?"

"I don't know why - but I would imagine it's not."

"It is not indeed, Ms. Liggett. So much for fairness."

Cann then decided to complicate things.

"But let's say, ladies and gentlemen, for the sake of argument, that I didn't give Mr. Cawley anything for this pen. Not even the nickel."

"Then you're a thief," came a shout from the rear.

"Not necessarily. And he hasn't filed any charges, has he." Cann shot back. "In the first place, as a general matter of criminal law, someone has to bring charges. Not always but usually." Cann looked around some more. "But more to the point, we're going to leave any criminal aspect of this matter out of the discussion for an even better reason." He looked at the faces around the room and said, "Why? Because it's my class, that's why. That's the law school equivalent of 'because I'm the mommy'." This time the class did chuckle.

Cann continued. "What we're looking for here is precisely what makes up the difference between the two scenarios." He surveyed the entire room.

A hand went up from a student on the right side about seven rows back.

"Walter Scott, here, Professor Cann."

"Thank you. Can you help us out of this tangled web, Mr. Scott?" Cann smirked.

"I'll sure try, Professor." The student smiled and Cann wondered if he'd gotten the literary reference.

"If you didn't give Mr. Cawley anything and he didn't press charges, wouldn't that make it a gift?"

"Would it?" Socrates would have been proud at the way that Cann bored in with the honored law school device of answering a question with a question.

"What about it, class? Let's pursue that. After all, if my goal is to own this pen, convince me - better still - convince Mr. Cawley that it's a gift."

"Ms. Liggett?" Cann called on the young woman again in part because even though he had intended no slight, Ms. Liggett appeared to be still smarting from what she perceived as being put down by the professor.

"For it to be a gift, wouldn't Mr. Cawley at least have to want it to be a gift?" she asked.

Cann welcomed the chance to smooth her feathers. "Excellent, Ms. Liggett, that's precisely it." Liggett beamed. "In fact, I will bend the rule a little and give you people a freebee. Simply stated, the law of gifts is as follows. A gift is dependent on the intent of both the donor and the donee and is complete upon delivery. In this case, delivery clearly took place and I, as the donee, am certainly willing to express the requisite intent that would allow me to keep it as such but I suspect that we can assume that Mr. Cawley did not intend this to be a gift." He looked down at the student. "May we assume that Mr. Cawley, or is this your gift to me?"

"With all due respect, Professor, I did not intend it as a gift."

"Well then, Mr. Cawley, if you say it's not a gift, then it's not a gift. Let's proceed."

Murmurs and shuffles.

"Okay. Let's see if we can't determine why I do - or do not - own this pen. What is it about this transaction, ladies and gentlemen - as it has occurred before you - that says that if I own this, it is by contract as opposed to by gift."

Scott opined. "You gave him something for it."

"Bingo," Cann pointed one index finger at Scott and the other at his own nose. "You got it. Another freebee. The legal term for it is consideration, ladies and gentlemen. Defined as something of value. The point here is that an essential element of a valid contract is the giving up of something of value on both sides. If that is lacking, there is no contract. Throughout your legal education and ensuing careers, be aware of the principal that a contract will fail based on - and I quote - "failure of consideration.""

"Now, Cawley gave up his pen and I gave up a nickel. Both items of value, are they not. So, do I own this pen?"

"But they weren't of equal value," a new voice from the left.

"Name, please?"

"Oh, sorry. Bronker."

"Well, who says they have to be of equal value, Mr. Bronker," Cann asked. The class already had learned to see a hypothetical coming.

"Let's say that you own a car, Mr. Bronker - a, oh, 1987 Pontiac Grand Prix. A decent car in decent shape with a market value of, say, two thousand dollars. You are now nearing the end of your third year of law school and have a balance due on your tuition of eight hundred dollars. If you cannot pay that balance, you do not get your law degree and without the law degree, you cannot accept that job offer with the Wall Street law firm which will pay you eighty thousand dollars a year to start." Cann paused to let the details sink in.

"Now, let's say I am aware of your situation so I offer you eight hundred dollars for your two thousand dollar car. Do you take it?"

When Bronker did not answer instantly, Cann went on. "Well, its my hypothetical and I say you do. Consideration on both sides but of unequal value. Is the contract invalid for "failure of consideration?""

"No?" Bronker said weakly.

"No, indeed," Cann confirmed. He included the whole class in his next statement. "Let me quote you verbatim the principle that guides contract law in this regard. 'Mere insufficiency of consideration - without more - will not render a contract invalid or unenforceable.' That's a fact, ladies and gentlemen. Everywhere you will practice."

Cann moved to the center of the dais, folded his arms, and rested his rump on the front edge of the desk.

"So, in this short period of time, we have learned that a contract does not have to be fair and the value of the consideration doesn't have to be equal. Our little scenario here of a nickel for Mr. Cawley's beautiful pen falls within those parameters so - why should Mr. Cawley get his pen back? What differentiates our scenario from the one I just posed to Mr. Bronker?"

Liggett was back in the swing of things. "Because even though in Bronker's case the value exchanged wasn't equal, under the circumstances, it was acceptable to both sides."

Cann once again put a finger to his nose and pointed at the student. "Keep going, Ms. Liggett."

"What I'm saying is that even though you had a bargaining advantage over Mr. Bronker, he could have said no. He decided voluntarily to accept or reject your offer. Whether the exchange was ultimately fair by some objective measurement, the parties freely agreed to it."

"Bingo. And exceptionally well put, Ms. Liggett."

The first-year law student beamed.

"So, it would appear that I have offered Mr. Cawley five cents for his pen. He may accept my offer if he wishes or he may reject it. Mr. Cawley?"

"Will my answer have any effect on my grade?" From Cawley's expression it wasn't possible to tell if he was kidding or not.

Cann answered most seriously. "Absolutely none. And if I had thought you might think so, I wouldn't have done this. The entire class is your witness, Mr. Cawley."

"Then I don't accept."

"Very good." Cann handed him back his pen and whirled around and wrote on the blackboard behind the dais - 'bargained for exchange'. He turned back to the classroom. "That, ladies and gentlemen, is as close as you will come to a synonym for contract. Barring some exceptions in the event of fraud or mistake, if you act freely and knowingly, you are expected to live with the consequences. You get what you pay for, but you also reap what you sow."

All around the room, Cann could see and be gratified by the looks of enlightenment of most of the faces. It told him that not only had the point had been grasped, but so had the Socratic method. Quite an accomplishment in a little over half an hour, he congratulated himself.

"Okay, listen. From here on out, this is how we'll deduce the points of law from the cases you'll read. Since it is early and this is your first day and your first class, let's cut it short."

As the din began to rise, he raised his voice, "For tomorrow's class, please read Owen v Tunison, Craft v Elder & Johnston Co., and White v Corlies & Tift. See you then."

Chapter Five

Cann watched the students file out of the classroom including the young woman who had been the last to come in and was the first to leave. With an eye and a memory trained to place everything, Cann knew that it was the same young woman he had seen the night before in the rec center.

It was not in his nature to allow separate facts and items to remain isolated and he had a natural facility - honed by years of training - to relate one thing to another no matter when he learned it or how irrelevant it seemed at the time of acquisition. It was a talent that had saved him many times - in the courtroom and elsewhere. But if one item couldn't be fit into an existing pattern or paradigm at a given moment, then it was filed away in Cann's mind from where it could be recalled when some other item triggered a connection. This had the added benefit of allowing Cann to focus on matters at hand without having his mind cluttered with isolated facts he could not yet use.

In this case, while Cann had placed who the young woman was, he had no frame of reference to explain her presence in his classroom. So he didn't bother himself about it. If it had significance, he would learn of it in due time.

He gathered up his books and materials to make room for the next professor and class who would be using the room. As he left the classroom, he noted that students were beginning to mill outside the door but as yet none had gone in.

"Well, at least it wasn't just me," he thought and turned down the hall and walked to the door marked 'Stairs'. It was just nine AM and his second class - also first year contracts - wasn't until eleven. Now was a good time to see what Roger wanted.

*   *   *   *

Janie Reston had a full hour before the first class of her college career but she had something to do in the meantime. After sitting in on Professor Cann's class as Dean Walder had suggested - she was glad she did - she hurried to the elevator where it seemed that every student in the building was waiting to take it down one flight. She found the stairwell, walked down the two flights to the first floor, and left the building.

She exited the Page Building and started across the Quad to the Gold Rec Center. Just as she stepped off the concrete walkway that ran all the way around the grassed interior of the Quad, she stopped in her tracks and stamped her right foot. She had left the key back in the dorm.

Janie had far less patience with herself than she did with others and called herself a few nasty names as she turned and walked north and out of the Quad to her dorm.

It took about ten minutes for her to reach the dorm. After initially starting out at an irritated power-walk pace, she relaxed and slowed down. She'd decided not to be quite so hard on herself for her lapse and to turn this trek that she had considered so frustrating at first into a tranquil stroll in the park-like setting of the campus.

The dorm that Janie had been assigned to was actually one of several converted buildings owned by the university. This particular one had been a transient hotel with a rather seedy past but the university had invested what was needed to make it a pleasant - if spartan - place to live. The other student residences that were on the original, pre-sprawl, campus were mostly of the glass and chrome variety reminiscent of the sixties. The 1920's decor and architecture of this dorm where Janie was to live for much of the next year was not of great significance to her but she did like the older style of the building she had been assigned to.

She bounded up the concrete stairway that was centered in the front of the red brick facade of the building, touching only every other step on the way up. Her final leap finished right at the heavy glass security doors that led in to the first floor hallway. Before her forward progress had even stopped, she had her hand on the round brass knob and used her momentum to push on it to gain entry. It didn't open and Janie slammed into the door banging the side of her face into it and dropping her knapsack. She was lucky she hadn't broken the glass. She quickly realized her mistakes. In the first place, the door needed to be pulled, not pushed. And in addition, there was the matter of security.

Each of the student residents had been issued a credit card sized electronic pass that had to be slid into an ATM-like device on the left side of the foyer at the entrance to the dorm. Janie rummaged through her knapsack and pulled out her wallet. She took out the security device and pushed it into the slot. The door buzzed alerting her to the fact that it could now be opened and she went in.

There were six floors in the building and each floor consisted of a narrow hallway with ten rooms on each side - twenty to a floor. Janie's room, which she shared with a junior named Gretchen, was on the fourth floor all the way at the end of the hallway on the right. Despite the stinging which she could still feel on her cheek where it had rubbed the surface of the outside door, she was unable to restrain the excess energy of her youth and again skipped every other step on the three flights of stairs up to the fourth floor. She made the required u-turn around the banister and started down the hall which appeared to be entirely empty and quiet. Janie reached her room, entered the code number which replaced a key, and went in.

She didn't even have to look for the key she'd left behind. It was right there on the dresser which stood against the rear wall of the room - exactly where she remembered putting it just before she picked up her purse and left earlier that morning. Checking

44

her watch, she noted that she still had plenty of time to see Sara and get to class. But even so, there was no reason to linger in the dorm so she scooped up the key and was stuffing it in her jeans pocket as she turned to leave.

As she went out of the room, she saw that the door to the room across the hall was open slightly. But it was enough to get her attention. A female student - she assumed it was a student - was seated on the dresser that occupied the same relative positioning as the one in Janie's room - against the rear wall. The girl was naked and seated on the dresser with her back to the wall behind her. Her head was tilted upward and her eyes were almost closed. Between her spread legs, Janie could see a man's head moving sometimes side to side - mostly up and down.

Janie didn't consider moving on or not watching. She was neither prude nor virgin even though her experience in sexual matters was limited to the bumbling and fumbling of youth. But she knew what arousal felt like and she felt a little of it now.

The girl in the other room was breathing deeply and rhythmically almost in synchronization with the movement of the man's head. Janie watched as the breathing became deeper still and began to be accompanied by a quiet moaning kind of sound. The girl never yelled or screamed but as her arousal grew, the breathing became even deeper and the arch in her back increased until there was a moment where she was curved away from the wall with only her head touching it as she emitted a series of whimpers which evolved into a crescendo of increasing then diminishing shudders. Then for a long moment, she was perfectly still. Finally, her shoulders dropped and her head tilted forward as she opened her eyes and looked straight ahead, seemingly without any feeling. It seemed strange to Janie that the girl wouldn't smile or at least look at the man who had apparently helped her to such pleasure. But then, she didn't know what she herself would do when it happened. She was pretty sure that she'd never had an orgasm. At least she hoped she hadn't since she'd never felt anything like what this girl had just seemed to.

The girl sat quietly on the dresser for a time then slid forward and placed her feet on the floor. She stepped forward away from the dresser and, for a moment, both of the people in the room were out of sight. Then Janie saw that the girl had her hands on the man's hips and was turning him around - reversing positions with him as he assumed a seated position on the dresser, very clearly aroused. Janie could now see that the man appeared to be in his middle or late twenties - faculty or graduate student maybe - with a dark complexion and a beard. Janie watched as the girl knelt on the floor - as the man had done before her - and placed her hands open-palmed on the sides of his thighs as she took his penis in her mouth and began to move up and down on it. Janie had tried that too - once - but it hadn't done anything for her. The young man she was with had seemed to enjoy it, though.

As the girl had done before him, the man was sitting with his head titled back against the wall. Then, as if he sensed that he was being watched, he slowly turned his head and seemed to look directly at Janie. It was not a sudden movement but one that was slow and deliberate. He had a glazed look in his eyes and a slight smile on his face and it occurred to Janie that he might not really even be seeing her. Even so, he never looked away from her even as the girl grasped the base of his penis with her right hand as she continued the up and down motion of her head.

For a long moment, Janie couldn't pull her eyes away from the man's. It was almost as she were being pulled into the sexual act as she stood across the hall. As the man's arousal increased, the intensity of his stare became more severe until, finally, his whole face started to quiver and only then did he close his eyes.

That broke the synergy that had been there and Janie shook her head slightly and moved off down the hall, bounding down the stairs and out of the building. She kept on running for a few steps more then slowed her pace, somewhat short of breath - not entirely from the running.

The return trip to the Quad only took her about half as long as the walk to the dorm. As she approached the Gold Center, she studied the dance room she'd been in the previous night - the scene of the crime, she thought sardonically. At that moment, the room was occupied by an aerobics class which also appeared to see no reason to draw the curtain across the window enabling Janie to see clearly how visible was their every move from the outside.

"Oh, boy. Step right up and see the show," she mumbled with a touch of chagrin and self-directed sarcasm. "I don't believe I didn't realize. What a jerk."

But there was nothing she could do about it now. She mentally shrugged. Spilt milk or crumbled cookies or something. She ran up the steps to Gold Center two at a time and went in.

She knew that the first door on the right was the dance room with the aerobics class and thought to herself that if she had half a brain she would have realized that the west wall of the building would have been an outside wall. Still, she reflected objectively that she really had no way of knowing that the wall was glass and not mirrors attached to a solid wall.

She walked past the door of the 'scene of the crime' and continued down the east-west hallway which bisected the building. On the left side of the hall which was the northern half of the building was the men's locker room then the basketball court and then the women's locker room after that. On the other side of the hall, opposite the double doors leading into the basketball court was a hallway to the right that ran the length of the entire southern half of Gold Rec Center with the staff offices lined up on the left side of that hallway.

Janie turned right and walked down the hallway to the door with the name 'Sara Furden' stenciled on it and walked right in.

Sara Furden, Assistant Professor of Physical Education, looked up from her desk and smiled broadly.

"Hey, Janie, what's up?" The Assistant Professor got up and came quickly around the desk and enveloped Janie in what could be called a bear hug except that they were both about the same size and neither could be described as a bear. Janie returned the hug.

"Hi, Sara. Not much, I guess. My first class is at ten."

Furden held Janie by the shoulders at arms length and looked at her. "Are you all checked into the dorm - with the rest of the jocks?" It was a little joke they'd made since Janie was 'kinda sorta pre-law' but Furden had insisted she live in the 'jock's dorm' where she felt she could keep a better eye on her.

Another hug. "God, Janie, I can't tell you enough how much it tickles me that you're here. My best friend's daughter - hell my own daughter, sort of. At least that's how I think of you. You know that. I'm going to take real good care of you while you're here. That's a promise to you and your mom."

"Well, you might have your hands full with that," Janie smiled ruefully.

Sara turned her head slightly to one side and focused on Janie's face trying to get a read on what was up. Furden felt that she knew Janie better than anyone. She had watched her grow from infancy to the lovely young lady who stood before her and as her mother's best friend from college to the present, she had participated in her upbringing at every step of the way.

And yet, because she wasn't Janie's mother, she had an access to her - even a closeness - that a mother, no matter how close or loving, wouldn't have. Sara was one part second mother and one part pseudo-sister and a large part best friend even though she was twice Janie's age.

She studied Janie's face and saw a look of concern that she was familiar enough with but which was, as usual, hard to read. Most children overreact and exaggerate their problems - not necessarily from deviousness but often in imitation of adults or at least in imitation of their perception of adults. But Janie had always been unusual in her reaction to pressure. She couldn't accurately be described as one of those strange babies that never cried. But when she did cry, it was not prolonged, it was always for a reason, and the reason was usually clear. She only did what was necessary in the context of the moment and always took the most direct route. But Janie had always been - what - cool. That was the only way to describe her.

At the age of six, Janie's bike had been stolen and she was pretty sure she knew who had done it. She had simply walked the half block - marching purposefully in her white size eleven tennis shoes, size six cutoff Oshkosh B'gosh jeans skirt, and red and white striped polo shirt - to Jason's house where she rang the doorbell and advised Jason's mother - she didn't know her real name - that she thought that Jason had borrowed her bike without telling her and could she look to see if it was there. Jason's mom had looked with her and, when they found it, Janie had ridden it home and Jason had gone to his room. And Janie had made it a point never to trust Jason again.

At age thirteen, Janie's best friend in the ninth grade at middle school had begun to get the reputation as the class slut - totally without reason or basis in fact. Janie watched as her friend grew more withdrawn and distraught as the stories got passed around with increasing frequency. Then one day, she had simply stood up in the classroom and asked the teacher if she could speak to the class. She was given permission to do so and told the class bluntly that despite all the stories, Emily was not a slut. She then spoke directly to the three boys whom everyone knew were spreading the stories and challenged them right there in the classroom to give the details of their encounters. The first boy tried to bluff his way through but Janie picked him apart with facts about where they really were at the time of the alleged encounter and other obvious discrepancies until the boy admitted his lies and that he had never touched Emily and didn't know anyone who had. After that, the other two boys didn't even try to maintain their stories and quickly admitted their lies. They ended up being the class buffoons for the rest of the year and Janie ended up being a hero to Emily and the other girls and most of the boys and even the teacher. To the present day, she says, she never saw anything like it.

So when Janie said that Sara may have her hands full with something, Sara thought that that was probably as circumspect as Janie had ever been in her life. "Is there a problem, honey?"

"You could say that," Janie replied and told her the story.

49

At first Sara's reaction was to want to smile. Yes, it was not a good thing to be running around in the buff where all could see, but it was hardly the end of the world. Janie and Sara both had essentially the same attitude towards nudity which was that it was certainly not evil in itself and, if one was seen in that state, so be it. Neither of them had any particular compulsion to expose themselves but, at the same time, their bodies were not something they needed to be ashamed of.

But the humor that Sara saw in the incident quickly dissipated as Janie went on to tell her about the arrival of campus security, the visit to headquarters, and the notification that a formal complaint had been filed and there would be a hearing.

"This is bullshit, Janie, pure bullshit." Sara was livid. She had at once become protective mother, big sister, and loyal best friend. "You're entitled to a representative at that hearing and I'll be happy to be the one."

Janie had not thought of that and hesitated while she considered if she was about to hurt her friend and mentor.

"Actually, I was going to have one of the law professor's, a John Cann, represent me." She went on to explain about the call to Dean Walder and her visit to Cann's class earlier that morning.

Sara didn't act hurt. "All right then. Well, that's great. If he'll do it. If not, I will. But I want to help. I know the people here and I know the system and if anyone tries to make more of this than it is, we'll kick some ass. They're not going to fuck with my Janie like this." She was really livid and meant every word.

Janie, who still wasn't entirely sure how seriously she needed to take all of this, was still very grateful for Sara.

"I just hope I won't get you in trouble for giving me the key, Sara. Do you want it back?"

"Nah. Hang on to it, Janie." Then she smiled. "But I think you might want to use the gym in the daytime till we find out where this thing is going. Okay?"

Janie nodded.

"And don't forget you have a 2 o'clock for me."

"Got it."

Chapter Six

The office of the dean of the Law School at Jefferson Legal Center was located in the northeast corner of the first floor of the Page Building. Dismissing as always the idea of taking an elevator down, Cann took the two flights on foot, entered the first floor hallway and walked almost its entire length to the mahogany door with the pane of frosted glass on which was written, "Dean of the Law School" with "Roger Walder" centered underneath in smaller print. Cann went straight in without knocking and asked Beverly Leeson, who had been Walder's secretary for as long as he had been Dean, if "the man" was in.

"No, but Roger is," she replied laughing. She looked over her shoulder and seeing that Walder was out of earshot remarked, "It's no fun to say stuff like that if he doesn't hear it."

"I'll be sure to let him know you said it," Cann laughed. "Can I go in."

There was no doubt in Cann's mind that he could have walked straight into Walders office without asking Beverly's permission and, in fact, Beverly was aware of the long standing relationship between the two men and wouldn't have objected if he had. Still, Cann was one who felt that the courtesies should be observed - unless there was a reason not to. Since Beverly had never given any such reason, it pleased him to abide by them. The secretary knew this and appreciated the gesture.

Walder was not at his desk when Cann walked in. Cann looked to his left and saw that he was sitting on the leather couch - which was genuine leather of course, a fact which Walder had pointed out to Cann during his first visit - and leaning forward over sheaves of papers on the coffee table in front of him.

"Welcome, John. How goes the first day?"

"Pretty good, actually. The first year contracts students really got into it right off the bat. It was kind of fun."

"Don't worry. They'll taper off soon enough when the novelty wears off," Walder counseled. "In no time at all they'll be spending more energy on avoiding being called on than they will be with discovering the essential points of law."

"Great to hear that," Cann said sarcastically. "It gives me something to look forward to - standing in front of 200 people doing all the talking."

"I didn't exactly say that, my friend. In fact, given the nature of law students, I doubt that has ever occurred in the history of any law school."

"Probably not," Cann grinned. "So why have I been summoned before your eminence this day. I got your note to see you."

"Ah, yes. I have a request to make. On behalf of an undergrad."

Walder explained to Cann the events of the night before as he had heard them from both campus security and Janie Reston. The fact was that there was little or no difference between the two versions. No material issue of fact.

"And you want me to represent her before this board?" He thought about it and then asked, only half joking, "Why? I mean, is this a role usually filled by a law professor?"

Walder shook his head. "No. In fact most students just bring their favorite english professor - or psych or sociology. If they bring anybody."

"Okay, same question, then. Why me."

"I guess for starters I've got no other reason than that she seems like a good kid and she might need some help."

Walder certainly knew what buttons to push with his friend. "What does she think about it," Cann asked. For the moment, he had not yet decided when - or whether - he would tell his friend about his own eye-witness version.

"Basically, she thinks it's much ado about nothing. I mean she's embarrassed more by the fact that she didn't realize she could be seen than by having apparently been seen. You should meet this kid, John. As we used to say, she really has her head on straight - especially for her age. She's as stable as they come and more than anything is a little pissed that someone is making an issue of this. She feels, and I strongly agree, that since no public spectacle occurred and nobody got hurt, why can't we let her forget about it."

"Why can't you?"

"Don't say "you" as in me, John. I think its as much ado about nothing as she does." Walder was serious. "But there's a written procedure and a complaint was filed and..."

"By whom?"

"We don't know. The procedure mandates that the identity of a complainant be kept confidential."

Cann's eyebrows went up more than a bit but he indicated to Walder with a flip of his hand for him to go on.

"Anyway, when a complaint is filed, the student disciplinary code requires that a preliminary hearing be held to determine if a formal board of inquiry should be convened."

"What's the charge against her?"

"That's one thing that the preliminary hearing is supposed to determine."

Cann's eyebrows arched again and Walder nodded even as he continued talking. "If it's determined that something occurred that violates university rules, then they bring formal charges and a formal hearing is scheduled."

Cann couldn't stop shaking his head. "Let me get this straight. This kid dances naked where she can be seen but as far as the University is concerned they don't even know if she was in fact seen." He would keep his secret for a while yet.

"Well, somebody filed a complaint, so I guess we can assume that she was seen by at least one person."

"Presumably," Cann conceded. "But, anyway, she is then picked up and brought to campus police headquarters where not knowing what - if anything - she has been charged with - , she is directed to give a written statement about her actions."

"That's right."

"All of this without the representation that even this code you mention allows her."

Walder waggled his finger. "Well, no, John. The code really doesn't specify when the right to representation begins."

"Why am I not surprised by that?" Cann's wry expression was matched by Walders own look.

Cann went on. "And presumably, if you didn't show up - if, by the luck of the draw you weren't the Dean on call last night - she would have given a written statement not knowing what charge or charges might be placed against her."

Walder interrupted. "Actually, I'm not so sure she would have. Like I said, she's a pretty sharp kid and seems to be one of those who won't budge if they think they're right."

"But she was asked - without representation - to potentially incriminate herself."

"Yes, and...." Walder thought he saw where Cann was going. "Don't get bogged down in Constitutional issues, John. This is a private institution don't forget."

"Yeah, I know." Cann paused briefly then continued. "But under these rules, an accused - no wait - a potential accused is brought before a board..."

Cann stopped and thought for a moment. Then he put up his hands again. "No. Wait one more time. You said the rules are unclear as to when this right to representation is triggered. Might a student go before this preliminary board without representation?"

Walder thought, then shrugged. "They might, I suppose. If nobody told them they were entitled to it."

"Does that happen?"

"To tell you the truth, I don't know. Possibly. I'm not familiar enough with the process to answer that. Or to know if the rules require that a student be advised of that right."

"Jesus Christ, Roger, who wrote these rules - Heinrich Himmler?"

"Seems like it, doesn't it?"

Cann gathered himself back in. "All right, Roger. Let's take a step back and put this in perspective." He took a breath before he began. "Notwithstanding that these rules are offensive - and they are - let's assume the kid is charged with something at the preliminary stage and the formal board finds her guilty. How bad can it be. I mean what'll they do to her. Make her stay in her room for a week - or write 'I will not dance naked' five hundred times on a blackboard?"

"Maybe," Walder said. "But maybe not. These things have been known to get nasty."

"Nasty how? Why?

"Because even though you may not look at campus life as real life, the people here do. And they take it very seriously. To the people here, this is real life - their real lives. Their departments, their viewpoints, their ideologies - especially their ideologies. Whatever happens anywhere else in anybody else's real world is important only to the extent that it affects their positions and perceived preeminence within their own real lives - no matter how unreal they may be."

"That's not so different from the rest of us. Or so evil."

"Right. Except for the way some innocent students become the cannon fodder in their turf disputes. They stake out their turf and they defend their turf. Make no mistake about that, John. They fight hard to protect what they feel is theirs - physical or ideological. Because they understand something about higher education that many of the rest of us do not."

"Which is?"

"That it's a business. They have a product and they make their living selling that product. Now listen up. This is the essential point you need to grasp to understand what I'm saying." Walder leaned forward. "The product of this business - these corporations - is not, as they would have us believe, education in general or even educated students. Despite what they would have us believe, students are not the product of this system. Hell, they don't even fall into the category of depreciable assets. They're consumables to be used in producing the product. They come and go and it matters not one whit what happens after that because there are always more where those came from."

"You sound bitter."

"Not so much bitter, I don't think. But I do resent the hypocrisy. They're constantly posturing about their goodness and self-sacrifice on behalf of the students but the fact is they know full well that they themselves – the faculty - are the product, John. And they'll go to any lengths to keep their not so little secret. They - not the students or anything else - are the reason they are in business. For them the important things are their tenure, their departments, their chairs, their reputations, their salaries to be sure, their currency among their peers. Haven't you ever found it ironic when academia criticizes corporate greed but says nothing about the professor who has a three hour course load and pulls down a six figure salary?" He saw Cann smirk and wasn't sure if he found this amusing. He shook his index finger at him. "This is no game to them and they play dirty to preserve the illusion and therefore the status quo."

Cann interrupted. "Roger, I understand your point. But why do you think it might get nasty with Janie Reston?"

"Because I found out today that Caroline Klein would be presenting the university's case at the preliminary hearing."

"And you are, of course, about to tell me who Caroline Klein is, I presume."

"Title-wise, she is the Chair of the Women's Studies Department."

Cann made a face that looked like a frown but was meant to be questioning. "Isn't that good," he asked. "I mean - forgive my indulging in stereotypes - but may I not assume that the Chair of the Women's Studies Department would be something of a feminist."

"Oh, you may indeed."

"Then wouldn't she be on Janie's side?"

"One would think so, wouldn't one. But let me tell you a story about Ms. Klein."

Cann held up a hand. "If this is going to take a while, let me get some coffee." Walder responded by tossing his head towards the outer office where the coffee pot was and sitting back in his chair. When Cann returned, Walder didn't wait for him to sit.

"Prior to coming here, Klein was an Associate Professor of Sociology at - well let's just say - a pre-eminent Ivy League institution. They had a similar disciplinary procedure as the one we have here and there was this incident involving a male student - a football player - and a female student. It seems that they had a little liaison in the female students room." Walder interrupted himself. "By the way, the version I'm relating to you is essentially the female student's version - not the male's - of what happened - which culminated in their having consensual sex. "

"Consensual."

"Undisputed and uncontroverted. There was no issue about that - at least not between the parties. Indeed, the only difference in the two versions was that the male asserted that he and the young lady had met in the lighted hall outside her room and gone in together while the young lady asserted that he had knocked on her door and been invited in to her unlighted room. After that, according to the female student, they had engaged in consensual sex and then talked for maybe half an hour afterwards - all in the dark. Suddenly the door opened and in walked the young lady's boyfriend. At that moment - and this is the young lady's version remember - then and only then, she said, did she realize that the male she had been with was not in fact her boyfriend. That she had participated in the sexual activity only because she had thought that she was doing it with her boyfriend."

Walder expected Cann to make some remark about the unbelievability of that premise but he surprised him. "How did the boyfriend react."

"Well, actually, according to the female student, he cried. Which is probably all he could do, John, since the football player was about 6'2" and weighed about 210. The boyfriend was no more than 5'6" and somewhere around 135-140."

"Kind of strains credulity, doesn't it?" Cann finally said.

"Indeed, in addition to which, the female student wanted to let the matter drop. It was the boyfriend who pressed the issue - who insisted that campus security be called. They arrived and the football player ended up being accused of rape. The campus police called the city police and the young man was arrested and initially charged with rape, and spent the night in jail. Not a very funny story."

"Now, as it turns out, the sexual crimes prosecutor in the District Attorney's office declined to prosecute the case. Her position was that even if you gave a jury nothing but the female's version, she didn't think they could get a conviction."

"Why do I think that's not the end of story?" Cann asked.

"Because I haven't gotten to Caroline Klein yet," Walder replied needlessly. "It seems Ms. Klein got wind of the accusation of rape and decided that something had to be done. Now, understand, John, that by now, the female student wanted nothing more than to have the entire incident forgotten and refused to participate or even testify. But Klein pressed the issue with rhetoric like "rape is too serious a crime to ignore."

"True enough, if there was a rape."

"That didn't even end up the issue. Since the female student refused to even attend the hearings, Ms. Klein presented a case against the football player that essentially said that the accusation was tantamount to the act. Somehow, more out of fear of offending Ms. Klein and her cohorts, I suspect, the young man was adjudged guilty of sexual misconduct."

"Penalty?"

"Ms. Klein would accept nothing short of expulsion. As it turned out the young man was blackballed throughout the entire Ivy League. Maybe even more widely. The young lady was harassed from both sides. On the one hand, she was ridiculed for her original story and on the other hand was harassed for refusing to "stand up for women's rights." She finally tried to set the record straight by acknowledging that she had in fact known that the man in her room was not her boyfriend and all she really wanted to do was spare her boyfriend's feelings. That didn't matter to Klein."

"And after all the ridicule at the beginning because of the original story, the other young man - the boyfriend - became such an even bigger laughing stock he killed himself."

"The saddest part of all is that Klein became a celebrity among her peers and parlayed the incident into the chair of the Women's Studies Department here. She actually brags about the incident and has never expressed the slightest regret or second thoughts about any part of it. She didn't care about either of the guys or the girl for that matter."

"And you think something similar might happen to Janie Reston?"

"I don't know. Maybe. It could." He thought for a moment. "Look, you said it yourself, John. If it wasn't for the luck of the draw, I wouldn't have even met the kid. But I did. And I like her. You can tell she's special. And I'm afraid that, for the slightest reason, or no reason at all, Caroline Klein will chew her up and spit her out if she sees something in it for her."

"And you want me to take her on."

"Everybody here is afraid of Klein. Hell, not just Klein. Everybody's afraid of everybody - or at least of the accusations they throw around like snowballs. You're new here. You don't know enough about being politically correct and I know you wouldn't care if you did. I hope that's good. I think it is. Anybody whose been here for any time at all has learned to back down from the buzz words. Accuse them of the right things and they'll join in the feeding frenzy to save their own ass."

Walder paused again. "So, what do you think? Will you do it?"

Cann nodded. "I'd like to talk to her first but yeah, I think so."

"Good." Walder smiled a bit sheepishly, "because I already told her to contact you."

"Well she hasn't but...she did sit in on my eight o'clock contracts class this morning."

"Well, that's something any........?" The bell went off in Walder's head. "How do you know that?"

"Because I was in my office last night when all of this was going on and saw the whole thing."

"You saw the.......Why didn't you tell me that before." Before Cann could answer, Walder shook his head and expressed his concerns. "Geez, I don't know, John. Maybe you shouldn't represent her after all. It could look like a conflict."

"To whom?" Cann replied. "Klein? Who cares? It wouldn't be a conflict in real life, Roger, and I'm not going to let it be one here either. The fact that I saw the incident for myself doesn't change a thing. Hell, you said yourself that there's no difference in the stories related by this Janie and the campus cops. Well, I can tell you that there's no difference between those two versions and what I saw. So looking at it from a lawyer-client relationship, the difference is that in this case I don't have to guess or hope that the so-called "defendant" is telling the truth. I am in the unusually comfortable position of knowing the truth myself. No conflict there."

Walder shrugged and said nothing.

Cann stood up. "How do I get in touch with her?"

"Well, if you haven't heard from her before then, she's calling me about 1 o'clock. What do you want me to tell her?"

"Tell her to come to my office about five this evening. We'll talk then."

"Okay, John. Thanks. Keep your guard up. Don't underestimate Klein. And keep me posted, too."

"Will do." Cann turned to leave, then remembered. "Oh, the message slip said you had two messages for me. What's the second one?"

Walder apologized. "Sorry, John. I forgot. A Milly called? From your office in Washington?" Walder made the statements into questions and then paused as if waiting for an indication of recognition from Cann who said nothing. "She asked you to call Arthur as soon as possible. She didn't leave a number."

Cann simply said, "That's okay. I've got the number." And left.

Chapter Seven

Janie survived the first college class of her life. But it was an eye-opener. At first, her impression of college was that it wasn't going to be all that different from high school. The professor seemed a little more laid back and the atmosphere was a little more casual but the subject matter was about what she'd expected for American History 203 - 1990's style.

For some reason in her earlier schooling, Janie had always found Ancient history fascinating but the more modern stuff - European and American had been by comparison boring to her. If for no other reason than it was closer in time - it seemed to her - it didn't have the excitement or exotic flavor of ancient Greece and Rome.

That was not to say, however, that she hadn't paid attention or learned anything. And it certainly was not to say that she felt that what she had been taught was unbiased and complete. But neither was she prepared to accept this professor's apparent assertion that the history of her country was one long string of evil deeds piled upon slaughter, fraud, and deceit. Janie's view was that the United States had done some bad and a lot of good.

Like John Cann in the first year contracts class she had sat in on earlier that day, this history professor started the class with an introductory talk about what they would do and where they would go. But unlike Cann, Professor Veltri's talk was not designed to prepare the students for the methods and methodologies they would encounter that semester. Professor Veltri announced that the status quo - meaning what they had come in with - would not be sufficient for a good grade in his course. They must question, question, question. Question everything - he said - the premise and the conclusion. For it would not be enough in his class - he said - to simply regurgitate the facts he gave them. They must show that they had absorbed the content and assimilated the meaning of that content. They would be required to leave his class at the end of the semester with a viewpoint all their own based on what they did in this course.

That, Janie thought, was an exciting way to do things.

Then Professor Veltri went on to tell the class - just like John Cann did - that they weren't in high school anymore. They were at a higher level where the search for knowledge was paramount. They would not be required - no - they would not be permitted to rely on the euro-centric propaganda that they had been subjected to throughout their earlier education. If they were to fully utilize the freedoms and tolerance of the academic community they must unshackle themselves from the trained reliance on accepting the premises that their teachers and others - yes, even their parents - had imposed on them. And he, Professor Veltri, would lead the way.

"Everybody's entitled to their own opinion," Janie thought, and she was prepared to listen and sort and sift through the information she would be given but she would reach her own conclusions. She noted sarcastically to herself that this Professor was asserting the same kind of authority he was telling the students to reject in others. But, as they had been told, they were now college students - young adults - and could make up their own minds. And so she would.

After what seemed like the professor's seventeenth reference to the euro-centricism of the founding fathers - 'I wonder if we're supposed to say founding persons, now', Janie thought - , accompanied by a figurative spit to the side and a crossing of his heart, Janie raised her hand.

"Professor, you keep focusing on the fact that our founding fathers attitudes were euro-centric. What else could they be? They were born in Europe."

"So they were, Ms....." he raised an eyebrow in inquiry.

"Reston. Janie Reston."

"Yes. Well, so they were, Ms. Weston but do you think that makes them good at everything?"

"It's Reston - with an 'R' but that's not what I was saying, Professor, I just meant that......"

"Perhaps you might wish to listen a little longer, Ms. Weston, before you challenge new ideas. I know that having your core beliefs challenged can be very threatening indeed, but please, be assured you have nothing to feel threatened about."

"I don't...."

"As the class goes forward, you will see that the new way we look at our own history allows us to place current situations and events in their proper perspective."

Janie felt attacked and wasn't going to back down. "But there's usually more than one perspective, isn't there professor. I mean who's to say what the proper one is - or if there is even just one proper one."

The Professor was exhibiting some irritation now. "That's what we shall see in the course of the ensuing semester, won't we. And I will be anxious to see, Ms. Weston, if you are at all able to leave mommy and daddy behind and expand your horizons."

Janie was, for one of the few times in her life, speechless.

Professor Veltri went on. "And this is a non-sexist class, Ms. Weston. The phrase we use here is the 'founding persons.' Try to remember that."

Professor Veltri didn't pause and quickly went back to his lecture. Janie stared for a long moment then realized her mouth was still hanging open. She sat back and took a breath. "Well, he kicked my butt on that one," she thought.

And she was right in the sense that the professor had won that one by silencing her. For the duration of the class Janie sat in thought, partly nursing her wounds and partly rehashing the dialogue and heard virtually none of the rest of the professor's lecture. But it was probably just as well.

When Professor Veltri dismissed them - excused them actually - it was exactly ten minutes to eleven and Janie had no break before her next class - second level English Lit, another advanced placement course.

"If they're all like this its going to be a long semester," she thought. "Maybe, I'll learn to keep my mouth shut and just listen." She pretended to herself to briefly consider it and then said aloud, "Naaah." And giggled to herself at her private joke.

*   *   *   *

After four hours of golf, Arthur Matsen and Carlton Bishop sat somewhat less than patiently on the fifteenth tee.

"I'm telling you, Arthur, this is getting ridiculous. This is going to be a five and a half, six hour round of golf. It takes the fun out of it."

"Such as it is, hmm, Carl?" Matsen smiled.

Bishop smiled back. "I know. Am I having fun yet?" He chuckled at his own expense. "It may not look like it, Arthur, but, overall, I do enjoy this game. And I'm getting better at it. My attitude if not my game, anyway. I haven't thrown a club all day."

"No, just tantrums. If conventional wisdom has any validity, at least you won't get an ulcer. Not from golf anyway."

The foursome they had been following all day was just now getting out of their carts to tee off on the fifteenth hole, the foursome in front of them having just moved far enough out of range to ensure that they would not be hit by a good drive. That meant it would be another seven to ten minutes before Matsen and Bishop would tee off themselves.

"Jesus, Arthur, this is nuts," Bishop started to say but was interrupted by the cellular phone. He shook his head less at the technology than at the context but said nothing further about it.

"Matsen here."

Milly briefly announced to Matsen that Brian Iverson was on the line.

"Thank you, Milly." He waited a moment. "Brian? How are you."

"Been better, sir," Iverson said. "I wanted to touch base but I don't have an awful lot just yet."

"Well, let's hear what you do have, then."

"Well, Ted was killed when he apparently missed a turn on Highway N40 in a little town called Sembach about fifty miles south of Mainz." He changed his tone. "I'm sorry, Arthur, I'm making assumptions about your Germany geography. Is it there?"

"It's pretty good, Brian. Mainz is what - thirty miles west of Frankfurt."

"Just about, yeah, - southwest actually but you've got it."

"Anyway, as you approach Sembach heading north, the road, N40, bears just a little left and the main street of Sembach bears a little right and there's this wedge shaped building right on the fork. It looks like he went into it at speed. Right now we have no idea why but it could be a lot of things. It's possible that he just fell asleep." Iverson shook his head and exhaled. "What a waste."

"I know. Any problem with the local authorities?"

"No, Gunther made the call. Sembach is so small, I was surprised it even had its own police force but it does. Two men. One chief, one indian. But they left the scene alone and they left me alone. Ted's on his way to Weisbaden and the car's on its way to Rhein Main."

"Do we know why he was there, Brian?"

"No idea. He might have just gotten tired of driving on the autobahn but there are other back roads closer to his route than N40. Not that N40 is a real back road but its no Autobahn either."

"I understand. Is there anything in the vicinity that might be of interest?"

"Above the village, there's an old US Air Force base that's empty now. But, at this point at least, there's no reason to think its significant."

"Do we know his route? When did he leave Geneva, anyway?"

"Friday at about seven PM."

"Help me on this part Brian. Its what - about 350 miles from Geneva to Frankfurt, isn't it. It doesn't take two and a half days to do it."

"Right. He obviously stopped along the way. We're tracing his movements now."

"That's why we have the locaters, Brian. Was Wagner's damaged in the crash?"

"It doesn't seem to be. But it shut down on Friday and didn't come back on until Monday morning - apparently around the time of the accident. A regular lost weekend - for now, anyway."

The locaters, by today's technology, were not terribly complicated devices. They were tied in to a combination of the American GPS system and the Russian GloNass network giving Loring, Matsen, and Gould the ability to monitor the movements and whereabouts of its associates anywhere in the world within one square mile. While the technology certainly existed to pinpoint objects or individuals within yards of their precise locations, the system that Loring Matsen used consisted of cellular type mile square grids within which the subject's presence would be fixed. Movement within the boundaries of a square mile grid, however, could not be monitored and thus would not be noted or recorded until the subject crossed over into an adjacent grid.

The locater itself was simply a transmitter which emitted a signal that allowed the wearer's position to be determined by the GPS. The location information was then relayed by satellite and received in the main office in DC where the information was recorded on rather old-fashioned reels of tape. In situations such as existed now with Ted Wagner's death, the firm was able to - or should have been able to - follow his path and recreate the trip from the tape they already had.

As an accommodation to the associates' sense of privacy, however, they had the ability to suspend the real time transmission of the data by simply pressing a small button on their watch where the locater was. For security reasons, however, Loring Matsen didn't advise the associates that their locaters also held a secondary chip that internally recorded the locations and travel of the wearer. The chip itself had no transmission capability but stored the information in its own memory. If and when needed, the information could be downloaded by technicians stationed in several Loring Matsen offices around the world - one of whom was in Frankfurt.

Iverson explained to Matsen that DC had already pulled the tape of the primary transmittals which showed that the locater was operating correctly until it was turned off - or went off for other reasons - at about 9:00 PM Friday night.

"We had him in Bern by way of the N1 highway when it went off at around 9 PM Friday. For now we have no idea what went on for the next 56 hours. It transmitted no signal again until early Monday morning around the time of the crash. We don't know why it was turned off or why it came back on again, for that matter. It could even be that the impact reactivated it. We just don't know."

"Where's the locater now?"

"Our tech's got it. We should have the travels in about 48 hours."

"Good. Did you glean anything else from the scene?"

"No, that ball's in forensics court. We'll have to wait on them."

"OK, get me everything as soon as you have it."

"Of course." Iverson went on to business. "What about the case?"

Even as he grieved for Wagner, Matsen hadn't forgotten the firm's business responsibilities. The IMF meeting - originally scheduled for 3:00 PM Central European Time had already been pushed back to 8:00 PM CET - thanks to Milly's efficiency.

Matsen explained. "Milly called Victor Kronman of the International Monetary Fund right after we first heard about the accident and advised him of Ted's death. Knowing the chip the Palestinians have on their shoulders, he didn't want any delay at all. I made it clear to him that we certainly didn't want to be the cause of any significant delay but this was an unusual circumstance. We had to have someone present at the meeting and would he please prevail upon the parties to accept this slight delay. For the moment, I'll oversee things from here and participate in today's meeting by teleconference. Kronman tells me that everyone's agreed to that. If any local activity is needed, you're it. I'll have the files sent over at once so you can familiarize yourself with the situation. You'll find that the loan application has been reviewed and the IMF has determined the terms the Palestinian Authority needs to implement and comply with before the World Bank makes the loan."

"Is that all the meeting is for - to give the terms and conditions to the Palestinians?"

"That's it. It'll be interesting. It always is. IMF conditions are always a hard pill for a country to swallow. This one may be different, though, because the Palestinian Authority doesn't really represent a separate country. They may be some day but right now they're only an autonomous authority - and that's only because the Israelis let them. And even that might change with the election next week."

Iverson nodded silently at the European end of the line.

Matsen finished his analysis. "Anyway, as far as the IMF is concerned, I suspect that instead of the usual conditions they put on borrower countries like wage and price controls, currency devaluation, and other austerity measures, we're going to hear them tell the Palestinians that they have to get their infrastructure in shape and control the extremists. Nothing surprising but not exactly easy either."

Iverson asked a question that had been nagging him. "Why is the meeting being held in Frankfurt, Arthur? Why didn't everybody stay in Geneva."

"In the first place, everybody's not in Geneva all the time. Most of the principals fly in to wherever the meetings are held. Ostensibly - and I have no reason at this time to doubt it - there isn't any significant reason for the Frankfurt location. The IMF tries to spread its activity around the lender nations and, since Germany has been underwriting more and more of the World

Bank loans lately, including this one, they put this meeting in Frankfurt."

"Will Arafat himself be at the meeting?"

"No. He'll be in the area but according to his aides that's just coincidence. There's a large Palestinian emigre population around Frankfurt which gives him lots of support. So he'll apparently be meeting with them while the IMF dictates its terms. My understanding is that he'll sit this one out and let his second or third in command do the listening. Malif, I'd guess. Maybe Raham. Maybe both."

"Does that strike you as at all suspicious?"

"Not really. A little I guess. As always, we need to be up on it, but I suspect at worst it's a matter of Arafat's enormous ego preventing him from personally sitting in on a situation where someone else is doing the dictating. He'll be told of the conditions by his aides, go through the usual posturing, and then let the terms go into effect - at least until he gets the money."

"And we hope he does?" It truly was a question.

"Well, the President has decided that we hope he does - and ours is not to question why now, is it?" Matsen paused. "To tell you the truth, I never thought I'd see the day that things would get this far towards peace in that region. So, we all need to be statesmanlike and do what we can to help things along. As I said, for the moment, I'll oversee from here and if local activity is needed, you're it."

Iverson started to say something then stopped - then said it anyway.

"Maybe I'm out of line, boss, but isn't John Cann the man for this job?"

"Always was, Brian. But it wasn't possible in this case." The words were spoken in a tone intended to close the discussion. But they didn't have the desired effect."

"Can I ask why not, sir?"

"You can but I won't tell you." Matsen was even more firm with those words. Then he relented a bit. He was a man who received loyalty and respect from his people and believed strongly that they needed to get the same in return from him. Iverson deserved a better explanation.

"Look, Brian, there were reasons that made sense in any other context than ours. But I don't feel free to discuss them - out of consideration for John among other things. Understand?"

The question at the end was even gentle. "But for your information, I do intend to see if he's available now. Don't count on it though."

"Yes, sir."

"And don't forget I'm going to be counting on you for assistance in this for now. In particular, I'm going to want you to be in on the teleconference so make sure you're in your office in - let's see - four hours? Is that right?"

"Eight PM CET - just under four hours. That's right, sir. I'll be here."

"Good. I may not be back in the office myself for another couple of hours so if you need anything, go through Milly."

"Yes,sir."

Matsen pushed the button marked "end" on the cellular phone. As he placed it in its holder in the golf cart, he looked up just in time to see Bishop sky another golf ball straight up followed by a curse and the slamming of the head of the treacherous three wood into the ground.

Chapter Eight

In between Cann's second Contracts class at 11:00 AM which, he was happy to say, had gone as well as the first one - and the 1:00 PM International Finance Class he had conducted with the second and third year students - some of whom were as intolerable as Walder had said they would be, he had actually had time for lunch. After eating, he had stopped by his office before the 1:00 o'clock class and found a message from Dean Roger Walder on his desk.

John:

Janie Reston came by about 12:15 and said she would come by to see you at 5:00 PM in your office. But she also said she would be in the dance room of the Gold Gym at 2:00 if you wanted to catch her there. First door on the right as you enter from the Quad. (But I guess you know that). Good luck. Keep me posted.

Roger

So Cann had dropped his class materials off at his office after the 1:00 o'clock Finance class and crossed the Quad to meet the remarkable Ms. Reston for the first time - close up at least. As he

71

crossed the Quad, he noticed that this time drapes were closed and wondered if it was Janie's idea.

He went through the double entry doors of the Gold Center which were hooked into eyes screwed into the walls behind them to keep them open. The first door on the right which of course he knew was the dance room where he had seen Janie the night before was closed. He knocked but knew that his rapping would never be heard over the music loudly playing inside the room.

He opened the door slowly and saw that an aerobics class was being conducted by none other than Janie Reston who glanced over as Cann stuck his head in the door. She smiled at him and raised her right hand in a wave. Then she summoned up a young man who had been exercising to the music in the front row of the class who took over leadership of the group from her.

She walked over to Cann where he was standing and said loudly in his ear so that he could be heard. "I'm Janie Reston, Professor Cann. Thanks for coming here to see me. We can talk in an office down the hall if you want."

"I think that would be a good idea," Cann shouted, just as a break in the beat of the music caused his voice to be the only sound in the room. But the music picked up again immediately and most of the exercisers didn't even appear to have heard him.

Cann and Janie smiled at each other at the incident and then Cann stood aside and held the door for Janie to exit the dance room.

Janie led the way as they went down the hall and turned right opposite the double door entrance to the basketball court on the left. As Cann followed her, he noted that she didn't appear to feel the slightest self-consciousness about herself. She wasn't wearing one of those colorful thong type aerobics outfits that seemed to be compulsory for a lot of people who took aerobics but she was wearing a simple pale beige leotard. Compared to the fashions of the day, it was bland - or would have been except for the fact that she wore it so well. It was made of fairly thin material - not so thin that it was transparent but thin and tight enough that it was extremely revealing of the shape and contours of the wearer.

Janie came to a stop at the door to Sara Furden's office and unlocked it before stepping aside to let Cann in first.

"We can talk in here," she said as she went in behind him and sat in one of the two rigid armchairs that faced Sara's desk. She gestured to Cann that he should sit behind the desk in Furden's chair but he chose to sit in the other armchair facing Janie on the diagonal.

Janie spoke first. "I sat in on your 8:00 class this morning, Professor. It was really interesting. I wouldn't have thought that Contracts would be."

"Obviously, its all in the presentation," Cann joked.

"No I really mean it," Janie protested.

"So do I." He laughed and she joined him.

"But, thanks, Ms. Reston. I appreciate the comment and the compliment." He went right on. "But before we do anything else, there's something you should know." Janie Reston nodded and waited for him to go on.

"How shall I explain this." He knew that he could and probably should just come right out and say it but he felt more comfortable easing into it. "My office is directly across the Quad from this building. On the second floor of the Page Building."

Janie nodded.

"In fact, my office overlooks the Quad."

"Um hm," Janie muttered and continued to look directly at Cann.

"And, - uh - I was in my office looking out the window last night about 10:00 PM," he said, then waited.

"Um hm?" Janie said again and still looked straight at him. It was only in her eyes that Cann could see the light begin to dawn. Her face and expression never changed but her eyes seemed to become more open and somewhat deeper as the point of what Cann was saying formed and developed and turned into a completed concept.

Still looking straight at him and without any change in her face at all, Janie said, "Oh, you saw me." It was a statement without any inflection that would make it a question.

"Yes, I did."

"I'm starting to wonder if there's anybody who didn't." Still she continued to stare right into Cann's eyes.

Then she asked, "So what did you think?"

Cann was taken a little aback not knowing if this was a sign of a certain brazenness or more evidence of her straightforwardness.

"About what?" he asked. He was genuinely unclear as to what she was asking him.

Intuitive beyond her years, Janie Reston laughed slightly and said, "Not my body, Professor. I'm asking if you think I did anything wrong."

Cann laughed at himself a little before he answered. "Absolutely not. In fact I was explaining to Dean Walder that I felt that was an advantage.." Janie grimaced..."no, I meant in the sense that I know for a fact what went on. I don't have to worry about any misstatements or omissions or lies by the client - you in this case."

Janie was serious. "Why would I lie to you. You're on my side, aren't you. I mean, you're like sort of my lawyer in this, right?"

"Yes, I am, Ms. Reston, but clients lie to their lawyers all the time."

"Why?"

"Lots of reasons. The only group you can be sure aren't lying are the innocent people who've been accused of a crime. On the other hand, the lawyer can never know for certain if the client is guilty or innocent because one other group you can be sure are lying are - by definition - the truly guilty who are going to trial because they are saying they're not guilty. Our system is such that we haven't given the lawyers the right or authority to make the final judgment so that the issue has to go to the test. Regardless of the slams the legal profession gets, if someone says they're innocent, they have to get the benefit of the doubt. The presumption of innocence is meaningless if the lawyers are allowed to short circuit the system by playing judge and jury themselves."

"Yeah. I've heard lots of people say that it's better for ten guilty people to go free than for one innocent person to be convicted."

"Well, I'm not sure I agree with that. Any number of guilty people going free in no way ensures that an innocent one won't be convicted of something he or she didn't do. In fact, it seems to me that if a given rule let's ten guilty people go free, it's probably not a good rule anyway. And there's not necessarily a connection between the guilty going free and the innocent being convicted. That phrase you quoted is just another one of those cute little rhetorical cliches that takes the place of thinking."

"What do you mean?"

"I just mean that too much of what passes for debate seems to consist of parroted cliches that don't mean what they seem to."

Janie shook her head at that and Cann felt the need to explain.

"Okay. There's this bumper sticker I've seen a lot that seems to say something profound but, like so many other superficial cliches, it doesn't stand up under analysis."

"Which one?"

"Well, the one I have in mind is the one that says, 'You cannot work for peace and prepare for war at the same time.' Have you seen it?"

"Yeah. I always thought it was a good saying. I mean aren't peace and war contradictions in terms?"

"Only if the definition of peace is restricted to mean only the absence of war. Always be careful, Janie, of letting others impose definitions on you. It restricts your ability to think for yourself. Always question the premise of what somebody is saying before you even think about accepting the arguments based on those premises."

Janie was listening closely and nodded.

"In the case of this saying, as you put it, of course you can work for peace and prepare for war at the same time. Only a fool would do otherwise. And there are plenty of actions that work towards both ends at the same time. History is full of examples of dead people and dead civilizations who failed to see that an inability to defend themselves was vulnerability. The simple fact is that there are 'bad guys' out there and all the 'good guys' in the world wishing it wasn't so, won't make it that way."

Janie was slowly nodding her head as she took in and digested what Cann was saying. Finally, she commented, "Cool."

Cann laughed. Not at Janie but at the way she reduced his hyperbole to its bare essentials with that one word.

"Anyway, we're way off the track. The point I was making was that people lie to their lawyers on the civil side, too. Mostly because the client knows better than anyone that there is another side to the story and that their opponent's case probably has some merit to it as well. So they 'fudge' a little bit - even with their own lawyer. The client sees it as putting the best face on their story. Some clients lie because they know they're flat out wrong and don't want to admit it. And then some others lie to try and trick the lawyer into making a mistake. That way, if they lose the case the first time, they can blame the lawyer and sue him or her - get a second bite at the apple as we say. It happens."

"Well, I'm not going to lie to you. What good would it do, anyway? You know for yourself what happened."

"That's right. I do. And I can tell you that it was nothing - period." He smiled. "Look at the bright side. At least you don't have to have me cross-examining you for the details. Although I do have a few questions."

"Okay."

"How did you get into the gym?"

"Sara Furden - this is her office. She's a Phys Ed professor here and a long time friend of my mother's - and mine too. I've literally known her all my life. She got me a work-study position as an aerobics instructor and gave me the key to let me work out and practice new routines. That's what I was doing last night."

"Why so late."

"I didn't get unpacked and everything until about 8:30 last night and, at first, I wasn't going to come over but I was a little keyed up and wanted to make sure I was loose enough." She giggled. "Well, maybe loose is the wrong word."

Cann laughed aloud and nodded, "Okay, I know what you mean."

"Anyway, I've been in Sara's office before but not the dance room. I mean I had only stuck my head into the dance room once and really didn't take a good look around. So when I went in last night, I flicked on the light and it looked like a mirrored wall to me. I admit I'm not the most modest person in the world but if I'd known it was a window I would have closed the drapes or gone to another room or something."

"And the first you knew of the problem was when the campus cops came in."

"Yup. I was just starting to go into my routine - well you know, I guess - when I turned around and this guy is standing there. Then a second one comes in. Uniforms or not, I got scared. I was only a little less scared when the female officer came in. I mean, you never know."

"Right."

"So, I was standing there trying to cover everything with only two hands - and the two guys were checking out everything they could in the mirror - when the woman cop tells me about the window wall. I almost shit. Sorry, excuse me. But I almost dropped my clothes when she told me. Then I got her to make the guys turn around - sort of - and I got dressed." She rolled her eyes and shook her head.

"But even then I didn't think I had done anything wrong. I still don't. I mean I feel like a dope and I hate to say it - a stupid kid - but that's what I was. And that's it. Criminy, I mean I didn't hurt anybody. Did I?"

For the first time, she looked vulnerable and Cann was touched by it. As strong as she may be, he thought, she was still a kid and this was uncharted territory for her. She was afraid - even if just a little. And he wanted to help. His paternal instincts - he was still surprised that he had them - came on strong and he spoke softly but with strength and conviction.

"No, Ms. Reston, you didn't do anything wrong. We both know that. And we'll see this through."

"Would it be okay if you called me Janie?" Janie asked.

"Sure. And I'd like you to call me John if your comfortable with it."

Janie smiled and asked him what he was just about to ask her. "Do we know who filed the complaint." Cann liked the idea that she used the pronoun 'we'.

"No, I was about to ask you."

"Can they do that? I mean what about my civil rights or something. What about - what's it called - the right to face your accuser?"

"Well, since this is a private institution, you don't have that right." Cann paused briefly before continuing. "I don't want to give a crash course in Constitutional Law right now but one thing you have to realize is that the Constitution was designed by the founding fathers to..."

"Founding persons..."

"Excuse me?..."

"Sorry, just a little joke...sort of. My history professor corrected me today when I used the phrase 'founding fathers'."

Cann raised his eyebrows at her. "Please tell me you're kidding."

"I can't because that's what he did. He told me they should be called the 'founding persons'." She giggled.

Cann closed his eyes and shook his head back and forth several times. "Dean Walder warned me that I would be in for some surprises. So far the biggest surprise seems to be how closely the professors fit the stereotype."

"Tell me about it," Janie said. "But you shouldn't be surprised, Professor - I mean John - us students have been getting it all the way through school. We're used to it. And don't worry. Most of us make up our own minds. These professors don't have half the influence they think they do. Not with students anyway. Maybe with each other."

Cann found himself being more impressed with this young woman every time she spoke. He could see why Roger liked her and he felt the same way.

Janie pressed him. "So what were you going to tell me about the founding fathers." She strongly emphasized the word 'fathers' for effect.

Cann smiled. "I wanted to make the point that the Constitution was designed as a document whose purpose was to protect individuals from the government - not each other. Except maybe as they work through government." He leaned forward a little in his chair and clasped his hands in front of him. "The key phrase in constitutional protections is 'state action'. That's what the founding fathers wanted to control. So the Constitutional rights we hear about - self-incrimination, the right to face an accuser, even due process - they don't apply unless the government is involved in the action being taken."

"I don't get it. I mean I know individual people sue other people based on their constitutional rights. Don't they?"

"Yes, but in most cases such a lawsuit is based on a law that's either already based on a constitutional right or is brought to defend a constitutional right under attack."

"Like what?"

"Well, take the famous Miranda rights for example. You know - 'you have the right to remain silent'?"

"Okay."

"If a police officer - an agent of the state - doesn't give an accused those rights, its a violation and, generally speaking, anything the accused says can't be used as evidence. But if - say - a private detective plays all sorts of tricks to get the same accused to talk to him, there is no violation. The information could - all other things being equal - be used as evidence in a court of law. That's because the Constitution isn't directed at the actions of private citizens towards one another. It's directed at the actions of the government toward private citizens. In the Miranda case, Miranda brought an action arguing that an existing constitutional right - his 5th amendment right not to be forced to incriminate himself - had been violated in a new way - by his not being advised of those rights when government officials took him into custody. The Supreme Court agreed and said it was."

Janie interrupted. "I consider myself kind of conservative and I'm not sure I agree with the Miranda rule. Do you?"

"Well, I don't like to be labeled since everyone defines things to suit them but, yes, Janie, actually I do agree with it. Don't buy into the concept that conservative equals anti-rights. I have no problem with the reading of the rights. It's the penalty - the exclusionary rule - which excludes all evidence which can be traced to the violation that I think is way out of whack."

"I guess you can't have one without the other, though, huh?"

"Sure you can. The exclusionary rule isn't in the Constitution. It's a procedural device the courts piled on top of the Miranda decision. And it's a crazy way of dealing with the problem. If a police officer does something wrong, why let the criminal go? Instead of suppressing evidence, just punish or discipline - or correct - the one who made the error. Simple enough."

With that, Cann raised his hand like a stop sign. "We're getting off the track here. I'm just making the point that because Charlestown University is a private institution, the Constitution doesn't require it to tell us who filed the complaint."

"Does that mean that the university can do anything it wants to me?" Cann could hear the concern growing in her voice.

"Only within limits." Cann sought to sooth the fears he was raising. "I don't mean to give you the impression that they can lock you up and throw away the key. Or flog you in the Quad. Those acts are against the law to begin with - for private citizens as well as governmental agencies. What I'm saying is that the university is not bound by the procedural mandates of the Constitution to follow certain rules of fairness that most of us have come to think of as basic. But that is not to say they can do anything to you that would violate other rights."

"Now you've really got me confused."

"It may not be as confusing if you think of the university as a private individual. They may not have to read you your rights under Miranda but they can't torture a confession out of you either. That's assault, among other things. That statement they wanted you to write last night before you even know what if anything you're being charged with is an excellent example. In a governmental context, that would clearly violate your Fifth Amendment right against self-incrimination. But the university didn't do anything wrong - constitutionally - in asking you to make the statement. I agree completely, by the way, with Roger's handling of that."

"Me too. I didn't know what to do about it but I had decided that I wasn't going to give one. What could they have done to me if I refused? Keep me in their headquarters all night?"

"I doubt it. In the absence of a criminal act, I don't see where they had any right to keep you in custody or even take you into custody in the first place. That might be something we should look into."

Janie's face showed how deeply she was thinking about all of this. "So what does govern this situation, then."

"Believe it or not - Contract. The nature of the relationship between you and the university is that of a contract between two individuals. You - or your parents - and the school. Within the limits of what is otherwise illegal - torture, false imprisonment, for example - the two of you have entered into a contract."

Janie held up her hand. "In your class this morning wasn't the point that whether it was fair or not, the parties have to agree to the terms of the contract?"

Cann couldn't be more impressed. "Yes."

"Well, I don't remember agreeing to any of this."

"But - in all likelihood, you did. When you - or your parents signed, presumably, some acceptance of admission, or other agreement. The basic agreement would be that you - in consideration........do you remember the discussion of consideration this morning?"

Janie nodded.

"Well in consideration of your paying tuition and, presumably, attending classes and meeting some minimum standards, the university would be obligated to provide you with the agreed upon instruction and, upon completion of the requirements, a degree. A bargained for exchange. Two items of value - in this case essentially fair value to each. In addition, I think it's reasonable to assume - but we'll check - that there was probably something about agreeing to abide by their rules of behavior - or Code of Conduct - or Terms in the Student Disciplinary Handbook - or some such thing."

"No doubt." Janie said that sarcastically.

"But the bright side is that the agreement also defines and limits what they can do to you. They can't sentence you to jail. Maybe - depending on the terms of whatever controls the situation - they could restrict you to your room though I tend to doubt that that's an alternative. But if its in the agreement, they could. It's pretty clear that the potential penalties in a case like this would be limited to the kinds of things they agreed to provide in the first place."

It was Janie's turn to lean forward and point. "So what you're saying is that if they determine that I've broken their rules, they don't have to keep up their end of the bargain. That's where probation or suspension or expulsion would come in."

"That's it. But let's not worry just yet. We don't know that there will be any charges of any kind. And, while I'm not the world's greatest optimist, I really can't imagine that this will be treated as being that big a deal. Okay?"

"I guess."

"Are you alright?"

"Yeah. I just feel so stupid. My first day - before my first day! - and I've got this hanging over my head."

"Well, I'm committed to helping you as much as I can, Janie. I promise."

That reminded her. "Oh, Sara - this is her office - said she wants to help in any way that she could. She's been at the school for five years now and thought maybe she could contribute something. She's a really good friend and she really wants to help."

"Good, I'm new to this place and never too proud to accept assistance. I'll get together with her before the hearing. I understand that its been set for 7:30 next Tuesday, right?"

"Yeah. Seven-thirty PM." She made a face. "I can't wait."

Cann stood up. "Don't worry, Janie. Time flies when you're having fun." Janie forced a crooked grin and Cann went back to being serious.

"Look, we can't predict what's going to happen so try not to worry about it. Okay?"

"I will. And thanks." She stood up and went up on her toes to give him a kiss on the cheek. "Is that okay? Do you mind?"

He didn't. "It's fine, Janie. I don't mind a bit."

She smiled and made a sort of half-skipping movement toward the door. "I have to get back to the class," she said, " - if they're still standing. Greg's a slave-driver when he leads." She stood with her back to the door and her right hand on the knob to let Cann pass. He stepped through the doorway and turned to wait in the hall to walk back with her. But Janie didn't wait for Cann. She pulled the door closed behind the two of them and cheerily said, "Bye" and actually skipped twice before breaking into a run down the hall. Cann shook his head with affection and amusement and watched until she turned left at the corner and was out of sight.

Chapter Nine

Cann exited the Gold Center and walked back across the Quad and into the Page building. He climbed the single flight of stairs and went into his office. He crossed the room and sat down, as always, leaning back in the large brown vinyl covered chair. After staring at the phone for several minutes, he lifted the receiver to call Arthur Matsen.

It wasn't that he was reluctant to call Arthur. There was certainly nothing negative between the two men. Quite the contrary. Arthur Matsen had plucked Cann from the field over a dozen years ago and mentored him through school and up the ladder at the firm. Now, while in some ways, vestiges of the mentor and protege relationship remained, in most other ways, they were peers and colleagues with full measures of mutual respect and regard.

It was that degree of respect and regard that made Cann the slightest bit hesitant to return the call to his mentor. There was something about the way he had been reached - at the university - on a work day - with a message to call Matsen at the office and not at home - that made it seem very likely to Cann that they would be going over ground already trod. Cann had already put Matsen in an awkward, almost untenable position by his defiance of a President who didn't handle defiance well. And he had gotten Matsen - or the firm anyway - caught in the middle. Matsen had backed him all the way, as Cann knew he would. But the situation had been difficult.

But there was no way Cann wouldn't return the call. So...

He picked up the phone and dialed the main number for Matsen, Loring. There was only one audible ring at Cann's end before the phone was answered. Cann heard Milly's familiar voice say, "Matsen, Loring, Gould. May I help you?"

"Hi, Milly. John Cann."

Milly who knew just about everything that went on at the firm - including exactly what the conversation between Matsen and Cann would be about - knew that the call would not be easy for either of them. But it was not her place to discuss the subject.

"Oh, John, it's wonderful to hear your voice. How have you been?"

"Good, actually, Milly. So far this academia thing has been pleasant. Kind of fun. How about you?"

"Well, I can't say I'd use the word fun right now, John."

"Why do I think that has something to do with why Arthur called."

"Because it does. Ironically, though, he's not available. Your timing is impeccably off. My orders were that he would take your call no matter where he was or what he was doing - except right now."

"What's going on right now? Can you say?"

"He's hooked up by phone to Frankfurt to sit in by teleconference on the IMF meeting over there. The Palestinian's are being given the old good news/bad news about IMF conditions for the $20,000,000 loan from the World Bank."

Cann was intimately familiar with the matter of the loan and the IMF and the Palestinians and knew now that his premonition about revisiting old territory had been correct. "Why is Arthur sitting in? Where's Ted?"

Milly told him.

"Oh no. I'm sorry to hear that. Ted was a good man." They had not been close friends but Cann had known and liked Ted Wagner. Still, he couldn't help but add. "I suppose Arthur is calling me now to take Ted's place?"

"Ted took yours," Milly said without thinking.

Cann was stung. "So I'm responsible for his death, Milly? I'd like to think not."

"I'm sorry, John, I didn't mean that. It's been a stressful day. I'm going over the limit even discussing it, anyway."

"No offense taken," Cann answered. But the remark smarted anyway.

"Actually, Arthur wants to discuss the entire matter with you. "

"Again," added Cann.

"Again," Milly responded. "His exact point?...I can't say."

"And wouldn't if you could, huh, Milly?"

"It's not my place, John. But listen to him, okay? Please?"

"You know I will. He'll call me back?"

"As soon as the meeting's over. Count on it. Maybe half an hour."

"No good. I have a 3:00 PM class to teach but I'll be back in the office right after it. Maybe 3:55. I'll wait for his call.

"Okay, John. I'll see that he knows you called."

"Thanks, Milly. You take care of yourself."

"You,too, John."

"I will."

*   *   *   *

As Cann hurried into his 3:00 PM Intergovernmental Relations class, Sara Furden sat in another office in another building on the campus watching quietly as Caroline Klein slowly finished reading a piece of mail she had picked up just as Furden came into the room. Finally, Klein put the letter down and looked across the desk at Furden and said, " Sorry to keep you waiting." Which of course she wasn't. "What can I do for you."

Furden characteristically got right to the point. "I understand that your going to present the university's case against Janie Reston."

"Is that the kid's name? Janie Reston? How cute." Klein's attitude - not unexpected - added to Furden's discomfort. "Yeah, apparently I am. Why?"

"So what is the university's position, " Furden pressed.

"How the hell should I know, Sara? I just heard about it today."

"And it only happened last night. Why so fast? What's going on?"

"You know as much as I do. Some kid - this Janie - exposed herself to the world and somebody blew the whistle. The rules call for a hearing. So what?"

"This Janie, as you put it, is a friend of mine." Klein raised an eyebrow and smirked but Furden continued. "I went to school with her mother and I've known Janie all her life."

Still smirking, Klein nodded and shrugged.

Furden went on. "This is a hell of a way to introduce a kid to university life. Let's just drop it. It was a simple mistake and she's embarrassed by it. Nobody got hurt. Right?"

"Well, that may not be for us to say, Sara. There may be a message to be sent here."

Oh shit, Furden thought. Her worst fears were about to be realized. "Come on. What message? A seventeen year old kid makes an error in judgment - no, not even judgment, an error in perception. What message can you take from that.

"It's not what message we take, Sara. It's what message we can give. Women arrive on this campus as babes in the woods? It's my job to change that - any way I can."

"Babes, Caroline? That's a word I didn't think you'd ever use."

"I use any words I want." Klein put heavy emphasis on the 'I' in the sentence making it clear that she was on a different level from the rest of the world. "As Chair of the Women's Studies program, it is incumbent on me to rid these 'babes' of the perceptions of their womanhood which have up to now been so structured and manipulated that they see themselves as reflections of an ideal created by a male-oriented society. From all I know of what happened last night, your friend Janie engaged in exhibitionistic behavior calculated to play upon the wrong attributes of women. It's entirely possible to use this incident to increase awareness among other females - especially among other freshman females -

that it's wrong to cater to the wants of males instead of taking what we want through our other strengths."

"But there was nobody around to see her, for crying out loud - how could she be influencing anybody. And it was a mistake. She didn't calculate anything - or intend for anybody to see her - male or female."

"But somebody did, didn't they. Somebody called security."

"Do you know who?"

"No, I don't. And I don't care. What does it matter anyway?" She was on her soap box. "Sara, I suspect that we feel the same on a lot of the issues confronting women. Or we should at least. This is one where, unfortunately the individual may have to suffer some discomfort - mild discomfort I would expect - for a greater good. We can use this incident to get out the message to this group of freshman women that they don't have to use their physical attributes to function in this world. That's important."

"Yeah I know," Sara broke in a sing-song cadence to her voice. "If we can save one other woman from this kind of situation, it will be worth it."

Klein didn't take to sarcasm. "Something like that," she snarled.

"Then let's save Janie. Why is the unknown 'other' more important."

"Because the concept is more important than the individual. That's why. Points need to be made whenever wherever and however they can. If there never is an 'other', it might be because we took this stand now." The look on Klein's face said "Checkmate."

Furden stood up. "Give the kid a break, Caroline. Is that so hard to do?"

Klein picked up another piece of mail. "I'll look at the facts and let you know what my decision is," Klein said shortly. "Close the door on your way out, please."

"Why is it your decision?"

"Because I'm making it my decision," Klein spat out. "Now why don't you cool it before you make it worse for your 'friend'."

88

Even though a big voice was telling her to shut up and get out, Furden blurted, "I'm not going to let her get hurt, Klein. I'll....."

"Yeah, fine." Klein interrupted. She waved dismissively. "Do what you will, Furden. You're out of your league. Believe it."

*   *   *   *

Cann hardly made it back to his office before the intercom buzzed. "Arthur Matsen on the line, Professor," said Sylvia.

"Thank you." He lifted the receiver to his ear. "Hello, Arthur. John here."

"John. It's great to talk to you. How is everything in the world of academia? Too dull for you?"

"Not really, Arthur," Cann laughed. "It's - well, let's say so far it's an experience."

The two men consciously prolonged the pleasantries. Not having spoken with each other for over three months there was much to say so it was easy. But when they inevitably ran out of social chat, it was Cann who broke the ice.

"I was sorry to hear about Ted, Arthur." He forced himself to stop there. Both men were acutely conscious of the fact that in any other conversation and any other context, Cann would have also said, "Is there anything I can do to help?" But in this case he didn't and they were both aware of the omission. It left a void in the conversation that seemed to hang for a few moments.

"Yes, it was a shame, John." Matsen finaly said. "A terrible waste."

There was silence on the line as both Cann and Matsen declined to bring the subject up or move on to something else. Cann pictured his friend agonizing over it and decided to open the discussion to the heretofore unspoken topic. "So where does that leave the firm on this one, Arthur?"

Matsen was relieved and grateful. Not only to have the subject on the table but also because he recognized the fact that Cann had brought it up to spare him the discomfort of doing so. He saw it as the show of loyalty and friendship that it was and appreciated it.

"Not unmanageable - yet. I was Ted's control for this one and so I've been kept informed. I'm as knowledgeable about it as he was. Or at least I'm supposed to be if he wasn't keeping secrets." The laugh was clearly forced.

"Ted was a straight shooter, Arthur. He wouldn't hold anything back."

"I know." Matsen paused then spoke. "We need someone there, John."

There it was. And as much as he would do - and had usually done - almost anything for Arthur Matsen, Cann still felt strongly about this matter.

Cann spoke quietly. "Are you asking me, Arthur?" Then, before Matsen could answer, Cann said, "I'm sorry, Arthur. I know you are and I don't want to make this difficult for you. But I hope you know how difficult this is for me, too. I feel like I'm letting you down."

"You're not let...."

Cann interrupted. "Of course I am. But I have no choice. You're the most principled man I know. And I pray to god that you know this is a matter of principle to me. My own principles and loyalty to Danny and the promise I made. Maybe it was a bad promise but I made it. And I can't take it back. That's why I can't do what you ask. I will not - I cannot - sit at the right hand of Yasir Arafat. It goes too far."

"I understand that, John, and you have my respect. You know that. For the moment, I am overseeing. Iverson's coordinating local activity. For now, I'd like you to be a resource. Background. General issues."

"It would have to be from here. Our illustrious President still doesn't want me in DC, right?" Cann said sarcastically.

Matsen shrugged unseen at the other end of the line. "In many ways, he's a pragmatist. I suspect if you took the assignment even at this late date, he'd be alright with it. That was the problem in the first place." Before Cann could speak, Matsen jumped in. "I know. I know, you can't."

90

"Come on, Arthur. He's no pragmatist. We both know that. Egotist, maybe. At best. If I were to accept the assignment - and I'm not - it wouldn't surprise me if he smirked and said, 'well, you can't have it, nyah, nyah." He laughed in spite of himself. "His ego's out of control."

"But, for good or ill, he's the man in the chair right now. And regardless of his attitude - or his inability to understand your position..."

"Or refusal."

"Or refusal," Matsen concurred, "he is the President. And he just might stumble or bluster his way into contributing to a solution in the Middle East."

"And taking all the credit no matter who really brings it off."

"Probably. But so what? If it happens, it's good. We're there to help that happen. With him or in spite of him."

In his office in Washington, Matsen leaned back in his chair and looked at the ceiling. "Look, John, you know I don't like the man either. I've known nine Presidents and every one of them, to one degree or another, could accept and respect another man's honor and principles - even when it meant they were disagreeing with the President of the United States. Not this one. I know. This one can't see past his own willfulness. But as slow as the process is going, at least right now there's a dialogue going on - and whether you like it or not, he speaks for the United States. We can frequently choose our allies. We don't often get to choose our opponents. We have to deal with what's there."

"The same can be said about Arafat, too, Arthur."

"Yes, it can. I'm glad to see that you realize that. Does it make you consider changing your mind?"

Cann's biggest problem was that he was fully capable of seeing the big picture. Peace in the Middle East - a permanent genuine peace - far outweighed individual considerations. He knew that. Still.......

"Arthur, you know how I feel about Arafat and you know why. Don't ask me to treat him as a respected world leader. He can never be that." His tone became deadly. "I'm telling you that if you put me in a room with him, I'll kill him." Cann was not posturing or exaggerating. He meant every word.

Matsen automatically said the things he had said before. "The region needs peace, John. Don't focus on Arafat. Think of the people. The Palestinians deserve a homeland."

"Come on, Arthur, I know you don't buy that as a justification. If that was the answer, this could have been over decades ago. To an awful lot of people, the King of Jordan is the titular head of the Palestinians and he's refused to give them any of his country - and Jordan is a lot bigger than Israel. Hell, he tossed them out. None of the Arab countries think a homeland for the Palestinians is important enough for them to give anything up. No, it has to be Israel." He stopped. "Come on Arthur, this is old polemics. Don't bait me."

"But if the old soldiers of Israel can sit down with the man, why can't you?"

"Obviously, I can't answer that. They made their decisions. I have to make mine. My gut wonders how Begin and Rabin and Peres could stand to be in a room with him at all - let alone shake his hand. For thirty years Arafat oversaw the murder of innocent men, women, and children all over the world. And the son of a bitch ends up with the Nobel Prize. For peace! Those tuxedos in Sweden are a pathetic joke. Arafat is what he always was - a coward and a terrorist. The so-called statesmen are always talking about sending a message. The message this sends is that there is nothing so evil that it can't go unrewarded."

"The world can forgive but you can't, is that it, John? That's a little egotistical, don't you think." But part of the problem Matsen had with winning this argument was that he essentially agreed with Cann. Being at the center of world crises for almost half a century, Matsen had often seen good come from evil - and vice versa. One man's Chamberlain was another man's Hammerskjold. As in so many crises, he felt that the peace process in the Middle East was more important than the individuals and personalities involved.

"There are a lot of people who say that Begin and Rabin, even Meir, and a lot of the others were terrorists at the beginning. They got a country and that legitimized them. That's the point that Arafat's at right now. When he gets a country, he becomes a statesman."

"Arthur, I'm biased. I admit it. But that's bullshit. I've heard that argument before and to me there is a huge difference between what the Haganah and the Irgun did pre-1948 and what Arafat and his PLO - and all their thug sidekicks - have done in their time. They - he - went beyond the normal terrors of war. You and I have both seen it. The poor bastard who gets killed in a pitched battle is just as dead as the civilian pushed out of an airplane. There's nothing pretty about either one. But there's a playing field that - even in war - used to be contained. These guys went everywhere and killed for the fun of it. Make no mistake about that. I've seen that, too - first hand - in their eyes - and in their smiles. They loved it, Arthur." He was shouting now. "And none of them - *none* - ever in their wildest dreams thought that what they were doing would lead to a country of Palestine - or cared if it did. They enjoyed what they were doing. That's it Arthur. Period. They took the battles outside the theaters of operation and murdered and maimed just for the fun and the visual effect. They killed people who had nothing to do with their cause or even their enemy's cause and made believe they were trying to blackmail people and countries into doing things that those people and countries couldn't do even if they wanted to. No, Arthur, I don't buy the song and dance that they are the same as the Israelis in pre-1948."

Part of Cann wanted to stop but continued. "And there's another difference. Begin and the others put their asses on the line themselves. Arafat is a coward who never placed himself in danger. The biggest sacrifice he has ever made is forgoing a complete night's sleep so that his sorry ass stayed in one piece." Cann slowed. "Please, Arthur, don't do this to me. Don't play devil's advocate on this one. It's personal. You know that."

Matsen searched for something to say.

"Look John. I know you can't see past Arafat in this but you have to try. What we're doing doesn't necessarily have to work to his benefit except indirectly. He is, for now, the head of the Palestinian Authority. Like we just said about the President. He's the man in the chair - for now. That doesn't mean that he always will be or that he will be even a year from now. What we're doing involves the process of helping the people of the region - the people - not any one leader. And if he happens to seem to benefit for a time - we have to live with it. To paraphrase someone we both admire, 'the good we do will live after him'."

Cann's smile was forced as he waited for the adrenalin rush to subside. "Nice literary turn, Arthur." He sighed and relented as much as he could.

"Arthur, I love Israel and the Israeli's. I make no bones about that. I want to see them live in peace as much as anybody - except maybe the Israeli's themselves. That's the prism I look through when the whole idea of Middle East peace is talked about. But I don't see how giving Arafat control over 20 million dollars is going to help Israel. I really don't see how helping him to build an airport in the middle of what is now Israel is going to help Israel. And deep in my heart, I believe that every time an honorable man treats that bastard as honorable, the entire process is diminished and Israel is endangered. The very meaning of the word 'peace' is dishonored. That's it. I can't help it. That's the way I feel."

"As for the President, I'll candidly admit to you that the idea of backing down and taking the assignment makes my skin crawl - for all the wrong reasons, I admit. I refuse to give him the satisfaction. For now the best I can do is meet you half way. I hope its enough - for now at least. Let me stay in the background. Call me anytime."

He gave out with a little laugh. "But try not to call me to Washington, will you? Mister President isn't too fond of me and I don't particularly want to see his face any more than he wants to see mine." Then Cann's voice went back to being glacial. "But I meant what I said about Arafat, Arthur. Please monitor the geographics carefully. I'll help every way I can. But don't let them hook me up with Arafat. I'm sorry. That's the way it is."

*   *   *   *

The large wood shingled house was set back about fifty feet from the north side of the street which dead-ended less than a quarter mile to the west and ran into State Road 53 about a half mile to the east. In fact, there were no other buildings on the north side of Rasen Street and there was only one house on the south side which sat about 150 yards to the east. And that house was empty. Which was surprising given its relative proximity to the Charlestown campus and the shortage of faculty housing.

The two men sitting inside the study of the house on the north side of the street were both smoking very strong cigarettes one after the other and the room was engulfed in a heavy odiferous fog. The smell of the smoke mixed with the heady sweet flavor of exceptionally strong coffee giving the room an exotic aroma which matched the visual scene. A westerner would probably remark that it was reminiscent of a scene from the movie Casablanca. To these men it was reminiscent of home.

The third man in the house at the time, Yousef Rahim, was laying sullenly on his bed in an upstairs room neither smoking nor drinking nor talking. It was he who was the subject of the conversation between the two men in the downstairs study.

"Where did you find him?" The man who sat behind the desk was asking the question of the man seated in a heavy leather armchair directly across the desk from him.

"I could not believe my eyes. I had just left the center and was not a hundred yards from the campus entrance when I saw him walking calmly along road 53. Not trying to conceal himself at all."

"Sometimes not trying to hide is the best concealment," said the man the others referred to as 'the chief'. "Did he have an explanation? Any reason for this breach of security?"

The man called Massoud shrugged. "He said he just wanted to get out. But then," Massoud hesitated, "he apparently met a girl and had sex with her."

"Allah help us," the chief threw his hands in the air. "So he left the house, walked to campus, and within a few hours met a girl and had sex. Just like that? Perhaps this is paradise after all, Massoud, heh?" Both men laughed. Then Al-Asif grew serious. "But we cannot have this. It is simply foolishness. Have you talked to him."

"Of course." Massoud was second-in-command. "But he is a simple man. Not stupid, Ram - but simple. He does not understand why he has stayed so long when he knows that the plan was for him to pass through quickly and be on his way. He has been here for almost two weeks and is - how do they say? - stir crazy?"

"But he is a professional, Massoud. He is not supposed to go 'stir crazy'. You must make him understand that we have an unusual circumstance which appears to be resolving and soon he will be on his way. His actions make no sense. He has endured far more difficult circumstances than this and not wavered. No?"

"Yes. But those other circumstances require focus and full attention or death can be the result. Here there is not that pressure. Here he spends too much time alone and has too much time on his hands."

The chief nodded. "I understand. But he must be made to understand that it is such things as what he has done today that bring down causes and men. One chance encounter - one random meeting. Something as simple as another girl finding him attractive and taking special note of him. Such things can come back at one time or another and destroy what we do here. Put it to him in those terms. Make him understand that what he has done has put us all in danger. This is not so different from the other circumstances you talk of. Survival is the issue now as well as then. When he exposes himself - when he reveals his identity or even his presence - he puts at risk his survival and our survival and the survival of the cause. This too is war and life and death.

He must see that this is an operation just like any other operation Make him see that."

"I will try."

"No, don't just try. You must succeed."

Chapter Ten

In the week following Ted Wagner's death, Brian Iverson delegated a great deal of the oversight of the day to day operations and routines of the office to others in the firm while he concentrated on the circumstances of Wagner's death beginning with an analysis of what, if anything, might have been done to prevent it.

Wagner had not - technically - been under Iverson's watch but Iverson had known that he would be coming to Frankfurt from Geneva for the Monday meeting. So despite the apparently random circumstances of the accident and also what his own objectivity told him, Iverson felt a degree of responsibility for Wagner's death.

Normal protocol - and common sense - dictated that Wagner would have come to the Frankfurt office of Loring Matsen before going on the IMF meeting. At that point, Frankfurt Security would have attached. Without a specific threat - or high tension status - it would have been loose but it would have attached nonetheless.

Of course, Wagner never made it that far and Iverson spent some time second-guessing himself and firm procedures in general. He had in fact already issued a memorandum to the DC office questioning whether there should be continuous and overlapping coverage of associates in transit from one office to another. But even as he wrote the memo, he knew that the expenditure in resources would be too great and concluded the memo with the statement that such an expenditure should be weighed against the costs. "What a political cop-out," he accused himself. But it was true. Short of assigning every associate on a case an individual permanent full-time 'cloak', there was no way to ensure the safety or survival of anyone. Accidents do happen. Anyway, Wagner's death was an accident.

Or so he thought.

Initially, there was no reason to think otherwise. In the darkness of the early morning hours, driving on an unfamiliar road in an unfamiliar country, a man who had possibly been driving all night, missed a slight bend in the road and smashed head on into a building. Sad but logical. And in almost every other situation, that is where it would have ended.

But Loring Matsen did not suffer the death of an associate without taking extraordinary steps to satisfy itself that it knew conclusively the details of every component of the event. Within forty-eight hours of clearing the scene in the tiny village of Sembach, Iverson had received preliminary reports from both the attending pathologist and the Motor Vehicle Technician going over Wagner's Austin-Healey. Both reported disturbing news.

The pathologist's verbal report to Iverson started out as Iverson would have predicted. Death appeared to be caused by massive trauma to the thoracic cavity and would have been instantaneous. Iverson listened to the rather gruesome description of the injuries with an impassive and stoic expression but his eyes widened imperceptibly when the pathologist - just as Iverson thought he was finished - said, "But..."

"But?" Iverson repeated.

"Yes. While the torso was quite destroyed, the extremities were intact and my first impression of the fingers and toes led me to a somewhat strange observation. Wagner's extremities were incipiently gangrenous."

Iverson figured he had to have misunderstood. "As in gangrene?"

He had not misunderstood. "Exactly. His hands and feet were in the early stage of dry gangrene at the time of his death."

Iverson remained incredulous. "Its September in Germany. No way have the temperatures been in that range. How in the hell....?"

The pathologist swayed back and forth in his swivel chair as he explained to Iverson in a perhaps more patient than necessary tone. "I said gangrene, Brian. Not frostbite. While gangrene can be one of the results of frostbite, it's not the direct result of cold. It can be the result of infection - called moist gangrene - or constriction of the blood vessels and muscles - dry gangrene. Wagner was suffering the dry type. Not caused bacteriologically - and not from cold. I need to get more deeply into this and other toxicology tests. I have some ideas - guesses really. Pure speculation right now."

"Okay. Anything else?"

"As a matter of fact, yes. In addition to the examination of tissues and structures, we drew some blood for testing from the patient." Iverson noted the use of the word patient, instead of victim. He found it an interesting affectation which reflected that, to the pathologist, the person on the table was still in a position to tell him something.

"Now," the doctor continued, "we're nowhere near finished with the tests - haven't really gotten started yet actually - but my lab assistant told me a minute ago that they found some unusual substance traces in the sample taken from Wagner's bloodstream. One of which has been identified as gamma-y-hdyroxybutyrate - found in a drug marketed as Rohypnol."

"Which is?" Iverson asked.

"Generic name 'flunitrazopam'. A sedative. Ten times more powerful than Valium. It's used to treat the most serious forms of anxiety and depression and has other legitimate medical uses as well. Unfortunately it's got a more nefarious claim to fame. You may have heard of it referred to as "roofies.""

Iverson had. "You mean the thing they call the 'date rape' pill?"

"Exactly. It has the effect of rendering someone who ingests it senseless in a very short time, makes them totally unaware of what's going on around them, and leaves them with no recollection of events while they are under its influence."

"Is it something someone would take to get a buzz or anything like that?" Iverson had never heard of Wagner being a substance abuser but he had to ask.

"Only if they got their kicks from the sensation of falling asleep almost instantly."

"So, could someone drive a car after taking it?"

"I don't believe so. Maybe very, very briefly, perhaps," the doctor said. "But I can't say I know enough about it to give you a definitive answer. Based on what I do know, I don't believe it's likely."

Iverson was already thinking that that could be an explanation of the accident. If Wagner had taken this Rohypnol - maybe thinking it was something else - then he could have dropped off as he got to Sembach and gone into the wedge of the building. It was possible. No less tragic. But possible.

"Will you be able to find out when Wagner took it?" Iverson asked.

"Sure. Like most elements, it breaks down at a predictable rate once it gets into the system. I can't give you an answer right now but we'll be able to tell you that and more after the full battery of tests are complete."

"Good. Thanks, doc."

It was a by-product of Iverson's job - and nature - for him to be suspicious. Even though his observations at the accident scene had given him no reason to suspect anything more than a car accident, he had, as always, reserved about 5% of his brain for suspicion - healthy skepticism, if you will. After the pathologist's call, the percentage had changed to around 65%. He still had no concrete reason to consider the event as more than an accident but the idea of someone trying to drive a car after taking an enormously powerful sedative set off the well-developed bells and whistles.

The suspicion quotient rocketed to virtual 100% when the motor vehicle technician phoned from the secured motor pool at Rhein Main airbase less than an hour later.

"You want my opinion?"

"Of course."

"This accident was no accident. Somebody made it happen."

Iverson leaned forward and picked up a pen from the side of his desk. "Why? What did you find specifically?"

"First, the motor mounts were all sheared off cleanly - indicating they had been cut or somehow weakened so that any significant impact would cause the engine to break free from the frame. Second, this car was in neutral when it hit the wall."

"How do you know that?"

"Because the gears are intact. There are toothed gears attached to the shift column that mesh with the gears in the transmission. You were at the scene. When this car hit the building, the entire drive shaft and rear end went back under the car as one piece. Remember, though, that the shift column stayed in place - right next to the driver. If the car had been in gear - any gear - the teeth on the shift column would have been meshed with the teeth in the transmission and the impact when the car hit the wall would have broken some of them off. It didn't. That says to me that the teeth weren't meshed."

"Couldn't they just have broken free at impact. I mean just pure happenstance or something?"

"Not in my opinion. These gears mesh very tightly. They have to or you'd be popping out of gear every time you hit a bump. And don't forget that when the car's in gear, the transmission is turning at very high rpm's. If there's an impact sufficient to shove the entire drive train assembly straight backwards, in the instant of impact the lateral forces on the teeth will be enormous. Hell, you've heard the sound it makes when people "grind the gears" when the car is standing still. We're talking hundreds of times the amount of impact here. No, this car was in neutral."

"I've heard of cars, popping out of gear by themselves. Any possibility of that?"

"Almost non-existent. We're looking at a high-performance car here. For its class at least. With a 'four-on-the-floor' set-up. The entire length of the shift column from knob to transmission is less than a foot. You just don't have the linkages between the shift and the transmission that would cause that problem. Plus, when a car pops out of gear by itself, it's because there's some pressure on the gears or linkages that cause them to do that. That kind of pressure leaves marks - and there aren't any. I looked long and hard for some."

Once again, Iverson appreciated and marveled at the thoroughness of this technician. "Anything else?"

"Well, this is more in the realm of speculation but there are marks on the trunk of the car that might explain how he hit the wall going so fast if he wasn't even in gear."

"Go ahead."

"He was pushed. And guided. The rear quarter of the body of the Austin is pretty much intact. A little buckling maybe but not much. All the impact was to the front. But we found chrome scrapings along the boot lid - that's what they call the trunk on these British cars."

Iverson knew that.

"Its indicative of a car with a higher ground clearance than the Austin has pushing it from the rear. There are even a couple of small depressions in the boot lid as if those chrome 'bullets' on the bumper of the pushing vehicle were pressing down as it pushed forward. Don't forget how low and curved the boots of these cars are."

"But those marks could be from an earlier time, no?"

"Possibly. But you're forgetting the way our guys treat their babies. Do you really think that Wagner would let his pride and joy go with blemishes for any length of time. This car would have been perfection."

"Good. But not conclusive on that point."

"I agree. Life's not perfect. But there were pressure depressions on the sides, too."

Iverson thought back to the parallel scrapes he had seen on the driver's side door which suddenly had greater significance. "On both sides?" He hadn't looked at the passenger side door.

"Pretty even. And they could match the height of any number of car bumpers in the world. My educated hunch says that there were three cars seeing to the force and the occurrence of this crash. One pushing from behind and one on each side to guide the Austin in and make sure it hit head on and full."

Iverson thought for a minute. "So your assessment is that Wagner was intentionally killed. What number would you give it?"

"My opinion - 100%. What can I prove - 90-95%, I think. In my mind, for what it's worth, I'm sure."

"I'll pass it on."

Iverson was very close to sure, too.

*　*　*　*

Iverson passed on to Matsen what he had to date - including the pathologist's preliminary observations with regard to the blood and toxicology tests - accompanied by the usual cautions that any conclusions at this point in time would be highly speculative. Iverson did offer the opinion, however, that the mechanical conditions of the Austin-Healey as related by the MV Tech were much less speculative. Closer to fact. So that regardless of the answers to the scientific and medical questions, Iverson was prepared to adopt the premise that Wagner's death was not a pure accident. Matsen's knuckles whitened as he read that part of Iverson's report. If Iverson accepted that, so did Matsen. He knew the manager of the Frankfurt office well. As with John Cann, Matsen had been the one who had brought Iverson into Loring Matsen. Unlike Cann, Iverson was recruited from the FBI - stolen by Matsen from the FBI might be more accurate.

Iverson had been a star at Northwestern Law School and had been actively recruited by the name firms not only in Chicago and the rest of the midwest but by many of the Washington and New York firms as well. He would have none of it. Long before he ever entered law school, he had decided to follow in his father's footsteps at the Federal Bureau of Investigation. For its part, the Bureau was delighted to get this outstanding prospect as an agent. His pedigree didn't hurt either.

As always, Iverson excelled at every step of the way even in the face of increasing antipathy - and worse, contempt - toward the Bureau and its work and history. It was an antipathy born in the arrogance and self-righteousness of the sixties and seventies which attained official sanction at the highest levels in the late seventies. A time when America's own leaders preached that everything about America was bad.

Things got a little better through the eighties - the bleeding was stopped anyway. But Iverson could never stomach the pervasive and incessantly negative hostility of the media and some others to the institution to which - for which - his father had given his life. The re-politicization and increasing abuses of the agency in the nineties finally disheartened Iverson to the point where he couldn't help but look at the Bureau as something appreciably less than the institution to which he had aspired.

Iverson had come to Matsen's attention on several occasions over the years when liaison with the Bureau had proven mutually beneficial. A half-flippant remark by Iverson to Matsen as they were leaving a presentation gave Matsen an opening to suggest further discussions and Iverson had accepted. The discussions led to an offer and Iverson joined the firm. Matsen's plan had been to keep Iverson in DC and groom him for the top. That was still the long-range plan but Iverson let Matsen know that he wanted to live in Europe for a while. It had always been a dream of his. And it was a good fit. In addition to the superb investigative and administrative skills Iverson possessed, the former FBI man spoke five languages and had acted as the Bureau's chief liaison with Interpol for over seven years. So, Matsen, in his wisdom, made Iverson an even happier man by making him the manager of the Frankfurt office. What that meant now was that the best man possible was already in place to investigate the death of Ted Wagner.

Matsen sent orders for Iverson to drop everything else and find out what happened. He also FYI'd Iverson's report on to Cann who spent a good part of the weekend going over it. The idea that Wagner's death had not been an accident was equally disturbing

105

to Cann. He questioned himself even more. Would Ted be alive if Cann had taken the assignment?

The answer was unavoidable. Almost certainly he would be.

Then the next question was, what could he do about it now?

That answer was equally clear. Nothing.

Nothing that would make Wagner be alive again, anyway.

There might be retribution if the facts warranted that. Cann would deal with that when it became reality.

So - with regret, to be sure - Cann moved on.

He had to consider that, when the process began to move again, he might be called upon to take Wagner's place. He was the best man for the job. The firm's first choice. Logically. Always had been. Now, in the absence of Ted Wagner, - if he was to help - it would be a question of how Cann could reconcile the demons within himself without betraying a promise to another fallen comrade.

Cann was not a specialist in the Middle East in the sense that a true specialist concentrates on one thing and nothing more. But for over twenty years, he had certainly spent more time on assignment there than anywhere else. It often seemed that assignments to other locations were just temporary duty away from his recurring activities involving the State of Israel. It never ended. Put out one fire and another sprang up. Cann had often commented in the last couple of years that, with the end of the Cold War, the Middle East had the dubious distinction of being the world's longest running continuous crisis.

Now - yet again - there were signs that the crisis could - might - one day - actually end. In moments of candor - or fits of pique - as it were, Cann was not as optimistic as some. Whenever it seemed that there might be some progress made, it seemed to Cann, it was only and always after Israel was being pressed to give something up.

There was no mistaking his loyalties. He was vigorously pro-Israeli. Period. And he still did not believe that the various parties who had sought to expunge the State of Israel from the face of the earth had reconciled themselves to its continued and permanent existence.

After the victories in the Hundred Hours, Six-Day, and Yom Kippur Wars, Israel's established geographical neighbors had - with uncharacteristic but understandable logic - eschewed direct military confrontation. But it was supplanted by what Cann felt was the lowest form of cowardice - sneak attacks on the most unsuspecting targets.

Cann was no naif. He had seen war and its results. He had seen death and injury and caused his share of both. He had long ago acquired the heart and mind of the professional soldier who sees death as one more certainty and accepts it as inevitable. It is only the time and place that are indeterminate. Known only - and then only perhaps briefly - to the determinator. It is - despite the apparent contradiction - a fact of life.

And Cann was also a student - of many things. Including history. And he knew that terrorism was not a twentieth century phenomenon. It was as old as the existence of fear - and the realization of the first terrorist somewhere back in time that a greater and wider effect could be achieved by the threat than by the act if the consequences of the act were terrible enough - and random enough.

But the terrorism of the past had been - in its way - confined. Most often used by the occupied to fight the militarily superior occupier, the weaker side would destroy a man or a thing of importance. The attacked would then become the attacker and extract some hideous punishment for the first attack. And on and on it would go. But there was to some degree a cause and effect. The occupier knew why the attack took place. And the occupied themselves knew that they were at risk for the acts of the attackers.

The enemies of Israel had removed the cause and effect aspect and taken terror to a new level - or depth. In exporting it beyond the borders of the conflict - to the world at large, they had articulated that their cause was paramount - not just to their enemy but to the most fundamental rules of human behavior and decency.

Over the years, Cann had faced - and faced down - many of the new terrorists. And he had found that less than a handful were true ideologues. None were soldiers. Soldiers died saving children they had never even seen before - not blowing them to pieces anonymously and without warning far from any arena of battle. Terrorists were not soldiers. Cann had looked into the eyes of many a terrorist and few were loyal to any cause other than their own sociopathy.

In contrast, soldiers had loyalties. To causes. To people. To promises. And to honor. Especially to honor. Long before there was an Arthur Matsen, or a law school, or a Loring, Matsen, and Gould in Cann's life, there was a promise to a fallen comrade on a runway apron in Entebbe, Uganda.

*   *   *   *

The terrorists were dead. The hostages were on the C-130. And the last of the Israeli commandoes were clearing the airport reception building which had - until less than thirty minutes before - been a prison to 104 people. 71 Israelis and 33 of other nationalities among the passengers. Five crew - all French.

Sadly, three of the hostages died in the beginning moments of the raid. Israel would mourn their loss. But given the enormity of the operation, that number was almost unbelievable. While, the hope had been for a complete rescue, the truth was that not a single one of the military personnel either on the raid or back in Tel Aviv would have anticipated such extraordinary effectiveness and low casualties. It had gone off better than the rehearsals. Everything and everyone had been exactly where they were expected to be. The few Ugandan soldiers who chose to fight were also dead. The rest who had been guarding the perimeter of the airbase were nowhere to be found.

The terrorists themselves had not put up much resistance at all. In fact, of the seven, four had thrown down their weapons at the first hint of trouble and tried to pose as hostages themselves. It was a particularly stupid thing to do but was apparently the flip side of what was known as the Stockholm syndrome - where the hostages began to identify and empathize with their captors. In this situation, the terrorists - with the help of a complicitous Idi Amin - had wielded such unquestioned power over their captives that now when they, the terrorists, were in trouble, they were unable to comprehend the effect of the change in circumstances. They had come to see their captives as sheep and had seen their compliance as a permanent condition rather than an effect of the guns at their heads. When the soldiers burst in, the terrorists had actually expected the hostages to hide them in their midst.

They were wrong.

One by one - and very quickly - the cowering ex-terrorists were identified to the commandoes by one or more former hostages and were shot where they lay. They had no time to suffer the misappropriation of hope that could hollow out the strongest of captives. In that way, the terrorists had received more merciful treatment than they had ever afforded their own captives.

Within ten minutes, the seizure operation was over and the retreat/escape was well under way. Colonel Daniel Shelanu stood outside the reception building waiting for the last of his soldiers to complete the clearance of the interior. All of the captives were accounted for and all - except for one who had been taken to the hospital earlier were on the evac plane. Shelanu reacted only slightly to the noise each time he heard a single shot from inside the building which indicated that one of the former captors' neutralization had become permanent and certain.

Shelanu watched with amusement and feigned irritation as the young American 'liaison' - the only non-Israeli in the operation - walked toward him across the tarmac.

"Go back to the plane, John," the Isreali Colonel of Commandoes said sharply. "You're violating the rules of engagement by being over here."

But he smiled as he said it.

"That's an interesting concept in an operation like this, Danny." The American in the unmarked fatigues and black beret extended his right hand to the colonel. "Congratulations."

"Yes," Shelanu replied, 'it went well. A textbook operation."

"Not from any textbook I ever read," Cann answered. "You wrote the book on this one."

"If only it were the final chapter, John. Despite our success, it may still be just the beginning of a new theatre."

"The world," Cann nodded. Behind them another single shot rang out. Both men glanced slightly back in the direction of the sound and continued their conversation.

"How does it end, Danny?" Cann asked.

"Maybe it doesn't. Ever. For it to end in this decade or even the eighties - if Israel lasts that long - the only solution is military. Israel conquers the entire Arab world."

"That isn't going to happen."

Shelanu nodded. "Of course not. And I'm not even saying that it should happen. What I am saying is that the Arabs who exist today have drawn a line in the sand - literally. And I don't see them backing off from their goal of wiping Israel off the face of the earth." He paused then said. "Which is of course the other military solution to this."

"Well, we're behind you, you know that."

"For now," Shelanu said then spoke quickly when he saw the look on Cann's face. "No, John, please. Understand that that was not an accusation of betrayal or even weakheartedness. But you must understand that - at this time - here in 1976 - the United States supports Israel because the Soviets support the Arabs - or vice versa - the chicken or the egg. What came first? That may change. Your leaders may change. Will change."

"But the heart of my country won't change. If nothing else, we're suckers for the underdog."

"I don't know that we would all agree with that characterization," Shelanu smiled, "but don't underestimate the pressures of world politics. I know you are familiar with our history but did you know that twenty years ago after what we call the Hundred Hours, we took all of the Sinai almost to the Suez Canal?"

"Sure, it's..."

"But do you know that it was Eisenhower - he alone - who made us give it all back and even threatened to stand aside if the Soviets attacked the State of Israel if we did not?"

"I've heard that. But the conventional thought in the military is that we would have stepped in if it came to that."

"Perhaps, but at that time, we could not take the chance and - who knows? - where would we be if Israel had a twenty year history as one of the larger countries in the Middle East - even if it was 70% desert - instead of a sliver along the coast." He put his hand on Cann's shoulder. "What I am saying is that we cannot predict the future. Obviously. And individual leaders have more of an effect on history than we sometimes can see or realize."

Cann spoke with a quiet that belied the intensity of his feelings as he looked around them. "And an individual with a bomb strapped to his chest or a gun in an airplane full of unarmed people can make some pretty heavy changes too."

"Ah, this." Shelanu waved his hand around. "This is the worst part of all. Even if good people want to stop the fighting, they in turn can be stopped by Arafat and people like him. This has to be stopped - and it cannot be stopped. Unless somehow Arafat is stopped."

"Even if he is, Danny, somebody else will take his place."

"Yes, and then that person must be stopped. And the next and the next. Isn't that better than the thousands of innocents who die if this one man does not?" He looked Cann straight in the eye. "We have both seen the results of his work. And I tell you, my good friend, it is my pledge on my honor and on yours that I will work to rid the world of this curse. Can you join me in that pledge?"

Cann looked hard into Shelanu's eyes and saw the determination and intensity behind the most scared of pledges. To swear on one's honor - among true soldiers - was to commit oneself to the most binding of promises. But to pledge upon the honor of another made failure a smear upon a comrade. And a

111

soldier who dishonored a fellow soldier of honor could have no honor of his own.

Cann was hesitant only because of the enormity of the charge. He too had seen the results of the terror - the limbless bodies of infants in the rubble of busses and homes, the old people frozen forever in pleas of submission that still had not caused them to be spared. Finally he said, "Yes. Danny. I join you in that pledge. On my honor."

"And on mine," Shelanu insisted.

"And on yours."

Shelanu nodded forcefully just as another single shot rang out. But this time his head didn't come back up. Instead, he seemed to sit down from his standing position and lay back until he was prone.

Cann looked down and saw the spreading red stain on the front of Colonel Daniel Shelanu's shirt. As he did so, he pulled the very non-regulation Luger 9mm pistol from the holster in the hollow of his back.

With extraordinary peripheral vision, he had seen the muzzle flash that had accompanied the shot that had hit Shelanu from the tower opposite where they stood. As he looked at the point where he had seen it, another shot rang out and Cann heard it thump into the prone Colonel. Not an instant passed before Cann returned a single round to the right and just above the second muzzle flash. He heard but could not see in the dark the clatter of metal as the sniper's weapon hit the tarmac below and he felt the involuntary gratification that came with a task accomplished. But it was short lived as he turned back to Shelanu who was already dead.

Behind him, several commandos rushed from the reception building with guns initially pointed at Cann who pointed up to the tower. Without a word they rushed over to the tower and went inside. Within one minute, there were several bursts of automatic fire and then a body in the uniform of the Army of Uganda was thrown off the tower. It landed in a heap on the tarmac very close to its gun.

Chapter Eleven

Things slowed down a little over the weekend for Janie. Her first full week of college was behind her and she felt that she had started out well - mostly. Her classes were about what she'd expected and her professors seemed to be pleasant enough albeit less impressive than she'd been led to expect. She was confident that she would do well and move on quickly to the next level. Even Professor Veltri had seemed to forget - or at least not mention - their prior discussion and had made no more references to Janie's inability to cut the apron strings. The same couldn't be said about his incessant references to euro-centricism and Janie wondered each time if she was being tested. But she passed on making any comments and the week ended quietly. She spent all day Saturday doing the things she had not done all week - like laundry and cleaning and even a little studying. But not much - not on a Saturday.

Saturday evening, Sara came by to take her to dinner and they went to a small place near the campus that served italian food, a favorite of both of them. Over pasta and the shared glass of wine that Sara let Janie sip from when the restaurant people weren't looking, they engaged in the same small talk that they always did. They hadn't really gotten together during the past week and had had no chance to talk so they were just catching up on the minutiae of each other's lives.

113

After a while, Sara told Janie about her conversation with Caroline Klein and apologized for the fact that the discussion had not gone well. This brought the issue and the hearing back to mind and tensed things up a bit.

Janie didn't understand what Klein's role was in the overall scheme of things. "I mean she's got no vested interest in seeing me get in trouble, right?"

"You have to understand that in many ways, she's what some people call a professional malcontent, Janie. I mean she has done some good things - I suppose - but she's one of these one-dimensional tunnel-visioned people that live for their cause and can't see anything beyond it. I don't imagine that she consciously wants to do you any harm. She just doesn't take something like that into consideration. It's irrelevant. If she hurts someone, she takes it absolutely for granted that the person injured is happy to be of service to her cause. And if they're not - well then they don't deserve her compassion anyway. I think I've heard it described as the Ayahtollah Khomeini syndrome - where the person is so convinced of the moral correctness of what they do, it is impossible for the slightest doubt to intrude. Anything is proper if it serves their end."

"My parents always said that the end doesn't justify the means."

"Well, not everybody lives by the same philosophy, Janie. Welcome to the real world."

"That sure doesn't make me feel any better about this," Janie moaned. "Professor Cann kind of told me what could happen and it just makes no sense to me. I made a silly stupid mistake." She shook her head back and forth slowly. "You know, I thought college was supposed to be more mature than high school. In high school, nobody would have made anything of this. I swear. "

Furden nodded. "The politics are different here. No doubt about that. But what did Professor Cann say to you. Is he scaring you too?"

Janie shook her head much more vigorously this time. "Oh no. He's really nice, Sara. He really is. And I really really feel that deep down, he's going to help me out of this - without too much scarring, anyway. There's something about him - a strength I guess - that makes me feel he's not going to let me get hurt."

Furden felt a little pang of jealously. "I won't either, you know, Janie. I made you a promise and I meant every word." Then she softened a bit. "Or do I sense a crush coming on here? Maybe I really should meet this Professor Cann of yours, don't you think."

Janie twisted her lips a little. "He's not 'mine', Sara. And he's kind of old. But you should talk to him. My 'dream team' defense needs to coordinate." She giggled. "I'll drop in on him on Monday and see if I can set something up. I think you'll like him." Janie's face crept into a sly grin. "He's a lot more your generation than mine."

Furden crumpled a paper napkin and tossed it at Janie's face but the projectile unraveled in flight and fell short of its target landing on Janie's plate. As they both watched it begin to absorb some of the puddle of red sauce in the middle of it, Furden noticed the mischievous hint of a smile beginning to appear on Janie's face.

"Don't you dare," Furden warned as Janie picked up the soggy mass in two fingers.

* * * *

Getting the internally stored locater data was critical to Iverson not just because of the absence of the real time information but also because the missing information might give some clues as to why the sender was turned off in the first place.

Unfortunately, and to his great frustration, Iverson had still not received it from the technical people by the close of business on Friday. Apparently, some of the inner workings of Wagner's watch had been badly jarred in the crash and that had caused a problem with the retrieval of the specific routing information Iverson needed. He was assured that he would get it as soon as possible and they regretted the delay but it was unavoidable if the retrieval was to be successful.

As a result, Iverson had spent the weekend in his apartment going over what information he did have available for his efforts to recreate Wagner's last days. At the moment, all the evidence Iverson had to work with - besides what he already knew from the autopsy and mechanical inspection of the Austin-Healey - was what he had been told by Loring Matsen's Geneva people.

On Thursday, Iverson had called Bucher, his Geneva counterpart, to direct an inquiry into Wagner's movements before he left Geneva on the previous Friday. That inquiry didn't appear to reveal any significant clues since Wagner had been in meetings from eight AM to just before six PM. Even his lunch had been a working session at which Wagner, his legal assistant, and several IMF staff had discussed the likely - indeed obvious - terms that would be imposed on the Palestinians at the Monday meeting in Frankfurt three days hence. Interviews with the participants in the meetings and the luncheon session revealed no obvious anamolies calling for investigative attention. The Loring Matsen legal assistant, a Lisa Harmony, said she had noticed nothing unusual about Wagner or his demeanor and hadn't seen him after the lunch concluded.

Bucher was able to determine that Wagner left the Loring Matsen Geneva office alone at 6:00 PM. A visit to the residence hotel where Wagner was staying revealed that he had arrived at the hotel at roughly 6:15. That would indicate a direct trip from the office. No delays. No stops.

Bucher interviewed the desk clerk who also remembered that it was not very long before Wagner came back down in the elevator and left the hotel with a small suitcase. The clerk couldn't be sure how much time had passed because the lobby was quite crowded with normal Friday evening in and out to dinner and entertainment traffic. It might have been as little as ten minutes.

'Did he recall anything about Herr Wagner at that time?' Bucher had asked the clerk.

'Only that he seemed quite cheerful and even excited.' The clerk had recalled that Wagner walked quickly - almost a run - out the front door to where the valet had brought his car and drove off at once. The valet confirmed this, could remember nothing else unusual, but did remark that Wagner had given him a 20 Franc tip, more than usual.

Wagner left his hotel at approximately 6:30 PM but the routing which had been transmitted in real time showed that he hadn't crossed a grid showing him leaving Geneva until just after 7:00 PM. Even accounting for traffic delays on a Friday evening, that indicated that Wagner almost certainly made a stop before getting on the N1 highway out of Geneva. And since the first grid crossover of the trip was the one occurring on N1 north, Iverson knew that the stop would have been somewhere inside the same grid square mile as Wagner's hotel.

Bucher had thoroughly examined Wagner's room. As with most transient locations, there was less to be found than would be expected in a more permanent residence. Often, there is something about transience that can make people more organized than usual and, since Wagner had been quite organized to begin with, nothing was out of place in his room. All items of clothing were hung or folded neatly in their appropriate places and papers were neatly stacked by the lamp and phone on the small writing desk.

Bucher also had the room swept electronically and found nothing. But he wasn't a slave to technology and took a degree of pleasure in using non-high tech methods to get information. So he picked up the message pad next to the telephone and, using a pencil, scraped the lead flatly on the top sheet of paper. Sure enough, the last writing which Wagner had done on the pad appeared as three lines of white lettering amid the dark gray of the pencil lead. The first line of three letters was quite clear. The second line consisting of two letters was a little less so but still readable. The third line appeared to be six numbers written on a single line in pairs but only the first three were discernible.

TBA
CG
22 0_ _

At Iverson's direction, Bucher made exact copies of the note pad page and faxed them to Frankfurt. That would be all the information Iverson would have to start with until he got the completed locater information and the rest of the test results from the doctor. It was better than nothing because it gave him something to do. Iverson didn't handle idleness well.

*　*　*　*

Caroline Klein padded out of the bedroom of her luxury condominium in huge furry pink slippers and a night shirt that barely covered the tops of her very long legs. She was five foot ten in her bare feet and quite slender but by no means skinny. She had sandy hair and an oval face with skin that was shiny and smooth enough for a woman carrying half her forty years. At most times of the day, she wore rimless eyeglasses but at the moment they were on the coffee table in the living room where she had just placed them as she made the walk from the bedroom to the front door of her condo.

She didn't bother looking through the security peephole before throwing open the door and retrieving the Sunday New York Times from the hall. Gathering the paper up in folded arms in front of her, she turned and re-entered her residence while at the same time giving a kick to the door to close it.

The automatic coffee maker had brewed the coffee as programmed at its Sunday setting of 10:00 AM instead of the weekday 6:00 AM so now, an hour later, it had acquired the roundness that she missed during the week. She poured herself a cup and took a deep inhale of the steam coming off it enjoying the scent of what she considered to be very strong coffee before she added the hazelnut flavored creamer she loved and went and curled up on the couch to read the paper.

She had completed the first news section and the comics and was about to start on the editorial page when she heard Ramadan moving about in the bedroom. After a minute or so of indistinct rustling, the door opened and he came out into the living room.

"So, you have beaten me up again," he smiled. Then he frowned. "No, wait, I have said something with the wrong phrase, no?"

"Not exactly, Ram," Klein said with a smile. She pronounced it 'rahm' not 'ram'. "What you said is right. It could be taken more than one way, though. 'Beat up' can mean that I 'got out of bed before you' or it could also mean that I 'physically inflicted violence on you'." She smiled again. "Not likely."

"I would hope that I would not give you cause to do such a thing," Ramadan smiled back. "May I help myself to some coffee?".

"Of course. But are you sure you can stand it? You always comment on how weak it is no matter how strong I try to make it."

"It is culture, Caroline. In the Middle east, we simply have a different concept of coffee. More like what is called espresso over here."

"I know but you don't expect me to buy an espresso maker just for you on Sundays, do you?" She immediately regretted what sounded like an inquiry into possible commitment and changed the subject.

"There's a fascinating article on page eight of the front section of the Times about the possibility of an Arab Summit after the Israeli election. I'd love you to read it and give me your impressions on the subject."

"Of course, Caroline. I would be happy to. But of what value are impressions compared to the reality we will know in three days after the election is complete. May I be so bold as to predict before I even read it that the writer of this article has simply stated his or her own opinions of what will happen if Yenahim wins or Shelanu wins. Such articles are nothing more than the self-indulgence of a reporter who wishes to show you what it was he or she would write about depending on the circumstances of the day. If they waited until after the election, they could only write half the article and that would not do. I suppose as predictions they have some value - but no more than the value of any other form of guess."

"Which is why I would like to hear your reaction to what it says, Ram. Your 'guesses' - and I only use that word because you did - as head of the Middle East Studies department, do have significant value." She smiled. "Especially to me."

Ramadan smiled back at her. "Thank you. But I fear that you are the exception to the rule." He took his coffee into the living room where he sat in an armchair opposite the couch where Klein had been reading the paper.

Pointing at the newspaper strewn about the couch, Ramadan Al-Asif asked Klein, "Do you know how many times I have been asked for comment by someone doing an article such as this?"

Klein didn't answer out loud. She just shook her head back and forth once.

"Never." He tilted his head slightly forward and raised his eyebrows in emphasis of the point. "Do you know why, even as Head of the Middle East Studies Department, I have never been asked to comment?"

"Because you might not confirm their preconceived notions, I suspect."

Ramadan shrugged one shoulder and said, "Exactly the opposite. It is because they assume they already know what I will say. I am an Arab. Therefore I am..." He hesitated and frowned, searching for a phrase. "'Pigeon-cooped?'," - he frowned again - "Is that the right term?"

"Pigeon-holed."

"Yes. Pigeon-holed, thank you, first and foremost as a terrorist and also as an anti-semite - a ridiculous term in relation to an Arab - who worships Assad and Hussein - either of them - and hates dogs. To them I am the 'camel jockey' who spends his nights with his male friends and his days beating his many wives."

"You paint with too broad a brush on that one, Ram." Klein's nature did not allow her to just listen during a conversation. "What you say is certainly true about the right-wingers but, as the right wingers themselves will tell you ad nauseum, most journalists are not on the right. And many are sympathetic to the Arab position in regard to Israel."

"And they already know what it is. So they do not ask. You help me make my point, Caroline. " He sipped his coffee. "Are you guilty , too, my dear?" Before she could protest he held up a hand and went on.

"Would it surprise you so very much to learn that I don't fit that stereotype. I don't mean the other things. By now, I hope you know I am not like that. I mean about Israel. That I feel there is much to admire about the Israelis. To be sure my loyalties lie with my own people but even a 'camel jockey' can be objective."

"I wish you wouldn't use that term, Ram. Stereotypes also offend me. Let's leave the pejoratives to the right-wingers."

"Leave the what? You exceed my vocabulary with that one," he said laughing.

"Pejoratives are negative characterizations - belittling stereotypes." Klein made the explanation in a straightforward way without rancor or patronization. It gave her genuine satisfaction to assist him with his English and when she did so, it was without smugness and with a degree of real affection.

The relationship between these two had actually come as an enormous surprise - indeed an impossibility - to her colleagues and all the others who just knew that a well known ardent feminist could never be involved with a man from one of the most sexist cultures in the world. Friend and foe alike imagined constant battles and tugs-of-war, or worse, between them as he did what comes naturally and she responded with years of training and conditioning.

But that was not the case at all and, truth be told, the success of the relationship was due more to Ramadan than Klein. When they first met, Klein had all her defenses up and - just as Ramadan had been saying - held the expected stereotype of him as an incurable and rabid sexist. But in their first conversation at a meeting of department heads, he had exhibited a surprising sensitivity and lack of arrogance. He had shown respect for her and admiration for her accomplishments - of which he already seemed to be aware.

It was a little thing but Klein was also taken by his unselfconscious acceptance of her help with his English. This was especially striking to Klein because she subscribed to the stereotype of men being incapable of asking for help and never - ever - asking for help from a woman. But at one point in their conversation he had made a reference to the Chair of the Math Department being 'as old as the mountains' and Klein had quickly - without thinking about it - corrected him saying that the phrase was actually 'old as the hills'. Once said, she had looked for the surliness that would surely come but it didn't. Instead he asked her about it and they had a light discussion on whether someone 'as old as the mountains' would be older than someone 'as old as the hills' and had had a good laugh.

They slept together that very night and frequently thereafter, both of them preferring her home because it was more comfortable and more luxurious than the house he shared with some other staff. It was also more private. They spent almost every weekend at her condo - and often found themselves in discussions such as the one they were having now.

"So when someone makes a pejorative statement," Klein continued, "they are saying something derogatory - or insulting. Get used to it , Ram, it's the American way. This country has a long history of one-dimensional stereotypes and bigotry. It is our shame - or one of them - and a burden that all of us are stuck with. Even those of us who have rejected racism and bigotry.

"Sometimes when you say such things, Caroline, I get the feeling that you take your objectivity beyond dissent to an actual dislike for your own country. Do you hate the United States?"

"I hate a lot of what it stands for. For the first two hundred years, we were a smug, self-satisfied arrogant bully imposing our will around the world. We congratulated ourselves on being god's anointed when what we had was due strictly to luck and coincidence and the ability to effectively steal all this land and natural resources from the people it really belonged to. Still belongs to. It's only in the last thirty or so years that we have managed to own up to our shortcomings and give compassion a foothold in our national psyche. And its still a precarious foothold. We could lose it at any time."

"Why?"

"Look at recent elections. We lost control of Congress and the right-wingers are undoing a lot of what we've accomplished so far."

"But if the people have voted them in - isn't that democracy."

"Democracy isn't enough, Ram. What was it Sartre or somebody said - 'People have to forced to be free'."

"Rousseau. The Social Contract."

"What? Oh, right. But listen. Democracy has its limits. You can't have majority rule and still be fair to the oppressed. Not if the majority is not fair to begin with. So they have to be led. If fairness is freedom, the people have to be forced to be free." Klein was warming to the subject and starting to lecture.

"The only way we were able to chart and steer the course we've been on was through the courts. You don't think the everyday citizen would have voted for the right thing, do you? We needed right-thinking judges to take the reins. The people would vote but they were electing the wrong people. We finally saw that the only way around that was to get judges who knew how to find a basis in the Constitution for what was right and then impose it on the other two branches of our government in the name of constitutionality. That's why this obsession with Constitutional Amendments is so dangerous to us. The value of the Constitution lies in its ambiguity. People burn flags because judges say the First Amendment lets them. That couldn't happen if the Constitution said, 'you can't burn the flag'. Listen if the issues of the last thirty years had been left to the legislatures - state and national - we'd still be segregated and women wouldn't have the vote."

"How awful." Ram was making a sarcastic joke. It was a rare slip for him.

Klein glared. Furden's characterization was correct. Klein's causes were everything and mere affection - which she knew would pass - did not displace them. There were taboo subjects and things that Ramadan - or anyone else - couldn't joke about in her presence. The fact that in his country women did not have the vote was bad enough. If he thought he could joke about it...

"I am sorry, my dear. Forgive me. It was meant only as a joke."

"Well, I don't find oppression of women funny."

"Nor do I. Can we lighten this up a bit?"

Klein was no longer glaring at him but her mood had changed dramatically. She turned her head towards the wall.

Ramadan sighed. He knew that Klein's funk would last several hours.

"Then perhaps I should go." It was not a bluff. Under the circumstances it was the only logical thing to do. He got up and walked toward the bedroom.

Klein spoke icily. "Perhaps you should."

Ramadan went into the bedroom and came out some ten minutes later fully dressed with a sports carryall that he used as an overnight bag. He walked up to Klein from behind and leaned over and kissed the top of her head. "Will I see you during the week?"

"Not Monday. We're having a Women's Outreach Monday night. But don't forget you're attending the Student Disciplinary pre-hearing on Tuesday."

"Ah, yes. I mean, no, I haven't forgotten. The young lady who danced naked in the gym."

"The issues are a little more global than that, Ram. You said you would attend. Solidarity is important. Everybody should be there. She has a lawyer coming with her. Remember that guy at the new faculty reception? The Johnson Chair in the law school?"

Ramadan seemed interested in that. "He will be with the girl?"

"Young woman, Ram, I've asked you before. Yes. He committed himself to representing her. He'll be at the pre-hearing. And probably his buddy Dean Walder, too. They appear to have adopted their own little Isadora Duncan."

"And so this matter keeps him here until Tuesday at least?"

Klein didn't understand the question. "He's the Johnson Scholar in the law school. He's here for the year I would think."

"It is normal for lawyers to be with the students at these hearings?"

"Actually, no. It's fairly unusual. Why?"

"Just curious." He paused seemingly deep in thought. "Well actually, since you are already angry with me, I may as well tell you what I am thinking."

"Yes, you may as well," Klein said coldly.

"I frankly do not understand why this hearing is even taking place. What the gir...young woman did was hardly terrible and it seems to me that this meeting on Tuesday only draws more attention to an event that would have been forgotten by now except for the reaction to it."

"Precisely. We don't want it forgotten. Every year there's something - there has to be so that we can make the point to the incoming women that they have the power now and they need to know how to use it. I'm sorry you don't see that - or agree with it perhaps. I would have hoped you were on my side." He protested with a gesture. "And I would have hoped that by now you would understand that the ramifications of...that the importance of an effect can far exceed the significance of the action that caused it."

"But other issues that have come up in the past have been more serious - assaults, harassment - more obviously critical to your point. This dancing naked, - don't you think many students will think she did nothing wrong."

"So?"

"So, in this circumstance perhaps this should be settled prior to the hearing."

"And lose our issue? I don't think so."

"You may lose more."

"How?"

"By making such a large issue of something that many of those you seek to influence do not find so bad. In my country, yes, a women's nudity would be a serious thing. But here. In the United States it is simply not so serious. This hearing is preliminary, no?

If you lose at this level. If no charges come out of it, that will be the end of it. No point will be made. Yes?"

"Not necessarily. The campus is already aware of the incident - mostly because of the upcoming hearing. In that way the point has already begun to be made."

"But if it ends at this stage without charges, then the greatest point that might be made is that this young woman was subjected to this process for no good reason. And even if charges are made against her, this matter will go to a formal hearing which does not occur for some time. Yes?"

"Maybe as much as sixty days. Why?"

"So the status quo lingers for that time. The case drags on. In which case your point also waits to be made for sixty days or more. Yes?"

"No. During that time, the matter is kept in discussion. Panel sessions. Open meetings. Recruitment. Outreach. We keep our position in front of the student body all the time."

"At this young lady's expense."

"There are casualties in every war, Ram." Klein breathed an exasperated sigh. She didn't like the phrase 'young lady' either but it was better than 'girl'.

"But what if, after all of that, in the end, she prevails. Is it not true that at the formal hearing, she has many more rights than she has at this stage?"

"Yes."

"So your chances of failing to get a determination against the young lady are increased if you to go to a formal hearing."

"Perhaps. But the final result is not the whole issue. The process and the time frame are also part of what we want."

"But that will be negated if, ultimately, the finding is that she did nothing wrong. Do you see my point? All your effort in the interim could then be perceived as unjustified persecution. You need to ensure your result."

"What are you getting at?"

"That you can more readily get what you want through negotiation. Give and take. Or put another way give and get. We learn it at bazaar by the time we are three years old. Get what you want - give what you don't really care about. And even better, get what you want right away without giving up anything to the girl that..." he raised a palm at her look..."she really doesn't already have. And you get your ensured victory right away."

"And the issue goes away. You don't seem to understand that we don't want it to go away."

"Yes, I do understand that, Caroline. You still get your year's worth of issue out of it. The young lady will give that to you. This whole thing must be stressful for someone so young and away from home. Clearly, she will wish to avoid this ordeal at all costs. So, part of the negotiated settlement is that she will counsel others - make speeches perhaps to groups of students - better still, agree to work under your supervision - to point out the error of her ways and the need to avoid such actions. You get the public point made - without the potential negative of a loss. She gets to avoid the process that is hanging over her head - both your heads, really."

Klein responded after a moment. Like Ramadan, it was beyond her comprehension to imagine that a student would not accept a compromise. "So, I offer her a way out that gets me what I want. It goes against my grain to compromise but - this isn't the strongest issue. You're right about that." She waggled her head in thought for a while then nodded abruptly. "I'll throw the option at this guy Cann - humor him a little. Make him think he's relevant." She looked curiously at Ramadan. "Why do you care about this hearing anyway?"

"Because if you settle this without a hearing, you will be free on Tuesday night. Yes?"

Klein didn't see that coming - and had to admit she was pleased by the ambush. "Get out of here," she laughed. "I'll call you about the hearing."

Chapter Twelve

The first time he attended a meeting in the Oval office some forty plus years ago, Arthur Matsen had decided to keep track of the number of such meetings he might find himself in over the years. No written list. No memoranda of dates and subjects. Just the number. Just in his head. In truth, it had been a rather arrogant decision since there was no assurance at the time that there would be more than one such meeting. But there had been. This early morning meeting on Monday September 16 was number 71.

It was also number 18 in this current administration. With less than a year to go in his term, the President had already summoned Matsen to more National Security sessions than any of his predecessors had done. Since Matsen was not a government employee, there was no 'ex officio' type of reason for him to be there and previous Presidents had only included him under extraordinary circumstances. But this President often seemed to require his attendance as a counselor, something Matsen would not have minded if he thought this President would take his counsel. For a time Matsen had even conjectured that the President perhaps sought the commonality of the legal profession in their backgrounds - but there were more than enough lawyers in the White House - including the First Lady. And this President had never practiced law, so he and Matsen didn't even have that in common.

Indeed, there was little if anything these two men had in common. Arthur Matsen was a going-on-elderly senior attorney cum statesman who looked the part of a Supreme Court Chief Justice. He was tall and slender with a full head of shining white hair, combed back, - a taller thinner Warren Burger. There had been a time not too long ago when the then President had briefly discussed the possibility an of appointment to the High Court for Matsen but both men had quickly dismissed the idea. The partisan climate would have turned what used to be a dignified confirmation process into a shooting gallery for the anti-intelligence community segment of the Senate Judiciary Committee. A new word would have been coined - 'Matsened' - to describe a process that went beyond being 'Borked'.

On the basis of the qualities that mattered - judiciousness, honesty, integrity, and intellect, Arthur Matsen would - in all likelihood - have made an excellent Supreme Court Justice. But those very qualities also caused him to argue against his own appointment. He quite simply knew too much about too many things and would be incapable of the obfuscation that would be required to obtain confirmation. Besides, he had spent forty plus years doing something he loved and he felt he had found his place to make a contribution. That President had deferred to his wishes because he had a quality in common to the best Presidents - not all - the invaluable ability to listen and heed others.

Arthur Matsen had personally known, to one degree or another, every President since Eisenhower. The mellow ones like Eisenhower and Ford - the charming one's like Kennedy and Reagan - the devious and sometimes cruel like Johnson and Nixon. But this one who sat in the Oval Office today was different.

Notwithstanding the different personalities of the inhabitants of the White House over the last forty years, they had all shared one characteristic - they led.

Well, except James Earl Carter. Carter had never seemed to Matsen - and many others - to have any capacity for real leadership and it was obvious to the insiders and the outsiders. Carter always had somebody or something else to blame for misfortunes - usually the American people themselves. Matsen still cringed when he recalled the "malaise" speech. He felt that had been the real beginning of the end of Carter's Presidency even though conventional political wisdom said that it was the public fiasco of his failure to deal with the Iranian hostage crisis.

To insiders, though, it was the appalling memory of the failed hostage rescue mission that was the hallmark of the Carter administration's impotence. The mission failed and the rescuers - good soldiers all - had their charred corpses put on display as examples of American ineptitude, when the true ineptitude lay in the inability of those in ultimate charge of events to let the mission succeed. Few people outside the inner sanctum knew that the mission failed primarily because it was called on and off time and time again. And it was during the last retreat - that the helicopters - low on fuel and perhaps even disoriented from the constant indecision and vacillation - collided. Matsen - and his like - never got over the disgust.

Sadly, the present incumbent seemed to Matsen to have many of the bad points of Carter. He never led. He followed - polls. Polls and focus groups. In truth, he was usually doing what he wanted to do - but not committing to it until someone else - by design or accident - articulated what he wanted to do in the first place. Then, if anything went wrong, he could blame his advisors. He could claim he didn't even know - that he was out of the loop. As if a President - at least any real President - could ever be out of the loop. Deniability - that hallowed Washington tradition - had been raised to an art form by this President. And that - perhaps more than anything - made him less in Matsen's eyes.

Every President - indeed every man worth his salt in life - took responsibility for the actions 'on his watch'. Not this one. Prior to this one, Matsen had never heard - and had never imagined he would hear - a President protest that 'he didn't know about it.' 'Nobody told me.' Previous Presidents - even Carter - at least had enough pride to eschew such a cowardly - even infantile disclaimer. But perhaps saddest of all, this President thought it was okay - no, that it was the smart thing to do. And that the people loved him all the more for it because he was never wrong but always there to take credit for things that went right. Perhaps no president in history, Matsen often thought, had a lower opinion of the people he was supposed to lead.

But then, who could blame him. Every step he had ever taken had led him to his present position. Every mistake and bad decision he had ever made had not stood in his way. And every device he had used to take credit and avoid blame had worked, standing smugly before cameras or people and saying things that no one really believed and that he didn't believe himself and that people knew he didn't believe and that people knew he didn't believe that they believed he believed it - but it didn't matter. If he said it, it became his and his followers' reality. And as long as enough people cared enough about their own interests to go along with the charade - regardless of the damage it might do - his devices succeeded.

Why wouldn't he keep on using these devices? They'd made him President of the United States.

So now the country had a putative leader who believed he couldn't make a mistake but, if he did, knew he could get away with it - and saw no contradiction in that philosophy. Like the legal theory of alternative defenses: "I didn't do it - but if I did it was an accident."

The President was working his way through the people in the room discussing - sometimes hectoring - the assembled aides with regard to the situation in the Middle East. Matsen never failed to note how much smaller the Oval Office was than it appeared on the news reports. Even so, it didn't feel crowded this day with only five people - not counting the President - in the room. The two women participants - the Undersecretary of State for Middle Eastern Affairs and the White House Press Secretary sat at either end of the couch opposite the President's desk. Between them sat the Head of the Middle East Section of the National Security Agency, a fiftyish man widely known for his roving eye - and hands. The President had purposely seated him between the two women - both attractive and in their thirties - because, notwithstanding the difficulties his own behavior had caused him in that regard, it amused him to watch the lech try to behave himself. Neither of the women - but especially the Press Secretary - would have tolerated even an accidental brush from him, so the NSA Section Chief sat with his hands folded in his lap and his shoulders bowed forward and scrunched together to avoid even the 'appearance of impropriety'.

To the right of the couch - the President's left - sat the Vice-President of the United States who was required to attend practically every meeting that took place involving the President. His and the Press Secretary's presence was mandatory primarily for one reason. When something was about to blow up in the President's face, the VP and the Press Secretary were the ones sent out to face the media with the story concocted to insulate the President from damage. The version of the facts presented for public consumption didn't have to be true - it frequently was not - but it was always presented by two people who supposedly knew first hand what had occurred in the Oval Office - because they were there. As a result, they couldn't later give a different version without destroying their own credibility and - more importantly - their careers. The Vice-President was hyped by the White House as being the most involved and 'inside' VP in history and it was a public image that the second in command enjoyed. But the hypocrisy and strain of the constant manipulation of himself as well as others showed in his face and the prematurely gray streaks in his hair.

Matsen was seated in a straight backed chair - Louis XIV or something like it - to the left of the couch. The President concluded his grillings of the Undersecretary and Section Head and was satisfied at their confirmation of his support for the way the peace negotiations in that region were going. He turned to Matsen.

"I understand we had a problem at your end, Arthur,"

"I'm afraid so. Our associate representing AramAir at the IMF talks was killed last Monday."

"So I understand. Car accident. Where does that leave us with regard to monitoring the situation?"

"Before we get to that, Mr. President, You should know that Mr. Wagner's death was apparently not an accident."

The President looked toward the ceiling. "It never is with you guys, is it. I think you've been hanging around the spooks too long, Arthur."

Matsen, as always, maintained his presence and decorum. "The preliminary medical examiner's report suggested drugs in the associate's system..." The President waggled his finger and clicked his tongue at Matsen. "...and other anamolies. And we've established that the car had been tampered with."

"Yes, I'm sure it was," the President exhaled. "And I suppose you found Mata Hari's fingerprints on his throat." He chuckled at his own humor and was annoyed when no one in the room joined him.

"Mr. President, there's no humor in this. To be sure, we don't know if Wagner's death is related to the negotiations at hand but it must..."

The President waved his right hand at Matsen. "Whatever. Nothing bad ever happens but that its got to have some nefarious external cause to it. It's never you're own mistake." He pointed a pencil at Matsen. "You sent a guy over their that likes to drive fast and he fell asleep at the wheel - or from what you just said - got himself stoned - and killed himself. Period. Face up to it. You will not waste this administration's resources on trying to find some boogie man to lay the blame on."

"Loring Matsen takes care of its own, Mr. President." Matsen emphasized and drew out the word 'Mister'. "We don't utilize the Administration's resources. We use our own. And will continue to do so as we determine appropriate."

The President was not used to sharp answers. "Watch your tone, Arthur. I may not control your budget directly but I have a lot to say about your biggest clients." He flashed a wide sarcastic smile and raised his eyebrows as if to say, 'Get the point?'. "Now how about answering my question. Where are we with regard to establishing a business relationship with Arafat?"

Matsen controlled any urge he might have to glare at the President and answered evenly after a thoughtful pause. "We're in good shape. Wagner has established - had established - a good rapport with Ali Mahad - Arafat's chief negotiator at the IMF meetings and through him with Arafat himself. Arafat remains convinced that when - not if - the Palestinian sector gains independent status, an international airport located between Jerusalem and Hebron will give the Palestinians enhanced credibility around the world. We're hopeful that Wagner's death won't hinder the inside track that Arab-American Air has obtained with them with regard to landing rights and servicing contracts."

"Who attended the meeting for AramAir that your guy missed?"

"I was able to cover it by teleconference and we had our local Frankfurt man available for in person activity but none was required. As it turned out, it was routine. The IMF advised the Palestinians that they needed to have their house in order but it was clear that the loan was a fait accompli."

"What was the Palestinian reaction. What did Arafat have to say?"

"We don't know yet. He didn't attend. And they haven't given their public reaction yet. Oh, its a virtual certainty that he'll huff and puff about independence and self-determination but he'll accept the conditions. There's nothing to them anyway. Nothing that he doesn't already want to do, anyway. But, as I said, he didn't attend the meeting himself. Our information was that he sat it out in a villa in Offenbach just east of Frankfurt."

"And what pray tell is the source of that information?"

"That's the explanation given by the Palestinian's themselves."

"And they're our best intelligence on this?" The President huffed.

"They were sufficient in this context, Mr. President. In the first place, Arafat's particular whereabouts - while always of concern -

were not paramount in the context of this particular meeting. Secondly, nobody keeps track of Arafat if he doesn't want to be kept track of. He was number one on the Mossad's hit parade for decades and they never got him. If the best intelligence agency in the Middle East - maybe the world - couldn't keep track of him, no one could. He and his people are very good at cloaking his movements. If they weren't, Arafat would have been dead years ago."

"Sounds like you're not really sure about your information, Arthur. Why do we pay your firm these exorbitant fees if all you're going to do is pass along information you learn from the Palestinian's themselves."

"Because we're not spies. We're a law firm and a good one. We are paid reasonable fees for high level legal representation of clients, Mr. President. While that representation affords us opportunities to garner - and perhaps share - other kinds of information, our primary responsibility remains the representation of the client."

"When you 'share' this information you get, Arthur, don't you ever worry about attorney-client privilege?" The President was smirking at the prospect of putting this arrogant citizen in his place. "I mean you find something out in the course of your representation of AramAir and - lo and behold - it ends up in this office. A little unethical wouldn't you say?" The President enjoyed making people uncomfortable and used it to his advantage. It was very easy to do because, regardless of the provocation, one does not usually answer a President in kind.

Usually. Not always.

"If you had ever practiced law, you would know, Mr. President, that there is not the slightest problem with attorney-client privilege in this regard. We discuss our representation - and share information - with our client. Only our client. In this case Arab-American Airways. If they then wish to share it with others - you for example -, that is entirely up to them. This firm, however, violates no privilege."

The President felt challenged. "Well, Arthur, AramAir is wholly owned by an agency of this government. That makes it a subsidiary of me. If I order you to tell me everything about the case, you will do so."

Matsen smiled and nodded. "Of course, Mr. President, as soon as you show me that my client, AramAir, has given me written permission to do so. Since they are, as you say, a subsidiary of you, that should not be a problem for you."

The President glared and briefly considered ordering Matsen to discuss the matter without such written permission. But he knew that Matsen wouldn't do it so he decided to take the out that Matsen had given him.

"You're damn right it wouldn't," the Chief Executive said. But he knew he'd been bested. "Well, at least it's one less bed you have to look under, heh, Arthur?"

"Pardon?"

"Well, if Arafat wasn't at the meeting, then your man's demise shouldn't have had anything to do with keeping him away from Arafat. One less nefarious motive to deal with."

"Mr. President. in the first place, I said that we don't know if the killing is even connected to the case, but that doesn't alter the fact that Ted Wagner was in fact killed. It was not an accident."

"Whatever," the President said in an annoyingly dismissive manner. "I presume you intend to replace him."

"Of course." Here it comes.

"With Cann?"

"If you will recall, he isn't with the firm at the moment. He is currently on unpaid leave of absence. At your behest."

"I recall. And I'm gratified to know that you recognize the measure of influence I have on your firm. However, as I said at the time, he can come back whenever he is willing to do what he is told."

"Frankly, I'm a little surprised you even remember his name."

"Don't be. I always remember the very few who refuse to follow my orders. I always remember disloyalty."

In four decades of dealing with Presidents, Matsen had never lost his temper - or at least shown it. That was not going to change now but it was difficult.

"You will never," Matsen said slowly, "find a man more loyal to his country or who has shown it more completely or more frequently than John Cann, Mr. President."

"Yes, well as long as I am President, disloyalty to me is disloyalty to the country."

Matsen declined to take the bait. "The fact is I talked to him a few days ago, Mr. President, and obtained his consent to be available as a resource in this matter - subject to your acceptance, of course."

"What about meetings with Arafat?"

Matsen shook his head. "It's still out of the question for him." The President sat up straighter and started to point a finger at Matsen who interrupted.

"Mr. President. Consider that an actual face to face with Arafat may never even be needed. Wagner only met with Arafat once in the last several months and even that meeting wasn't critical. John's position is a matter of conscience for him, Mr. President and could easily be accommodated. I would hope you could understand and accept that. Why is it so important that he agree to do something that may never be necessary?"

"Because I need to know that he knows who's the boss. Period. Who else have you got?"

"Nobody in John Cann's league. Not even close."

The President leaned forward and placed his elbows on the desk. He folded his hands in front of his face and tapped the first knuckle of his right hand against his upper lip. After several moments of total silence in the Oval office, he looked hard at Matsen and said. "You know, Arthur, when I got this job, I didn't expect to have to sit here and negotiate with the hired help."

Matsen stiffened.

The President held up a hand. "I don't mean you. I mean Cann." Matsen was not mollified in the least. "We both know I have enormous resources and - assets is the word, isn't it, Arthur?

137

- at my disposal. It seems to me that I may just have to send out one of those assets to convince Cann that he doesn't have a choice but to do it my way. What do you think of that?"

Matsen stared back at the President and replied evenly. "I think, Mr. President, - I know - that it wouldn't work. The fact is that the only 'asset' who might bring John Cann in is John Cann."

The President's dislike for this man was increasing with every exchange. He couldn't understand how his predecessors tolerated this set up. There was no control. For now it was time to close the subject. "Then I guess we'll have to do without him, won't we. Find someone. Whatever it takes. But don't let me see Cann on the team unless he's ready to do it my way."

"I'll do my best," Matsen said. "We've got a little time. Nothing further is scheduled until the end of next week - after the election."

"Which our guy is going to win. Right?"

In spite of himself, Matsen was amazed at the way this man could change gears.

"Israel is a sovereign nation, Mr. President. Whomever the Israeli's choose will have to be 'our guy'."

"Don't count on that. With the amount of aid we give that country, we'd better have more influence than that, Arthur. The prestige of this country - and mine - has been placed squarely behind the re-election of Prime Minister Yenahim. His defeat would be a disaster for the peace process. And me. Don't you agree?"

"There is no question, Mr. President, that Prime Minster Yenahim will continue on the road and the track and the timetable that has gotten us to this point. But I don't see where Shelanu and his party would go back to the previous conditions either."

"Yes, well, don't you forget the public position of this administration, Arthur. Shelanu's election will throw the Middle East back into chaos. The Palestinians won't stand for it and the Arab countries won't stand for it. There will be an immediate throwback to the cycle of attack - counter-attack - intifada - street bombings - death and maiming if Yenahim doesn't win."

"With all due respect, Mr. President, I don't think that will happen."

"Neither do I, Arthur, but that's our public position. Nobody in their right mind would go back to the status ante quo. And Lev Shelanu is in his right mind - and bright. While he may not turn back the clock, he'd at least let it wind down before re-setting it. Shelanu has made it clear that he would slow the process and rethink some of the agreements already made. And I can't have that."

"He has a point. Israel has already given up a lot of territorial security for promises that may or may not be fulfilled down the road, Mr. President. Shelanu wants to make sure that Israel doesn't get in a position where she can't force those promises to be kept."

"Not my problem, Arthur. I've got a re-election of my own coming up and I want to run on bringing peace to the Middle East. Maybe even a Nobel Peace Prize. Shelanu's election probably delays any progress past November. So this administration - that's me in case anyone has a question - and that means this government and this country are placing all their eggs in Yenahim's basket. If we haven't made it clear already, we are going to make sure that the Israeli's know that if there's a Shelanu victory next Wednesday, they may not be able to count on the further support of the United States of America."

While the other four people in the room showed no reaction, Matsen was aghast.

"Mr. President! You cannot conduct international blackmail from this room. Israel is a proud nation and rightly so. Such a position - especially publicly articulated - may have the opposite effect to what you want."

"Well, it better not. And how dare you use the word 'blackmail' to me?"

"Mr. President, you need to start listening to your advisers. They've got..."

"My adviser's are with me on this, Matsen." He looked around the room. "Right, people?"

The four others in the room nodded without enthusiasm.

"See? A carefully thought out and well supported position of the United States government. This is political hardball, Arthur. I would have thought you'd be used to it by now. You've certainly been around long enough." He smiled. "Maybe too long, heh?"

"All right then, Mr. President, think politically. Lyndon Johnson had a favorite saying: 'Never tell someone to go to hell unless you have the wherewithal to send him there'. Don't make threats you can't carry out. You're backing yourself into a corner with this position. You'll have no place to go with it if Shelanu does win. Have you thought about that?"

"Let the Israeli's think about it. I won't accept it."

"How can you not accept it. You won't have a choice."

"Sure I do - we do. The word to Israel is that its my way or the highway. That's it." He stood up. "I trust I have your support as well, Arthur." He didn't wait for an answer. "This meetings adjourned."

Chapter Thirteen

At long last, the locater information was hand delivered to Iverson at 2:30 PM Monday afternoon. It was in the form of a time/date printout of the GPS/GloNass information that had not been transmitted real time but had been stored in the chip in Wagner's locater.

The printout was in a column format with the date and the time indicated on the left side of the green and white horizontally striped paper and the grid coordinates of Wagner's locations indicated on the right side of the paper.

As soon as he got it, Iverson went into the large conference room at Loring Matsen Frankfurt and made an initial examination of the printout. The memory chip was designed to store seven days worth of location information so that it predated Wagner's death by a week. While not disregarding the possibility that information prior to Friday September 6 could be of value, Iverson skipped ahead to the activities of the Friday Wagner left Geneva to drive to Frankfurt and scanned the listing for the entire weekend. Then he picked up the phone, pressed the intercom button and punched in the number 17. The research assistant who picked up the phone only nodded at the other end while Iverson talked and then said OK when he was done.

Within ten minutes - during which Iverson sat impatiently looking over the printout again and again - two sets of maps of Germany and Switzerland were delivered to the conference room.

One set consisted of the latest, most up-to-date highway maps put out by the European Automobile Association. The other set were high detail, satellite imagery enhanced topographical and surveillance maps of the same two countries. The research assistant also brought Iverson the clear plastic GPS/GloNass grid overlays for the sectors of the country he had requested.

Initially, Iverson put the more sophisticated topo and surveillance maps to the side. Over the years, Iverson had frequently been called upon to conduct training classes and seminars. One of the first things he always stressed - especially to new investigators - was that it was extraordinarily rare for an investigative breakthrough to come from some kind of brilliant Holmesian deduction based on an incredible insight on the part of the investigator. Many investigative successes were the result of noticing everyday sorts of things and seeing how they fit into a pattern. People were people and no matter what they might be doing, it was human nature to take the path of least resistance. Whether someone was engaged in legal or illegal activities, most people acted simply and logically.

Thus, one of Iverson's investigative tenets was 'always try the easy way first'. Accordingly, Iverson decided he would first track the locater data along the major highways that coincided with the passing of the locater signal from grid to grid. Based on what he knew so far, there was no reason to expect that Wagner had gotten off the major road systems on this trip. If he had, the job of tracking him would be more difficult, since the locater information only revealed when a subject passed from one mile-square grid into another. If the person whose steps were being examined were in wilderness, for example, or some other situation without normally defined routes, then a crossover could be at any point along the mile long boundary between the two grids.

On the other hand, if the person were known to have started out on a highway, and that highway continued along the general path of the crossovers, one might reasonably assume that the person was making the crossovers where they coincided with the highway being traveled in the previous grid. Of course, it was possible for a subject to change from one road to another while in a grid and still cross into the same adjacent grid on a different road than the one he entered on. But such a change would show up fairly quickly. The investigator would see a crossover into an unexpected grid somewhere away from the previously assumed route of the subject. In most cases, the route could then be tracked backwards and corrected.

According to the computer printout, Wagner had left Geneva on that Friday evening at 7:00 PM a fact they already knew. He had headed north out of Geneva on the N1 highway and at Lausanne at the northern tip of Lake Geneva had switched to the N9 which headed generally in an east-southeasterly direction.

At first glance, that might have seemed odd for someone heading north to Germany from Geneva but Iverson knew that staying on the N1 - which was a direct north route - would eventually mean traveling on some secondary and even lesser roads north of Neuchatel. Indeed, as far as super-highway status went, the N1 disappeared entirely for a while and reappeared again in Bern. So it was not unusual for a traveler to take the N9 across to the N12 and head north from there picking up the N1 again at Bern and then the N2 into Basel - superhighway all the way.

Iverson hadn't forgotten Wagner's desire to open up the Austin-Healy on the roads of Europe and knew that could be a factor in his choice of superhighway routes as well. But he decided that it was an unlikely reason for his choice of route because Switzerland has - and enforces - a 75 mile per hour speed limit on its major highways. Wagner undoubtedly knew that Loring Matsen didn't appreciate an associate offending a host country by way of speeding tickets or other disregard of their laws.

Iverson knew that Wagner had reached Bern just after 9:00 PM Friday and that was when and where the real time sender had been turned off. Looking at the computer printout, Iverson now knew that it was also there that Wagner's route had deviated from the expected. According to the printout, he left the N1 and headed east mostly on secondary roads all the way to Lucerne where he stayed until about noon the next day.

Iverson felt a mild sense of satisfaction at the locater's confirmation of an earlier assumption he had made that Wagner might have gone to Lucerne. Another thing he had often told investigative trainees was that, while assumptions must never be conclusively relied upon, no investigation can be pursued without them. Based on how little - or how much - information one had, the investigator would construct a paradigm - a fancy way of saying make a 'guess' or a 'set of assumptions' - and then build on those assumptions until they were either confirmed or became insupportable. At any given point, a new fact could come up which would do one or the other and, at that point, the effective investigator would objectively measure the new fact or item against the previous assumptions and other known facts. The effective investigator will always – always - be fully prepared to abandon the discredited assumption without regret. Never, Iverson had said in every training session he had ever conducted, let your assumptions become anything more than a tentative signpost written in erasable ink. And do not confuse the signposts along the way with the destination.

The first assumption - or guess - that Iverson had made before getting the locater information was that the numbers on the second page of the hotel note pad sent to him by Bucher in Geneva might be a telephone number. In Switzerland, telephone numbers are written in three sets of pairs and 22 is one of the city codes for Lucerne. Simple enough. Given the time frames involved in relation to Wagner's anticipated movements and - assuming the numbers were a telephone number - it was possible that Wagner had gone to Lucerne.

But this was by no means the only alternative. Even given the starting point of Geneva and the fact that Wagner did in fact end up in Germany, Iverson knew that Wagner could also have headed elsewhere - west into France, for example. In the old days, a simple call to the Gendarmerie Frontiere would have told him if

Wagner had crossed the border but, with European Union, unrestricted passage was the norm.

And Wagner could have traveled even further still. Using other modes of transportation than his car, the external limits of the possible travel area were enormous. But, for now, there were no indications of that and Wagner would check his simpler, more obvious assumptions before expanding the parameters of the investigation.

Iverson had opted for the Lucerne guess because two assumptions that coincide are better than one. Lucerne fit by way of geographical proximity in relation to the possible significance of the set of numbers. France, with a population some nine times larger than Switzerland's, has many times the number of phones that Switzerland does as well. As a result, French telephone numbers contain seven digits, not counting the country codes while Switzerland's telephone numbers contain six. So Iverson's guess of Lucerne was the result of two related assumptions which might or might not mutually confirm each other.

Frequently, however, even information which negates a prior assumption can be of value. If, for example, the locater information had shown that Wagner had diverted to France, then Iverson would also know that the numbers were not a telephone number. He would then have to move onto other assumptions about the number - a lock combination? - a birth date? - even a code. Because the possibilities were so many, Iverson dearly hoped his first guess was correct - it often was. But, if not, he was fully prepared to drop it and move on to the next set of assumptions.

So, he was gratified - but not smug - that the locater showed the trip to Lucerne because it also increased the possibility that the numbers were a telephone number - and that was much more public information than lock combinations and birth dates - and certainly codes. It was not determinative of anything yet, but it was a good start.

Iverson now knew that Wagner was in Lucerne for roughly 12 hours. He had arrived before midnight Friday September 6 having taken Highway 10 from Bern to Emmenbruck just north of Lucerne and then taking Highway 2 southeast into Lucerne. Wagner had then driven into the heart of the city on the Baselstrasse which runs east to within a mile of the main train station - the Hauptbahnhof - which sits on a corner of land on the western boundary of the Vierwaldstatter See - otherwise known as Lake Lucerne.

Much of the western part of the City of Lucerne straddles the north and south banks of the Reuss River where it empties into the western end of the Vierwaldstatter See. Iverson placed the locater coordinated overlay on top of the exactly scaled map of the City of Lucerne. The grid within which the locater indicated that Wagner had stopped and spent virtually all of his time in Lucerne was the mile square that was bordered on the east by the lake and on the north by the river. The square extended south exactly one mile into the newer residential area of the city and was bordered on the west, where Wagner had entered it, by the deep semi-urban forest called the Gigeliwald.

According to the locater, at no time during his stay in Lucerne did Wagner cross the Reuss into the northern part of Lucerne. There were only two places in the vicinity of his activity where he could have done so. Within the Hauptbahnhof grid, there were five bridges over the Reuss but only the Seebrucke which crosssed directly in front of the Hauptbahnhof carried vehicular traffic. The other four bridges were all the picturesque covered wooden structures including the famous 14th Century Kapplebrucke connecting both halves of the Old City. Iverson thought he recalled that the original Kappelbrucke had burned in 1992 but it had been restored. Even so, it was still only used for pedestrian traffic as were the other bridges north and west of the Seebrucke.

Following the course of the River Reuss back northwest from the lake, the next vehicular bridge where Wagner could have entered the northern part of Lucerne was the St. Karli Brucke. But a crossing there would have caught Iverson's attention because it was even further north than the Seebrucke and outside the grid where Wagner seemed to have stayed while in Lucerne. There was no crossover that indicated that.

So Iverson felt that he would be able to limit his investigation to the square mile south of the River Reuss and west of Lake Lucerne. This was so even though the locater data had shown a series of crossovers back and forth from the Hauptbahnhof grid into the immediately adjacent grid to the west. Rather than complicating things by expanding the area of the search to a second square mile grid, however, Iverson felt this was more good news for his investigation.

The reason for that assumption was that if Wagner had crossed from one grid to another - and not continued on into yet another grid after that - Iverson's investigation would logically concentrate on the last grid entered. On the other hand, if Wagner had crossed into a different grid but come back into the previous grid and stayed in that one, Iverson would have concentrated his search in the first one. But with Wagner appearing to have crossed back and forth between two adjacent grids frequently and in very short periods of time, that indicated to Iverson that Wagner's activities had been concentrated in a location right on or close to the line between the two. This would allow Iverson to - initially at least - base his search in a much smaller area than the mile square he usually had to contend with.

Sitting in a conference room in Frankfurt, that was about as much information as Iverson felt that he could get from the locater information about Wagner's time in Lucerne. A quick call to the Swiss National Telephone System confirmed that the 22 exchange did in fact cover that portion of the city of Lucerne. So Iverson was confident that the information he had at that point was sufficient confirmation of his previous assumptions to justify a trip to Lucerne.

But not everything was falling so neatly into place. As always, one of the first things Iverson had done at the beginning of the investigation was to put Matsen Loring's EI - Electronics Investigations - section on the case. He knew that in this day and age of the information superhighway, EI could often get the information they needed instantaneously from nothing more sophisticated or esoteric than the Internet. If they didn't find what they wanted there, they would exit that superhighway onto other roads. By reviewing restaurant, service station, banking, and other commercial transactions, it was amazing how much information could be garnered in an amazingly short period of time. Given the fact that they were also connected via the information superhighway with Interpol and the individual police forces and intelligence agencies of many if not most countries of the world, it was clear that, except in the most unusual circumstances, someone could run but they couldn't electronically hide.

That electronic search had revealed an odd hole in the information coming in to Iverson. There was no record of Wagner's having checked into a hotel or engaged in any financial transactions of any kind while in Lucerne or anywhere else for the entire weekend. This was in itself cause for suspicion because it didn't fit in with the simple and logical manner of the way people go about normal routine. It was not at all unreasonable to assume that Wagner would have checked into a hotel or pension or inn and would - all other things being equal - have no reason to avoid using his credit cards. Loring Matsen was exceedingly generous with expense accounts so Iverson would have fully expected Wagner to have used that card. But the credit card records showed no use whatsoever for any of Wagner's cards in Lucerne for the entire time the locater indicated he was there. Not even a restaurant charge and it was fair to assume he had eaten. Iverson - for the moment - made no assumptions about the reasons for that except that Wagner - apparently by design - had taken pains to cover his tracks. Very out of the ordinary. Very disturbing. It was up to Iverson to find out why. He would leave for Lucerne in the morning.

But even though he would start his search in Lucerne, Iverson also wanted to try to get as complete a picture of Wagner's entire last trip as he could. So he continued his examination of the locater time/date printout which showed that Wagner left Lucerne around noon Saturday September 7 on the N2 highway which ran all the way to Basel on the Swiss border with Germany. The printout revealed no variance from the route followed by the N2 indicating that Wagner drove straight to and through Basel without stopping and that he continued on the German Autobahn 5 which ran directly north all the way to Frankfurt and beyond.

But Wagner didn't drive straight through to Frankfurt even though he could easily have. From Basel to Frankfurt is barely a four hour drive - at reasonable speeds - so that had he chosen to do so, he could have arrived in Frankfurt at a perfectly reasonable time in the early evening hours of Saturday.

However, around 4:00 PM on Saturday afternoon, Wagner exited Autobahn 5 at the city of Karlsruhe which is about an hour south of Heidelberg and continued north on Highway 65 toward Ludwigshafen. After passing through that large industrial city, he continued still further north on Highway 65 until it intersected with Autobahn Number 6 near the wine center of Bad Durkheim in the Rheinpfalz region of Southwest Germany.

Iverson knew the area. He had even attended several of the famous wine festivals in the Stadt Park where stood the enormous 1,000,000 litre wine cask that had actually been used for that purpose in the past and was now a restaurant and bar which could seat well over a hundred people.

As in Lucerne, the locater information indicated that, once inside Bad Durkheim, Wagner apparently didn't move around much at all. According to the printout, he stayed the entire time within the same grid he initially appeared to stop in.

Again, also as in Lucerne, there was no credit card or other similar activity for the duration of his stay and once he'd arrived, there had been no crossovers between grids. The result was that Iverson had no clues to Wagner's activities in Bad Durkheim and no trace of his movements until he left the following day around 6:00 PM at which time, Iverson noted, he didn't head back west to the north-south Autobahn 5 to Frankfurt or head north at all. He got onto Autobahn 6 and continued his journey further west stopping in the city of Kaiserslautern around 7:00 PM Sunday evening. Iverson noted soberly that Kaiserslautern was at the southern end of highway N40 approximately 10 or 12 miles south of Sembach and the spot where Wagner was killed.

Wagner appeared to have stopped somewhere in the center of the large city but - again - once stopped, there was no movement shown on the printout. No EI information either. No credit card or other electronic payment evidence of a check in to any hotel, inn, or gasthaus. No purchases of any kind, not even meals.

Then, around 8:45 PM, that Sunday night, Wagner left Kaiserslautern and drove straight north on the N40 to the village of Sembach. From that point on, there was no indication of any movement whatsoever until the next morning. That was when the real-time sender came back on - 5:08 AM. Iverson wondered if that was the very instant of Wagner's death.

He picked up the phone and, even though it was Sunday evening, dialed Gunther Abel at his home. He brought the BSK colonel and friend up to date on the circumstances of Wagner's death, including what he knew of the medical and automotive evidence. After Abel expressed his official condolences, Iverson requested his assistance.

The crash had occurred on a federal highway so it was entirely appropriate - if unusual - for the federal security official - to look into it. Abel had the all the jurisdictional authority he needed to conduct an investigation and would do so while Iverson was on the road 'at the other end' for a few days. They would get together and compare notes when he returned. Viel gluck.

*　*　*　*

Some of the more light-hearted third year students in Cann's 1:00 PM International Finance class brought in a cupcake with a candle on it to celebrate Cann's one week anniversary as a law professor. Cann jokingly offered to share it with the class which unanimously declined so he brought it back to his office with him. He grabbed some coffee in the outer office area and brought it in with him to enjoy with the cupcake. He was just finishing it and licking chocolate frosting off his fingers when the intercom buzzed.

"Professor Klein on the line, Professor."

There was a brief moment of non-recognition before the synapses in Cann's brain selected the relevant information and brought to his consciousness the identity of the caller as well as the information Roger Walder had given him about her a week ago.

Cann had not forgotten about Janie Reston or the hearing scheduled for the next day. But, under the circumstances of the situation, there had been nothing to do about it and nothing to prepare so he had not really thought a lot about it. All in good time. Like now, he guessed.

"Professor Klein? John Cann here."

"Professor Cann. Nice to talk to you. How do you like the world of legal education." That was an oxymoron to her but she didn't say so out loud.

"So far, so good, Professor. Please call me John. What can I do for you."

"First, you can call me Caroline. I'm calling about the disciplinary hearing tomorrow night regarding the woman who danced nude last week. I understand that you will be representing her?"

"Janie Reston. Yes, I'll be there with her." Cann stopped there. It was second nature to him not to volunteer information.

Klein paused for a moment expecting more but nothing came.

"Well, John, you should know that I've been selected to present the university's case at the hearing and it occurs to me that perhaps we can simplify things a great deal beforehand."

"That sounds great, Caroline. Amicable solutions are always preferable to confrontation. Actually, Janie and I still don't know what the university's problem - or, rather, position is. What exactly is it that the university is looking for."

"As an overall principle, what the university always seeks is the maintenance and betterment of the college community through reasoned guidance of student behavior while carefully guarding the tolerance for diversity and encouragement of expression and formulation of new ideas."

'Jesus Christ, do people really talk like that?' Cann thought to himself.

Out loud, however, he said, "Personally, I prefer the practical approach. A philosophy perhaps of, 'No harm done. No big deal. Let bygones be bygones.' Something like that?"

Klein's voice took on a lecturing - albeit pseudo-kindly - tone. "In another context, perhaps, that might be possible. But you're new here, John. You don't understand that a large part of our responsibilities to our students involves exposure. And, yes, I am aware of the irony of that word in this context. We expose them to new ideas and expose the fallacies of the old. We expose them to their strengths and their uniqueness while at the same time protecting them from those parts of themselves that are the products of years of indoctrination."

Klein seemed to be gathering a head of steam so Cann interrupted.

"Then let's apply that to the situation at hand, Caroline. You've already mentioned two terms that are relevant to this incident involving Janie Reston - 'tolerance' and 'expression.' We both know that dance and, for that matter, nudity, are forms of expression that from time to time have needed varying degrees of protection from repression and intolerance. Can we agree that nothing of what Janie did was intrinsically wrong?"

"Actually, no we cannot. Because we can't look at the actions without examining the motivations."

Cann tried to interject, "Why not?" but Klein was charging forward.

"Why did she dance nude? Why didn't she close the drapes? Who did she want to see her? Why did she want to be seen? Does her behavior indicate a lack of self worth that requires her to draw attention to herself in such an inappropriate manner? Does she need to........."

Cann had to raise his voice to be heard. "Whoa! Take it easy. You've posed a lot of questions there and they all have answers if you care to hear them. She danced nude because she felt like it. There's nothing wrong with that. Why did she want to be seen? She didn't. She didn't even know she could be seen. Does she have a lack of self- esteem? It sure doesn't seem like it to me. But if she does, wouldn't exposing her to potential ridicule certainly be detrimental to her as well as intolerant?"

"I resent being accused of ridiculing anyone, Professor Cann," Klein said haughtily.

"That's not what I said. Surely you can see..."

"I'll decide what I can see. And what to do about it. Look, I called to tell you the best way for this to be handled." Cann raised his eyebrows at that. "I'll present a case at the hearing to make the point that this young woman represents a still large segment of our female population that has been indoctrinated to think that they are bodies and not minds...."

"Wait a second. Have you ever even spoken to Janie?"

"I have not. It's not..."

"Spend five minutes with her. You'll see that not only does she have a mind, she has an extraordinary mind and she knows it and she's proud of it. If it happens that she's also physically attractive, that doesn't lessen her mind one bit. The two are not mutually exclusive, are they?"

"As a matter of fact, there are those who feel that the two cannot co-exist, Professor. But she wasn't dancing around exposing her intellect. You seem to be forgetting that?"

"Not at all. But she's entitled to do that. As I said before, what she did is not intrinsically evil or even improper. And it does nothing to diminish her mind or intellectual worth. Or value as a human being - or a woman."

Klein actually paused for a second, then recovered. "Well, even if that's the case with this particular young woman, there are too many others who may not be so unusual and may not be able to see the distinction. It is that group that I must reach."

"And in the process harm this one?"

"If she is as strong as you are saying, she can handle it, can she not? Most of the others cannot."

"And you think that's your call? With all due respect, Professor, aren't you granting yourself a rather large amount of judgmental latitude in this? Whatever happened to the benefit of the doubt."

Klein made very sure Cann could hear her expel her breath in exasperation. "This discussion is becoming tedious, Professor Cann. I called to do you a favor. Not argue with you. Just listen. At the hearing, I will lay out a position that makes the point that women don't need to do what this young woman did in order to gain attention or have worth. The board will vote that she be charged with conduct detrimental to the university. Rather than schedule a full formal hearing, you can get up and say that she realizes it was wrong now and won't do it again. The board will waive the formal hearing and impose a penalty of probation conditioned on a semester of sensitivity counseling. The board can then vote to accept a plea from the young woman and that will be that."

Cann was silent. Not because he was considering the proposal. But because at that moment, he couldn't think of a single thing to say that didn't have the phrase 'fuck yourself' in it.

But he didn't want to say that. Not yet, anyway. Instead he said, "I don't find that to be a very reasonable reaction to the facts of this case, Professor Klein. However, it's Janie Reston's decision and I will put it to her. I want you to know, however, that I will strongly recommend to her that she not accept it. Frankly, I don't think my recommendation will even be necessary. She is an extraordinary person, Professor. Once you've met her, I hope you will allow yourself to see that."

"You sound a little enamored of this young woman."

"She has a name, you know. Janie Reston."

"That should be Ms. Reston to you. Do you let her call you, John?"

"As a matter of fact, I do."

Without missing a beat, Klein said, "Well, such familiarity with students can get you in trouble, Professor. Or is there more to this than we know? Perhaps you might need to disqualify yourself."

Cann's brain marveled at how facile Klein was when it came to this kind of psuedo-intellectual skirmishing. But that was overwhelmed by the knot in his gut that accompanied his genuine anger.

"It makes no sense to reduce this discussion to a level of innuendo, Professor Klein. You inference is sheer nonsense. And you're right. I am new here. That means you may not be used to someone who doesn't buckle under to your efforts at intimidation."

"Very well, Professor Cann. The hearing is at 7:30 PM tomorrow. The Student Congress room in the Union. I don't think you fully understand where you are or what you're dealing with. Be assured that I intend to see what you're made of."

"Yes, well, you will, Professor Klein. You will."

He put the phone back into its base and looked up to see Janie Reston standing in the door. She had a slight crooked smile on her face but her brows were lifted in question.

"Professor Klein?" she asked.

"Afraid so. And I may have made matters worse." Cann shrugged his shoulders. "I think I just pissed the good professor off."

Janie walked to the chair opposite Cann's desk and sat down. "Join the club," she sad calmly but a little sadly. "Sara got into it with her last Friday, too. You guys make quite the pair."

"With friends like us you don't need enemies, huh, Janie?"

"Then why do I seem to have one?" She was genuinely perplexed.

In a way, so was Cann. He didn't have an answer for her. But he tried. "Actually, I don't think you do. I've met people like Klein before - in different contexts but basically the same. They're one dimensional - a type that can't or won't see the forest for the ideological trees. There are basically two kinds. The ones who like to hurt people and the ones that don't really have that as their goal but don't really care if they do. I suspect Klein is the latter type."

Janie smiled. "Boy, that's weird. That's almost exactly what Sara said the other night. I guess it must be true, huh?"

155

"I guess," Cann agreed. "That reminds me, I said I wanted to talk to her before the hearing. Think we have time to get together?"

"That's why I'm here. I wanted to invite you to join me and Sara for lunch tomorrow. My treat." She sat back in her chair with an inquisitive look on her face as she waited for an answer.

Cann found that he couldn't look at her without smiling. "I'd love to. But you're the struggling student. Why don't you let me treat?"

"Okay," Janie said without hesitation and smiled even more widely.

Cann shook his head in mock sadness. "Played me like a fiddle, didn't you?" But he was smiling too. "Do you like, Italian?"

"Yeah, but Sara and I did Italian Saturday night," Janie responded. "How about Chinese?"

It wasn't one of Cann's favorites but he agreed. "You pick the place then. Let me know before noon tomorrow."

Chapter Fourteen

Cann rearranged his schedule in order to make the lunch date with Janie and Sara Furden. He taught the two morning Contracts classes but asked a colleague to go to his 1:00 International Finance class and make the announcement that he would be unable to attend that day and would like the class to use the time to have a round table discussion among themselves covering the cases read for that day. Cann would, the colleague was to announce, discuss their conclusions with them during the first part of the next class and then move on to the cases originally scheduled for that day. That way, the students would be happy to know, they would not fall behind in the scheduled sequence of cases for the semester.

There hadn't been any messages for Cann when he'd arrived at his office in the Page building just before 8:00 AM that Tuesday morning but, when he'd returned to his office after the 8:00 AM Contracts class, there was one from Janie telling him that she had spoken with Sara who said that the Imperial Garden was good and not too far from campus. The message went on to say that Sara was already going to be in the vicinity of the restaurant around noon so would Cann be able to pick Janie up at her dorm and give her a ride to the restaurant. If she didn't hear otherwise from him, she would be out front just before twelve.

But it was the message that Cann found slipped under his door when he returned from the 11:00 AM Contracts class that really got his attention.

It was on the usual pink 'while you were out' style of message paper Cann had received all his other messages on but, unlike the others which had been handwritten by the faculty receptionist, this one was typewritten. It read: "You may want to see the police report before the hearing."

That was it. Nothing more. Unsigned. While the note didn't go into specifics, there was no ambiguity in it as far as Cann was concerned. He read it twice then tossed it onto his desk as he passed around it to sit down. He reached down into the lower right hand drawer of his desk and extracted the campus phone directory remembering that the one and only other time so far that he had done so concerned this business as well.

Cann dialed the extension of the campus security headquarters and asked to speak with someone in charge of records. He explained the situation to them and who he was and requested that a copy of the security report regarding the Jane Reston incident be made available to him as soon as possible. He was not entirely surprised - but still angered - when he was told that he would not be allowed to see the report prior to the hearing. It was 'confidential'.

Cann then demanded to speak to the Director of Campus Security but was told that she was unavailable. He left a message saying who he was, what he wanted, and why and hung up the phone. Rather firmly.

As soon as the phone hit the cradle, Cann was up and around his desk and walking down the hall to the stairwell. He went down the single flight of stairs and straight into Dean Walder's office. Beverly waved him through and he walked in to see Walder behind his desk reading some papers.

"John, to what do I owe this honor.?"

Cann tossed the message slip on Walder's desk. Walder picked it up and took just over a second to scan it. He looked up at Cann.

"Janie Reston?'" he asked.

"Who else?" Cann told Walder about his conversation with campus security and asked if there was anything he thought could be done to get the report.

"Roger, I've about had it with these rules that seem to get adjusted to fit the circumstances of the moment. The only consistency I've seen so far is that Janie's the only one without any rights."

He also told Walder about his conversation with Klein and by the time he was finished, he was leaning over Walder's desk jabbing his right forefinger down onto the surface of the desk as he spoke.

"I'm fully aware of the constitutional issues - or the lack of them - in this kind of situation. But you and I both know that there is a minimal threshold of due process rights that apply even here in academia and it's about time that somebody let these people know it. It will give me great pleasure to disabuse them of the notion that there are no rules binding them in any way. I'm getting pissed and I'm going to show them - Ms. Klein included - that, contrary to their apparent beliefs, there is a higher authority than them." He slapped the desk simultaneously with the word 'them' and stood up. Then he said only a bit more quietly, "although I suspect they will find that hard to believe."

"No doubt they will," Walder answered. "Opposition is pretty rare. They're used to getting their way." He was glad to see that Cann was heating up. He had told him not underestimate these people but he suspected that up till now, Cann had.

"I don't know what I can do," Walder advised, 'but I'll give it a shot. Let me call the University General Counsel and see if she can give us a hand. She's good and she's fair and has at least one foot in the real world."

Cann took a breath and said a little more calmly. "I'm on my way to take Janie and a faculty friend of hers to lunch. But I'm not going to say anything about this till I get back and talk to you - and see the report." He expelled some air through pursed lips and shook his head to calm himself down. "I'll check in with you when I get back. Thanks."

He turned to leave and as he reached the doorway, Walder called after him. "I've always enjoyed a good fight, John. Glad you're on our side."

Cann didn't say anything. His own feeling was that fights weren't meant to be enjoyed. And there was no such thing as a good one. Only a well fought one. His philosophy was that if you did get into one - win it.

* * * *

Janie had also rearranged her schedule for the day of the hearing by skipping all her classes, planning to sleep in until about 10:30. Her roommate Gretchen had left for her first class at about 8:40 AM and so there was nothing to disturb Janie until she woke on her own. She hadn't set her alarm and as a result, she slept until 11:40 AM.

Even after awakening, she lay in bed for a few minutes until she thought about her lunch date at noon with Furden and Cann. She turned her head slowly to the left and up towards the head of the bed and glanced lazily at the clock. It took a couple of seconds for the time on the clock to register that she had slept as late as she had and as soon as she realized how little time there was before Cann was to arrive, she leaped from the bed.

Janie slept nude. So did Gretchen for that matter and, since the events of a week ago yesterday, they had both made several jokes about their lack of inhibition in that regard getting them into trouble. But it didn't change anything. And since each room in this dorm had its own shower enclosure, there was no need to dress until one was ready to leave.

The shower was at the rear of the room opposite the door. Just as Janie started to turn to her left and take the five or so steps that would lead her to it, she noted out of the corner of her right eye that the door to the room was partly open. Gretchen, who perpetually ran late, had a habit of flipping over the dead bolt on the inside lockset as she flew out the room, pulling the door behind her on the assumption that it would engage itself as it hit the door jamb - but never checking to see if it had. As long as the button was down on the lockset, the spring mechanism would allow the tongue of the lock to compress and take its place inside the lock's counterpart on the door jamb. But if the button on the lockset was in the up and locked position, the tongue could not withdraw into the lockset and would simply bang on the jamb and not engage.

Janie had mentioned this to Gretchen several times but it had made no difference. Now she felt angry and upset. It wasn't a question of prudery or modesty. It was a question of privacy and security. She was even starting to wonder why these things kept happening to her - to question her own motives. She hadn't thought of herself as an exhibitionist but was wondering now if she had some kind of problem that got her into these situations. Here, in what should have been the privacy of her own room, she realized that for about two hours, anyone who had walked by the door could have seen her sleeping in bed. Even though she had been covered by a sheet, she still didn't know if she had maybe tossed and turned and thrown the sheet off herself for a time. At least the room was at the end of the hall where traffic was almost non-existent. She made a mental note to talk to Gretchen again. The door was about half open and only about three feet away. Janie took a long step toward it and reached out her left hand to push it shut. At that moment, the door across the hall opened and the man she had seen in that room a week earlier stepped out. His eyes widened as he looked at Janie standing in the open doorway with her left hand on the back of the door and the rest of her standing fully exposed in the opening. She quickly tried to throw the door into the frame but the spring mechanism was still locked and, again, the door bounced back open, even wider than it had been before. Janie stepped behind it and fumbled with the small button in an effort to free the spring. Her own haste made it take longer than it normally would have but eventually she got it and slammed the door closed.

Although it had seemed like an eternity to Janie, she had actually taken no more than five seconds between the time the man came out of the other room and the time the door slammed shut for the second time. The man's reactions were delayed, first by the sight of Janie, then by the moving door, and again by the unexpected re-opening of the door. By the time the man had made his decision, Janie had freed the mechanism and finally succeeded in getting the door closed. Because she had been behind the door by then, she had not seen the man reach behind himself and take a sudden step to the door just as it slammed forcefully in his face.

While Janie stood for a moment on the inside of the door taking a deep breath and then heading for the shower, the man in the hallway took a step back and raised his right leg in preparation for a kick. At that moment, voices came from the stairway at the other end of the hall and he stopped himself. He quickly calculated that he could not break in Janie's door with one kick - if at all - and thought better of it. He decided to take the obvious approach and walked down the hallway to where the voices were coming up the stairs. As he knew they would, the students coming up to the fourth floor didn't even look at him as he passed them on the stairs. They went down the fourth floor hall and went into several rooms about two thirds of the way down leaving their doors open so that they could continue to communicate as they prepared for lunch or their next class. The man continued down to the first floor where he doubled back quickly and placed himself under the stairs to wait for the interrupters to leave.

Janie finished her shower and dressed as quickly as she could. She had managed to put the incident - or at least the primal fears it had brought up - into a corner of her mind. She looked at the travel alarm on the table at the head of her bed and saw that it was almost five minutes to twelve. She wanted to be out front when Cann arrived so she ran to the door. She hesitated for a moment and looked through the peephole in the door. The fisheye view showed no one in the hall but she could see open doors a little way down. Nothing unusual there. She opened the door, checked the hall again, and stepped out. She turned back and checked the lock to make sure it would catch this time then pulled the door shut behind her and gave the knob a turn and the door a push to make sure it was secure. She then turned, skipped twice, and broke into a half run down the hall.

The man under the stairwell heard the loud thudding of footsteps coming down the stairs and assumed it was a much larger person than Janie. She reached the first floor still at a run and was against and through the large outer door before he could react. Janie came to a stop on the top step at the front of the building and looked around for Cann, realizing for the first time that she didn't know what kind of car he drove. The man inside came around from under the stairwell and moved to the door at the same time reaching around behind himself again for something. As he reached the door, Cann pulled up in front of the building and gave Janie a wave. She instantly recognized him not least because he had the plexiglass top off the car and was clearly visible in the driver's seat. Janie took a brief moment to admire the sleek Corvette and muttered, "Cool!" to herself as she bounded down the stairs.

The man inside the dorm stepped back from the door as Janie ran over and got into Cann's car in one fluid motion. He took his hand out from the small of his back and tried to be as unobtrusive as possible as he withdrew from the light of the outside. Cann was watching Janie run toward his car but still noticed the movement inside the door. He looked closer but was able to see only the silhouette as it drew back from view. He looked back to Janie who was already sitting in the passenger seat of the Corvette with a 'let's get this show on the road' look on her face. Cann smiled, put the car into first gear and accelerated away.

*　*　*　*

To Janie's mild dismay, the lunch didn't go as well as she had hoped. Sara was standing out in front of the restaurant with a rather dour look on her face when Cann and Janie pulled up. After Cann parked the car, he and Janie walked over to Furden and Janie made the introductions. From the start, she sensed a hostility - or at least a reserve - on Furden's part towards Cann and she didn't know why.

It didn't get much better throughout the lunch as Furden threw question after question at Cann about why he was so anxious to help Janie and what he thought he could do for her. Twice Janie had interrupted to quietly ask Furden to 'lighten up'.

Cann, for his part, remembered that Janie had told him about the longstanding relationship she and her mother had with Furden and tried to be understanding.

Still, he couldn't help resenting the inquisition. At first, he answered Furden's questions in a friendly open manner but as Furden continued to bore in, he began to close himself off. Eventually Furden's questioning tapered off and she and Cann even exchanged reports of their respective conversations with Klein. But it never became a friendly conversation and by the time the check came, there was an awkward silence among the threesome.

Cann paid the check and walked out to see that Furden and Janie were already walking toward Furden's car. As she got to the passenger side door, Janie turned back to Cann and shrugged her shoulders with her palms up and mouthed, "I'll call you." She smiled, wiggled her fingers in a wave and then grimaced and got into Furden's car.

*   *   *   *

Cann drove back to the campus and went straight to Walder's office. It was about 1:30 and Beverly often took a late lunch so that she could be there to handle the Dean's noontime traffic so Cann walked right in.

Walder looked up and lifted a sheaf of papers in his hand. "You're not going to believe this," he said. Cann could tell he was fuming.

Cann took the security report on the Janie Reston incident and sat down on the couch in Walder's office. It was only a few seconds before he involuntarily began to sit up and lean forward as he read. It took him only about two minutes to read the entire report. Then he looked at Walder with an expression that seemed blank on the surface but in which Walder could see a quiet ferocity that made even him nervous.

"How..." Cann began and then stopped. "What do they..." Walder could not ever remember Cann being at this much of a loss for words.

Cann took a breath and started again. "I have never..." but he still couldn't get it out. Finally, he said, "This is obscene. Roger, this - and what they want to do to that kid - is obscene. There's no other word for it."

Cann looked down at the papers and began to read what was written about halfway down the first page:

"When this officer arrived on the scene, the student perpetrator was standing completely naked in the middle of the dance room fondling her breasts and engaging in acts of self stimulation in clear view of the entire Quadrangle. Before I and the other responding officers could make our way inside, the student had come to the wall, which is entirely made of glass, and pressed herself - her front - hard against the glass. She then reached down and penetrated herself with the middle finger of her right hand and then placed that finger into her own mouth simulating, in this officer's opinion, the act of oral sex."

Cann looked at Walder and said nothing for a moment. When he spoke he forced himself to sound objective. "No such thing happened, Roger. Not even close. Her actions were absolutely antiseptic." Cann was, for all of his experiences, completely uncomprehending for the moment.

"I know, John. Remember, the very same officer who wrote that report gave me a completely different story the night of the incident."

"And that original story matches what I saw. And matches Janie's story as well. This is insane." Cann took a breath. "Alright, let's look at this. They don't know I saw the incident. But they do know that you went to campus security that night and they have to know - at least the security officer has to know - that you were told an entirely different story. How do they think they'll get away with this?"

Walder answered thoughtfully. "Because they get away with it all the time. They look you in the eye and lie to you and the key is they don't care whether you believe them or not. Unless you can slap them down - and they don't think anybody can - it doesn't matter to them. Fail to agree with them and they'll accuse you of intolerance. I've tried to tell you but until you see it for yourself, you really can't believe it." Walder paused in thought for a moment before going on. "I think I said to you before that these people determine their own reality. It is what they say it is. But it goes further than that, John. They enforce their own reality. Woe befall the member of this community that fails to march to the drummer of the day."

"But how can they keep so many people quiet."

"Come on, John. You know better than that. The whole point in a situation like this is that they don't have to keep 'so many' people quiet. Look at this case. How many people know the truth. Janie and you for certain. You two were the only real 'witnesses' to the incident." He paused and cocked his head a little. "By the way, does she know you saw her?"

Cann nodded.

"That's good. Okay, so, aside from you, the campus security people have some first hand knowledge after a certain point. Obviously they've already been co-opted. Then there's me. But I got my information second hand. Pure hearsay. And that's it."

"I beg to differ, Roger. It's only hearsay as far as the truth of what Janie did. It's not hearsay when you talk about what the security officer said to you. You can't testify as to first hand knowledge of what Janie did but you can testify as to first hand knowledge of what the security officer told you she did."

"Thanks for the class on the hearsay rule," Walder said sarcastically. "I've got a JD, too don't forget.?"

"Sorry, Roger. Don't get sensitive. The point is that you can say that the security officer had an entirely different story the night of the incident. Do they really think you'd go along with this - crap?" Cann paused. "You wouldn't, would you?"

Walder was genuinely hurt and at the same time angry. All he said was, "Let's both forget you said that."

Cann was chagrined by his lack of faith in his friend. "Right. You didn't deserve that." A moment of mutual silence passed between them while the truce took hold. "But the question remains. Why would they think you wouldn't speak up?"

"First, because almost no one does. It's that simple. It's the trade-off mentality. I'll let you get your 'scalp' and you'll go along when I'm after one for myself. Then, if someone doesn't go along, there's the ostracization. Sometimes it gets to looking like junior high. Adults picking up their dining room trays and moving to another table when the transgressor sits down. Turning their backs on the outsider. And if you really piss them off, there's the discrediting. The out and out attacks. The ruination of careers. Suddenly the rumor starts that so and so did such and such at some time in their past - smears, insults, phone calls in the night. Many people have skeletons. The ones that don't, they lie about. In any event, there's almost no one who didn't say or do something in the past that they'd rather not have brought up. It can be devastating for even the strongest of people. Believe me, there's a lot of bright, good former teachers who got chased out just because they wouldn't play the game - or toe the line. Don't forget what I told you when you first called me. Despite the PR, these people care about their little club and their paychecks and their status. Certainly not the students. They're expendable. An endless supply of sacrificial lambs."

"This is the second time I've heard that speech, Roger. It's pretty contemptuous of the system. Why do you stay?"

"As a matter of pure principle I don't have a good answer to that. I suppose it's mostly because we're somewhat insulated from the infighting in the law school. Most of the graduate schools are. Some of the people are afraid of us - think we'll sue at the drop of the hat. Actually, we'd probably be the last to sue. We know what a pain in the ass it is. Some others think of us as more of a trade school - which we are if you think about it. We aim straight toward a specific career and minimize the ideology - at least we're supposed to. In any case, I haven't found myself in the fray very often. And, as Administration, I'm a little less vulnerable to the faculty pressure." He winked. "Besides, I told you I love a good fight."

"Well, there's going to be a fight over this crap, you can bet on that. First off, I want to talk to this campus security officer to find out about this change of story. And I will find out."

"No. Don't do that. It's not the right way - as satisfying as it might be." Wilder leaned forward. "Listen. One of the big reasons this crap I'm describing to you doesn't get squelched is that it usually doesn't extend beyond the university. Therefore the endowment doesn't get hurt and therefore the university doesn't care." He waved the security report in the air. "This is different. I don't know why but they really crossed the line with this one. This is defamation - libel - and it's clearly malicious. Even if we couldn't beat the system on campus, we've got a killer case in court. And the judgment would be against the school as well as the individuals. And its nasty enough for punitive damages. Big hit on the endowment. This is one the powers will want to do something about." He tossed his arm forward waving the report like a flag bearer leading a cavalry charge. "Let's go see the good General Counsel. I think we're going to have some powerful allies in this one. It should be fun."

As Cann followed Walder out the door, he called after him, "You have a strange idea of fun, my friend."

As they exited Walder's inner office, they saw that Beverly had returned from lunch by then. She had the telephone handset in her left hand and up to her ear and as Cann reached her desk, she put up her right index finger in a sign telling him to wait one moment. "Go on ahead, Roger," Cann said as he took up a position by Beverly's desk.

After a brief moment, Beverly put her right hand over the mouthpiece of the phone and said, "I ran into Sylvia on my way to lunch and she told me to tell you if I saw you that she left you an important message on your desk."

Cann went straight to his office and picked up the pink slip which was sitting on the corner of his desk. It said simply, 'Arthur Matsen. He said it was important'.

Cann picked up the phone and dialed the DC office of Loring Matsen. The phone was answered after three rings by one of the staff receptionists who put him straight through to Matsen.

"John, thanks for getting back to me so quickly."

"No problem, Arthur. What's up?"

"I may need you here in Washington."

"Uh-oh. You remember what I said?"

Matsen nodded even though Cann couldn't see it. "I remember. But it gets even better. It's the President who wants you here."

"Is that supposed to make me feel better - or important."

Matsen's voice showed some exasperation and he spoke sternly. "You know, John. It might be time for you to remember that we all have a job to do - including you. You're still a member of this firm. At one time or another, all of us - you, me, everybody - has had to bite the bullet and get past personal feelings to get the job done. I admire your principles but now you're starting to act petty. It isn't principle any more - now its just a grudge. I would have hoped you were above that."

Because it was Arthur Matsen saying it, Cann heeded the message.

"Well said, Arthur. Maybe I needed that. What's the problem?"

"Did you catch the President's press conference at noon?"

"I didn't know there was one."

"It was a bit of a rush but he's lighting fires."

"Meaning?"

"Knowing you and your feelings, I assume you're following the Israeli election." Now Cann was nodding at the other end of the phone. "So you know that the polls have Lev Shelanu drawing even with Yenahim."

"Right." The more conservative Shelanu had been trailing in the polls from the beginning of the Israeli campaign but continued

169

terrorist attacks and unkept commitments from the other side had made Shealanu's message of a 'secure peace' much more attractive to the Israeli voters. "Is that supposed to be bad?"

"The President thinks it is."

"What did he say?"

"Well, he's made it pretty clear all along that he wants to see Yenahim continue the process as it's been going."

"Right. Land for peace. Bad idea, in my opinion."

"I know. But it's not a bad idea to the President. He thinks it should continue. But that part was no surprise. He went quite a bit further today."

Cann could feel the knot in his stomach start to tighten as Arthur related the discussion that had taken place in the oval office the day before. "Now he's thrown down the gauntlet here by formally endorsing Yenahim and stating flat out that the United States will have to rethink its committments to Israel if Shelanu wins the election."

"Good."

Matsen blinked. "I beg your pardon?"

"Listen, Arthur. More than maybe any other people on earth, the Israeli's can't be pushed around. When the US and the European countries were bending over and pulling down their pants every time some bunch of crazies with the word 'red' or 'black' in their names made a demand or committed an atrocity, Israel calmly told the world - in more diplomatic terms, of course - that if you fuck with us, we'll fuck with you. And they made good on it. It made El Al the most secure airline in the world and even - considering the circumstances - Israel a pretty secure country. That should have taught us something." Cann warmed to his subject. "What other major country had virtually no problem with terrorism? The Soviet Union. Why? Because the first few times it was tried, the terrorists said 'we'll blow up one of your planes'. And the Soviets said, 'Go ahead'. And they meant it. But the terrorists didn't do it. They didn't want to die. So the Soviets waited them out - or stormed the plane - and when the terrorists were taken into custody, they were led off the plane, knelt down on the runway and executed on the spot. The message was clear: 'blow up the plane - and your dead. Don't blow up the plane - you're still dead. It makes no difference to us. So, don't bother'. And they didn't."

"Isn't that sinking to the level of the terrorist?"

"So what? Why not? All we've done to date - publicly at least - is handcuff ourselves by sticking moral restrictions into a totally immoral situation. There's only one rule, Arthur - 'There are no rules' - or at least there's a new set every time somebody gets a new idea. The only way to handle it is to let the other guy make the rules, then play the game by his rules - just better. Simple. If that's sinking to a level, so be it."

"But why did you say 'Good'?"

Cann explained. "I want Lev to win, Arthur. And he's no extremist - unless wanting to look out for your country and your people is extremist. But then that definition would apply to both Lev and Yenahim. They have different views of the route to be taken. But they're both good men and they're acting in good faith. I can't say the same for our President. It's bad enough that he would insinuate himself into another country's election - but its worse that his motive is just to get a trophy for his own re-election bag. I'm sorry, Arthur. I know how you feel about 'respecting the office' but the guy's an asshole."

Matsen interrupted. "So you're saying that the President's ultimatum may have the opposite effect from what he wants."

"You bet. I'm saying that I'll make you a wager that he single-handedly gave the election to Lev. I'll have to thank him when I see him."

"Please don't. Remember what he told me yesterday - that he wouldn't accept Shelanu's election."

"What did he mean? What does he think he can do?"

"I don't know," Matsen said. "But he's got something up his sleeve and he doesn't seem to consider himself bound by the normal rules."

"Where do I come in?"

"He didn't say but I'm hoping he's got enough sense to be thinking about using you to open up channels of communication with Shelanu if he does win."

"Do you believe that?"

"Nope."

"Neither do I. But listen. I'm in the middle of something here that I've committed to. It's not a world crisis but its just as important to the people involved and I need to see it through."

"Well, I don't know when we'll need you - or even if he's going to call for you. Can you work around this other thing if need be?"

"Actually, this particular issue could resolve today - I hope. Even if it doesn't, I'll find a way to work everything in together, though."

"Alright, John. I'll let you know if you're needed."

Cann hung up the phone and paused for a moment thinking about the conversation he had just had with Matsen. He looked at his watch - 1:55 PM. Roger probably hadn't yet reached the General Counsel's office and even when he did, he would very likely have to wait a bit before he got in to see the very busy General Counsel of the university. He - Cann - didn't need to wait with him or even be there when they started. There was no need for him to rush right over. Maybe he'd run an errand of sorts on the way.

Chapter Fifteen

Iverson left Frankfurt for Lucerne by car at 8:00AM CET and, without straining the engine, made the trip in just over five hours. Once he passed Karlsruhe, he was aware that he was following the same route that Wagner had taken when he was coming north - but in the opposite direction. After passing north and east of Basel, on the German-Swiss border, he got on the N2 which would take him all the way to Lucerne. At Emmenbrucke, just north of Lucerne, he found himself following exactly the same route that Wagner had taken both into and out of Lucerne.

Iverson exited from Highway N2 into the city of Lucerne and headed south on the main thoroughfare of the Baselstrasse just as Wagner had done. Before he'd left Frankfurt, he'd estimated that the boundary between the two grids he was concerned with ran due south from the Reuss River on a line east of where the St. Karli Brucke crossed the Reuss and just about where a small street named the Fahrestrasse met the river. The locater system was good but it didn't pinpoint locations to the inch and Iverson knew there was a spread of about 30-50 yards either way from his estimated boundary line that would have to be covered. He didn't consider that bad at all. He'd begun investigations with greater unknowns than that.

As always, he wanted to get a sense of the area he was about to explore. His search area was near the main train station - the

173

Hauptbahnhof - and he decided to leave the car there and walk around. He continued driving east on the Baselstrasse until it ran into the Hirshengraben which itself ends at the Pilatus Platz named after the 7000 foot high mountain just south of the city. From Pilatus Platz, the Pilatus Strasse runs briefly in an easterly direction right up to the Hauptbahnhof which had, as Iverson had suspected, a large parking area where he could leave the car. After securing everything in the trunk except maps and his notes, he walked west away from the Hauptbahnhof along the Bahnhofstrasse which ran directly alongside the river. He first passed the famous Kappelbrucke across the river on his right and then passed the next wooden bridge called the Rathaus Steg, so named because, quite logically, it was the footbridge that led to the old city hall on the north side of the river. He continued up the Bahnhofstrasse and along the river for several hundred yards before the street veered left to join with and end at the Hirshengraben. Iverson didn't take the left but continued on along the river as the path shrank into a series of narrowing concrete walkways until it ended at the Zeughaus at a point where the Spreuer Brucke crosses the Reuss. Since he could go no further, and he had reached the point where the Baselstrasse commenced at the Hirschengraben several yards to his north, Iverson turned left walked through the Kasernen Platz at the front of the Zeughaus and took a right.

Up to that point, as Iverson had walked along the river, he had seen only the backs of the buildings along the bank. Now, he was walking directly on the Baselstrasse which was a main thoroughfare lined with shops of every description on both sides of the street. The only exception was a few hundred yards down and across the street where a funicular sat with its base on the Baselstrasse and its tracks heading up the steep slope behind the shops. The tracks for the cog train pointed straight up the hill and dissappeared into the woodlands of the Gigeliwald above. The forest became so thick so quickly that Iverson couldn't see the train's destination. He filed the item away in his mind and continued westward on the Baselstrasse.

But this was not just a leisurely stroll. The investigation had begun. In addition to the locater information, Iverson was looking for 'CG' and 'TBA'. He didn't know what either was so he had to consider everything. Before long, he was surprised and a little annoyed to notice that in the several hundred yards from the beginning of the Baselstrasse to his estimated boundary line between the two grids, Iverson counted no less than ten places of business with the initials 'CG' - and that was just on the Baselstrasse itself. No 'TBA' but ten 'CG's".

There were five chocolate stores alone. Chocolat George's, Grande, Godiva, Gallant, and Grenache. In addition, there was a gift shop called Casa Grande, a jeweler called Casa Gucci, two restaurants, Chez George and Chez Germaine, and a watch specialist, Cartier Goldschmidt. He noted that the names were predominantly, but not exclusively, French even though Lucerne is a German speaking city. But then, he thought, the idea of 'Paris chic' is a universal sales tool.

After he had settled himself into a hotel later, Iverson planned to look in the phone book for the telephone numbers of the places he had seen and the other places he assumed he would find with the suspect initials. While he had confirmed that 22 was a telephone prefix in the area he was searching, he had also learned that it was not the only one. So, any of the shops that had a phone number beginning with a prefix other than 22 - and there were several - would be eliminated. For now. Iverson, as always, was fully aware that his initial premises could be faulty but he would work them until they led somewhere - for good or ill.

As he approached the estimated boundary line, he saw a telephone kiosk in front of a small dress shop called 'Le Chemise de Gigi. Great, another possibility - so he decided to check his premise. Of the ten possibles - eleven counting 'Le Chemise de Gigi" - only four had telephone numbers beginning with 22. An encouragingly low percentage to follow up on.

As he turned away from the telephone kiosk, he looked across the street and beyond the single layer of shops that lined Baselstrasse on the south side. Beyond the shops and up the slope, the entire search area to the south appeared to be woods - the Gigeliwald. As long as his current working premise remained - that he would look for Wagner's activities on main streets and existing structures - then the Gigeliwald would be an area that did not need to be searched. If his premise was nullified, then he would have to consider a reason why Wagner might have spent the night in the woods and - eventually - he might even have to search every square foot within the grid boundary - the Gigeliwald included.

Iverson was looking upwards. This was Switzerland after all and Lucerne sits amid foothills and mountains sloping steeply away from the valley floor and lake. Above the shops of the Baselstrasse clinging to the side of the slope slightly to Iverson's right, there was a structure set amid the woods of the Gigeliwald. It was a sprawling castle-like building that Iverson initially assumed to be a private residence of some business tycoon or member of royalty. It had no lettering or identifying marks on it - at least none that were visible to Iverson from below. Iverson also noted that he could see no roadways or paths leading up the structure and thought back to the funicular he had passed a few moments earlier.

He crossed the Baselstrasse and headed back the way he had come but this time on the other side of the street. Perspective can be a funny thing and Iverson knew that it was entirely possible - almost likely - that he would notice something from one side of a street that he wouldn't have seen from the other. Distance adds perspective as the saying goes. But sometimes so does proximity.

It didn't take long for Iverson to find himself approaching the funicular he had seen earlier from the opposite direction and from across the street. What he had not seen in his initial observation of the cog train was a small polished brass plaque on the west wall of the tiny shelter that sat at the base of the tracks.

'*HOTEL CHATEAU GROESCH*' it read. That made twelve initial possibles with seven of the shops eliminated.

Once again, Iverson sifted through his options for his next move. Two of the chocolate shops had phone numbers that began with '22'. Was it possible that Wagner drove all the way to Lucerne for some chocolate? Sure. Less likely than other possiblities, however. Switzerland is noted for its chocolate and every other city, including Geneva, Bern, or Basel, has vast numbers of confectioners and chocolatiers to choose from. Iverson would check them out if he hadn't made a breakthrough before he got to them. But they wouldn't be his first guess.

Cartier Goldschmidt also had 22 as the initial pair in its telephone number but fine watch establishments were as common as chocolate shops in Switzerland, They were everywhere. Cartier Goldschmidt might be checked out. But not yet.

The other '22' prefixed establishment was Chez Germaine. Everybody eats and, if Wagner's stop in Lucerne had been just a few hours, or, if Iverson had to choose among the first eleven 'CG's', then Chez Germaine would have been his first stop.

But Wagner had been in Lucerne for 12 hours and overnight at that. Common sense, logic, and normal human behavior said that he had slept for part of that time. Maybe it was in a private home or apartment. Maybe even in his car. There was no credit card record of Wagner's checking into a hotel, but that didn't mean it didn't happen - or that he hadn't paid cash. If Wagner didn't want it known that he was there - and that was a possibility - Iverson needed to cover all the contingencies. For confirmation or to eliminate them one by one.

And anyway, Iverson needed a place to stay himself. He was not leaving Lucerne until he knew what Wagner had done there - or until he had totally run out of leads and was at a complete dead end. Iverson had never had such a failure and he wasn't planning to have one now. So he needed to establish a base for himself and it seemed to him that, even if it was not the 'CG' he was looking for, the Chateau Groesch - sitting right in the heart of his search area - was the logical choice.

He made his way back to the Hauptbahnhof, this time staying on the main streets - the Baselstrasse to the Hisrchengraben and then left on side streets until he met the Bahnhofstrasse again where it ran in front of the Stadt Theatre. Along the way he made no further striking observations that would displace the Chateau Groesch from its first position. He unlocked his car, got in, and sat inside making a few notes before he drove out of the Hauptbanhof Parkplatz and back toward the Baselstrasse.

Iverson was capable at times of a certain self-deprecating humor and it was that which caused him to mutter several remarks at himself about being such a 'crack investigator'. It was prompted by his inability to find a way up to the Chateau Groesch. He had driven a good distance west on the Baselstrasse without finding a left turn that seemed to lead up to the Chateau. The only left turn off the Baselstrasse was past the St. Karli Brucke and even that road was not truly a left - it was more like a fork that barely branched of the Baselstrasse and continued west northwest at an extremely obtuse angle from the main road, quickly disappearing into the woods. After several fruitless round trips, Iverson was sitting in his car on Baselstrasse opposite the funicular wondering if that was the only access to the hillside hotel. He was about to return the car to the Hauptbahnhof Parkplatz and walk back to the funicular when a Stadt Polizei car pulled up behind him. It was obvious that parking was not allowed on the Baselstrasse and the Swiss police are famous for two things - efficiency and humorlessness. Iverson explained his dilemma to the officer who nodded knowingly while commenting that the Chateau Groesch is a very exclusive establishment indeed. He then explained that the left Iverson had seen past the St. Karli Brucke was indeed the road to take to reach the Chateau Groesch. One takes it until it disappears into the woods. After a short time, there is another left that takes one to the south and then yet another left - unpaved - that brings one back in an easterly direction. That road is private and ends in the Chateau Groesch's 'eigene Parklplatze' - its private lot exclusively for guests. Iverson offered the police officer a hearty 'Dankeshoen' to which the police officer responded with a quiet 'Bitteschoen' followed by 'Unterschrieben Sie hier, bitte, mein Herr,' handing Iverson his pen along with a citation and a receipt for the 10 Swiss Franc fine he was required to pay on the spot. Iverson decided he would absorb the loss himself and not put that charge on his expenses.

Iverson followed the police officer's directions and found his way up the hillside and onto a dirt road that he hoped was the one leading to the hotel. It wound through the woods for about a half mile before opening up into an unpaved park-like setting in front of the Chateau Groesch. Iverson saw the valet/doorman standing in the uncovered entryway of the main building but decided to park the car himself. In spite of the fact that the parking space he selected was a good eighty yards from the building, by the time Iverson had turned off the engine, the valet was at the car opening the door. As Iverson exited the car, he gazed past the hotel complex to its right and got his first glimpse of the breathtaking view of the city of Lucerne and the lake to its east spread out below him.

Iverson turned back to the valet and was a surprised to see that the attendant was - well - quite elderly and he was concerned about allowing his bags to be carried by the much older man. He opened the trunk and then held up his hand to indicate that he would carry the larger bag but the valet simply ignored him. Without the slightest hesitation or difficulty, the valet removed the overnight bag and the briefcase from the trunk. Iverson took the laptop computer himself and the other black bag and followed the valet into the hotel. The valet waited with the bags by the elevator while Iverson went to the front desk.

In response to Iverson's inquiry, the young woman behind the reception desk advised him that the Chateau Groesch usually required reservations but there was a room available overlooking the flower garden and the lake - 'one of our best' - for three hundred francs a night. Iverson took the room without hesitation and handed over the Loring Matsen gold card. As the clerk swiped the card through the magnetic reader, Iverson idly picked up a matchbook with a picture of the Chateau on it and, among other things, its phone number. The numbers matched the readable numbers found on the pad in Wagner's room. The clerk completed her task with the pleasant efficiency for which the

Swiss are noted and, after marking the authorization code on the imprinted credit slip, handed Iverson a key, a piece of chocolate wrapped in gold foil, and a small box containing a decorative three inch plate with a picture of the Chateau Groesch on it.

"Wilkommen zum Chateau Groesch," the young lady smiled.

Iverson smiled back, said, "Danke," and took out the photograph of Wagner he had been carrying in his front shirt pocket.

'Did the lady remember seeing his friend who had spent a Friday night here about ten days ago?'

Without looking at the photograph, the clerk asked, "What night, mein herr?"

"The night of Friday, September 6," Iverson replied.

"Verzeihung," the clerk apologized. 'I was not working that night. Perhaps the valet could help'.

Iverson went back to the old man and asked him if he would be willing to examine a photograph and tell him if he had seen the man.

"Aber naturlich."

But he could not. He seemed to study the picture very carefully before shaking his head and Iverson felt the first stirrings of doubt about his premise. Iverson advised the valet that the man would have arrived very late on Friday September 6 and had left about noon the following Saturday.

"Do you work Saturdays?"

"Bestimmt, mein Herr." 'To be sure'. But, he explained, the valets work only six hours shifts and his ran from 13:00 to 19:00 hours six days a week. Perhaps the night man who comes on at 19:00 hours could help'.

Iverson thanked him and followed the valet to his room where he gave him a very generous tip indeed. It was now 5:30 PM - half 18:00 in European parlance - one and one-half hours until the night valet came in.

Iverson walked over to the french doors that led out onto a small balcony. The view from this room was even more extraordinary than the one he had seen from the parkplatz.

Directly below him was a courtyard overflowing with flowers of what seemed like every color imaginable. Looking out over the garden and to the east, he could see the entire city of Lucerne and the Vierwaldstattersee for as far as it ran in that direction.

Iverson sat down to enjoy the view for a while and drank a bottle of Stella Artois, a mild Belgian beer, from the mini bar in the room. Unlike many who find beer filling, for Iverson, it whetted his appetite. He finished the bottle and left the room taking the tiny elevator down three floors to the main level where he had come in. He had seen the dining area off to the right opposite the reception desk during check-in but when he approached more closely, he saw that it was the breakfast and luncheon area only. As he turned back toward the lobby, he noticed a glass case on the wall with several flyers and brochures in it announcing 'things to do' and available excursions. Also, he noted, was a list entitled 'Ereignis" - 'Events' - for the month of September.

Iverson considered everything a potential lead and always tried to ensure that nothing was overlooked or ignored. So even as he considered that the brevity of Wagner's visit indicated that he might not have come for some particular scheduled event, Iverson looked back toward the beginning of the monthly listing to see what might have coincided with Wagner's visit.

He saw and noted that at 9:00 hours on Saturday September 7 an auction of rare German wines was held in the breakfast area of the Chateau Groesch.

A connection.

Another coincidence.

And investigations make progress because coincidences keep occurring until they are no longer merely coincidences.

In addition to his love of his Austin-Healy, it was well known within Loring Matsen - and to Iverson - that Wagner was an afficionado of rare German wines - a rather esoteric interest.

In all of recorded history, German wines have never reached the ranks of the outstanding and extraordinarily expensive vintages. No container of German wine has ever commanded a price even remotely close to the $30,000 plus prices of a Chateau

Lafitte or Mouton Rothschild and certainly not to the 1787 Chateau Lafitte claret which brought $131,250 - a price attributed in large part to its having been initialed by Thomas Jefferson.

One of the reasons for that - in general - is that German wines have traditionally been produced by small farmers for local consumption and simply not thought of as something to keep for long periods of time. Also, the wines produced have in fact been mostly consumed locally - as intended - so that there was little to keep for aging even if someone wanted to. And - due to the multiplicity of growers - there was little consistency of the qualities that make a wine notable among the numerous small vintners. A national attempt at consistency and quality was made with the passage of the German Wine Law in 1971 - with some improvement - but German wines - mostly white - still do not reach the historic proportions of price and reputation that the others do.

A result of that was that someone like Wagner who, while fiscally comfortable, was by no means wealthy, could indulge in the speculative collection of wines whose prices topped out in the range of several hundred dollars instead of the tens of thousands that the truly 'great' vintages commanded.

Could Iverson be sure that that was what brought Wagner here? No. But his premise remained intact for the moment. And it was a reason to continue to pursue the premise.

Iverson asked the valet who had carried his bags where the dining room - for dinner - was. He was directed to go through a long narrow tunnel that sloped down into what may have been the dungeon of the chateau in past centuries. Iverson finally emerged into a large dark room with perhaps thirty tables spread around it. He was seated at a small table for one directly next to a slit in the wall which he could see was on the same side of the building as his room because from where he sat he had a similar view of the city and the lake.

After a dinner that approached the level of a gourmet experience and which was presented with the understated graciousness of the Swiss, Iverson walked out to the lobby and saw that the valet he had dealt with had been replaced by another man who also appeared to be at least in his seventies - or more - and perhaps should not have been carrying other people's luggage either. But, like the other valet, the man was managing his tasks with ease. 'It must be the mountain air,' Iverson thought.

When the night valet had returned to the lobby from delivering the guests and their luggage to their room, Iverson repeated his inquiry and handed the man the photograph of Wagner. The valet looked at it only for a moment before advising Iverson that, yes, he remembered this man coming in a week ago Friday before midnight.

"You can be so sure of the time?"

"My memory is excellent, mein herr," the old man pursed his lips and puffed his chest proudly.

"And he checked into the hotel?"

"No, he did not, mein herr." Iverson's premise was in danger. "The young lady with him checked them both in."

Iverson had already considered the possibility. A tryst. A rendezvous. Iverson had mixed feeling about this bit of information. It was consistent with the premise and that was good. But it was inconsistent with what was known - and thought - of Wagner. He wasn't know to be a womanizer and it was out of character. But then, things like that happen.

'Could the kind valet describe the young lady?'

'Early twenties. Very pretty. Black hair. Dark eyes. She appeared to be very tanned. Excellent figure.' The old man could tell because she wore very tight blue jeans and a black leotard top. Very shapely', he assured Iverson as he winked and bounced his brows.

'Did he take them to their room?'

"Aber naturlich. There is only one valet on duty at a time. It is more profitable that way," the valet said with the candor found mostly in the very young and the very old.

'Did he notice anything more about them?'

'Not really. They did nothing strange. They did not touch or even talk very much on the way up to the room. He assumed they were married.'

Iverson knew that Wagner's wife remained in Virginia. And, in any case, the description didn't fit Wagner's wife whom Iverson had seen once at a reception. Carrie Wagner was an attractive woman but with sandy hair and light skin and Iverson thought she was in her mid-thirties.

So the most likely inference to be added to the paradigm was that Wagner had an assignation - perhaps even an ongoing affair. But who was the woman?

Iverson went to the desk clerk and asked if there were any way he could see the check-in records for the night of Friday, September 6.

The same clerk who had checked him in shook her head with a severe frown on her face. "Ach nein, mein herr. Es it nicht moglich. This would not be possible. Such information is private and confidential."

The Swiss reputation for concern with regard to privacy is justified and it extends well beyond their banks and other financial institutions. Iverson was aware of this even as he asked the clerk for the information but, since she was right there, he'd figured it was worth a try.

Even without the information he'd just asked the clerk for, the investigation had reached a point where it had gone beyond a mere premise. It was time to make the first attempt at unifying the structure of the premise to see if it made sense.

Iverson knew that Wagner had come to Lucerne and stayed in the Hotel Chateau Groesch. It was likely - a valid inference for now, anyway - that Wagner's reason for the trip had been the wine auction or the woman or both. Only 'song' was missing from the trilogy, he mused.

At this point, from a security standpoint - the other major concern of the investigation - the reasons for the detour to Lucerne were benign. Mrs. Wagner may not think so, but......

Iverson went back to the valet and asked if he knew which valet had worked the morning of Saturday September 7.

'Indeed. he did,' the old man explained, 'it was he who had worked an extra shift that Saturday morning. Could he be of further assistance?'

'Did the kind valet see the couple at all in the morning?'

'Not before or at breakfast but he did notice them going in and out of the breakfast room later in the morning. He had no direct contact with them, however, until they called about half 12:00 for him to get their bags.'

'How did they act?'

'Normal. No - quiet. Perhaps they may have had an argument. Not a serious one, mind you. A small disagreement, perhaps. The old man had been married for 51 years and knew the coolness when he saw it.' He winked again and clicked his tongue. 'But if so, it was not serious.' He pursed his lips and shook his head. 'No nothing serious at all. He was quite sure.'

'Did they do anything out of the ordinary?'

'Nothing at all. They went straight out to their car. The woman drove and the man got in the passenger side with one of those large covered coffee cups with a handle. He looked like he was in some discomfort. A headache perhaps. Or maybe he was just tired.' He winked yet again. 'I would be too with that young lady.'

Iverson gave the man a second large tip for the information and went back to his room.

The Stella Artois had been replaced and a couple more added to the mini bar and Iverson took one out onto the balcony and looked down at the lights of the darkened city and thought about what he had so far.

Nothing he had learned up to this point gave a direct clue to the reason Wagner was killed. The visit to Lucerne and the woman he was with could be completely unrelated to his death - an innocent encounter. Well, perhaps innocent wasn't the word for it. But he wasn't prepared yet to draw an adverse inference in that regard.

He needed to know who the woman was and when she parted company with Wagner. The valet had them leaving the hotel just about noon which confirmed the locater information. Unless the woman was a resident of Lucerne and Wagner had - for example - picked her up and dropped her off at the Hauptbahnhof - which would not take very long - the indications were that she accompanied him all the way to Bad Durkheim at least. If she'd accompanied him the rest of the way to Sembach, then it was very likely that she knew about - and very possibly had something to do with - Wagner's death.

So who was she and how would Iverson find out?

The obvious way, of course. It was Iverson's first principle.

He picked up the room telephone and called the Geneva station for Interpol. He read his identification number into the computer when it asked for it and was transferred to a live human being. He indicated what he needed and then gave the person at the end of the line his hotel room phone extension so he could be reached. While he waited, the Interpol clerk in Geneva placed a call to the duty chief of the Stadt Polizei for the city of Lucerne who in turn placed a call to the head of security at the Hotel Chateau Groesch. Twenty minutes later, Iverson's room phone rang and he was invited by the Chief of hotel security to come down and look at the check-in records for the night of Friday, September 6.

Iverson took the elevator down to the level below the lobby and when it stopped and the doors had opened, he stepped out and turned left toward the security office. He knocked once on the plain door that had the single word 'Direktor' stenciled on it in small letters and a voice called. "Komme."

The two men shook hands across the desk and exchanged greetings after which the security chief handed Iverson a sheet of paper without saying an additional word. Iverson took it and nodded his thanks to the man and sat down in the chair in front of the desk.

The Swiss are almost as famous for their efficiency as they are for their concern for privacy and the list of guests who had registered on that Saturday was neatly typed out with the name of the guest in the first column, the number of people in the party in the second column, the manner of payment in the third column and, since almost everyone paid by credit card, the account number in the fourth column. All the way to the right, the room number was printed on the sheet as well.

The list was arranged in chronological order so - since it was almost midnight by the time Wagner had arrived - Iverson started at the last entry - and recognized the name at once: Lisa Harmony.

So it appeared that Wagner was having an affair or relationship of some sort with one of the legal assistants in the Loring Matsen Geneva office. Surely not the first time that something like that had occurred.

But small alarms were starting to go off in Iverson's head. He recalled that Bucher had told him that Ms. Harmony had said that she had not seen Wagner after the lunch meeting on Friday the 6th and had indicated that she didn't know him very well. Of course, that was an understandable position for someone who was having an affair with a married man and didn't want it known. And if that's all it was, Iverson had no intention of making more out of it.

But Iverson also remembered Bucher's description of Lisa Harmony's demeanor during her interview with him as being quite nonchalant - almost overly so - and as having shown little concern when told of Wagner's death. It could have been an act and it could even have been shock but Iverson noted it for future reference.

Iverson asked for and was - reluctantly - given a photocopy of the register sheet. He also asked to see the phone log for the room which revealed that no calls had been made from that phone in the time that Wagner stayed at the hotel. He thanked the security head and asked if he could see the room that Wagner and Harmony had shared. "Aber naturlich," he was told, 'but it has been cleaned every day since the visit and also occupied on three separate occasions by two couples and a businessman.'

Iverson wanted to see it anyway but the head of security's analysis was accurate and there was nothing to be found. Iverson thanked him for his time and cooperation and returned to his own room.

Before he settled in for the night, he made two phone calls. The first was to the Loring Matsen EI section. The credit card that Lisa Harmony had used at check-in was, like Loring Matsen cards, a gold level charge card. But legal assistants, while they are valuable employees of the firm, do not normally get company gold cards. Iverson read the credit card number from his copy of the register and asked EI to get back to him as soon as possible with all relevant data.

The he called Bucher again in Geneva. 'Would his colleague be so kind as to place surveillance on Ms. Lisa Harmony?' He explained his reasons. 'They should also do an "A" security check on her,' he advised the Swiss. Loring Matsen legal assistants, depending on their assignments, were normally subject to less stringent security checks - "B" or lower. But in special circumstances, like this, the highest degree of scrutiny was called for.

Bucher agreed at once. 'And may I suggest that a review of her recent work and phone records would be in order as well. Yes. We will be discreet.'

Chapter Sixteen

By the time Cann got to the office of Elizabeth Buffinton, General Counsel for Charlestown University, it was 2:30 PM and Walder had been in with the Chief Legal Officer of the university for about ten minutes. It had been enough time for Walder to outline the situation and for Buffinton to read the campus security report and have the report's author summoned to her office. The secretary to the General Counsel had been advised that Cann would be coming and that he could be sent in but she still buzzed Elizabeth Buffinton on the intercom and announced him. The amplified voice was tinny as it came through the speaker. "He can come right in."

Buffinton sat behind a large mahogany desk that appeared - and probably was - very old. As Cann came through the door into her office, she stood up to shake his hand and introduce herself. She was a slight woman - maybe five foot three and 100 pounds, late thirties, with a pleasant angular face which was at the moment smiling politely.

"Nice to meet you, Professor Cann. Dean Walder was telling me about you."

Cann was immediately struck by the speaking voice of the woman. His first thought was that she should get a new digital intercom that didn't distort her deep modulated tones so much. She had the voice of a commercial voice-over star, deep without being masculine with precise diction and no trace of an accent.

189

Despite her physical dimensions, she radiated strength. He found himself being overly conscious of speaking from his own diaphragm as he had been taught to do in his college speech classes.

The General Counsel went on. "Dean Walder has explained to me his view of the situation. And that this," she picked up the papers Walder had brought with him, "is substantially at odds with what he was told the night of the incident. Is that correct?"

"Well, I certainly don't take issue with what Roger said, Ms. Buffinton, but I have no first hand knowledge of what he was told by security that night. I'm personally sure that what the Dean says is true because I know him. But I wasn't there when he talked to security."

When lawyers get together, unless they're close friends, it's an occupational hazard that every conversation takes on elements of a cross-examiner/witness confrontation. The speaker frames his or her question carefully in an attempt to elicit the precise answer he or she wants without allowing evasion of the essential point. The answerer in turn makes an instantaneous decision as to what part of the question contains the essence of the inquiry and whether or not that is information they wish to provide. They choose the part they feel is safe to answer and then decide on the minimum amount of information they can disclose without seeming evasive or lacking in professional courtesy and openness. The answerer also decides on the spot what part of the question is the trick part calculated to lay the basis for further, more difficult questions. It isn't even conscious. It's part of the profile.

Cann's answer to the General Counsel's question made the point that he couldn't know - first hand - what the security guard said to Walder. He could say with absolute certainty what Walder told him the guard said but he couldn't know if what the guard said was true - except from his own observation.

Buffinton laughed softly. "This isn't a deposition, Professor. I'm not trying to get you to engage in hearsay. Dean Walder tells me that you were an actual eyewitness to this incident. Does what you observed comport with the Dean's position that the true facts bear little resemblance to this report."

"Absolutely. The nudity part is accurate but the business of any lewd behavior is a total fabrication."

"You're sure of that."

Cann remained cautious. "Yes. Why?"

Buffinton's tone remained purely conversational. "Dean Walder points out - quite accurately - that there is a severe liability issue for the university in this matter. I concur. And that - and that alone - is my official concern."

Buffinton then spoke directly to Cann. "As I said before, Professor, Dean Walder was telling me about you. But that wasn't entirely necessary. I know of you. Or at least I've heard of you and your corporate and government representation. Your reputation says you're good. Very good. So am I. And I would like to hope that we could approach this matter from the same viewpoint."

Cann hoped that this meant that she was on Janie's side. But he wasn't yet prepared to drop his guard.

Buffinton continued. "Because of the nature of your work and your clients, I know you'll understand my role as General Counsel. Just as you are corporate counsel to your business clients, I am corporate counsel to this university. There is no difference between us in that regard. My primary duty is to my client. I'm the lawyer for the school. It's my job to look out for and defend its legal interests. So when someone," she nodded toward Dean Walder, "tells me of an exposure to liability for my client - or even of potential exposure - it's my job to be concerned and to limit - or eliminate - that exposure."

Cann understood perfectly. Buffinton paused but signaled with her hands that she wasn't finished. Cann and Walder didn't try to interrupt. They could see that she was carefully formulating her sentences. Finally she continued.

"None of that is meant to imply that I feel no sympathy or empathy towards this student. I want you to know that, on a personal level, I frankly believe Dean Walder and, by extension, this," she looked down at the police report, "this Jane Reston. I think they should just leave the kid alone."

"Here, here," Walder quietly supported her statement.

Buffinton smiled. "But the university also has to operate in a certain context, gentlemen. And it's a context that's unique to the university setting." She looked back at Cann. "Our respective corporate representation differs in one very large respect, Professor. Image. Corporate America - or big business, if you will - has a profit oriented image. Some consider that good. Others consider it very bad indeed. But that's the image. In contrast, the image that corporate academic America wants to project is that of a selfless compassionate caring plato-like tutor nurturing the minds of innocents in a vicious and selfish world. And corporate academic America has been successful in promoting that image. It's a textbook public relations triumph that has led to non-profit status - which simply means that as long as you spend your money on yourself it's not considered profit. The result is a holier than thou attitude that would gag a maggot."

In spite of himself, Cann burst out laughing at the phrase as well as her frankness and the General Counsel joined him in it. Then, perhaps realizing the extent of the cynicism reflected in her statement, she pointed her finger at both men and told them, "If you ever say I said what I just said, I'll call you both liars to your face." They laughed a little more but she was still not finished.

"What I'm trying to say is that everything we do - every action taken - is examined and often challenged within the context of concepts like academic freedom, tolerance, diversity, freedom of expression, and god knows how many others. I'll not comment on the sincerity of those who bring them up most of the time, but the result is that we can't just make a business decision for sound business reasons. We have to take into account that someone's ox will be gored and they will at least try to use some issue - real or imagined - to protect their own perceived interest."

"Hence, the ubiquitous balancing test," Walder offered.

"Exactly," Buffinton replied. "And the 'other side' gets powerful support. The faculty will support the unions, the staff will often support the faculty, and the students support whoever gets to them first and convinces them that the 'other side' is the new authority figure in their lives. But you can be certain that all of them will support each other in frequent opposition to the administration. And often it is an unfortunate fact of academic corporate life that not making a sound business decision is the soundest business decision."

Cann was growing a little impatient although he was determined not to show it. "So where does that leave Janie."

"Well let's do the balancing act, Professor. Caroline Klein is pushing this, right?"

"According to her, she was dragged into it but now is being guided by higher motives."

"Right." The sarcasm in the General Counsel's voice was unmistakable. "But Ms. Klein is a formidable opponent. And may attempt to exact costs from the university if she is thwarted - strikes, boycotts, damages - certainly confrontational publicity calculated to persuade like-minded alumni and others to withhold their financial support. So we have to examine the legal liability of the university if we let Klein go after Ms. Reston compared to the costs if we stop her."

The General Counsel held up the index finger of her right hand.

"First, let's say that the security report is an accurate depiction of the students actions." Cann started to protest. "For the sake of argument only, professor. Let's assume it's completely true. The first issue could be one of invasion of privacy. In my opinion, the university could probably prevail on that one because she made no attempt to conceal her actions from public observation."

Cann opened his mouth to speak but again Buffinton held up her hand and went on. She was used to having the floor. "I know, Professor. She didn't know she could be seen and, as we all know, a question of invasion of privacy turns on the expectation of privacy one is allowed to have under the circumstances. If someone voluntarily and knowingly walks through a crowded mall without clothing, their expectation of privacy is nil. If someone is in a closed room - and is observed - they may have a valid expectation of privacy. The key issue is the reasonableness of the expectation. I said I think we would prevail on that question - but it would by no means be certain."

Cann agreed that the privacy issue was the weakest argument that Janie had and here the General Counsel was saying that she wasn't entirely sure of winning even that. He was encouraged and so said nothing. Over the years, he had often recalled a bit of advice a first year civil procedure professor had given him on the subject of argument. 'Have your argument ready. Have your cases ready. Be prepared to argue every point as strenuously as you can. But know when to shut up. If it appears that you're already winning - keep your mouth shut'.

"On the other hand," Buffinton continued, "if, as you say, this report is a total fabrication, then we now have a question of a whole other set of very severe liabilities. We are talking about libel - and particularly malicious libel at that. That's my gravest concern. Since it would go to her moral character - and be untrue - we're talking 'libel per se'."

Cann was impressed. Not so much that she would be seeing all the issues. That's what lawyers are trained to do. It's also what forms the basis of so much of the criticism that lawyers create problems when in truth they are doing exactly what they have been asked to do by finding potential problems no matter how obscure.

What Cann was impressed with was the objectivity and thoroughness with which Buffinton was discussing the issues with him and Walder. Both pro and con from the university's perspective. Again, that's what lawyers are supposed to do for their clients, but she was being especially candid and frank and it was appreciated.

The 'libel per se' Buffinton referred to was of special importance in her discussion because it allowed for unlimited punitive damages even if a plaintiff had no actual damages.

It is a common misconception among the general populace that if someone does something wrong they are automatically on the hook for huge amounts of money. Not generally true. For someone to be awarded a judgment, there are two things that must occur. First there must be a wrong - a tort. Secondly there must be damages related to the wrong - monetary damages or some otherwise compensable injury and they must be proven. If, for example, someone trespasses on someone else's land, they have committed a tort. But if they leave immediately without doing any harm, there are no damages. So, the landowner could sue but even if he or she won, they would be awarded nothing or perhaps one dollar in 'nominal damages'.

The same is true in most libel cases. If someone lies about someone else in a way that causes no compensable injury, there are no damages. But libel law states that there are certain lies which do not require proof of actual injury. The two most common are libeling someone in their profession and libeling someone's moral character. If the act of libeling - the tort - is proved, no proof of damages is needed. A judge or jury may award an amount sufficient to punish the perpetrator of the libel. The more assets they have, the larger the judgment would have to be to make its effects felt by the wrongdoer.

So Buffinton was quite right to be concerned about a heavy hit against the university if it were found liable for such an act - and she was fully aware and correct that even if the administration of the university was unaware of the acts of its employees and indeed totally opposed them, it could still be held accountable for their acts.

Both Cann and Walder could see where her line of thought was leading and neither of them were about to interrupt.

"So, gentlemen, let us assume that security insists their report is true. What proof of the untruth of the statement exists. We have Ms. Reston, of course. Her testimony is readily attackable as self-serving. She would also have the most reason to lie."

Again, Cann opened his mouth to speak but was placated by a gesture from Buffinton. "We also have Dean Walder's testimony that he was told an entirely different story the night of the incident and that testimony would of course carry more weight than Ms. Reston's because the Dean has no reason at all to lie - that we know of." She made yet another placating gesture to indicate that she was speaking again for the sake of argument and not accusing him of anything. "But there is also the point that the security guard has no apparent reason to lie, either."

"That we know of," said Walder.

"Right. That we know of." Buffinton agreed. "But let me finish."

"Clearly, the strongest evidence against the statement is that of Professor Cann. An outside observer who has no discernible vested interest in the case. Maybe."

Cann cocked his head slightly to the right and squinted at the General Counsel. Again, she held up her hand in a gesture indicating 'wait'.

"You say you have spoken with Professor Klein about this, Professor Cann. I would be very surprised if she has not already previewed one of their favorite tactics towards males who oppose them. May I ask if she has implied any - shall we say - closeness between you and Ms. Reston?"

"She has indeed."

"I'm sure she has. And therein, Professor, lies the vulnerabilities of your testimony in this. These people play hardball."

Cann surpressed the urge to look at Walder who had used exactly the same phrase in the past.

"Your testimony will be subject to both personal and logical attack. May I demonstrate?"

Cann nodded. "Be my guest."

"Professor Cann, you state that you saw the entire episode from your office window. Is that true?"

"Yes."

"And is it your testimony that Ms. Reston did not perform the acts that are stated in the security report."

"That is my testimony and it is the truth."

They were both getting into the role playing.

"And you never took your eyes off her for a moment."

Cann hesitated.

Buffinton came out of character and became the General Counsel again.

"I can tell that you see where I'm going. Its the old 'rock and a hard place' line of questioning. If you say that you never took your eyes off her, you're going to be vilified as a dirty old man ogling this girl - not glancing away for a second. Getting your thrills by watching a near child who doesn't know you're there. Actually that's probably the least of what they'll accuse you of doing.

"On the other hand, if you answer that question by saying that you did look away at any time, then they'll jump all over you with the point that, 'Well, if you weren't watching her all the time, how do you know she didn't do what the report says she did during one of those times when you weren't looking. You just testified that you weren't watching all the time'.'Rock and a hard place'."

Cann replied. "Well done. But my testimony is - and will be - that I did look away briefly to see if I could maybe find a way - phone her or something - to let her know she could be seen but at no time did I look away for a long enough period of time for her to do the things the report says she does. And as I tried to look up a phone number, I glanced up fairly consistently. And even if I looked away for long enough for the series of acts to have taken place, they were so out of character with what she was doing before and after I had looked away as to be impossibly inconsistent. And finally, the acts described in the report all took place after the officers arrived. I saw every second from then on. None - none of what that report says occurred did occur. Period."

Buffinton smiled and nodded. "Very good, Professor. I'm impressed. I didn't think you could get around that but you did. That's the best handling of the 'rock and a hard place' tactic that I've seen so far."

The intercom buzzed and the secretary announced, "Sergeant Pescary is here, General."

"Thank you. Send her in."

The door opened and the campus security duty sergeant walked into the inner office of the General Counsel and stopped in the center of the room. Cann and Walder had been occupying the two armchairs directly in front of Buffinton's desk and they stood when the officer walked into the room.

Pescary looked warily at Cann and then turned her gaze to Walder. At first her face was blank and then it began to show recognition. From recognition, her expression evolved into one of resignation as she realized the implications of the meeting.

Buffinton broke the silence. "Please sit down, Officer." She indicated the left chair in front of her desk which Cann had taken when he came in. He went to the couch against the left wall of the office while Walder retook the chair on the right.

"I'll get right to the point." Buffinton handed the report over to Pescary. "Do you recognize this?"

Pescary briefly examined the papers and nodded.

"These gentlemen tell me it is essentially a fabrication."

Buffinton waited for a response but none came. "Well, is it?"

Pescary took a deep breath while the three others in the room held theirs. Then she looked at Walder, who asked, "Do you remember me?"

Pescary nodded again. "Dean of the Law School."

Walder said. "You told me an entirely different story that night."

Pescary shrugged.

Buffinton indicated Cann sitting on the couch. "And this gentleman here was an eyewitness to the incident."

Pescary turned and looked at Cann who just stared back at her. She looked briefly again at Buffinton then looked down at her hands which were folded in her lap.

Buffinton pressed. "Please respond to my question, Officer Pescary."

A pause. And then, "It's...um...not all true. No."

"In what way. Please be specific." Buffinton was not being harsh but she was all business.

Pescary started slowly but it did not take long for her to confirm Walder and Cann's version of the events of the night of September 8 as they involved one Ms. Jane Reston.

When Pescary finished her story, Buffinton asked almost gently, "Do you have any idea of the seriousness of what you've done? Or the liability to which you have exposed this university? Not to mention the harm you would have done to this student."

Silence.

"Why did you do this?"

Pescary was silent for a long while but no one else in the room spoke. They waited. Finally, the officer said, "The message wasn't strong enough. Or the issue wasn't strong enough. Or something like that. Everything was too innocent. We had to dirty things up a little."

Buffinton said. "Go on. I don't understand." But she did.

"Every year, some student, usually a new one, does something really stupid and usually offensive. Something that can be used to send a message to the student body in a way that gets through a lot better than a lecture or a pamphlet - or even a demonstration. Last year we had the transfer student who was a hooker at her last school and the year before we had that basketball player who had a history of beating up his girlfriends. This year, this was the best we had. And we were afraid that it wasn't enough."

"Who exactly is we?" Buffinton asked.

Pescary shrugged.

Cann said quietly, "Klein."

"That's a little too easy, isn't it?" Buffinton asked.

"Not when the officer here sounds like a recording of a conversation with her?" Cann replied.

Buffinton probed. "Is Caroline Klein part of this, Officer?"

"I run incidents with possibilities by her. She makes the judgment on whether they're useful."

Buffinton sounded genuinely shocked. "Am I to understand that you give Professor Klein access to the confidential security files of the University Security Department?"

Pescary nodded.

Buffinton was blunt. "I suggest you consider yourself under suspension, Officer. I don't have direct authority to do that but as soon as I get off the phone with your Director, I think such a thing will be in order."

Pescary stood and looked at Walder and then at Cann.

"Before you go I have a question." It was Cann. "Was it Klein who called in the complaint in the first place?"

"Yes."

"How do you know?" interjected Buffinton. "Hell, how did she know it was even going on. Her office is on the other side of the campus."

"I don't know how she knew. But I know it was her because I've talked to her on the phone a hundred times. And she said it was her."

Buffinton looked back and forth at Cann and Walder then spoke with finality. "If either of you gentlemen have no further questions...?" She made it a question herself. After both men shook their heads, she said, "Then you can go, Officer Pescary. Please check in with Director Oldham when you get back to security."

After Pescary had closed the door behind her, Walder asked, "Now what?"

"Now we talk to Professor Klein," Buffinton said. She pressed the button on the intercom and asked Betty to please try to get Professor Caroline Klein on the line.

While they waited to see if Betty would get Klein, Cann mused, "You know, I don't mean to be thick but I still don't see how they thought they could get away with this."

Buffinton answered. "I guess its because they have before." She looked at each man individually. "Professor - Dean, I can tell you that right now I'm sick to my stomach. I've been here seven years and Pescary is right. Every year there's been at least one situation like this. I'm thinking back to past years and students who went through this process and I have to wonder how many of them were set up too. I remember one girl who sat right here in my office - in that chair - in tears - utterly broken by the process - and protested to me that she hadn't - would never - do what they said she did. And I dismissed her as a good actress or a spoiled brat. The poor kid came to me for help and I ignored her." Buffinton was truly and visibly shaken. "How do they get away with it? It's not because they have such high credibility. They don't. Until this moment I never realized how much the rest of us just don't take it that seriously. A lot of the fault lies with our - 'they're just kids, they'll get over it' - attitude." She shook her head with intensity. "No more. The rules will change. Bet on it." She shook her head one more time, "God, right now, I want to throw up." She actually looked like she might.

The intercom buzzed. "I have Professor Klein on line 1, General."

"Thank you." Buffinton gathered herself and said to Cann and Walder, "I'm going to put this on speaker but I would appreciate it if you would allow me to be the only one who talks. Any problem?" Both men shook their heads in the negative. Buffinton then hit the button on her phone that activated the speaker and said, "Professor Klein? University Counsel Liz Buffinton here."

"Ms. Buffinton? What can I do for you?"

"Well, first of all, I'm calling to tell you that there will be no disciplinary hearing on the Janie Reston matter tonight? Or any other..."

"Say's who," Klein interrupted.

Cann and Walder looked at each other.

"Says me, Ms. Klein, the Chief Legal Officer of this university."

"I don't think you have that authority, Ms. Buffinton. Or the proper realization of the importance of the issues involved here." It was as if Klein was incapable of comprehending that she was not in control.

"Oh, I have that authority, Ms. Klein. Rest assured of that. And even if I do not, the President of the university does and he will act on my recommendation. Does that register?"

"Please explain."

Buffinton did so but without mentioning Officer Pescary by name. When she was finished, Klein was still not prepared to back down.

"What you're telling me is nonsense, Ms. Buffinton. I did not make any such call and I certainly have played no part in altering the record. I did not hear of this incident until the Associate Dean of Students called me the next day about presenting the university's position. And the version that you are telling me is a fabrication is the only version of the incident of which I am aware. If it's inaccurate, then I have been as deceived as anyone."

"Then you should have no objection to the cancellation of the hearing." Buffinton was good.

So was Klein. "To the contrary, I have every objection. Now we have two versions. And we need to know which one is true. I thought you attorneys believed in having hearings to establish facts. Or is that only when you are being paid handsome fees?"

Buffinton was also tough. "You might want to consider cutting the bullshit, Klein, before you go deeper into it yourself. There will be hearings all right to get to the truth. But Ms. Reston won't be the respondent."

"I welcome them." Klein didn't even sound like she was bluffing. "But that doesn't alter the fact that the hearing scheduled for tonight will go on - with or without Ms. Reston present. And with or without your sanction."

The three lawyers in the room couldn't believe what they had heard. But Buffinton retained her equanimity. "It will be of no consequence to anyone - especially Ms. Reston. Whatever you do will not - repeat not - be validated or condoned by the university. You will be acting completely on your own and contrary to the express direction of the chief legal officer of Charlestown University. Do you understand the significance of that, Ms. Klein? Any liability accruing for any further actions you may take in this regard will be yours and yours alone."

"I doubt that. I believe that the legal concept here is that the security guard who gave you your information is the what - agent, isn't it - of the university. And therefore the university is responsible for his or her actions. True?"

"Only to an extent. But since you've ventured onto my turf, pay attention. Up to this point, the university may be responsible for the acts of its agents but here and now we have taken steps to nip it in the bud before the greatest damage has been done. And if the university gets sued over this, rest assured that we will plead you in. Do you know what that means, Professor Klein?" She didn't wait for an answer. "Let me tell you. Ms. Reston sues the university - and I can't say that I blame her. We then sue you - you become what's called a third party defendant. The case will be entitled Reston vs Charlestown vs Klein. We will not be on your side and we will not pay for your lawyers. Our position will be that any liability that the university has up to this point is your responsibility. It will be the reverse of what you and so many have come to expect. And if there is a judgment entered against the university, we will go after you to pay it."

"I do not..."

Buffinton wouldn't let Klein interrupt.

"That's not all, Ms. Klein. I'm not finished. That only applies to liabilities up to this point. You are on notice - and I will put it on the record - that from this point on, the university disavows what you are doing and demands that you cease and desist. Any liability from here on is yours. That means that any judgment for damages will look toward your lovely condo and your savings and pension and even that Lexus you are so proud of and all of the other material things you no doubt profess not to care about but have gone to great lengths to acquire."

For once Klein did not try to interrupt.

"And let me advise you further. Behavior such as we are discussing places this university in a very bad light, Ms. Klein. And such behavior can be grounds for your dismissal - severance of your contract. Desist, Ms. Klein, or I will recommend your termination."

Klein snorted. "I have tenure."

"Tenure does not protect you from dismissal for cause, Ms. Klein. For cause. And as chief legal officer, I will issue the opinion that the acts we are talking about constitute such cause. That will be my legal opinion, Ms. Klein. And that's the one that counts. The only one. Have I made myself clear, yet, Professor?"

"You've certainly tried. But I'm not that easily cowed, Ms. Buffinton. We shall see what we shall see."

"Do so at your peril, Ms. Klein." The General Counsel reached over and hit the button that terminated the call. The three people in the room looked at each other in silence. They didn't know whether to be impressed or dumbfounded. Or both.

Chapter Seventeen

Cann had cancelled his 1:00 International Finance class to take Janie and Sara Furden to lunch but hadn't done the same with the 3:00 Intergovernmental Relations class. It hadn't crossed his mind that he wouldn't make that one. But it was 3:10 PM when he left the General Counsel's office and, without stopping to pick up his books, he rushed to the classroom to try to catch the students. He should have known better. Only two students remained - one reading the case book - the other reading the newspaper. Cann offered his apologies to the two students and went down to his office.

He sat on the edge of his desk and picked up the phone. He dialed the number that Janie had given him for the phone in her dorm room. There was no answer until the phone company 'personal secretary' program stepped in to advise him to leave a message. The reality was that Cann didn't want to tell Janie about the cancelled hearing by leaving a message on her phone. A little self-indulgently, he wanted to tell her in person and see her face when she got the news. But as he started to leave a rather minimal message for Janie to return his call, it occurred to him that if she didn't do so in time, she might still show up at the 'hearing'. There was no doubt what Klein would do with that opportunity. And if she tried to return the call but he wasn't around, the same thing would happen. Besides, not telling her as soon as possible only prolonged her agony. So he left a short but complete message telling her that the hearing was off and she should relax and enjoy herself and give him a call and he would explain the details then.

He left his office and went down the single flight of stairs and out of the Page Building into the Quad. He crossed the grassy area to the Gold Rec Center and went into the west entrance that faced the Quad.

As he entered the glass doors that were again hooked to the wall so they would remain open, he stopped to confirm what Pescary had actually told him by examining the perimeter of the metal door frame beginning at the center and working his way out and down the sides and to the center at the bottom. When he was finished, he stood up straight and went into the building itself. On his right, he noticed that the door to the aerobics/dance room was open and the room - for the first time that he remembered - was empty. He made a similar examination of that door frame and then took the right turn off the hall that led to Sara Furden's office. He thought it was time for them to have a long frank talk but her door was locked and there was no answer to his knock. He turned and left.

*   *   *   *

Yousef Rahim wasn't bored despite the fact that he had by now spent over four hours in the small janitor's closet under the stairs of the dormitory. It was the perfect place to watch for the girl's return. The door to the closet opened towards the front door of the dorm and the inside stairs were of the open-plank style that allowed him to see straight through. His field of vision from where he sat on a five gallon drum of cleaning liquid allowed him to see all the way to the street from his vantage point. As people approached the door, he simply closed it until they had gone past or up the stairs and then opened it just a crack again to watch for the girl.

He wasn't bored because he had made the conscious decision to treat what he was doing as a mission - and missions required endurance - especially that particular form of endurance called patience. Patience was an accomplishment in itself and he prided himself on his accomplishments.

That was why he was so bored in the house. When he was there, he had no mission - no duties - no goals. He was accomplishing nothing.

It was such boredom - and resentment at his own forced inaction - that first caused Yousef to leave the house against instructions. It invigorated him to walk about amid the enemy and breathe their air as freely as they did.

The first time he had just gone onto the campus and observed the area while being sure to make no contacts with any people. But, he confirmed to himself, there was little danger of his being recognized. Here more than other places it seemed that no one looked at anyone else.

It was on his second trip away from the house that he had met the girl by the soccer field who had shown such interest in him. They had talked and then, early in the day, they gone to her room and had sex. Good sex.

It was not as if Yousef would have gone without sex in the house. He had been told when he arrived that a man's needs are important and that he could have a girl sent to him if he requested it. He had twice made such a request. But it was not the same to have sex with someone who was doing it on assignment as it was to do it based on raw attraction.

But sex was just a diversion. Yousef was a man of action. He told the chief at every opportunity that it was a waste of the skills he had acquired - and often utilized - for him to just sit in a room or anywhere else in the sprawling house or watch television or do anything that had no immediate result to it. He needed a mission. He did not feel complete when he did not have one.

His last had been a milestone in their struggle. He and the others had shown the Americans that they were not safe in their fabled homeland. Over and over since the bombing, the newspapers shouted about the 'lesson' that had been brought home. 'How dare the Americans have thought they were so safe', he smiled to himself.

207

It was true that the others had been tracked down and captured and were on trial or about to be and he was free. But he didn't feel guilty about that. To Yousef, it was additional proof that his destiny was to lead the struggle. He knew that he was allowed to remain free so that Allah could use him as the instrument of his comrades' freedom or an instrument of their vengeance. Indeed, it was the fact no one appeared to be working toward that goal that most disturbed him. Or worse, that if they were, he was not part of it. That would be shame for him as he felt strongly that this was his destiny at this time in eternity. He would not allow that.

He thought of himself as brilliant - and in the ways of his missions, he was. An objective analysis would more accurately describe him as single-minded. His thought process was technical not intellectual. If he was at point 'A' and the mission concluded at point 'E', he would progress relentlessly to 'B' then 'C' then 'D' then 'E'. No shortcuts but no stopping either.

He had little formal education and resented that the safe house had been placed at a location such as this and wondered if it had been chosen to make him feel so completely out of his element. He knew and accepted that he was not learned enough to go to the center and play at the role of research assistant or adjunct professor. His lack of formal education left him unsuited to such intellectual pursuits - even as a subterfuge.

For himself, he was sure that he did not need any more education than the one he had acquired in the desert camps and the cold classrooms that taught weaponry and death. He was a man of action. He thought of himself that way and it was true. So every chance he got, he pressed the chief to send him back into the field - or to the homeland. On a mission. It almost didn't matter what.

Yousef's relationship with the man he and the others called 'ray-yis' was strained. The chief was a man of learning and leadership and was in charge. Yousef believed in the chain of command even as he believed that his ultimate destiny was to be at the head of it. He gave the chief the proper measure of respect in that regard.

But to Yousef, the chief was not a man of action. So he would be unable to understand a man of action - or understand that a man of action had to act.

For his part, the chief considered Yousef to be the consummate soldier. Yousef would have been pleased by that until he learned that the chief used the word 'soldier' in the sense that he was a journeyman - a worker not a leader. The chief knew of Yousef's accomplishments and took satisfaction from - even admired - the successes. At the same time, the chief gave Yousef - and his like - credit only for following the plans of others, like himself.

But the relationship between the two men was most strained because, like all good leaders, the chief could see through and beyond the words and actions Yousef employed to show respect and deference to the chief. The chief knew that Yousef saw him as a thinker not a doer and did not truly defer to the chief as a man or as a warrior. This did not concern the chief as a matter of ego or conceit - but it concerned him as a matter of control. Yousef had already defied the order to remain concealed and in so doing, he risked the mission and the organization. The American authorities were still on heightened alert. Even here at Charlestown University, the chief was certain they were being watched.

Yousef didn't know - because there had never been reason for him to - that the chief was in fact a man of action as well as a man of planning. And a man of caution. Always caution. And in the name of caution, the chief was capable of the most decisive action. He had all too often witnessed how the slightest vagary of chance had destroyed men, goals, and ideas.

That was another thing Yousef didn't know about 'ray-yis' - that the chief had never hesitated to order ruthless action based on the possibility - or mere suspicion - that the mission might be placed in danger. Had Yousef realized that, it would have changed the relationship. Not because it would have engendered any fear. The 'soldier' would have had increased respect for the chief.

The two men were on a collision course. The chief knew it - Yousef did not. The chief would not allow further risk to the mission. Massoud was to make that clear. Massoud thought that he had done so - that he had gotten through to Yousef that the trip outside the house - they only knew of the one - could harm the cause. And no one questioned Yousef's devotion to the cause.

While Massoud was right about Yousef's devotion to the cause, he miscalculated Yousef's almost child-like propensity for hearing what he wanted to hear and acting accordingly. As a result, Yousef decided that Massoud's words were not a warning. Yousef understood that Massoud's words were an order. He had a mission. A mission to undo his own deeds, perhaps. But a mission nonetheless.

He didn't like what he had to do but he had been ordered, had he not. The mark of the true warrior was not only to do what needed to be done but to do even that which one may not wish to do. Even though he was used to death - and to inflicting it - it pained him somewhat to kill the girl in the dorm. But it had to be done. Orders.

It was easy. She let him in when he buzzed and they made love one more time before he ended her life. Then he went to leave and - of course - Allah was on his side.

He hadn't really even remembered the second girl who had seen his face until he saw her for the second time in the dorm. Then the memory had come back to him and he knew that must be done as well. It would have already been done if the others had not come up the stairs or if the girl had been one step slower in the hall or if the man in the expensive looking car had arrived five seconds later.

So he had to wait. And while he waited, he thought about the girl standing in the doorway - naked and defiant. And he thought about the child's face on the woman's body and dreamed dreams of the virgin handmaidens that would be his in good time.

The hours of waiting had given him too much time to think. If the girl had returned in the first or second or maybe even the third hour, Yousef would have done his work and been away. But the passage of time caused him to think too much. And he had finally decided that it would be a waste of this lovely virgin for him to simply put her in the room with the other one and leave her there. The mission would be expanded on. A field decision. And the added challenge would make the mission more interesting.

At 4:30 PM, Furden's car pulled up in front of the dorm to drop Janie off. After the lunch with Cann, Janie had told Furden of her intention to skip the entire day's classes and, while Furden felt constrained to indicate mild disapproval, the two had quickly agreed to spend the afternoon at Furden's apartment complex lounging by the pool.

They hardly talked at all but the silence wasn't tense. They had known each other for so long that they could handle the absence of active communication. Furden mostly read a book and Janie alternated between floating on an inflatable mattress and laying on a lounge chair. At one point, Janie had tried to engage her older friend in a discussion of Furden's apparent hostility to Cann but Furden had dismissed her inquiries by suggesting that Janie was just reading too much into it.

They didn't talk at all about the hearing until it got to be about 4:00 and Sara said they had better think about cleaning up and dressing for it. Then Janie got the knot in the pit of her stomach that was as much a result of not knowing what was going to happen as it was fear of what might.

Yousef was watching for Cann's Corvette so he didn't pick Janie up visually until she had turned and started up the walkway toward the stairs. His plan had been for him to precede her to the fourth floor as soon as he saw the car pull up and be waiting for her in the room across the hall when she arrived at her own door. Now there would not be time and he would have to try to follow her down the long hall and hope she didn't turn around and see him before he got to her. Or wait for yet another opportunity.

But, as always, Allah was with him. After a few steps toward the dorm, he saw Janie turn back toward the car in apparent response to a call from the driver. He watched her return to the car and as she bent forward and leaned through the passenger side window in conversation, Yousef quickly and quietly slipped out of the closet and stealthily climbed the stairs to the fourth floor, went down the hall, and used the blade of the small knife to re-gain entry to the room across the hall from Janie's.

As soon as he was inside the room, he discerned the beginnings of the telltale aroma of death coming from the young woman he had murdered earlier that day just as they had finished making love. He looked at her lying on the bed just as he had left her - and then turned without another thought of her to look out the peephole in the door.

Janie finished her conversation with Furden, agreeing that she would meet her outside the Student Union just before seven. Then she turned and ran up the walk and to the top of the stairs before stopping to insert the security card to gain entrance.

She climbed the stairs, made the u-turn, and walked purposefully down the hall. As she reached the door to her room, she glanced at the closed door opposite just to assure herself that no one was coming out of it this time. She unlocked her door and pushed it open. As she stepped in, Yousef opened the door to the other room and in two quick steps placed his hand on the edge of Janie's door to stop it from closing.

Janie didn't fully realize at first that the door hadn't closed but after the events of the morning, she wasn't about to leave it to chance. She turned and it was then that she saw the fingers wrapped around the edge. Without conscious thought, she threw the entire weight of her body against the door slamming it on the fingers. But it didn't close.

Yousef had a high tolerance for pain and wouldn't be dissuaded even if his fingers were broken. He had endured much more than that for the cause. He put his right shoulder into the door and was surprised when it opened as easily as it did throwing Janie across the small room and into the closed door to the bathroom.

Janie lost her balance when she hit the door and found herself sitting on the floor looking up at the man she had now seen three times but didn't know. Yousef put out his hand to restrain her from whatever she was considering next and that made her hesitate. He took three quick steps across the room and leaned

212

over Janie and grabbed her wrists in his hands and pulled her up. When he did that, he felt the stab of pain in his right hand and knew that at least some of the fingers were broken. Unlike many people, this didn't make him angry. Things like that happen and they would heal. He didn't blame the girl. She was doing what she felt necessary. So was he.

Using his strength - which was considerable - and the element of surprise, Yousef suddenly spun Janie around and threw his left forearm across her neck. Janie felt terribly frightened and wished for Cann to be there. But he wasn't. Yousef carefully tightened the pressure on Janie's carotid artery until he felt her go limp. When she was unconscious, but not dead, he laid her down on Gretchen's bed. He went into the bathroom and filled a glass with water and took something out of his pocket. Then he sat down and waited for the flow of blood to begin to return to Janie's brain. It didn't take very long and he was ready. As soon as she stirred, he reached over - looking if someone could have seen - like a caregiver as he cradled her head and offered her the glass of water. As Janie started to drink, she reflexively gagged on the solid object he had placed in her mouth and almost coughed it out. Yousef was ready for that as well and simply placed his right hand behind her head and his left across both her nose and mouth. Unable to breathe any air, Janie instinctively tried to gulp it and, in the process, ingested the pill. Her eyes looked fearfully into Yousef's with all of the unspoken questions she felt. But he didn't care to answer.

Unconsciousness was quick although not instantaneous. Through both fear and resignation, Janie didn't fight it. In just a few moments, she began to feel her consciousness slipping away but knew there was nothing she could do. She had thought she was about to die before when the man had started to choke her. But then she regained consciousness. She wondered now if she was going to die this time - whether the sight of this man looking down at her would be the last conscious thought she would ever have. Janie misread the absence of emotion on his face as a gentle expression and tried to form a smile at him but couldn't. Then she went to sleep.

*   *   *   *

At 6:15 PM, the chief turned the black Land Rover right off Higway 53 and onto Rasen Street. He drove the half mile to the house and turned right into the driveway and pulled all the way up to the wooden doors of the barn turned garage.

"Welcome, gentlemen." He glanced over at the man seated in the bucket seat to his right and then looked up into the rear view mirror at the three others on the bench seat behind him.

A couple of the men nodded but no one spoke. It had been a long trip but the men still weren't all that tired. Their silence now was more a residue of their day long self-enforced isolation from each other and their studied avoidance of any meaningful contact with the public.

The chief opened his door and stepped down, first onto the metal step beneath the door and then onto the ground. He took a couple of paces toward the front door of the house and then turned back to the vehicle and gestured with his left hand at the door, like a maitre'd showing a group to their table. Massoud stood in the open doorway with a hand raised in greeting.

The men came around the front of the vehicle and passed between the chief and the house. "Go on in, gentlemen. I will be with you shortly." But the chief didn't follow immediately. He was looking at the doors to the garage. Or more accurately, he was looking through the space made by the ill-fittedness of the aged doors at the yellow vehicle he could see inside.

He turned with a questioning look on his face to Massoud who gazed back with a very serious expression on his. As the four newcomers filed past him into the house, Massoud looked hard at the chief and tossed his head to the right indicating that they should talk apart from the arrivals.

The chief went into the house as Massoud showed the visitors into the study to the right. "Make yourselves comfortable, please, gentlemen," Massoud said as he closed the door behind them. "We will be right in." He pulled the door behind him and went immediately to the kitchen at the rear of the house where the chief waited.

The chief was talking before Massoud got all the way into the room. "Is there a problem. What is that vehicle in the garage?"

"It is Yousef I am afraid. He was out again today."

"The fool. Out? Why out? Where? I cannot tolerate these actions." He looked even harder at Massoud. "I thought you had made him understand."

"So did I. I see now that he understands what he wants to understand. I told him that it was vital that he not be recognized by anyone. He is now saying that he took that to mean that I was ordering him to eliminate those who had seen him when he was away from the house."

The chief went pale. "Are you saying he has killed people here?"

"Ey-wa, ray-yis. According to Yousef, he has eliminated the girl he had sex with in the dormitory. And there is also a dead cab driver in the vehicle you saw in the barn."

"Ki-feh-ya ki-da! Enough! The man is crazy."

"There is more."

The chief just looked at Massoud. "May Allah show us mercy. What more is there?"

"Apparently there was another girl who saw him closely enough to recognize him."

"Another girl he had sex with?"

"I don't think so. Just one who saw him closely enough to recognize him."

"And he has killed her, too?"

Massoud grimaced. "No. He has brought her here."

The chief was a stolid man not given to displays of emotion but at that sentence he thrust his face forward and his body actually convulsed as if he were gagging. "He has what?" His voice was a vicious gravelly hiss.

"He has her in his bed in his room. She is drugged and asleep. He insists that no one has witnessed his acts and that he has cleared any traces of his presence or activities."

"Does he indeed," the chief said. "What does he propose to do with her - as if I can't imagine. And what was he planning to do about the taxi and driver?"

"He sees no reason why the girl cannot be kept here under sedation for the pleasure of us all. And he said that he would dispose of the cab and driver after dark in a place and a manner that will make it look like an accident took place."

"Yes. And so he will, Massoud. And so he will. You will assist him in this, of course."

"Perhaps our visitors could assist as well," Massoud said.

"Indeed."

"And the girl?"

The chief pondered for a moment, then said. "First things first. Secure the girl in the room. Make sure she does not awaken. Then bring Yousef to the study. To meet our new friends. Tell him they will be joining him on a mission." He paused again. "Give me some time with our guests."

Both men left the kitchen. Massoud turned and went up the stairs and the chief went directly to the study. When he walked in, the four men were in different places around the room. Two were sitting on the tufted upholstered gray couch that ran along the wall opposite the desk which faced the front of the house. One of the others was standing looking out the window into the front yard while the fourth was looking up at the floor to ceiling bookshelves that covered most the interior walls of the room.

The chief strode in purposefully saying, "Allah ak-bar." The others muttered their response.

"Welcome to America, gentlemen. Welcome, welcome." He crossed the room and leaned back against the edge of the desk.

"Gentlemen, you have, of course, been fully briefed on our operation here and you know what your roles will be. It has taken us two years but we have now been accepted - and funded - as a full department of the university. We now occupy the on-campus Middle East Studies Center and have done so for over a month."

The chief pointed to the two men sitting on the couch. "You, Sami and Basheer, are permanent full-time faculty members - one Assistant and one Associate Professor of Middle Eastern Studies. Naji and Abdullah are Research Assistants. You have been chosen for these positions because you are qualified for them and you have the credentials. It is important that you take these positions very seriously. These are not merely roles you are to play. This is what you are. You must act in every way as if they are your only careers. At all times and in all places you will be professors and academics as if you will never be anything else. Fight for your raises. Demand tenure. In all ways, this is your life. And no discussion of anything other than those roles will ever - ever - take place anywhere but here. And even here, gentlemen, you - we - are to exercise total caution. Take nothing for granted. We are each other's only allies. Never forget that. Assume you are always under surveillance and that everyone is the enemy."

He paused and smiled. "But as is often said here in America, 'Now for the good news'." The four men were attentive.

"While we must trust no one but ourselves, I believe it is safe to say that you will be amazed at the assistance you will receive - wittingly and unwittingly - in this country. You see, gentlemen, our biggest ally - our greatest advantage lies in the fact that America is a land of cowards." The chief smiled as did the other four men in the room. "Fear runs rampant at every level of life in the United States. And those who choose not to fear have the advantage. Use it at every opportunity."

"The time will come when you - we - will be called upon to act for the cause. When that happens, you will see what cowards this country has. They will swagger and talk of how much power they have in their efforts to dissuade us. And why not? It used to work for them - until it became clear that they would do nothing with it." He laughed again.

"America has enormous power, gentlemen. Make no mistake. But what good is it when they are afraid to use it. Instead, they claim it is noble to turn the other cheek. Good. When they do, we slap that one too." They all laughed again. "And others who may actually wish to do something, say that they can do nothing because they are not absolutely and conclusively certain of who their enemies are. They are fools. Your enemy is who you say he is."

He clenched a fist and shook it at them. "Imagine what we could do with the power of America, gentlemen. And try to imagine that we would not use it if we had it." All the men in the room nodded in agreement. Then the chief lowered his voice for emphasis.

"Glory in the differences between us and the Americans, gentlemen. While America says that 'if it costs one human life, it's not worth it' we say, 'if the cause is just then what do a thousand lives matter'. We are more powerful than America because the power we are willing to use far exceeds the power that America is willing to use. America has come to believe that nothing is worth dying for and in so doing ensures its own death. Perhaps a quick death - perhaps a slow death. But in either case, a horrible death. The worst kind of death. A death without honor. Be thankful, gentlemen, that America is our enemy. You would not want them for a friend."

The four listeners were silent at the chief's eloquence. He folded his hands in front of him and lowered his head. "But first, gentlemen, I am saddened to say that one of us is endangering the cause." The four men looked around at each other.

"No, not one of you. One who has preceded you here." The chief then explained the situation as he wanted them to understand it. When he was done, they nodded their assent and quietly waited, Sami and Basheer still on the couch and Abdullah sitting in the armchair. Naji, the largest of the group and the only one larger than Yousef, picked up the heavy walking stick that had been leaning against the desk and examined it while the five men waited for Massoud to arrive with Yousef.

When the door to the study opened, Yousef strode in ahead of Massoud offering his hearty and sincere greetings to his comrades. He was truly glad to have other men of action around him. As he bent over the couch to embrace Basheer and then Sami, Naji swung the walking stick in a circle that began by his side and went up above his own head and continued down and around until it struck Yousef full at the base of his skull. The blow only stunned the powerful Yousef who instinctively lashed out at the men in front of him. Both Basheer and Sami punched out at Yousef themselves with both men hitting him in the face at the same time. Yousef reeled from that double blow and the four men in the room pushed him to the floor on his back while continuing to rain blows on his face.

Finally Yousef stopped struggling and the chief felt his neck for a pulse. It was faint but there was one.

The four men lifted Yousef and carried him out of the house to the barn and placed him in the back seat of the taxicab. Yousef had killed the driver by banging his face repeatedly into the steering wheel until the man was dead. His plan had been to stage an accident on one of the back roads of the county and the chief had decided that was as good a scenario as any - but with a passenger.

After the men placed Yousef in the rear seat of the taxi, three of them went back into the house and Naji climbed into the rear seat to Yousef's left. Naji then took the back of Yasouf's head in his right hand and threw it forward as hard as he could smashing the face into the rigid frame of the seat in front of him. It took several such throws before the chief could detect no pulse. Naji was sent back into the house and the chief stayed for another ten minutes checking Yousef frequently to ensure he was dead.

Only after the chief was sure did he go back into the house where the four men were sitting. The room was quiet and the men seemed thoughtful although none of them were upset by the recent events. They had all killed before and took it as a fact of life.

The chief spoke to them. "I know our training is meant to be directed against others and not one of our own. But I assure you that what was done needed to be done. I apologize to you for asking this of you and thank you for your service to the cause."

The chief took a breath, "And if you will excuse me, I unfortunately have a meeting to attend. Thank you again."

The men nodded and the chief said. "Please go with Massoud. He will show you something more pleasant and which is at your service. Perhaps this is not the time after" - he flipped his head toward the barn outside - "this, but it is available to you if and when you like."

The men were curious and followed Massoud out of the study and up the stairs where they turned left and walked single file down to the last door on the left. When he reached the door, Massoud turned and said, "There is much to be enjoyed about this country, gentlemen." He threw back the door and said, "Welcome to America."

Basheer was first in line and stood in the open doorway looking at Janie who lay face up and naked in an 'x' position with both her hands and feet extended and tied at the four corners of the bed. The purpose of the ropes that held her was not restraint - Janie was incapable of resistance or escape. She was tied the way she was for purposes of display.

The other three men pressed in behind Basheer to get a look and all four ended up standing at the foot of the bed looking down at Janie. After only a few seconds, it was Abdullah who mumbled something about 'not letting this go to waste' as he undid his pants and walked around the side of the bed.

Chapter Eighteen

Cann tried to reach Janie at 5:00 PM and again at 6:15 without success. He left a second message adding at the end of it that he really needed for Janie to give him a call so that he would know she had gotten the message. When he still didn't reach her on the third try, his concern turned to the possibility that Janie would show up at the kangaroo hearing anyway. And if she did, he had no doubt that Klein and her cronies would not bother to bring Janie up to date on the situation as it really existed. He put his tie back on, grabbed his jacket, and headed for the Student Union.

* * * *

Elizabeth Buffinton always worked a little late so it wasn't unusual for her to be in her office at 6:30 PM when the Director of Campus Security finally got back to her.

The two women had spoken briefly earlier in the day just after Cann and Walder had left. The university General Counsel had first briefed Director Oldham on the actions of Sergeant Pescary and also gave her opinion that a suspension might be in order.

"At the very least," Oldham had said. "Just let me pull the original file and confirm the facts before we go further. I'll call you right back."

But it had been about three hours before the return call was made.

221

Buffinton listened as Oldham confirmed that the original hand-written narrative confirmed the version attested to by Walder and Cann.

"According to the facts as written in the report I have in front of me, the student may have been guilty of bad judgment - or just ignorance of her surroundings - but that's it. You say that Pescary admitted writing the second version."

"Today - in my office - to my face."

"Then she's history, Counsel. Do I have the legal basis for termination?"

"Based on the facts that I'm aware of, there's no question that you do. The university will back you."

"Good." Oldham was a professional and was all business in her outward appearance. Inside she was livid. "This isn't the way I run my shop, Counsel. I just want you to know that."

"I do," Buffinton said. "Now we have to figure out how to deal with Klein on this."

"Caroline Klein? Director of Women's Studies?"

"That's the one."

"What's she got to do with it?"

Buffinton was growing wary. "According to Pescary, it was Klein who put her up to altering the report. And called in the complaint in the first place."

Oldham hesitated then spoke. "I'll see about the altered report, Counsel, you can count on that. It won't happen again. But according to this - and I have the original in my hand - Klein didn't call in any complaint. This was a silent alarm call. Apparently, the student set off the silent alarm when she went in at that time of night." There was silence as the Director of Security re-read the report. "Yup. That's what I thought I'd read. Nobody called in a complaint. I see the dispatch notation right here."

"I see," Buffinton said. But she didn't.

* * * *

In Weisbaden, Dr. Barry Dimsen refused to leave the lab despite the late hour as he pored over the raw toxicology reports from the Wagner autopsy. The initial finding of the gamma-y-hydroxybutyrate had been confirmed which established to the pathologist that the decedent had ingested flunitrazepam - sold in Europe under the brand name Rohypnol - in the last twenty-four to forty-eight hours of his life. But the amounts indicated by the tests also showed that it wasn't - or shouldn't have been - a lethal dose. And Dimsen was looking for a cause of death.

If Wagner had died of the injuries to his thoracic region, Dimsen knew that he would have placed the Rohpynol in the context of being a possible agent that allowed - or caused - him to go into that wall and be killed. But the tissue analysis and other methodolgies employed in the autopsy had already told the pathologist that the massive trauma that Wagner had experienced had not been the cause of death. By measuring tissue degeneration and chemical breakdowns, they had already established that Wagner had been dead for as much as several hours before the accident - the accident that wasn't an accident.

So it wasn't the collision that killed Wagner.

But it wasn't the Rohypnol either. There was no question that in a sufficient amount, that drug could be lethal but as far as they could tell, there just hadn't been enough Rohypnol in Wagner to kill him.

And what did the gangrene have to do with it - if anything? Dimsen searched the toxicology report for something that would leap off the page at him and make the connection.

In addition to listing isolated elements on a printout, the computerized analysis program automatically cross-referenced possible combinations with the Physicians' Desk Reference and other medical references and listed them under their brand names on the print out.

In Wagner's case, other than the most miniscule trace of Tylenol - and the Rohypnol, of course, - the only other substance with a significant presence in Wagner's system was the prescription drug Migramol. Off the top of his head, Dimsen knew that Migramol was a prescription treatment for migraine headaches. He didn't recall seeing that Wagner suffered from migraines but that was easily confirmed in Wagner's medical file which had been couriered over from Washington several days before.

It was at times like this that Dimsen disliked the computer program because it listed the brand name rather than the ingredients. He would rather know what the components of Migramol were than the brand name of the drug itself. It wouldn't be hard to find out, of course, but it was that much more work for him. He went back to his office and checked his PDR.

Logically, he found it listed under the general heading of Migraine Preparations and under the subheading of Ergot Derivatives and Combinations.

Ingredients? Migramol was a combination of ergotamine and caffeine.

Ergotamine. Dimsen knew it came from the mold 'ergot' and that triggered a vague recall of a disease called ergotism.

Medical dictionary.

Ergotism: a disease of humans and animals caused by an excessive intake of ergot characterized by mental disorientation, muscle cramps, convulsions, and dry gangrene of the extremities.

"...dry gangrene of the extremities..."

Bingo. One step closer.

But still...The listed side-effects were caused by 'chronic and excessive use'. According to his medical history, Wagner had suffered from migraines for many years - Dimsen supposed you could call that chronic - but for that very reason, Wagner would have been - or should have been - fully competent in the self-management of his medication. That would not indicate a tendency toward 'excessive' use.

Of course, the reference books didn't anticipate its use in conjunction with something like Rohypnol.

So Dimsen conjectured that the ergot based Migramol could explain the gangrene if its effects were exacerbated by the cardiovascular depressor effects of the powerful central nervous system depressant, Rohypnol.

Dimsen knew the reason for the Migramol use. He still had no clue as to why Wagner would have taken the Rohypnol.

Well, the why wasn't a medical question. Dimsen was after the how. He now thought he knew the how of the gangrene.

But damn it! It still didn't explain why Wagner was dead.

*   *   *   *

The Student Congress room in the Student Union was a bare large room with four long metal tables arranged to form a square in the center of the room. Each of the four tables had five chairs each allowing for twenty people to be seated around the perimeter of the square formed by the tables. All the chairs were occupied.

More chairs were arranged in rows against the walls of the room for observers and overflow at meetings. Many of those seats were ocupied this evening as well. True to her word, Klein had not advised anyone of the cancellation and had even confirmed the time of the hearing to those who had asked.

Missing of course were the Administration attendees, notably the Assistant Dean of Student Affairs who moderated all such hearings 'ex officio' under the regulations. But everyone else was present.

As a result, the crowd in the room consisted of the usual representatives of the various departments, the university support and counseling groups, several other groups often lumped together under the term 'activist groups', and the faculty liaisons for the several different unions that represented the employees in food service, groundskeeping, janitorial, and transportation.

Since most of these attendees regularly sat in on and participated in these hearings, they were familiar with the procedures involved and knew there was something different about this one when Klein insisted on starting without the Assistant Dean - or the student for that matter.

They also saw that Klein looked drawn.

This had been an unusual day for her - perhaps the most unusual of her career. Of course, the others didn't know that. Nor did they know that she'd been challenged. It had been a very long time since anyone had challenged her and it rattled her.

She'd learned early on how to play the game and had become so good at it that she'd never lost at it. The down side of that was that, as a result, she'd never learned how to lose at the game.

And it was a game to her. She took it seriously, to be sure, and played it like a world-ranked grandmaster plays chess - investing her heart and soul into the checkmate and then savoring the humiliation of the opponent. With each victory - no draws - she became addicted to the power that came with being feared. And as she continued to set and control the conflicts and strategies, even the challenges to her power faded away.

So she had also forgotten how to deal with challenges, internally as well as externally. The only strategy she knew - it had never failed - was full head-on assault. Continue to charge forward. Never retreat. Control the debate. Impose your will. They - the ubiquitous 'they' - will always back down.

She began the 'hearing' a few minutes after seven and laid out the facts - as she felt they needed to be known - in a monologue that didn't allow for interruption. No one questioned the absence of two of the principals. Klein was in friendly territory. The listeners would of course assume that there were good reasons for the way this was being handled and, whatever the reasons may be, first and foremost they all knew they had to stick together.

"Solidarity, people. That's what this is about." Klein was putting things into the proper perspective for them. "This goes beyond one student and even the message it sends. If you realize nothing else, realize that the university has declared war on us."

Political Science Professor Patricia Gruber was the first to ask a question. "You say, Caroline, that the university cancelled this hearing without consulting you?"

"Totally unilateral. I got a call this afternoon from Liz Buffinton and the first words out of her mouth were there would be no hearing."

"Did she say why?"

"The excuse she gave was that the charges were trumped up and the university didn't want to risk the liability. We've all heard that song and dance before, haven't we?"

The contentious but principled Jacob Reiser from Religious Studies - irreverently called 'Relly Stew' by the students in the program - interjected. "Hold on now. Trumped up you say? How so?"

"Buffinton said..." Klein placed heavy emphasis on the word 'said' to indicate its untruth "...that the facts as contained in the police report were not true. That the student didn't do everything the report says she did."

Reiser shook his head. "That's a serious accusation, Caroline. Doesn't it only make sense that such a potential embarrassment to the student - not to mention ourselves - and the university - be looked at carefully before proceeding."

Klein jabbed in. "Yes it does. But it wasn't just a matter of false allegations in the report. Buffinton accused me of complicity in the falsification. Hell, she even accused me of calling in the complaint - which is ridiculous." Before Reiser could jump in, Klein pressed on. "That's what I mean about solidarity, folks. If they're willing to come after me, you know they won't hesitate to come after any of you." Klein was oblivious to the arrogance of the statement. But the fact was that the others agreed with her. It was simple fact that Klein was the most feared - or one of the most feared - people on the campus in terms of political clout. "If the university can squelch me or shut me up or intimidate me - and I won't go down without a fight - then you know they'll be willing to go after anyone here."

Ramadan Al-Asif spoke up. "Caroline, you know we are all with you but - as I have said previously - perhaps this isn't the issue to pick the fight over. There will be stronger..."

"We are not 'picking the fight', Professor Al-Asif. The university has already picked it. And as I thought I had already made clear, this student isn't even the issue anymore - or her behavior. They attacked me. Everyone has to pick a side. There's a line drawn in

227

the sand, folks - no pun intended, Ram," she said sarcastically, - "and if we don't cross it, thirty years of progress goes down the toilet."

"A particularly apt reference, Ms. Klein - and a good place for it." Cann had been standing unnoticed in the doorway for a while.

When he had arrived, his only concern had been to look for Janie. On the way over, he had had visions of finding her chained to the wall or confined in some sort of dock while Klein and the rest of the coven danced around her chanting incantations. He was relieved when he saw that she wasn't in the room. Apparently she'd gotten his message.

Klein looked up at him and without missing a beat said, "Who invited Charlestown's newest resident Nazi?" The reference made Reiser and some of the others flinch.

Cann had a thick skin. His frequent forays into a world that contained intense stresses and often physical violence had the effect of placing verbal attempts at injury in their proper perspective. A kind of 'sticks and stones' philosophy of life. The equanimity that came with it continued to serve him well after he was culled from that very small group and chosen for further training and eventually law school. It remained of value to him over the next two decades as he witnessed the demise of professional courtesy among the members of the legal profession - a demise as lamented within the profession as it was celebrated outside it. But the sum total of his life's history had left him with a deep disdain for the verbal barbs of others.

But he had to give Klein credit. She really could piss him off. In no time at all, she had overcome the sense of mellowness that the university setting itself and - he had to admit - the brightness and innocence of Janie had brought out in him. Some stupid game like this directed at him would have been nothing. But Janie had brought out surprisingly paternal feelings from deep inside that in turn brought out a 'knight in shining armor' complex he had sometimes been accused of having in the past. So he didn't like Klein to begin with.

And he didn't like Nazi's. But most of all, he especially didn't like people who had no idea of the horror the world was capable of using words like Nazi for no other reason than they liked the sound of it and liked the way it put people who did know and care on the defensive.

So he had to exert some effort to retain his usually automatic equanimity. He was helped by the fact that he already understood a lot of the game. He knew that he would score a point in this round of the academic 'dozens' by not rising to Klein's bait. So he looked around the table and the room at the assembled group and said, quite calmly, "Ms. Klein, of course, has not been fully candid with you."

He then proceeded to advise the assembled throng about the altered security report. And he was pleased to see that it had the desired effect. He watched the looks of concern grow on the faces of the people in attendance. He had no illusion that they were offended at the injustice of the situation. But he could see each of them toting up the plusses and minuses of the situation in the light of their own concerns and vulnerabilities. And there really weren't any plusses for them - other than the absence of Klein's wrath.

Of course, Klein was not silent while he talked. In fact, for the entire time he talked so did she, mocking what he was saying by repeating him and laughing at his words. When Cann continued on calmly, she adopted the tactic of asking, "Says who? Says who? Says who?," over and over and laughing as if his words were, of course, quite ridiculous.

It didn't take Cann all that long to lay out the issues of fraud and libel and misrepresentation and dishonesty as well as the potential consequences to the credibility and the futures of the members assembled. He was especially pleased with the unanimity of their horror when he related Elizabeth Buffinton's explanation of the university postition vis-a-vis their own personal liability and tenure. He had their full attention despite Klein's continuous attempt at interruption.

"No one here expects you to have the slightest ability to understand what this is all about, Cann." Klein appeared to be incapable of a polite sentence. "The issue is solidarity and..."

"Okay then, it's solidarity." He looked at the rest of the crowd. "Jump right in folks. Show your solidarity with Ms. Klein here. And follow her down the chute. You're going to lose if you back her up in this charade. In a lot of ways. Forget the legal liabilities for the moment. What about your image? How much of your perceived power comes from somehow managing to convince these kids that you're on their side. Wait till this comes out. A student does nothing wrong. No problem. We'll just lie about it - and for no better reason than to make a scene."

Klein was the only one not listening as she engaged in a droning monologue in the background which served no purpose other than to let her ignore Cann out loud.

"Make no mistake, folks. What Ms. Klein has done is not just unethical or immoral. It's illegal. If that's a bandwagon you want to jump on, do so at your peril."

He turned back to Klein with every intention of rubbing it in as hard as he could. He wasn't at all sure if his primary motivation at the moment was to protect Janie or humiliate Klein.

"Leave the kid alone, Klein. Drop the issue. You've had your ass kicked. And you've been beaten at your own game." Cann knew what he was doing. He wanted to get her as angry as possible - it was worth points.

And Klein was in fact reduced to an almost juvenile rage. "None of what he says is true, of course, people. Or are you all as stupid as he is?" Cann maintained a placid smile on his face as Klein began to unravel. "You're falling for the big lie. That's what this is, isn't it." She turned back to Cann. "Isn't it, Adolf? Or is it Hermann? Martin?"

"Caroline, please," Reiser protested.

"It's John, actually," Cann said evenly. "Oh, but I told you that before. Do you have trouble remembering things accurately, Ms. Klein?"

Some of the others laughed at that. That was the worst thing of all.

"Fuck you, Adolf."

Cann felt the bile rise in his throat yet again. But he was too close to beating her at her own game.

"Now, now, Caroline." Cann placed his finger against his lips and pretended to struggle to recall something. "You know, there was a thing on CNN the other night about how it's so terrible to call people Nazi's because it diminishes the evil that the real ones did. Maybe you didn't see it. Were you busy re-writing security reports or something? Anyway, it was about how this conservative talk show host is so awful because he uses 'nazi' as a suffix on a word to describe a radical fringe group. And the point of the report was that it's such a horrible misapplication of that terrible name. Don't you find that odd, Caroline? I mean for thirty years people like you have used the word to describe anybody you disagree with - like you're doing now." He waggled his finger at her. "But now it's a no-no, Caroline. You really need to catch up. You're actually being politically incorrect. Aren't you embarrassed."

"I don't embarrass easily."

Cann couldn't resist. It was too easy a shot.

"No kidding," Cann rejoined.

There was even more laughter at that and Klein glared around the room once more. "Okay folks, divided we fall it is. But I don't fall alone." She took several moments to look into the eyes of some of the other people in the room. "You know where your skeletons are and so do I."

Then she turned back to Cann. "And where is your little honey anyway, Cann? You've gone to such great lengths to protect her. Shouldn't she be here to enjoy the triumph." She looked around the room intending to play on the inference of a sexual connection between Janie and Cann. Then she thought better of it. "Fuck it. But don't think you can protect her all the time."

Cann wasn't happy with that. "Care to elaborate?" he asked.

Klein was too angry to see the look in Cann's eyes. Or perhaps too angry to care. "You can't be everywhere, Cann. And maybe - just maybe - something will happen to her that even her much older knight in shining armor can't protect her from."

The gentleness of Cann's tone didn't mask the threat in his words. "You had better hope that doesn't happen."

Klein was reinvigorated knowing that she had hit a nerve. "Is that a threat, Mr. Cann?" she smiled, waiting for the expected protests of denial.

There were none.

"Indeed it is, Ms. Klein. Indeed it is."

The smile faded back to anger and Klein said, more foolishly than she could ever know, "Well, shit happens, Mr. Cann. Even to little girls with big protectors."

Klein figured that if she had really exposed a nerve, Cann would explode and she waited with the hint of a smirk on her face. If she knew Cann better, however, she would have been more concerned by what she didn't see. The more angry Cann became, the less emotion he exhibited. At this moment in time, Cann was devoid of any discernible emotion.

"I should probably assume that you're not thinking too clearly at the moment. But, as you just said, fuck it. With that stupid and very - very - ill-conceived statement, you've crossed a line that separates this insulated little sophomoric universe you should have stayed in from one you could never comprehend. You're standing on the edge of my world, Klein. And you don't want to come in."

Klein huffed. "You still don't understand who I am and what I can do."

"To the contrary. I understand perfectly. It's you that don't understand. You've had your ass kicked on your own turf. Why would you think in your wildest dreams that you could survive or even play on mine? You've lost Klein. You're reduced to making threats of violence against an innocent kid. Look around you. You don't have an ounce of credibility left - if you ever had any at all."

Klein looked around and only then did she realize that more than the meeting was over. Half the people had already left and the rest were filing out of the room without even looking at her and Cann. Some were even involved in obviously mocking conversations in which Klein appeared to be the object of derision. It was beyond her comprehension.

She lashed out her right hand in an attempt to slap Cann who caught her wrist easily in his fingers. She went to take her hand away and realized that she couldn't move it even a fraction of an inch. She looked at Cann and eventually focused on his eyes. It was his eyes that finally got the message across to her.

She was no less angry. For too many years, her anger had been her strength. But for the first time in all those years, there was an offsetting emotion. Fear. Followed by defeat.

"May I go," she said, attempting to sound haughty. But her voice cracked and it nullified the attempt. Cann let go of her hand but never took his gaze off her face.

* * * *

By the time it was 10:00 PM, Janie had been raped nine times. Twice each by Basheer, Sami, and Naji, and three times by Abdullah who was not about to let his comrades forget his prowess. Actually, Massoud had serviced himself when he was preparing Janie before he brought the others up to her. So the number of rapes was actually ten.

Abdullah had been the first and had climbed on top of her as she lay on the bed still bound to the corners by the ropes. After he had finished, it was clear that the bindings were unnecessary and they had been undone. This allowed the men to turn her over for the second round of rapes. Naji had also tried to indulge himself by placing his penis in Janie's mouth but her state of unconsciousness was such that he got no satisfaction from it and re-penetrated her in a more conventional way.

The Rohypnol Janie had been given, kept her in a state of near unconsciousness and immobility but, as the hours passed, the effects diminished sufficiently to cause her to become the slightest bit aware of movement on and about her even though her brain was unable to process the details of what was happening to her. An unfortunate result of that was that she would occasionally stir during one of the acts which the men in their ignorance took to be response and they found it arousing.

Between the acts of rape, one by one, the men drifted downstairs to the game room which was across the foyer from the study. There they had eaten sandwiches and drank whatever liquor they had acquired a taste for in their travels, except for Basheer who drank his strong aromatic coffee every moment of the waking day. Then, after a while, their thoughts again turned to the young woman upstairs and someone wondered if perhaps she should be tied up again, should she regain enough of her senses to escape.

"And wouldn't she look so pretty running naked around the campus," Basheer laughed. The others joined in. But Naji went up to check and about five minutes later, returned with Janie still completely naked and thrown over his shoulder.

"Why leave her up there alone?" he laughed. "Our company is so much better than nothing, is it not?"

The other men all laughed and Abdullah swept the pool balls to one end of the table. Naji bent over and sat Janie down on the edge of the table and held her up in a sitting position for a moment. Then, with a chuckle, he pushed two fingers into her chest. The men watched as her upper body slowly fell back onto the table and, as her shoulders hit the surface of the table, her head slammed backwards into the slate with a sickening hollow 'thunk' sound.

In the wild, after the prey has been brought down by the adult predators, and the initial hunger has been satisfied, the young of the wild often play with the victim - or parts of it - in innocent play. There was nothing innocent about these four men who, if they had ever had any humanity at all, had had it trained out of them. Like the beasts that they were, they began to play with their prey.

For a time, they propped her against the rails of the pool table with her legs spread outward until they were almost perpendicular to her torso and amused themselves with shooting pool balls into her groin. At one point, Abdullah started to see if he could fit the cue ball inside of her but he was stopped. Not out of decency or because of any distaste for such an act - but only because the others feared it might 'stretch her out' and lessen their pleasure. They did experiment, however, with both the small and large ends of several pool cues. All of this - and more - was recorded for later amusement with the video camera Sami brought down from his room for that purpose.

When they tired of these games - one after the other - they all raped her again. By this time Massoud had returned from disposing of the taxi and its contents and he joined in - his second round. It was the fourth for Abdullah and the third for the rest.

Finally, around midnight, Massoud announced that the chief, who had returned at about 9:00 PM but had declined to partake of the amusements, had ordered Janie secured for the night and that the men should get some rest. "Do not worry," Massoud had announced. "Unless the chief has other plans for the young girl, she will be available for future pleasure."

"No need to use it all up at once, hey?" Basheer had chortled.

Massoud had carried Janie back to the upstairs bedroom and actually drawn a warm bath and washed her before re-tying her to the bed and administering enough of the drug to keep her through the night. As he left, he locked the door - as much to prevent entry as escape.

*　*　*　*

When Cann got back to his apartment, he was in strange mood. He felt satisfaction from his defeat of Klein - but nothing that could be called elation. Many times in the past he had seen that most ultimate sign of victory - the moment when he could see clearly in Klein's eyes that - finally - she knew she had been bested. It was the one single sign of complete victory - the moment when the vanquished becomes incontrovertibly aware of their own defeat.

But the victory was tempered by the absence of a message from Janie - or even Furden - on his machine.

There had been one from Arthur Matsen. 'We need you in Washington. ASAP. Catch the first plane after you get this message and come straight to the office. If you have questions, don't even call. Ask me in person when you get here."

He had checked with the airlines. There were several flights into Dulles leaving around 9:30 PM. Given a choice he preferred to fly into National. However, late arrivals were restricted at National, so he'd have to try to get an even earlier flight to go there and, even if he dashed out at that moment, he didn't think he could make it to the airport in time. So he didn't book a seat on any flight for that night. There were just as many flights at 7:00 AM the next morning which would get him to DC before the start of the business day. It would also give him time to ask Walder to arrange for his classes to be taken care of. He was sure Roger would say something about this not becoming a habit and he didn't blame him. It was true. He had made a commitment and needed to live up to it.

He also hoped that maybe he'd hear from Janie. He had as yet no sense of foreboding or concern for Janie's safety. The fact that neither she nor Furden had shown up at the hearing indicated to him that they'd gotten his message. So, for the moment, Cann felt only disappointment that he hadn't yet been able to share in the joy of the result - and his feelings were hurt just a little bit.

He was also disappointed that he still hadn't talked to Sara Furden about something else. He'd gotten what used to be called 'bad vibes' from Furden at lunch but he was willing to ascribe them mostly to his resentment at the third degree she'd tried to give him. Still, he wanted to ask her what she had against him.

Or in store for him.

Chapter Nineteen

Iverson had turned in about 11:00 PM CET after muting both the cellular phone and the cellular fax that he had set up on the small table in his hotel room. It had been a productive day in Lucerne and now he was waiting for responses to his inquiries. At the same time, he had no reason to anticipate that anything that might come in during the night which would require his immediate attention. And if it did, his emergency pager was on so that he could be reached in that event. But he didn't need to be bothered by things that could wait till morning.

On many occasions in the past, Iverson had gone without sleep for days at a time during an investigation and he knew that he could handle it if he had to. But he preferred a good night's sleep and there was no question that any investigator would operate more efficiently when rested. Besides, Loring Matsen was paying three hundred Swiss Francs for this night's sleep. It was his duty to get a good one.

At 6:00 AM CET, as programmed, the hotel phone beeped several times to wake him. Iverson picked up the receiver and held it to his ear to hear the computerized message he had selected the night before wish him a good morning and good day. He hung it up and after consulting the plastic directory beside the bed phone, dialed 5 for room service. He ordered coffee and croissants and lay back in the bed to wait for the knock that would signal the arrival of his breakfast.

After a moment, he raised his head until his chin pressed his chest and looked over to see if there was anything hanging out of the fax machine. There was. Curiosity won out over languidity and he got out of bed to see what had come in.

There were three messages.

The first was from Arthur Matsen. It asked him to phone or fax a progress report on whatever Iverson's investigation had given him so far at his earliest convenience. Iverson looked at the top of the page to see when it was sent - 11:00 PM Tuesday September 17, meaning that it came in to Iverson's hotel room at 5:00 AM Wednesday, September 18. The message advised Iverson that he, Matsen, would be in urgent White House meetings beginning early Wednesday and extending to who knows when. If Iverson could not contact him before 7:00 AM Washington time, it was very likely that he would be unreachable at all for some time after that. Iverson checked the clock again. 6:13 AM Central European Time - it was still just after midnight in Washington so he had plenty of time to get Matsen his report.

The second fax was from the pathologist at Wiesbaden and consisted of a brief update from Dr. Dimsen. Iverson snatched that fax up immediately and wished his coffee would arrive. He took the pathologist's summary across to the small couch and turned on the lamp next to it. He read it quickly.

'So at this point, we are certain that while the massive trauma to the thoracic area suffered by the decedent would have been sufficient to cause death, it was not the actual cause. We have determined that the decedent was, at the time of the accident, already deceased and had been for several hours. We continue to attempt to pinpoint the cause of death and are focusing on substance traces found in the blood and tissues of the decedent. I can confirm to you that there was a significant amount of the drug Rohypnol - the powerful sedative I described to you in our previous phone conversation - in the decedent's system. Although Rohypnol is a strong central nervous system depressant, that substance, by itself, in the amounts found, should not have been sufficient to cause

238

death. However, the tests also indicated the presence of a prescription drug used in the treatment of migraine headaches called Migramol which is a combination of caffein and an ergot alkaloid called 'ergotamine' which is derived from the sclerotium of the mold ergot. A check of the decedent's medical history reveals that he did in fact suffer from migraine headaches and had a refillable prescription for Migramol. However, once again, although it has been demonstrated that the interaction of an ergot derivative with a strong central nervous system depressant like Rohypnol can be dangerous, if not closely managed, we simply do not have the evidence to conclude that this interaction of Migramol and Ruhypnol was the the determinant cause of death. Our investigation remains open and, regrettably, at this point in time, we must admit we do not know the exact cause of Mr. Wagner's death.'

There were three short raps on the door to the hotel room followed by a muffled voice calling, "Room Service!" Iverson went over, checked through the peephole, and opened the door to let the young man carry the tray in. When the small pewter coffee pot, porcelain cups, and metal covered tray of pastries were properly arranged on the dresser where Iverson had indicated, he signed the bill and walked the server to the door.

He poured himself a cup of coffee and buttered half a croissant and went back to the couch and re-read the report. He would like to have had more but - you go with what you've got.

The third fax came from the Frankfurt office of the Bundes SicherheitsKraft with no signature but a notation at the bottom indicating that it had been sent on behalf of Oberst Gunther Abel. It read simply:

Preliminary query to Brian Iverson:

'Does the name Dr. Ahmed Quefar have any known connection to your present investigation or mean anything to you in any other way. We have connected this individual who is a Palestinian emigre with current residence in Kaiserslautern to an apparent unauthorized use of a portion of the abandoned

American Air Base above the village of Sembach. We are running a full identity check on Dr. Quefar but any connection with your investigation at this time is purely speculative and is based solely on his Palestinian nationality as it relates to the middle eastern connection to your investigation and, of course, his presence in Sembach. Nothing more. Please advise. Call Frankfurt office. They will patch you through at once.'

Leave it to Abel to squeeze a ton of information into a small paragraph, Iverson thought with admiration. The feeling was mutual. The two men had a long standing and professionally close relationship and had worked together or assisted each other so many times that a request such as Iverson had made was not a matter of reciprocal favors or a quid pro quo situation. They had long ago stopped counting who did what for whom. They just helped when they were asked.

After speaking with Iverson on Monday evening, Abel devoted Tuesday morning to clearing his desk and drove to Sembach early Tuesday afternoon. His first stop, of course, had been the small Sembach police station where he paid the professional courtesies before beginning.

'Had the local officers conducted any investigation of the accident of the previous week,' he had asked.

'None whatsoever,' he was reminded. 'He had directed them to turn everything over to the American investigator. Had Oberst Abel forgotten that?'

'Not at all and he thanked the local polizei for their cooperation in this very sensitive matter. But - had they not perhaps heard of any unusual circumstances or situations observed by the local people on that day and around the early morning hours? This was a farming community after all and it would not be at all unusual for someone to be up and about and seeing or hearing something out of place.'

The local commander commented that no one even appeared to have heard the crash but that was not so unusual since most of the residences are several streets back from the Hauptstrasse and N40. And, he smiled ruefully, such crashes were not all that rare.

The other officer who made up the rest of the local police force offered, however, that one of the local farmers had reportedly observed some unusual activity at the abandoned air base above the village.

'The morning of the accident?'

'Nein. The night before. About 9:30 PM. A neighboring farmer was hunting varmints in his north field and saw a small automobile which could have been the one that was later wrecked being driven up the hill and through the main gate.'

'Any other vehicles? '

'Yes. Two other cars and a truck. An old Opel diesel with no trailer attached.'

'Did this farmer see where the vehicles went?'

'Only that they continued on into the base and then turned right and pulled up to the one story building that sits opposite the old barracks.'

'And had the local officers investigated this?'

'Aber nein, naturlich. The base is still American territory and they had no jurisdiction to even enter let alone investigate.'

'Of course. Quite right.'

Technically the officers were correct. The base property was still American territory but as a practical matter, the United States had written it off and was not concerned with it. At the same time, the high precision ingrained in the German character would not allow for them to simply step into this vacuum of sorts which left the base in a sort of quasi-international limbo. As far as German jurisdiction was concerned, Abel was quite certain that he had all the authority he needed but it would do no harm to avoid stepping on any toes.

He borrowed the phone and called Iverson's office in Frankfurt which arranged within the hour for Abel to be escorted onto the former airbase accompanied by the Squadron Commander of the Air Police Squadron at nearby Ramstein Airbase which was still active. He would also be accompanied by the local Office of Specials Investigations (OSI) agent who was also peripherally attached to the Defense Intelligence Agency (DIA). That agent had

241

it emphatically pointed out to him by his own superiors that he was to act as liaison and - if needed - assistant to the German Security Officer.

The local farmer was located and questioned by Abel.

'Is there frequent activity on the base?'

'Ja. But not involving vehicles, Herr Oberst. Some 'fremden' have taken up residence in the empty buildings. But I see them usually only during the day and they do not own cars.'

The word 'fremden' meant strangers or even 'strange ones' and in the past had been the common term for foreigners. Current political correctness called for the more modern 'einwander' to be used when referring to 'immigrants' but the farmer was old and set in his ways.

'Is there activity all over the base or is it limited to a particular location?'

'I cannot see all over the base, mein herr, so I cannot tell you for certain. All that I see is what I see from where I do my work. I do not sniff around. The only activity I see is around the building which sits behind the barracks buildings in the middle of the base.'

'Do you know what they do?'

The old farmer shrugged and snorted. 'Nothing. I have always assumed that they live there for nothing so they do not need to work. But I do not know.'

Out of courtesy, Abel framed it as a request, but he required the farmer to accompany him to the base to assist in their search. The old man retraced the movements he had seen and Abel and the others found themselves behind the barracks and in front of what used to be the base hospital.

The former American air base was not very large and neither was the former hospital. It was more like a medium sized clinic. If the building had been locked in the past, it wasn't now and so the party of men were able to just walk in the front door. Just inside, there was a central receiving/reception area with corridors running away from it to the left and right. The right corridor contained examining rooms and doctors offices while the left corridor led to other examining rooms, laboratories, and a small operating room. Even when Sembach Air Base had been open, serious cases had been taken to Ramstein or even Weisbaden.

The Air Police commander had brought two Air Police enlisted men with him so all together there were five men - not counting the farmer - who spread out to look around the building.

Most of the rooms in the building appeared not to have seen any use for a long time. But the first two rooms off the left corridor were noticeably cleaner and smelled of antiseptic. Abel examined both rooms personally and thoroughly but found nothing he would be willing to call evidence.

He walked back to the center reception area where the rest of the men stood waiting for him. Through the dirty glass of the front doors, Abel saw that several children had gathered on the sidewalk and were peering into the building. He smiled and waved at the children then turned back to the assembled group.

"Gentlemen," he said in English, "please smile and wave at the children but pay them no further attention." The group did so.

"I want to talk to them, but if we run outside they will no doubt scatter. Please let us stay in here for a few minutes but every so often, please make some sort of visual contact with the children so that they will, hopefully, remain when I walk outside."

Abel was right. The children saw that the men inside had little interest in them and seemed friendly enough so they relaxed. After a few minutes, Abel walked causally to the door and, when they still stayed where they were, he went outside.

"Tag," he said to the group of five children who were all dark skinned males with curly hair. Abel took them for Turkish, the largest of the immigrant groups referred to by Germans as their 'guest workers.' All appeared to be in the seven to nine year old age bracket and they all looked up at him and said, 'Tag' in unison.

"Can anyone tell me what this building is used for, please," Abel asked.

Most of the children just looked at one another but the tallest said, "It is the hospital."

"Well, I know it used to be but what is it used for now?" Abel gave the child his friendliest smile.

"It is still the hospital for us and the others in the area who cannot go to the doctor," the child responded. "Dr. Quefar comes here to look after us because the German doctors will not see us."

Abel surpressed his irritation at the explanation that was to him pure propaganda. Germany has one of the best health care systems in the world and it is open to everyone - including 'guest workers'. But 'free clinics' were constantly springing up which, it was universally acknowledged, provided a level of care that did not even approach the care given at the national clinics and offices.

But the people who opened the 'free clinics' used the mere fact of their existence as proof that there was a need for them whether there was or not. Abel looked at it as a cynical misuse of the people the clinic personnel claimed to care about. He also took it as a personal affront to his own sense of duty and pride in his country.

But all he said was, "Dr. Quefar?"

"Yes," the boy replied, "he gives us our pills and takes care of us." He pulled a piece of paper out of his pocket and showed it to Abel. It was a prescription form with the name Herr Doktor Ahmed Quefar printed across the top with a Kaiserslautern address and phone number printed underneath the name.

Abel quickly memorized the spelling of the name as well as the address and phone number and handed the paper back to the boy with another smile. "Dr. Quefar must be a very good man," he said.

The boys all nodded, some smiling, some serious.

Abel looked at his watch. 16:45 CET. He was curious about this Dr. Quefar but he had no concrete or significant reason to seek him out - just yet. His original plan when he started out had been to return to Frankfurt for the evening even if he wasn't finished in Sembach. There was barely an hour's distance between the two locations and he could pull the papers on this Dr. Quefar from his office and contact Iverson from there as well.

Abel said goodbye to the boys and then made all the appropriate thank you's to the men who had assisted him, walked to his car, and left the base.

*   *   *   *

Iverson had never heard of Dr. Quefar and would so advise Abel. At the same time, he made a note to have the name run through the computers, even though he knew that it was very likely that Abel would come up with all they needed to know about this Palestinian doctor. Germany keeps fairly close tabs on its own citizens. But it keeps very close tabs on its 'guests'.

He finished his coffee and croissants slowly with his head resting on the back of the couch and his mind at ease to facilitate the absorption and coordination of the bits and pieces of information he had. Both for his own use and for Matsen's report, he was arranging his thought process on a chronological continuum - a time line starting on the evening of Friday September 6 and ending in the early morning hours of Monday September 9.

What did he have so far?

Wagner left Geneva on Friday evening and arrived in Lucerne later that same Friday night with Lisa Harmony. They appear to have driven straight there and they apparently slept together - or at least shared a room - that night. They left together the next day around noon. As of now, Iverson didn't know how they had spent the morning hours although his premise now was that it had something to do with the wine auction. He would look into that today.

At the other end of the continuum, Abel was working his way back toward him. A classic 'pinzer' movement, Iverson thought with satisfaction. With the best in the business.

They knew that Wagner's crash in Sembach apparently took place around 5:00 AM or so. According to the pathologist, Wagner was already dead when that occurred. They also knew that, according to the locater information, Wagner had been in Sembach since the night before. Why?

Investigations have the 5 w's in common with journalism. Who, what, where, when, and why. Add to that the how.

The 'what' was Wagner's death.

The pathologist seemed to feel that they were very close to the 'how'. Iverson wasn't sure that they didn't already have it but were being overly cautious. And he wouldn't have it any other way.

They knew the 'when' of Wagner's death but the precise 'where' still remained a mystery.

The 'who'? Iverson had nothing on that other than the most vague and abstract rudiments of a premise as yet so undeveloped that it had not begun to penetrate his conscious. Maybe Abel was on to something there. Iverson hoped so but for now, he needed to follow up with Bucher on this Lisa Harmony. That could lead somewhere. He would see.

Then there was the 'why'. The questions were all important but, in some ways, it was the 'why' that bothered Iverson the most. Why did Wagner have to die?

He shook his head to clear it. He didn't have any answer to the 'why' either.

Time to go back to work.

He showered and took care of the other universally required, if not always performed, morning personal tasks.

He finished the last of the coffee and croissants as he picked up the small computer and began to type his report to Matsen on it. When he had finished inputting all the items he had just gone over in his head and the details behind them, he hooked up the fax modem and sent the memo on its way. It would be waiting for Matsen when he arrived at his office in the morning.

*   *   *   *

What Iverson didn't know - indeed what Cann didn't know either and if he had known it would have made him change his flight plans - was that Matsen was pulling an all-nighter.

Even though Cann didn't take it that way, the message Matsen left on his machine had been intended to convey that Matsen wanted Cann in DC immediately - at whatever hour of the day or night he could get there.

It was 1:00 AM Daylight Saving Time in DC - 7:00 AM in Frankfurt and Geneva and Lucerne and Sembach. And it was 8:00 AM in Tel Aviv and Jerusalem. The voting booths were already in operation.

Matsen had as much regard for the opinion polls as Cann did. Virtually none. But neither of the men had any specific knowledge that would have allowed them to discount the pre-election polls that had shown first the Yenahim lead and then the catch-up by Shelanu that appeared to be taking place as election day neared.

But the President believed in the polls. He swore by them. Hell, he lived and died by them.

So while Matsen's reaction to the final pre-election polls taken during the twenty-four hours of imposed campaign inactivity that immediately preceded the Israeli election was one of 'I hope it's true but I'll wait for the votes', the President was - in the words of one of his younger aides - 'going postal' - 'ballistic' in the more traditional saying.

The pre-election polls had Shelanu not just catching up but surging into a big lead. It was a trend that - if true and if it continued - would result in a landslide - one of the most lop-sided margins in the short history of that small country.

Matsen would agree with Cann that such a result would be good for Israel but the President had apparently stormed out of a meeting with the poll results in his hands screaming at aides to set up a series of meetings on this crucial issue for the first thing in the morning. One of his orders was to get Matsen in and 'make sure the old bastard brings that arrogant son-of-a-bitch Cann with him.'

So Matsen had decided to spend the night at the office - which was not exactly roughing it by anybody's standards. He had his television set to CNN and his PC unit tied into Israeli television to follow the elections himself in real time. Soon he would let himself fall asleep but for now he was watching closely. He didn't speak or read Hebrew but he could understand the names and read the numbers next to them. Most of the day was yet to come and things could change but for now, the exit polls were bearing out the pre-election polls. The Israeli voters were giving Shelanu a mandate - and the President of the United States the finger.

Chapter Twenty

It was a little after eight AM CET when Iverson approached the young woman standing behind the front desk of the hotel. It was the same one who had checked him into the hotel the day before and who had also twice declined his requests for information. Iverson thought he perceived a difference in attitude this morning - a heightened deference perhaps - but he couldn't be sure.

"May I ask you some questions, Fraulein?" he said.

"But of course, mein herr," the clerk responded effusively. "I had no idea who you were yesterday or I would have helped you directly. I am sorry you were put to such trouble."

So she did know about his calls and his meeting with the head of security. He couldn't know if she had gotten into any trouble. He hoped not but it was water under the brucke, he supposed.

"Danke, Fraulein," he continued, "there was a wine auction or something here a week ago Saturday. Are you familiar with that?"

She looked pained - almost as if she wanted to say, 'Ask me something I know about'. "No, mein herr, I am so sorry. I do not." She paused for just a second and then went on, "I mean I know what you are talking about. I was on the desk that morning but, I know nothing of the auction and so little about wines. Perhaps there is something else I can help you with."

Iverson decided that he really wanted to give her the opportunity so he asked, "Well, do you know anyone else who might be able to help me - the person who conducted the auction, perhaps?"

The clerk brightened. "Of course, mein herr. Moment, bitte." She picked up the phone and punched in a three digit extension and waited. After a moment, her face registered contact at the other end of the phone and she spoke crisply into the mouthpiece. After a couple of "ja's" she wrote something down, thanked the other party, and hung up the phone.

"The event you ask about was managed by Herr Walter Specht of the local wine society. He has a wine shop just down the Baselstrasse about half way to the Hauptbanhof. He may be able to assist you." She looked pleased and relieved as she handed the piece of paper with Herr Specht's name and address on it to Iverson.

"Thank you so much, Fraulein. You have been most helpful," he smiled.

She beamed back. "If there is anything more I can do for you, mein herr, please only ask."

"Thank you again."

Iverson looked at the address and thought he remembered seeing the wine shop during his exploratory walk of the previous day. If he remembered the location correctly, there was no need for the car.

He walked out the exit on the east side of the hotel which led to the funicular. It was a self-serve operation and the car itself sat at the bottom of the track where it had been left by its previous passenger. He pushed the green button on the wall of the open carport-like shed at the top of the track and heard the gears kick into action and saw the train begin to slowly climb the steep hill. It reached the top and stopped automatically. Iverson got in and pushed the green button inside the car and again the machinery whirred and the car was lowered by the undercarriage cable to Baselstrasse.

When the car stopped, Iverson exited the small covered kiosk that served as a weather shelter and walked east on Baselstrasse for several hundred yards before he saw the sign for Weinstube Specht across the street.

Herr Specht was a delightful old man who loved his work and, judging by the floridity of his complexion, the product of his work. But it was barely 9:00 AM and there was no evidence that he had been tasting yet that day.

Iverson's questions were brief and to the point and Walter Specht was happy to answer them without hesitation.

'Yes, he had conducted an auction of rare German wines on the morning of Saturday, September 7 at the Chateau Groesch. He had been somewhat surprised and disappointed that the crowd was not larger. He had hoped for perhaps as many as fifty or sixty bidders or more but, ach, there were at most only perhaps thirty or so serious collectors there. Still, he had made several thousand francs for himself and more for the owners of the auctioned items.'

"Would a wine auction usually attract many active bidders?"

"No. But this was not a normal auction. A Herr Reinhardt Conrad of Bad Durkheim in Germany had consigned his 1976 Trockebeerenauslese to the sale." Specht paused and looked at Iverson. "Is the gentleman familiar with German wines?"

"A little." Iverson explained that he knew that the 1971 German wine law dictated that German wines be categorized according to quality with what was called 'Qualitatswein' as the lowest level, except for wine consigned as mediocre 'table wine'. All the other wines were grouped in a category called 'Qualitatswein mit Pradikat' - quality wine with certain characteristics. Those wines were allowed to designate themselves as such with a 'QmP' on their label to show they were of a higher quality than plain Qualitatswein.

QmP wines were then further divided into five categories - in general according to their quality as defined in terms of their sweetness and, sometimes, alcohol content. The lowest of the QmP's was Kabinett followed in ascending order of value by Spatlese, Auslese, Beerenauslese, and Trockenbeerenauslese. So Iverson knew enough to know that Herr Conrad's consignment was the highest possible level of German white wines.

Specht was impressed.

"But what exactly makes a Trockenbeerenausle so special, Herr Specht?" Iverson asked.

He could tell the wine merchant was about to warm up to his subject by the way he paused and hiked up his pants before he began to speak.

"Ah, it is the sweetness, mein herr. The glorious, wondrously dry quality that is the result of the time it is left on the vine. The vineyard must have many days of sunshine - more than usual - and then the noble rot begins to do its work."

"Noble rot?" Iverson asked, thinking that doesn't sound so appetizing.

"Yes, mein herr," Sepcht continued. "There is a mold called 'botrytis cinerea' which begins to act on the grapes giving them the extra sweetness that makes them so special. The first of such affected grapes that are picked become the 'auslese' - a marvelous wine in itself. The next batch becomes the 'beerenauslese' - truly wondrous in its sweetness. But there are grapes that are allowed to remain on the vine until the precise moment when the effect of the noble rot is at its highest. Each grape is examined individually on a daily basis and only when each is exactly ready is it gently removed by hand from the vine - not in batches, mein herr, but one by one and set aside. Some days only a few individual grapes are harvested and some days none at all are chosen. It is these rarest of grapes that become the glorious 'Trockenbeerenauslese' - the nectar of the gods, in my opinion."

"What does a Trockenbeerenauslese usually command for a price, Herr Sepcht?"

The wine vendor pursed his lips. "Oh, as you may know, German wines are simply not that expensive. In a normal year - if there is any Trockenbeerenauslese produced - some years there is none - it may command a price from fifty to several hundred Deutsch Marks."

Iverson did some quick calculations at an exchange rate of 2 marks to the dollar and arrived at a price range in dollars from perhaps $25 to as much as a several hundred.

"But this was a 1976." Specht spoke the year with reverence and looked at Iverson to see if he understood the significance of what he had just said.

He didn't. "Was 1976 a good year?"

Specht rolled his eyes. "Good?" He laughed. "It has never been equaled let alone surpassed. No, it has never even been approached in quality. It stands alone. This wine has great value on its own and there were fewer than a dozen known bottles of it left. Herr Conrad's bottle was not one of the known items which indicates that it was perhaps bought in the vintage year. All of that gave it further value far and above what even the intrinsic quality dictates. If the right people had attended, it was possible that this bottle could have set a new record for a German white wine."

"What did it go for?"

"It didn't go for anything. Herr Conrad had set a reserve of 2500 DM on it and the highest bid we got was from an American gentleman at almost 1500 DM. A very nice bid, indeed. I wish we could have taken it but," he shrugged, "we had a reserve. I tried to tell Herr Conrad that his reserve was too high - even for this gem but..."

"Do you know this Herr Conrad well?"

"Only by this transaction - and only by phone. I have never met the man. If I knew him better, I think perhaps I might have been able to persuade him to be more reasonable with his reserve."

Iverson took out the photograph of Wagner and showed it to Specht. "Ja, that is the young man who wanted the wine so much. You know him?"

"Yes."

"Did he get the wine. He was very determined about it."

Iverson looked at Specht. "What do you mean? I thought you said you couldn't accept his bid."

"I couldn't. But your friend decided that he wanted to deal directly with Herr Conrad himself."

Iverson asked him to explain.

"The young man appeared upset that I could not accept his bid. He even seemed to be in a little pain. I found that understandable. He had made a very good bid. I explained again about the reserve to him but he seemed determined to get the wine. He said he was traveling to Germany anyway and he asked me to give him Herr Conrad's address and phone number."

"Did you?"

The wine merchant pursed his lips and shook his head. "That is simply not done. It is why auctions such as these are conducted anonymously. So that the owner will not be bothered by unsuccessful bidders. And frankly, mein herr, it did not please me to consider the possibility that a sale would be made on this item with no commission for me but...," he shrugged yet again.

"So what happened?" Iverson asked.

"Well at that very moment, Herr Conrad called the hotel to see what had happened with the auction. An unusual coincidence, no? I told him of your friend's bid and again suggested he might lower the reserve. It seemed to me that even if I couldn't tell bidders the exact amount of the reserve, if I could just state that it had been lowered, we might receive higher bids."

"And?"

"He refused." Specht frowned. "And then he asked me to put the high bidder on the phone. I can tell you, mein herr, I almost refused. I did refuse at first, actually. This is also not done. This is a slap in the face to me. Any reputable auctioneer - or merchant - resents deeply to be used just to get a reading on the market value of an item. It is enormously more insulting to then be told to step aside while the owner deals with the bidder. I can tell you this, Herr Conrad will never sell another bottle of wine through this shop - or any other that I can influence."

"Did you put Herr Wagner - that was my friend's name - on the phone?"

"Was, mein herr?"

"He died in an auto accident in Germany the following Monday."

"Mein Beileiden. How sad." Specht's condolences seemed genuine. "Yes, I did - in a way. I am a quiet polite man, mein herr, and I have never hung up on someone in my life. I simply walked away and left the phone hanging by the cord."

"And he went over and picked it up?"

"Yes. The young lady with him was watching even more closely than he and she practically pushed him over to the phone when I walked away. Did he get the wine?"

"I don't know. He was in that general area before the accident though. So perhaps he did. Do you have Herr Conrad's address and phone number?"

"But of course." Specht went into a small area at the rear of the store and came back with the information scribbled on a small piece of paper.

Iverson read the name and adress and then looked at the other information on the paper - especially the reference that Specht had made to the Trockenbeerenauslese. He looked up at the wine merchant, then back at the paper, then up at Specht again. "Is this the usual abbreviation for Trockenbeerenauslese?" Iverson asked pointing on the page to the initials 'TBA'.

"Jawohl, mein herr. The full name is a bit unwieldy so it is almost always referred to as 'TBA'."

Iverson was actually a bit disappointed that the initials hadn't referred to a person or been a lead of some kind but at least it resolved a question - and it supported the premise. As always, it was better than a dead end.

"By the way, what happened to the Trockenbeerenauslese, Herr Specht. Did you send it back to Herr Conrad?"

Specht laughed a little. "Ach, nein, mein herr. It does not work that way. The wine itself stays in the hands of the owner. We auction certificates here. There is too great a danger that the wine will be damaged in transit. So, no, I did not have to send it back. It was already there."

Iverson nodded and thanked the wine merchant for his help and purchased a bottle of a nice Riesling - about 12 DM - before he left.

Iverson walked back to the Chateau Groesch and again approached the clerk. "It seems that I do need your help again after all, I am afraid," Iverson said.

The clerk was delighted.

Iverson told her that, as she probably knew, he had already been allowed to see the billing sheet and other records for a couple who had checked in about ten days ago.

'She acknowledged that she was aware of that now and, as she said before, if she had only known...'

'It was quite alright,' Iverson assured her, 'but right now he would like to know if the hotel kept a record of phone calls involving the lobby telephone?'

'Indeed we do, mein herr. We have state of the art equipment throughout the hotel but the lobby phones are internal phones only and - by design - must come and go through the switchboard. We had a problem with unpaid for calls, you see.'

"Of course.'

"So the desk person must put the call through and log the number being dialed."

"And is there a record of the incoming calls, as well?" Iverson asked.

"As I said, mien herr, we have state of the art equipment in the Chateau Groesch - including what is named 'Caller ID'. So we record the numbers coming in as well as going out."

Iverson asked if he could see the records for telephone calls made from the lobby on the morning of Saturday, September 7.

'But of course,' he was told, 'one moment, bitte.'

The clerk returned with another sheet of the ubiquitous green and white striped computer paper on which she had circled a fairly small section of the entire list. "I have taken the liberty of circling the calls made from the lobby phones between 8:00 and 12:00 that morning."

"Thank you," Iverson smiled. The list, even though computer generated, was simple enough. In the first column on the left side of the page was the time of day. Next to it was the telephone number followed by a notation - 'ank' for incoming or 'weg' for outgoing. Next to that was a space for phone card or credit card numbers and the fourth column gave the length of the call. The list was chronological so Iverson ran his finger down until he came to the calls in the later part of the morning.

Iverson first scanned the calls with the reference 'ank' next to them and found nothing. No incoming calls to the lobby phone at all between 10:38 and 12:17. Interesting.

He looked back over to the 'time of day' column and concentrated on the hour between 11:00 and noon. Five calls, all outgoing. He took out the piece of paper on which Herr Specht had scribbled the phone number for Herr Conrad and compared it to the numbers called from the lobby phone. Bingo. There it was. Conrad had not called Specht. Someone had called Conrad. And Iverson would be willing to bet that it was Lisa Harmony.

Even more information was available on this computer sheet. Next to the number and the 'weg', was a phone card number that the call had been charged to. Another tidbit for EI.

Iverson thanked the clerk and made her day by telling her she had been enormously helpful and he would make it a point to advise her superiors of her kind assistance.

The clerk smiled and radiated gratitude. "There is one other thing, if I may, mein herr?"

"Of course."

"You are inquiring about the couple who stayed that night in Room 317 are you not?"

"Yes. How did you know that?" Iverson figured he already knew.

The clerk spoke hesitantly as if she was uncertain whether she had spoken out of turn. "Herr Niebauer, our Director of Security, advised me of that when he called me to his office."

That's what Iverson had suspected. "Well, I hope he didn't find any fault with you, Fraulein. You were doing your job."

She smiled yet again, this time with relief. "Danke, mein herr. That is what Herr Niebauer said to me also. But he did tell me to cooperate in every way with you in the future."

"And you have." Iverson paused and waited for a second before asking. "You were going to tell me something else?"

"Yes. As they left, the young lady asked me if there was an Apotheke nearby."

So Harmony - or Wagner - wanted a drugstore. Interesting. "And is there one?"

"Yes. I told them of the the Apotheke Buhlmann just up the Baselstrasse from here. But I have no way of knowing if they went there."

"No matter, Fraulein. I do."

Iverson decided not to waste time trying to get a Swiss to reveal information to a stranger - especially medical information. He took the elevator down one level and walked to the Security Office for the second time where he explained to Herr Niebauer what he wanted to know. The Director nodded curtly and made two phone calls - the first to the Stadt Polizei who advised him to wait just a few minutes before making the second call. Iverson and Niebauer filled the brief time with idle chat after which the Director of Security phoned the Apotheke Buhlmann.

The Apotheker on duty had been called by the City Police and he would be happy to cooperate and answer whatever questions they might wish to ask.

Niebauer thanked the 'drogist' and handed the phone over to Iverson who asked the only question he had at the moment.

The drogist took a moment to check the Apotheke records and then came back on the line and confirmed to Iverson that an American named Wagner had re-filled a prescription issued in the United States for the drug Migramol on the 7th of September.

Having confirmed what he wanted to know, Iverson was about to thank the drogist and give the phone back to Niebauer. But while he had been sitting and chatting with the Director of Security, Iverson had been recalling a previous case he had worked on in which the solution had turned on an American prescription having been filled in a European drugstore.

On an impulse he asked the drogist to tell him exactly what was in Migramol.

The Swiss pharmacist took a moment to find the page in the European PDR and read the ingredients off to Iverson.

"It is made up of ergotamine, an ergot derivative, caffeine, and belladonna alkaloids, mein herr. Is there anything else you wish to know?"

Iverson had no other questions for the drogist. He didn't know if this information was going to be of help to Dimsen but he would forward it on to him as soon as he got to his room.

He thanked the Apotheker and he thanked Niebauer and he went back to his room.

As he walked in the door, he saw that a fax was coming in and another sheet of paper was already on the floor. He left the first piece on the floor as he grabbed the second one before it started to fall.

He read the second one first. It was from Bucher in Geneva:

Lisa Harmony has not appeared for work this morning. I have sent some security officers to her apartment to see if she is merely home sick or has disappeared. We have commenced the 'A' check on her and are examining her papers and records as I send this. I will be in touch with you very soon.

Iverson was not really surprised and, in a way, he was not even disappointed. He had been around enough investigations to know that something like this could often be an investigative break. If she wasn't just home sick - and Iverson didn't assume that to be the case - then something had tipped Lisa Harmony off. In addition to his other leads, he could now look for what that tip-off was - and if he could find it, it would in all likelihood lead him to something else.

What was the tip-off? Iverson had spoken only to Bucher about the surveillance and he had no reason to distrust his colleague. It was possible that Bucher had told someone who had in turn told Harmony. He would ask.

His call to Bucher went through without delay.

"Guten morgen, Brian."

"Morgen, Franz." Right to the point. "What happened?"

"Nothing here, Brian. After we spoke last night, I made my plans but I have spoken with no one about this, if that's what you are asking."

"What about the surveillance."

"I did nothing last night. I intended to have the team pick her up when she came to work this morning. That appears to have been a mistake. I'm sorry."

"What about your phone?"

Bucher was a little annoyed. "Please, Brian. I have my phones checked as frequently as you do - maybe more. And I have had it checked again. It is clear. Can you say the same for your cellular?"

That last question let Iverson know that he had in fact insulted his Geneva colleague. All the cellulars had built in scramblers which activated automatically so the question was meant as a 'dig'.

"Sorry, Franz, please don't take it personally. Just asking. Just keep looking for something in her work - and for a clue to the leak."

"It may not be in Geneva, Brian." Bucher was still annoyed.

"Right." Iverson was not inclined to argue. "I'll be in touch."

He hung up the phone and bent over to pick up the fax on the floor. It was from EI. 'Finally' thought Iverson.

> To: Iverson
> From: Vasigny/EI
> Re: Your Inquiry
>   Credit Card #:   7312 4086 3992 6619
>   AmFar Gold
>   Issued to: Lisa Harmony
>   Address: Rue des Fleurs 364
>   CH-6847 Geneva
>   Switzerland
>   Bill to: P.O. Box 3918
>   Franklin, VA 22102

Very interesting. Lisa Harmony has a gold card issued directly to her. Not a Loring Matsen card though. Loring Matsen pays its legal assistants well but...and she could of course have money of her own. Still...

Most interesting was the information that the bill gets paid by someone else. 'Daddy maybe?' A possibility. But Daddy usually doesn't have a post office box. Not unheard of, of course. It could be. But still...

Faxes are great but he needed to talk to EI. He phoned Vasigny, knowing that the people who work in the Electronics Investigation Section have been known to stay at their desks for days when they are on a quest, as they call it. So he wasn't surprised when Vaisgny answered the phone even though it was the wee hours of the morning where he was.

"Something's afoot here, Brian. Too many levels of complication for a straight deal."

"I'm beginning to see that. Were you able to trace the PO box?" It was not as easy as a lot of people think. The Post Office is very proprietary about the privacy of the owners of their PO boxes. With everyone. Government agencies. Law enforcement. They do not willingly release that information - almost never without a court order. While well intentioned, it worked to the advantage of those who had something to hide as well as those who did not. It was one of those things that struck Iverson as a great irony. The fact that - if there was some illegality here - and he was now working on the assumption that this was something more than just a romantic tryst - the protections of a free society would be of equal advantage to a wrongdoer.

But then they didn't figure on people like Vasigny.

"Oh ye of little faith, Brian." Vasigny laughed.

Loring Matsen wasn't a government agency. And they weren't going to court over this. Iverson had no doubt that Vasigny had the know-how to hack into the Postal Service Computers for the information - but that was a crime in itself - to be utilized only as a last resort.

So Vasigny had gone with the old fashioned method. He called a friend who was a mail handler. He got the information within an hour of his call.

"Post Office Box 3918 in Franklin, Virginia belongs to a branch of the First Bank of Manassas. The bills go directly to the bank. I figure there's an authorization for direct electronic payment."

"Jesus," Iverson breathed. "Dead end?"

"Oh ye of no faith at all, my friend. Au contraire - a piece of cake."

"You talk funny, Greg," Iverson laughed with both amusement and relief.

"All of us gnomes do. It keeps us sane amid all of these non-human - and therefore unquestioning and trustworthy - devices with which we live." Vasigny explained what he was doing as he punched the keys.

"We can't get directly into the bank's accounts - well, we can but Arthur doesn't like it when we do. And it's unlikely that the bank cross references their account number with the credit card number in its computers. Since electronic payments are simply another form of 'wire transfers' between banks or accounts, we could try to get the information we want from the Federal Reserve - but that's a no-no, too. And, in any case, every transfer made anywhere is in there - the electronic equivalent of a needle in a haystack. So, logic tells us to look where we know the account number is cross referenced with what we do know - the credit card number. The credit card company. So we," Iverson could hear the keys clicking over the phone as Vasigny continued, "truck on back to the issuer and match up the credit card number with the method of payment."

"You can do that?"

"It's not even that difficult, Brian. Don't misunderstand, the credit card companies are very security conscious, too, but they leave much of the account security to outside firms whose focus is on misapplication of funds or theft of numbers. The programs they use with regard to electronic payments monitor the account at the beginning to make sure that the payments get made and nobody complains. After that, there's not a lot of concern on their part about that aspect of the relationship. What gets monitored the least is when something goes back to the payer. I mean, people

262

question debits, not credits. So," more clicking, "lets look for credits from the credit card back to the bank account."

Iverson knew Vasigny well enough to know that he had probably already gone through this process but he would let him tell it in his way. Besides, Iverson found it fascinating.

"So. Here we are. Looks like somebody brought something back to Sears. OK. So where did they put the money? And," - click, click, click - "bingo. $127.59 into account number 7499 012 220 at First Bank of Manassas."

Iverson jumped in. "Can we find out who owns the bank account?"

"Patience, my man, patience. Would you say it was vital to a Loring Matsen interest to do so?"

Iverson knew that Vasigny was looking for authorization to cross the line even though he had already played so fast and loose with the system that it didn't matter. But Iverson wanted the information.

"Yes. It is. Need it in writing?"

"Not from you, Brian. Some others maybe. But not from you. Let's go in." He went back to the keyboard. "Once again, there is less concern with money coming in than going out. So let's make a deposit."

"Won't that leave a record?"

"Only for a while, I make a deposit of $0.00 which will register and let me get the name of the account holder. But these accounts are continuously reconciled and the next reconciliation will wipe a $0.00 deposit off the record as a useless anomaly."

'Amazing', Iverson thought.

More clicking. Then silence. Then, "Well, well, well."

"Well, well, well, what?" Iverson almost shouted.

"Does the name Center for the International Support of Palestine ring a bell?"

It did.

Every investigation has critical points along the way where the entire nature of the investigative process changes. It can be halted or redefined or intensified or altered in any number of ways. This was one of those points for this investigation. Up to this point, whatever this was all about, Iverson had developed no evidence that indicted this was anything more than a private matter.

That was no longer true. The person who spent at least part of the last weekend Wagner ever lived and may have been the last to see him alive - and may have played a role in his death - was now connected to the Center for International Support of Palestine. That meant that the entire investigation - and the death of Wagner - now had an international - perhaps even a terrorist - dimension.

Iverson knew that the Center for the International Support of Palestine was represented to be a charitable, non-profit think tank operation dedicated to the improvement of relations between the United States and the Islamic world - especially Palestinians.

But, through his contacts, he also knew that European intelligence had developed some information that the Center for International Support of Palestine was somehow connected to the more extremist splinter groups as well as the mainstream PLO and others. Because they had found no evidence of any European activity or other direct connection between CISP and any operations in Europe, the agencies had concluded that it had been established solely for activities in America.

In the United States, CISP had reportedly been under investigation for about a year by the FBI and other agencies interested in allegations of fund raising on behalf of terrorist groups and the smuggling of terrorists into and out of the United States under the guise of academics and researchers. Iverson had shared what little information he had with the American agencies but without the active assistance of the other country's intelligence operations, the investigation had not borne any significant fruit. As a result, CISP was still operating freely.

Iverson dwelled for a moment on this other irony involving the fact that CISP had been under investigation - for an entire year - and was still operating freely. Any other country on the face of the earth when confronted with the prospect of a terror campaign that had already begun would not be so inclined to give a suspect or group such a benefit of the doubt. Only in the United States, he mused, would the authorities bend over backward to afford Constitutional rights and guarantees to groups that have declared their antipathy to - and a virtual state of war with - that very document and the people it was intended to protect.

Iverson let Vasigny know how impressed he was and how much his work was appreciated. The self-described 'gnomes' worked as much for that as for their paychecks. Before hanging up, Iverson gave Vasigny the phone card number and asked what could be done to monitor its traffic. Vasigny advised that he would be able to give Iverson reports on any calls charged to the card but if he wanted to know the contents of the calls, he would have to talk to their friends at Langley and the NSA. Finally, recalling his conversation with Bucher, Iverson asked Vasigny to check on recent usage of Lisa Harmony's credit card account. Especially, travel items. 'Let's see where you went to, Ms. Harmony' he thought.

Before the phone line disconnected, Iverson was working on the follow-up fax to Matsen. They needed to know how CISP fit in with Wagner's death and the investigation in general. John Cann was the Middle East man in this firm. Iverson hoped that Matsen would be able to get him involved in this. They needed him even more now.

Chapter Twenty-One

At 5:15 AM EST, the automatic coffee maker in Arthur Matsen's office began to spurt and gurgle. Fifteen minutes later, the gentle beep of the alarm drew Matsen out of his sleep. He got up from the bed which would fold back into a couch and poured himself a cup of the blend of Dominican and Jamaican coffees he had added to the appliance a few hours earlier.

He walked over to his desk and picked up the phone and dialed Cann's number at Charlestown not really expecting it to be answered. But it was and that raised some annoyance in Matsen.

"Why are you still there?" he said without saying hello.

"I'm just on my way out the door, Arthur. I'll be in DC," he looked at his watch, "in about two hours."

"I wanted you here last night."

"I didn't realize that."

"Why do you think my message said don't even call. Just get here."

Cann knew that the message didn't exactly say that but he never enjoyed sparring with Matsen. "Arthur, I didn't get the urgency in the message that you intended. I'm sorry. But there's nothing I can do about it now except get there as soon as possible. Let me get to the airport."

"Well, by the time you get here, I may already be at the White House. Go straight to the office as soon as you get in." Before Cann could say anything Matsen said, "No. Wait. I'm sending a copter to pick you up. You're coming into Dulles, I presume?"

"National. At 8:00 AM - if its on time."

"National." Matsen repeated. "Well, forget the copter. A limo will get you from National to here as quickly as the copter would - there'll be a car waiting for you when you land. It'll bring you to the office or the White House - wherever I happen to be at the time."

"What's up, Arthur? This almost sounds like 'national emergency' stuff."

"I'm not prepared to go that far quite yet, John. We'll see what happens today."

"About what?"

"Have you had the news on? Heard anything about the Israeli election?"

"No. Down here at this time of morning all you get is elevator music."

"Shelanu is kicking ass."

Despite the polls, Cann hadn't really expected that and all he could manage to say was, "Cool."

"Maybe. Maybe not. Some predictions of that started coming in yesterday and I'm told that the President went through the roof. After that the early results started to confirm the polls. I've got Israeli television on right now - it'll be noon soon over there - and it looks like it's really going to happen."

"Where do I come in?"

"The President specifically ordered me to bring you to the White House with me."

"Great. Hot seat time again."

"Well, it'll be hotter if I show up alone. And when you get here, keep your cool. Treat the man with as much deference as you can muster..."

"That won't be..." Cann had intended to say 'much'.

Matsen interrupted sternly. "...difficult. That's what you were going to say, wasn't it. It won't be 'difficult'. Look, I'm serious. Listen to me on this. Don't make things any worse. He's the President of the United States and he doesn't like you, anyway. If he had his way, he'd probably have you shot on the White House lawn."

Cann didn't disagree. "So, you think he wants me to deal with Lev Shelanu for him."

"I hope that's what it is. He seems close to irrational on this subject though. Look, just get off the phone and get to the airport. Hopefully, we'll have time to talk before any meetings."

"Right. See you in a few hours, Arthur." He hung up.

Matsen leaned back in his chair and closed his eyes. He wasn't really tired even though he was operating on four hours sleep. It was something he'd gotten used to over the years which he was able to deal with thanks to an ability to store reserves of sleep when it was available and then call on them when needed.

His eye caught the white of the papers in the black plastic receiving tray of the fax machine. He got up and walked over to it and picked up the two sheets. He had a practice of making sure that he always read faxes in the sequence in which they were received so he looked to the tops of the pages for the page numbers. This time they both said 'page 1 of 1' so he knew that they were two separate messages which had come in at different times. He looked again at the tops of the pages. One said 7:29 CET - it had come into the office about 1:30 AM. He had dozed off watching the election results and now he knew roughly when. The second fax was marked 9:57 CET - just before 4:00 AM. He saw they were from Iverson - the progress report, he figured. For a brief moment, he started to put them down without reading them. He needed to stay focused on the matter at hand. But then, he had made a specific request that Iverson get this report to him before his meetings and it was only fair that he read them now. Who knows when he might have another chance to look them over.

*   *   *   *

Iverson knew that the investigation needed to move to Germany. It was already almost 11:00 AM and, since he figured on about five hours to Bad Durkheim, if he was to have any chance of getting there during the business day, he had to get on the road.

He couldn't get away. The phone kept ringing. But each time it did, it gave him a little more information.

First it was Bucher calling to tell him that there didn't appear to be any clues to Lisa Harmony's activities in her desk or phone records. Everything seemed in order. They were, however, able to get an excellent set of fingerprints from her work station which were now being run through Interpol and its affiliated agencies.

Iverson brought Bucher up to speed on what he had learned from Visigny at EI about Harmony's credit card and her apparent connection with CISP. The information did nothing to improve Bucher's frustration over her disappearance but it did let him know that whatever was going on was bigger than he had previously thought.

Both men commented on the effect this would have on future screening procedures of prospective employees at all levels, but, for now, they needed to focus on the immediate problem.

Iverson hung up the phone and finished putting his things together. Just as he was about to leave the room, the cellular fax went off. Iverson unzipped the black leather case so that the paper could come out of the machine freely and sat on the bed to wait for the transmission to finish.

As soon as the machine emitted its concluding beep, Iverson tore the sheet off and looked at it. It was from Vasigny and contained a list of telephone numbers that had been charged to Lisa Harmony's phone card.

The list was not very long which tended to confirm Iverson's premise that this card was used only for CISP business. That fact also made the phone numbers that much more significant.

He looked down the list of 9 calls that had been made in the past two weeks. There were only three phone numbers on the list. Five of the calls were to the same number in the 703 area code which Iverson knew to be the area of Virginia bordering

Washington, DC. He would be very surprised if that number was not CISP.

Three of the other calls, two from Geneva and the one made from the lobby of the Chateau Groesch - the only call not made from Geneva - were to Herr Specht's wine collector, Reinhardt Conrad.

The last call on the list, made from Geneva at 11:00 AM Monday, September 9, was to another number in Germany. Iverson knew the 49 country code but he wasn't familiar with the city code. In the old days, he might have just picked up the phone and dialed the number to see who answered. But in this day and age of 'caller ID', it was too easy to put a subject on alert. Gunther Abel could - and would - help with this.

Iverson finally got out of Lucerne about 11:30 AM CET. By then, he was too impatient to take the time to make another call from the hotel so he just headed out and as soon as he reached divided highway north of Lucerne, he placed a call to Gunther Abel at his Frankfurt number.

Abel was in his office in Frankfurt. If there had been a good reason, he had been prepared to return to Sembach that Wednesday morning but so far it appeared that he had learned as much as he could in the tiny village. The identity information on Dr. Quefar had come in during the night and he read it over coffee and made a few calls when he was done. Even though there was no glaring item of information regarding Dr. Quefar in the documents he had seen, Abel's instincts wouldn't allow him to dismiss the physician from his thoughts. So he was anxious to hear back from Iverson and took the call immediately when it was put through.

"Morgen, Brian. Wie gehts?"

"Morning, Gunther. Thank you so much for your help."

"It is nothing."

"It is not nothing, my friend. Listen, I'm on my way back to Germany right now, heading for a place called Bad Durkhein - do you know it?"

"But of course. I like my wines, too. What is in Bad Durkheim? Besides wine, of course."

Iverson related to Abel what he knew so far of events in Lucerne and how those events now indicated that the investigation should be picked up in Bad Durkheim.

"It all fits so far, Gunther. Even the location fits in with the data we got from the GPS/Glonass system. Wagner drove directly from Lucerne up the highway - just as I'm doing now - ducked off at Karlsruhe and went straight to Bad Durkheim."

Iverson then gave Abel the information he had on Herr Reinhardt Conrad - phone number and address - and asked if he would be able to check that out while he - Iverson - was in transit.

"But, of course. Also, Brian, give me the other number you said was called by this Harmony person. I will find out to whom it belongs."

"Thanks, Gunther."

As soon as Iverson read off the numbers, Abel erupted with a guffaw.

"You see how efficient I am Brian, I can aready tell you to whom that number belongs."

As though in competition with Abel, Iverson's brain reflexively attempted to process what information it had and anticipate what it was that Abel was about to tell him. The only logical answer was just beginning to form as Abel said, "That is the telephone number for our friend, Dr. Quefar - in Kaiserslautern. The plot thickens indeed."

The two men signed off but Abel didn't hang up the phone handset. He severed the connection with Iverson by pushing down on the button in the receiver and then entered a three digit extension. He told the man at the other end to get his car ready and have it out front. He left his office and walked down the hall to the elevator stopping only long enough to stick his head inside another office and crook his finger at the two men inside who immediately stopped what they were doing and followed Abel from the building and down to his car.

When Abel had driven to Sembach the day before, he had gone west from Frankfurt through Wiesbaden and then down through Mainz and then down the N40 directly to the village. If he were heading straight to Kaiserslautern, he would have taken the same route through Sembach and into the larger city.

But he was taking things in sequence. He was heading first to Bad Durkheim so he took the number 5 Autobahn south from Frankfurt to Mannheim where he exited onto the number 6 Autobahn and headed west to an exit marked by the town of Grunstadt. Bad Durkheim was a few miles south of that.

He was not ignoring Sembach or Kaiserslautern. He was a thorough man and learned from other people's mistakes. Iverson had told him how Lisa Harmony had disappeared before Bucher had gotten surveillance on her and they still didn't know how she knew she was under suspicion. So, before he left Frankfurt, Abel placed a call to the Kaiserslautern Stadt Polizei and asked them to keep an eye on Dr. Quefar's office and report any movement. As long as nothing unusual occurred, keep a wary distance.

As far as Bad Durkheim was concerned, Abel already knew that the address for Reinhardt Conrad that Specht had given to Iverson was a phony. It had taken only seconds for his team in Frankfurt to learn that it simply didn't exist. He was not surprised.

It had taken a few moments longer for the team to find out that the telephone number was what is known as a 'centrex drop' - effectively a number with only an electronic location inside the computers of the telephone company. The only purpose of a 'centrex drop' is to receive calls and instantaneously pass them on - forward them - to another number at a real location. It wouldn't have taken as long to get that information as it did except that the number had been cancelled the morning of September 9, 1996.

It only took an authorization from someone of Gunther Abel's rank and position to require the telephone company to release the number to which the calls were being forwarded and the location of the receiver. It was not that Germany took the privacy or the rights of its phone users more lightly than the United States - Abel would be held personally and severely accountable for any misuse

- his career would be over. But partly for that reason and also for other reasons found in the German psyche, the initial benefit of the doubt in such matters was given to the police.

So they drove directly to the address provided by the phone company. Abel figured he should not be surprised to find that it was a wine stube or a restaurant or even a winery. Not just because of the connection with the Trockenbeerenauslese and Conrad. Bad Durkhein lies in the heart of wine country and probably half the businesses in the city depended to one degree or another on wine.

And he was right. The abandoned vinyard was situated about half a mile south of the city limit. For reference, Abel compared the location to the locater grid map sent by fax modem from Iverson's Frankurt office to Abel's. It confirmed that this was the square mile grid where Wagner spent his entire time in Bad Durkheim.

Abel looked around before getting out of the car. There were two buildings on the site, one a residence and the other a barn, both in extreme states of disrepair. Surrounding the buildings on all four sides was an expanse of terraced land containing innumerable empty wooden stakes with an occasional withered vine hanging down. It was clear that it had been a long time since any grapes had been harvested here.

Abel and the two men with him exchanged mutual cautions among themselves and moved out to examine the premises.

First, they thoroughly searched the barn and established that it was empty. The only sign of recent activity was a set of tire tracks directly in its center and just inside the door. It was readily apparent from the width of the tracks that they had been made by a small car - like an Austin-Healey perhaps. Abel made a note to get some forensics people in here along with someone who knew more than he did about 1960's British sports cars.

They moved their examination then to the former residence. A large, two-story structure, it too for the most part gave the appearance of a long period of disuse. Throughout it, however, there were areas where one could see that the accumulation of dust had been disturbed and one room on the second floor was exceptionally clean - too clean - almost antiseptic. As if someone had wanted to remove all evidence of whatever activity had taken place there.

Abel was anxious to get on to Kaiserslautern and Dr. Quefar. He was prepared to operate on the assumption that the tire tracks were from Wagner's Austin-Healey. If so, that would combine with the locater grid information and the forwarded telephone number to make him confident that, until and unless something made him change his mind, this was where Wagner had spent a twenty-four hour period from the evening of Saturday, September 7 to the evening of Sunday, September 8.

But if there was more to be learned, he wanted it.

In the half mile between the vineyard and the city proper, the terraces of vines extended for a few hundred yards. After that there were several houses on either side of the road, then an automobile repair shop, and then the usual assortment of shops and other business entities of a medium sized city.

Abel directed his men to walk back to the city and stop at each location along the road to ask if anyone had seen any unusual activity on the weekend of September 6-9.

As his men headed out on foot, Abel took another look around but as far as he could tell, they hadn't missed anything. Nothing glaring at least. The forensics people would be better equipped to come up with the less obvious clues if any existed.

He went out to the car and called in his findings and updated instructions and advised his office that they should not hesitate to share any and all information with Brian Iverson.

When he finished, he started the car and headed back towards the center of Bad Durkheim. As he approached the automobile repair shop, Heilman, the senior of the two men he had brought with him waved at Abel from the right side of the road. Abel stopped the car next to Heilman and pressed the button on the armrest to his left which opened the passenger side window to his right.

"There was no one in the houses, Herr Oberst, but the man in here," he flipped his head in the direction of his right shoulder and toward the shop, "has some information that might be helpful."

On the trip down from Frankfurt, Abel had given Heilman and Leider a fairly complete but generalized summation of what they were doing and what they were looking for. He had also given them the sternest of directions to disregard nothing and bring anything and everything to his attention. He would make the judgment whether something was important or not.

"Like what, Heilman?" Abel asked.

Heilman related to Abel that the mechanic inside had stated in response to Heilman's questions that the vineyard had been abandoned for almost three years. But not too long ago - he wasn't sure but he was pretty sure that it would have been around the weekend they were asking about - on that Saturday - early - he had seen two cars - drive up the road and - he wasn't paying that much attention of course and the road turns just where the entrance to the vineyard starts - but he thought they had turned into the vineyard.

'Well, that couldn't be clearer,' Abel thought.

Heilman continued. "But because he had looked up just then, he did notice another truck come along right after the two cars and this one he was sure turned into the vineyard. He even walked up the road a bit and saw it parked in the driveway with the two cars.

"Did he notice anything about it - any markings or anything?"

"Yes. That was why he paid so much attention. He thought it very odd that a medical supplies truck would be going to an abandoned vineyard."

That got Abel's attention. "Did he get the name?"

"I have it written down here, Herr Oberst," Heilman said proudly. "The mechanic even remembered that it was from a company in Ludwigshafen. That was printed on the truck as well."

275

"Excellent, Heilman. Did he see the sports car by any chance." He consulted his copy of the locater printout. "It would have been in the evening. Probably not so late."

"Unfortunately, no, Herr Oberst. He closed up around 16:00 hours that day, he said."

"Schade. Please thank him for me."

Abel then explained to Heilman that he had called for the forensics people and also that he wanted Heilman to remain in Bad Durkheim and oversee the continuation of the investigation. "Be sure to talk to as many townspeople as you can. Who knows what someone may have seen. But for now," he scribbled something on a paper he had taken from the glove compartment. "Here is a voucher for hotel and expenses. There is a very nice Parkhotel up on the hill there." Abel pointed up and to his left. "Stay there and have a good dinner and some of the local reisling. Not too much, though," he smiled. "The hotel may bill the office directly. We will be reimbursed by a very generous American firm. So enjoy yourself and keep me posted with what you find."

"Dankeschoen, Herr Oberst. Vielen dank."

For only a moment, Abel considered driving east to Ludwigshafen and finding the medical supplies company himself but by now his instincts were screaming at him to get to Kaiserslautern. So he told Heilman to get the medical supplies company on the phone and find out what their business had been at the vineyard. Call him on the car cellular as soon as he had anything. "Anything at all. Understand?"

"Ja, Ich verstehe, Herr Oberst."

*   *   *   *

Janie wasn't aware of it but the day had started out peacefully for her. That was only because Massoud had locked the door the night before.

As each of the four men had awakened, they came down the hall and tried the knob on the door. The first two, Sami and Basheer, simply shrugged and went away content to wait a bit for their pleasure. Naji tried a little harder but he too left without going in.

But Abdullah had lain in his bed thinking of the naked young girl and the events of the night before and had gotten himself thoroughly aroused. So that when he first jiggled the knob and nothing happened, he simply turned to his left and put his right shoulder into the door. It opened easily. He nodded his head abruptly as if to say, 'just as it should be'. Then he walked in - once again - reaching inside his pants as he approached the bed.

'He must be sure to tell the others that the gate of heaven has been opened once again.' he laughed to himself. 'When he is finished, of course.'

*   *   *   *

Sara Furden called Janie at 7:00 AM Wednesday morning and again at 8:00 AM and again at 9:00 AM. She was beginning to get really worried.

After she had dropped Janie off at her dorm the previous afternoon and returned to her apartment, Sara had begun to think about the pressures on Janie as the time of the hearing approached. She decided that she didn't want to leave the poor kid alone for the next couple of hours to imagine all the terrible things that might happen to her.

So, around 5:45 PM or so, she phoned Janie's room to tell her that she would pick her up. When all she got was the recorded message, she assumed that Janie was at dinner or had perhaps even left early for the hearing. Before leaving her apartment, on an impulse, Sara called the number for Janie's message retrieval. As her 'in loco parent', as they had kiddingly termed the situation, Janie had given Sara the phone code as one more way for them to communicate. Sara hoped that maybe Janie had left a message for Sara on the recording. She hadn't.

But she did retrieve Cann's message to Janie, and, despite the hostility she felt toward him, Sara couldn't help but be pleased at the news that the hearing was off, and, if she understood correctly, the charges were dropped. Great news. What a relief.

But there was a downside, too. In the message, Cann also told Janie to stop worrying about who had called in the complaint. He told her about the silent alarm. Now Sara was afraid that Janie hated her for giving her the key and not telling her about the alarm. Or for not telling her since.

That was probably why Janie hadn't called her with the news? Wouldn't you think that would be the first thing she would do. It ate at Sara that her initial reaction to the story as Janie told it to her that morning had been one of amusement. Then before she'd even finished laughing, it had suddenly dawned on Sara that she'd never thought to tell Janie about the alarm. Oh God, what if that was it? If it was the alarm that summoned security, it made it all Sara's fault.

But according to everybody, it wasn't the silent alarm that started the whole thing. Somebody called security. That's what they said. I mean even if it was the silent alarm, that wasn't what caused the problem. If it was just the silent alarm, there wouldn't be a hearing because there was no complaint. So it wasn't her fault.

But now Cann was saying that it was the silent alarm. And Klein had been evasive when Sara had talked to her about who called in the complaint. Sara had asked her if she knew who had made the complaint and Klein had just said that it didn't matter. If there was no complaint and it was the silent alarm, then that meant Sara's airhead stupidity had handed Janie to Klein on a silver platter.

God, maybe it was the silent alarm after all and it was my fault that Janie went through all of this. And then I couldn't do anything for her. And Cann comes through and saves her instead. Nice 'in loco parentis'. All 'loco' - no parent.

At least it's over.

Of course, Cann gets all the credit.

She hadn't really been able to do much for Janie in the whole matter. And it ate at her that it might have been her fault in the first place.

And that was how Sara's Tuesday night had gone until exhaustion brought sleep. Or several fits of it.

She got up at 5:30 AM Wednesday and had to force herself to keep from calling Janie's dorm room right then. She waited until 7:00 but only got the recorder again. Of course, they probably have it on silent answer so as not to be disturbed.

Then she thought of Cann again.

Of course.

The bastard.

He probably made a big deal about how he saved her and took advantage of her gratitude. Janie's cool. But she's still a kid. A cute, sexy kid less than half his age. Why else would he go to all this trouble for her? The bastard.

She looked up Cann's number and called his apartment. No answer there either. Naturally.

She dressed quickly and drove over to Janie's dorm. Gretchen was still in bed and buzzed her up. Sara's panic and anger grew when Gretchen said that Janie hadn't been in all night. As far as she knew. 'Hadn't seen her since yesterday morning. Funny thing though, Gretchen's bed was a little messed up but Janie's wasn't. It wasn't like Janie. She was obsessive about respecting Gretchen's space. And there was a glass on the floor next to her bed when she got back to the room yesterday. Empty. Just lying on the floor by the bed. Strange.'

Sara was going beyond panic.

Where was Cann, damn it? He probably had the answer to this. She was even beginning to hope so.

It was getting close to 10:00 AM. Sara knew Janie's class schedule and knew her history class would be starting soon. She left her car parked at the dorm and ran to the Potter Building. "Please show up for class, Janie. Please."

She waited until 10:20. She was in agony. By now she was prepared to accept - almost hoped - that Janie was safe in Cann's arms. She would hate him for it but she it was better than what she was starting to imagine.

At 10:45, she called the police.

Not campus security. The real police.

Chapter Twenty-Two

At 11:00 AM, Matsen and Cann were still waiting for the President to call them into the Oval Office.

Cann had gotten into Washington National a little after 8:00 AM and was met at the end of the tunnel by the driver holding up the sign that said 'L-M'.

"Where're we going?"

"The White House, Mr. Cann. Direct. No detours. No delays."

"Sounds like Arthur is in a mood."

"I wouldn't know, sir."

"Okay." Cann put his head back against the seat and watched the driver skillfully maneuver through the rush hour traffic all the way into the city proper. Even though the distance isn't great in miles, it was approaching 9:00 AM when the limo pulled up to the East Gate of the White House. The gate attendant leaned down and looked hard into the faces of the occupants of the car and checked their ID's carefully. He then consulted his list of authorized visitors and found Cann's name. 'Just like the good old days,' Cann thought. He remembered being welcome without feeling so.

He went through another check by the Secret Service Agent manning the desk just inside the east entrance. There would be other checks throughout the building. The President was in residence and that meant that the highest level of security was in place. One of the inside jokes in the world of federal security was that if you ever want to commit suicide, just make an unusual move when security was at 'in residence' level. Except it wasn't a joke.

Finally Cann was brought to an anteroom not far from the Oval Office where Arthur Matsen sat cooling his heels. He had been cooling them since before 8:00 AM.

Like many of the rooms in the White House, this one was tiny - not much larger than a medium size walk-in closet with barely enough room for the three straight backed chairs arranged against the three walls that didn't have a door.

"Morning, Arthur. Sorry I didn't get here last night."

Matsen stood up and gripped Cann's right shoulder with his left hand while he shook right hands with him. He was genuinely glad to see his friend and protege for the first time in months and regretted his sharpness on the phone earlier.

"Why, John? So you could sit and wait all this time with me? Don't worry about it. I was much too brusque this morning. You're here now and the President won't have that to bitch about at least."

"What's going on, Arthur? When does he want to see us?"

"Who knows? He sent for me at 7:15 this morning and I came straight over. I haven't seen him at all but the hallway has been all hustle and bustle since I've been here. The Secretary of State and the National Security adviser have both been running back and forth like a couple of errand boys. Even DCI Onger had some pace to his step today." The Director of Central Intelligence was famous for what he considered deliberateness but others thought of as just plain slow.

"State? NSC? CIA? I'll say it again. What's going on?"

"John, I don't know what he's got up his sleeve but I don't like all this activity. It's got something to do with Shelanu's election. Of that I have no doubt."

"But what can he do?"

Matsen put his hands out to the side, palms up. "John, be prepared for anything. That's all I can say. But I suspect no matter what it is, you'll be the conduit to Shelanu. For now, all we can do is wait."

Matsen reached into his briefcase. "In the meantime, I want to pick your brain about something. What do you know about an organization called the Center for the International Support of Palestine?"

"Not much. I know of it. A think tank in DC. Virginia, actually. Supposedly dedicated to the betterment of Arab-American relations."

"Supposedly?"

"Well, don't read too much into my use of that word. All I mean is that all of these 'centers' have ulterior motives. At the very least they're fund-raisers and lobbyists - registered or not. And it's not just Arab or other Middle East groups. Everybody does it. Everybody. No matter how much people hate the golden goose, they all want some of the eggs."

"Are you aware of any terrorist connections with CISP?"

"Am I personally? No. But as I said, I really don't know that much about them. They've only been around for about a year and a half - maybe two. And if they are a front, you can bet that they'll be squeaky clean for a while before they get into anything. Don't forget that I've been - shall we say - away from the arena for a few months now." Cann looked hard at Matsen. "Are there any?"

"Any what?"

"Terrorist connections."

Matsen nodded. "The word is that they're at least loosely connected with most of them. That they're positioning themselves as a conduit for whomever needs logistical support here in the United States. Fund raising and lobbying, too, as you said. The rumors are that they're establishing a network among Middle East Studies departments at universities around the country. Even smuggling in operations people - terrorists - as academics and researchers."

"How do we know that?"

"Iverson. His contacts in European intelligence gave him that info a while ago. We turned it over to the agencies and they've been looking into it. But I checked and they haven't made any solid connections yet."

"Let me guess. There's been no official help from any of the foreign intelligence agencies that might have the information. Right?"

"Very little unofficial help either, John. If it wasn't for the fact that Iverson is so highly thought of in Europe, we wouldn't have even gotten what we did."

Cann shook his head. Despite some progress, the United States was still a pariah in the international intelligence community. It was a condition that had its roots in the Carter administration's decision that the gathering of intelligence was both unnecessary and immoral. In an elitist form of racism - elitist in that it was deemed acceptable by those who decried it elsewhere - decisions were made on the basis that it didn't matter if the rest of the world did something - the poor unfortunates didn't know any better. The rule-makers of the United States had already evolved to a higher level and as a result, our participation at the same level as our inferiors was beneath us - grounds for penance on our part. In those days, in intelligence as well as other areas, the national uniform became sackcloth and polyester.

Cann had lost colleagues and friends. It made no difference that they had acted under the imprimatur of their country - even with high motives. They were quite literally abandoned and left to their fates because their leaders had 'seen the light'. Those left 'out in the cold' apparently should have - somehow - known better and if they failed to see what was coming - well then they deserved their fates. Fates that included being tortured and murdered. Well, that was okay. In another example of their ability to subhumanize others in relation to themselves, those who had made careers out of decrying violence seemed to have no qualms about the violence occurring to those who had - perhaps - disagreed with them.

To be sure, there were rescue attempts - all unsanctioned - some failures, many successes. But even the successes failed to become known because that would have impaired the myth of the unreachability of the terrorists. Other attempts would have become expected.

The rest of the world - especially those parts where principles such as loyalty and consistency still meant something - watched appalled as the United States let its agents, its station chiefs, members of its military, citizens, anyone and everyone be taken and abused - as a matter of official policy. The world looked away in disgust as former allies of the United States were left to wander nationless - even denied medical help for terminal illness - in a vacuum born of cowardice. For ultimately the world saw the facade of morality for what it really was - sheer and total cowardice. The net result was that nobody trusted the United States intelligence community anymore. And plenty of others hated us for what we had done or not done.

"We need to know what this is about, John." Matsen was staring hard at Cann. "You might be able to get a little help from your friends - either officially or unofficially. I'd like you to see what you can do."

Cann knew that Arthur was very selective about asking Cann to presume upon his connections - and high level friendships - but if Arthur felt that the stakes were high enough...

"If there's anything to these people or these rumors at all - hell, even if there isn't - you can bet the Israeli's are keeping an eye on them. I can make some calls but understand that the Mossad isn't going to share anything with us - not officially anyway. Neither is Shin Bet or Unit 154 or any other arm of Israeli intelligence. This Pollard thing is a real wedge between us."

Only a couple of months ago, for the third time, the President had refused to pardon the man sentenced to life without parole for spying on the United States on behalf of Israel. It had been a foolish and arrogant thing for Israel to do but it was an action born of an inability to trust that the United States wouldn't suddenly turn on its most steadfast ally in the Middle East.

Matsen pressed. "Well, see what you can do, would you?"

He knew Cann would. "I'll ask, Arthur. But under the present circumstances, I have no idea what to expect. It would be best not to expect anything, I suppose. Israel may be our ally officially but they look very darkly on the unauthorized release of their intelligence information without very good reason - even to good friends. I'd hate to see my contacts getting into deep shit. What's the deal with CISP that makes it vital to know right now?"

Matsen handed Cann the two fax reports he had received from Iverson earlier that day and a synopsis of the information compiled during the investigation of Ted Wagner's death. Cann read it quickly but carefully and then looked up at Matsen.

"This CISP was involved in Ted's death?"

"So it would appear. And the ramifications go beyond even that. Such involvement would indicate that not only has CISP gone from a legitimate or semi-legitimate front to an operational player in some serious events. And in the European arena. That's another major development." Matsen nodded somberly. "Properly played, that might give us a stake to get back in the game over there."

"So we're talking murder here?"

"Actually, we're still not sure. Dimsen's the pathologist on this and he's a good one. Right now, he's leaning to a combination of drugs with a lethal result. On purpose or accidental?" Matsen spread his hands out with their palms facing up. "He doesn't feel he's got enough to definitely say one way or the other just yet."

Cann had a look on his face that Matsen had seen before. "Yeah. Well unless Ted took the drugs of his own free will - and I don't believe that for a second - it doesn't matter a bit whether the result was accidental or not. If somebody drugged him and he died, their intentions don't mean a thing to me."

"Nor me," Matsen commiserated.

Cann looked down at the reports. "I've heard of this Rohypnol. It's a powerful sedative, isn't it?"

"Right. A real knock-out drop. A regular Mickey Finn."

Cann smiled inwardly at the archaic reference. But there was nothing amusing about the situation.

"And Dimsen thinks it interacted with this...," he searched the memo for the name of the drug, "...Migramol and killed him?"

"That's what he wants to conclude but he's borderline obsessive about making it definite until he's 100% sure."

286

Cann had a puzzled look on his face. After staring at the documents in his hands for another minute, he looked up at Matsen. "Why were we even looking for another cause of death, Arthur. From what I understand, the injuries from the collision were pretty major. Why did anybody even look for another cause?"

"Gangrene."

"I beg your pardon?"

"Well, all the traumatic injuries were to the torso and the thoracic region but during the autopsy, Dimsen noticed a slight discoloration in Ted's feet. His examination revealed it was the earliest visible stages of gangrene. That raised enough question for him that he decided to run tests he might not otherwise have run." Matsen pointed at the papers in front of Cann. "As you've read, he looked for and found evidence that Ted was dead before the Austin-Healey ever hit the wall."

"And, of course, the fact that somebody - CISP presumably - was around and came up with the idea of making it look like a car accident is just further indication that some sort of foul play was involved." Cann nodded in admiration. "I'm impressed. A lot of doctors would have missed or ignored the discoloration. Ascribed it to lividity or some such thing - whatever lividity is. But now the question is why. I know what Ted was working on..."

"Sure. It was supposed to be your assignment."

Cann flinched again. "Arthur, at one point, Milly implied that Ted's death was my fault because I should have been there and not him. Do you feel that way?" The question was posed without defensiveness or confrontation. Cann really cared what his friend thought.

Matsen was emphatic. "No, John, I absolutely do not feel that way. As the saying goes, shit happens. If you had taken the assignment, Ted might have been killed in a car accident on the beltway."

"Thanks."

"And anyway, we still don't know with absolute certainty that his death is even related to the assignment. A middle eastern connection - to be sure - but the case Ted was on was routine - another IMF loan - a fait accompli. No intrigue. No mystery." Matsen bored his finger into the air, "But, at a minimum, we still owe it to Ted to find out what happened."

Cann agreed.

*   *   *   *

Iverson was still about an hour away from Bad Durkheim when Abel turned off the Baumstrasse in Kaiserslautern into the Arzt Platz where so many physicians had their offices. In the late afternoon, he had expected to see a lot of traffic in the parking area which formed the center of the square around which the various medical arts buildings were located. But it was civilian cars he had expected to see. Not the dozen or so police cars parked at every which angle with their blue lights still going.

"This is not exactly what you would call a 'wary distance', heh, Leider?" The assistant merely nodded.

Abel pulled up to behind the green striped white car that had the stylized crest of the local police chief on the side. He and Leider stepped out and went up to the officer with the highest peak on his cap and showed the chief their credentials. He nodded.

"What has happened?" Abel asked.

The Major of the Kaiserslautern Police replied with deference. "When you called for surveillance this morning we sent cars to observe the front and back of Dr. Quefar's building with instructions - as you said - to observe only and keep their distance. We also put the trap on the phone that you requested." Abel nodded in agreement. That was what he had asked.

"About forty-five minutes ago, however," the local officer went on, "the trap intercepted a call coming in that told the doctor that," he consulted his notes, "'inquiries were being made' and he should 'check to see that there is no connection remaining from recent events.' The caller said he must go at once. And the doctor was out the door in three minutes."

Abel nodded again. "So you decided to move in? Is the doctor inside?"

The major cleared his throat. "No. He is not. I made a judgment, Herr Oberst. I thought it would be best to let him go. I hope you will agree."

The police major advised Abel that since the call did not seem to be ordering Quefar to disappear but only to check on something important, the officer had decided to allow Dr. Quefar to do what he was told to do and see where it would lead. The surveillance teams were ordered to lay back and follow him when he left. The teams had followed Dr. Quefar and an aide to the abandoned airbase outside of Sembach. "It is a little village about..."

"I know of it, Herr Major. Thank you. And I do agree with your decision. You did well." Abel made a mental note to remember this man. Initiative under pressure is rare. "Is Dr. Quefar still at the base, do you know?"

The major made a wry face. "He is now in custody, Herr Abel. My teams managed to remain concealed from his view until he entered the base hospital but they were concerned that he would destroy evidence inside. So they tried to get as close as possible to observe what the doctor was doing inside. As they were maneuvering towards the windows, it seems a group of children began to throw rocks at them and otherwise raise quite a disturbance. The commotion alerted Dr. Quefar who decided to run for his car. My men decided that it would be better to detain him."

"Your men are very well trained, Herr Oberst. This is to your credit. Now I would like to talk to this Dr. Quefar. Will you accompany us? You have been of such assistance already." Abel was quite sincere in his praise.

"For the moment, I would prefer to finish here but please allow me to send a couple of cars to assist you." Abel accepted the offer. The two men shook hands and Abel and Leider turned to go to their car while the local officer waved his hand to signal two cars to go with the Federal Oberst.

Abel turned back to the major. "By the way. Did your trap show where the telephone call came from?"

"But of course, Herr Oberst." He flipped back the pages of his small notebook. "The number was 0271 4936. A Ludwigshafen exchange. Belonging to a company called, 'Ausrustung Klinical, GmbH', a medical supplies company."

*   *   *   *

At 12:30 - five full hours after Matsen had been ordered to get to the White House right away - the President was ready to see him and Cann.

When they walked into the Oval office, the President was sitting behind the desk leaning back with his hands clasped behind his neck, elbows pointing straight out to the sides. He had a slight smile on his face - more of a pleased expression - and he didn't significantly acknowledge Matsen and Cann's entrance into the room. Just a slight nod to Matsen and a stare at Cann.

The room was crowded. Standing directly to the President's left, by the desk, facing the President with his hands folded in front of him and his gaze on the floor, was the Secretary of State. Just to his right and a pace behind him was the Under Secretary for Middle Eastern Affairs who was, at the moment, looking out the window towards the Washington Monument. Also in the room were the National Security Adviser, the Secretary of Defense, and the Director of the Central Intelligence Agency. As always, the Press Secretary and the Vice President were present.

"Thank you for coming, gentlemen. I'd ask you to please be seated but..." He waved around the room to indicate there were no empty chairs.

"As you can see from those whom I have in attendance here, there have been some rather weighty discussions going on in this room this morning." He shifted his gaze to Matsen. "Arthur, I'm sure you realize they are directly related to the Israeli election that is already effectively over." He looked at his watch and did some quick figuring. "The polls will be closing soon but there is no question remaining as to the result."

Matsen nodded.

"I have made no secret of the fact that it has been my sincere belief that the Middle East peace process would have been far better served by a Menahim victory." The President turned an icy stare at Cann. "I am aware that you are - shall we say - unusually close to Lev Shelanu, Cann..."

Cann interrupted. "There's nothing unusual about it, Mr. President. I was with his brother when he died. I've been a friend of the family for years. Even you should be able to understand that."

Cann felt more than saw the sharp turn of Matsen's head at his last remark.

"Well, by unusual I meant that it is unusual for a private citizen to be friends with an elected head of state."

"Perhaps it shouldn't be, Mr. President. Not in a democracy."

Matsen jumped in before the President could explode. "Mr. President. I'm sure we all agree that it is in the best interests of all to wait and see how this election actually affects the peace process. It..."

"We know how it affects the peace process, Arthur. Shelanu has made it clear throughout the campaign that he would grind it to a halt."

"Slow it down maybe - take a closer look at some of the concessions being made." That was Cann.

The President turned to Cann. "Mr. Cann, you seem incapable of following protocol but try to remember you are in the office of the President of the United States - that's me and don't forget it - and until I ask you to speak, kindly keep your mouth shut."

For once, Cann did not retort but he made no effort to hide the cold hard look on his face. Matsen breathed an inward sigh of relief that Cann had restrained himself. But they had a long way to go.

The President took a breath and folded his arms on the desk in front of him looking and sounding as if he was beginning one of his televised speeches. "I am personally confident that I have consistently made it clear that the United States has no desire to intrude into the affairs of another country. However, it seems to me that 'intrusion' can occur not only in the form of criticism and interference but also in the form of contribution and support." He grinned and gave an abrupt nod of his head that indicated 'if that's the way they want it'.

"It now seems clear to me that while successive Israeli governments have welcomed United States aid, the people of Israel themselves appear to consider it something of an intrusion. I have decided therefore that there should be a significant change in our position toward the parties."

"Mr. President." It was Matsen and his voice was somber. "With all due respect, and regardless of any personal affront you may feel at this moment, there is no pressing reason to do anything precipitous. It sounds like you're considering a shut-off of aid to Israel. That would be..."

"Wrong, Arthur. I can't do that without Congress and it would take too long. Oh, I could just stop spending the appropriations but...Events need to be responded to much more quickly."

"I disagree, sir. We have the time. Why not at least wait until you've talked to Shelanu. Man to man."

Cann didn't say any of the things that crossed his mind at that moment.

The President leaned across his desk and jabbed his right index finger into the top of his desk as he spoke. "In my view, it's dangerous to wait. The damage to the relationship between the United States and Israel is irreparable. This election is nothing short of a derailment of the peace process and it will take a bold and dramatic step to force the train back onto the track." The President leaned back in his chair and tossed the pen he was holding onto the desk.

"I have decided to grant full diplomatic recognition to the State of Palestine."

"Oh for Christ's sake," Cann spat out as he shook his head from side to side in utter disgust.

"You have a problem with that, Mr. Cann?" The President smirked at Cann and slowly turned to Matsen who looked like he was choking on something. In a way, he was.

"State of.........Mr. President, what State of Palestine? There isn't one." He looked at the Secretary of State who immediately looked away. "Bart. For god's sake, this is insanity. Haven't you...?"

"It's my decision, Arthur. Don't question him about it." The president adopted a mock conversational tone. "You know, in a way, I'm glad for Shelanu's election."

Cann huffed.

"No really. If this hadn't happened, I probably never would have rethought the relationship between the United States and Israel. Instead of just continuing policy that has been written in stone for fifty years, I looked at it objectively and saw that it's been an entirely one-sided relationship for all that time. We do for them and support them. What has Israel ever done for the United States?"

It was Cann who answered. "They've only been our sole ally in the most persistently volatile region in the world, that's all. And a good friend."

"A good customer, maybe. With money we send them. But not a friend. They've never done anything for us. They didn't even help us out in Vietnam and..."

Cann laughed without humor and more than a touch of contempt. "They helped us more than you did. I can't believe you of all people would bring up Vietnam."

"I bring up whatever it suits me to bring up. And right now I'm bringing up the fact that all we've ever gotten out of our continued support of Israel is the enmity of the rest of the region. And now terrorist attacks that are hitting us at home."

"So throw in the towel? Is that what this is about? Surrendering to terrorism." He emitted a scornful grunt. "Why am I not surprised?"

"It is about leveling the playing field, Mr. Cann. It is now the official position of the United States of America that we have heretofore taken a much too one-sided stance in the area. Henceforth, that will change."

"You're not going to level any playing field. You'll probably level the Middle East."

"By forcing peace on an intransigent Israel? I don't think so, Cann. Israel will just have to accept this. What can they do?"

"It's not what they *can* do, it's what they'll have to do."

"Like what? What's that supposed to mean?"

Cann lectured the President. "If you do this, every Arab state will feel compelled to immediately follow suit. Even if they don't want to, they'll have to. It's what they've screamed about for all these years. And all the accords and treaties of the last several years between them and Israel will go by the boards. In one stroke, you will have re-united the Arab world against Israel and gutted the heart of a country that has always been a good friend. You, Mr. President, will have destroyed the peace process - not the election of Lev Shelanu."

"But that's not how the American people will see it."

"They're not as stupid as you think they are."

"Sure they are. But even if they're not, the press will portray this as a bold move on my part. No matter what happens, they'll treat it as a master diplomatic stroke. If Shelanu toes the line and accepts this development, I get credit for moving the process forward a hundredfold. If there's any damage to the peace process, it'll be blamed on Shelanu's intransigence. "

"And if there's a war. What about the people who die?"

"I don't believe that will happen. But, either way - with or without an Israel - there will be peace."

That statement stated so cavalierly almost stripped Cann of the restraint developed over thirty years of training and discipline. He and the President stared at each other for a long moment, Cann's eyes growing cold and deep. The President's look was one of mocking smugness - the look of a man who feared his opponent but knew he couldn't be reached.

Cann decided to try another tack. He took a deep breath before he went on. "Just where is this State of Palestine you're about to recognize?"

"Right where they say it is now." He pointed to the shaded area in the central part of Israel that was labeled 'Proposed Palestinian State'.

Cann continued. "I assume you know that's still part of Israel. And it's not yours to give away."

"But historically it was the country of Palestine."

"No, Mister President." Cann contemptuously overarticulated the title which did not go unnoticed by anyone in the room. "Historically, there was never an organized fixed political entity called Palestine. It was a region that corresponded with Israeli territory and a lot more that was - or is - part of the other Arab countries. Why don't you give the Palestinians some of those countries too, if you're sincere in what you say." He looked around the room at the advisers. "Haven't any of you bothered to tell him even the basics of the region's history?"

The Under Secretary for Middle Eastern Affairs mumbled, "He knows," earning a hard stare from the President. She went back to looking out the window.

Up to that point in the conversation, Cann was operating on a sort of automatic pilot. He knew that he was being played with and that what he was doing and saying would be ignored. But every time the President stated a point, Cann was unable to keep from responding. Finally, the futility of the exercise took over and he put up his hands.

"Look. Why am I even at this meeting? You certainly don't need my approval and you're obviously not looking for it. Why am I here?"

"Because I know how buddy-buddy you are with Shelanu and that you'll run out of here and call him as soon as you get the chance."

Cann shook his head. "Why would I? He'll get the message through normal diplomatic channels and - despite what you think - he doesn't consult with me on policy."

"Maybe. Maybe not." The President was thoroughly enjoying himself at Cann's - and in Cann's opinion - Israel's expense. "If you don't call him, he'll call you - after he hears you were at this meeting. And he will hear about that. And when he calls, you can tell him - as his bosom friend - that he should make no mistake. This is personal."

Cann wanted to just walk out but the setting demanded a minimal adherence to protocol that only barely overcame his anger. "Personal? Then meet him face to face." Cann laughed mirthlessly. "But that wouldn't even occur to you, would it." Cann shook his head for the umpteenth time in this relatively brief meeting. "This is crazy. The man ran for office in his own country - and won. What did you want him to do. Clear his candidacy with you before he ran?"

"Well, obviously it's too late for that, of course." The President put an expression of feigned earnestness on his face. "But he could resign before he gets sworn in. He could say that the campaign took too much out..."

That was too much even for the constraints of protocol. "You're out of your fucking mind." Cann made a quick move that was nothing more than the beginning of a turn to leave the room. But it made the President flinch in his chair behind the desk.

"Keep still, Mr. Cann. You're making these fine Secret Service gentlemen a little nervous." Actually, the trained guards had not been unduly alarmed by Cann's movement. "This may even work out for the best. Bold moves are always risky."

"Of course, once you've determined that all the risks are to other people."

"Knock it off." The President was stung partly by the barb but mostly by his inability to cow the man across from him. "Once again I find that you have trouble understanding where your loyalties properly lie."

Cann grew icier by the minute. "My loyalties have never been questioned and you certainly don't have the credentials to do it."

"Careful, Cann. You're on thin ice. Don't forget who you're talking to." He smiled and said, "Maybe I'll just have you locked up for a while - an unregistered agent of a foreign power. How does that sound?"

Cann raised his eyebrows and looked coldly at the President.

The President continued. "We have a nice holding cell in the basement and I'll see to it that you're tossed in there until you learn to show the proper respect."

"Mr. President, I believe that I'm showing you all the respect you deserve."

Matsen interjected quickly. "Mr. President. Stop and think for a moment about what you're doing. You're about to desert one of the United States' oldest allies - in this century anyway. And side with a people who - rightly or wrongly - will never accept America as a friend. We will be accepted as a benefactor perhaps - but never a friend. The hatred goes back too far. In doing this, you're disregarding what I am convinced is the unified opposition of your advisers - never a wise move. And now, you are threatening the summary confinement of a private citizen of this country for disagreeing with you?"

"When such disagreement impairs our national security, then I shall do what is required of me. As I see fit. And that includes throwing this guy's ass in the can - no pun intended."

Cann continued to stare at the President with an odd smile on his face as he spoke to Matsen. "What do you figure, Arthur? Can he do that?"

Matsen also looked at the President while he spoke to Cann. "It's probably the most unwise thing I've ever heard a President say, John, and that covers a lot of ground. But," he never took his eyes off the President, "the Secret Service does take its orders directly from the President and I suspect that if he tells that rather large gentleman standing in the corner to take you downstairs and lock you up, the large gentleman will be inclined to seek to comply."

The President grinned even wider at Cann.

"And we all know that he would be unsuccessful in his attempt if you did not wish to comply."

The President's expression soured appreciably.

"But being the gentleman - and loyal citizen - that you are, I suspect you would go quietly, would you not?"

"Yes, I would," Cann agreed.

"And, of course, I would have you out of there by writ of habeus corpus issued by any one of nine justices of the United States Supreme Court within fifteen minutes. Unless our President wished to have a nice big fat constitutional crisis on his hands."

The President was red-faced at this mockery by Cann and Matsen. "So maybe I'll put you in with him, Arthur." The President smiled and Matsen glared. There was silence as the standoff lingered. Finally, the President waved his hands in front of his face and said, "Look, I have no intention of locking anyone up. But don't think I can't. The fact is my preference is for the two of you to be out of the White House immediately. I have business to attend to." He stood up and looked at Cann. "So do you." Then he announced to no one in particular, "The meeting's over. You're excused," and turned and walked out the door without looking back.

Chapter Twenty-Three

Iverson had made good time and was approaching the Grunstadt exit off Autobahn 6 just north of Bad Durkheim when he decided to confirm Abel's location. He assumed Abel was still in Bad Durkhein but in fact the German official's cellular phone twittered just as he was getting into it to drive from Kaiserslautern to Sembach.

"No, Brian, I left Bad Durkheim some time ago and am now leaving Kaiserslautern for Sembach." Abel related in some detail what he had found so far that day and what he soon hoped to accomplish by learning everything that Dr. Quefar could tell him.

"Don't bother with Bad Durkhein, Brian. I think it is better if we conclude this together."

"Conclude?"

"Yes. I think we are that close. At least to finding out what happened to Herr Wagner. It would help if you are present when I meet with Dr. Quefar."

If that was Abel's opinion, it was good enough for Iverson. "Where are you?"

"At the moment, I am in Kaiserslautern but we are leaving for the air base above Sembach. Do you know it?"

"I've never seen it but I've been told where it is."

"Good. Just stay on Autobahn 6 and get off at Kaiserslautern. Go north on N40 and then through the village and up the hill. You will see the airbase from there."

It took Iverson less than an hour to get to the village of Sembach. As he approached he found himself heading directly at the vee-shape that had cost Wagner his life. Or rather where the accident was staged. He bore right off N40 and headed up the slight incline through the village. At the far end of the village, he turned right and up ahead off to the left saw the cluster of buildings at the top of the hill that was the former military installation. He drove a short distance more then turned left onto the sloping approach road that led to the main gate of the base. He drove through the untended entrance and up the road to the second right as Abel had instructed. As he turned onto the street where the hospital was Iverson saw the small cluster of police cars parked in front of the glass doors.

As he turned off the ignition and started to get out of the car, he was startled by a sharp bang on the side of the car and, by habit and instinct, dropped to one knee inside the open door and placed his hand on his sidearm but didn't take it out. He could see nothing and as he scanned the area, he heard Abels's voice behind him.

"The children are throwing stones, Brian. Come in. But do it quickly."

Iverson turned toward the hospital building and trotted to the doors and went inside. "What's all that about, Gunther."

"The children have seen Dr. Quefar in our custody and they have decided to show their displeasure. One child shouted at us they would have their own 'intifada' right here. It is not serious but watch your head when you go out."

Iverson stood by the door with Abel and Leider and looked across the central reception area at the four uniformed city police who were on either side of a small moustachioed and handcuffed man standing against the wall. "Dr. Quefar, I presume," he said quietly to Abel.

"Yes. The rather uncommunicative Dr. Quefar as a matter of fact. How is your Israeli accent, Brian?"

"Good, Gunther, quite good, I think." Abel grinned slightly and nodded. The two men walked over to Dr. Quefar. Abel spoke to the man in German.

"Dr. Quefar. We are really quite anxious to get answers to our questions. Are you willing to cooperate?"

The physician did not appear arrogant but simply shook his head.

"Schade. Pity. We are quite pressed for time and I fear we must be on our way. We have several leads to look into. You will be taken into federal custody at this point and we will expect you to confirm our findings for us when we have completed our investigations. Do you understand that?"

Quefar just stared.

"In the meantime, we are - as you can see," he waved his hand around the room at the seven men gathered around the lone individual, "quite short handed." The physician's eyes narrowed at that."And so we will ask our good friend here to take care of you for us." He pointed toward Iverson. "Perhaps you will be more comfortable with him."

Iverson smiled and nodded at Quefar and said, "I am sure we will become very good friends." He spoke in fluent Arabic with a purposely discernible Israeli accent.

Quefar blanched.

The group of police gathered themselves around the doctor so that he could barely be seen. They exited the building and walked Quefar to Iverson's car moving quickly to get to the car before the shower of stones began to fall. They shoved the physician in through the driver's side door and across to the front passenger seat. Leider followed quickly into the driver's seat and Iverson got in the back seat and slid over to where he was directly behind Quefar. "Eyes front," he barked. Quefar was familiar with the circumstances and wondered if he would feel the bullet when it penetrated his skull.

* * * *

301

Ramadan Al-Asif was in the stairwell of the Sanger Building peering between the frame and the exit door that he was holding open just a crack. He could see down the hallway to Caroline Klein's office where a uniformed police officer was standing outside the open door. Al-Asif had been on his way to discuss the previous day's hearing with her when he saw the officer and, out of caution or premonition, - he wasn't sure which - he ducked into the stairwell to observe what he could.

After several minutes, a man in a suit came out of the office and came down the hall. The uniformed officer reached in and closed the door to Klein's office and followed the plain-clothes detective. Al-Asif gently closed the stairwell door and waited until he was sure they had passed then slowly opened it. He took pains to ensure that the hallway was clear and then walked to Klein's office and went in.

She was sitting at her desk with her face in her hands and looked up as Al-Asif walked in. He had never seen her look the way she did. Her hair was stringy and her eyes seemed to have sunk deep into the sockets so that they looked almost blackened. In the past, the angularities in the shape of her face had given her a sculptured classicism whereas now she looked merely craggy.

"What's wrong, Caroline? Was that the police I just saw leaving?" He knew of course that it was.

"The system thinks it'll beat me." She said this to no one in particular and then focused on Al-Asif's face. "All my life I've fought the system and now they think they're going to take me down. Not me."

"Caroline, what did the police want?"

"I don't care what they want, Ram. How do I make that clear to you - and them and everybody else. Somebody thinks they can pull a fast one on me. It's Cann. I know it. He thinks I'll just slink away in defeat after last night. No way."

"What does that have to do with the police being here." Impatience was uncharacteristically evident in Al-Asif's voice.

"They're looking for the kid," Klein finally said.

"What kid?" Al-Asif really didn't know what she was talking about.

But Klein was back to her own issues. "First the university pulls the rug out from under me on the hearing. But no, that's not enough. They accuse me of fraud and deception and that bitch Buffinton even threatens my job. Me? Do you believe it?" She didn't wait for an answer to the question. "Then Cann pulls his smug little fascist display of testosterone overdose and those cowards who've always come to me when they need something slink away and hang me out to dry." She glared. "You're one of them, Ram. You were there and you didn't help. That makes you part of the problem. I won't forget it."

"Caroline..."

"Shut up. I know where your skeletons are too."

"Caroline you said that last night, too, and it concerns me. That's why I am here. I need to know what..."

"And then this morning that little she-jock shit Furden calls me up and starts asking me about the kid - like where is she? Did I do anything to her? Did I know she was missing? God damn. Like I'm going to waste my energies on that. I'll save my guns for the big boys. I always have."

"Caroline, what 'kid' are you talking about? Who is missing?"

Klein gave Al-Asif a sneering look and said nothing.

"God damn it, Caroline, answer me." He slammed his fist onto the desk.

Klein looked surprised but not frightened. "Get the fuck out of here. Who do you think you're talking too?" She snorted. "Oh I get it. You think I'm vulnerable now, too. So you're going to join in the feeding frenzy. Well, I'm top shark here, Abdul. You're the one who's going to get eaten."

"Meaning what? I'm trying to tell you Caroline that you should not make threats that have consequences you cannot imagine." Al-Asif spoke quietly. "Now, please. I'm losing my patience. Answer my question."

Klein emitted a derisive laugh. "Or what, Abdul?"

Al-Asif shook his head. "You stupid woman." The way he said it, it was obvious that he intended the word 'woman' to be the insult. Klein swung her open palm at him but he just pulled his head back a short distance and the attempt at a slap missed. Then, in a single set of motions that didn't take more than a second, Al-Asif reached his left hand behind Klein's head and pulled it towards him. At the same instant, with his right hand, he picked up the letter opener that was on her desk and pressed it against the white of her right eye just hard enough to cause the vitreous fluid to begin to seep out. "What kid, Caroline?"

Klein still didn't say anything but now it was because of shock. First it was the shock of him even challenging her. That was quickly followed by her shock at his physical strength and then at the realization of what he was actually doing. Even so, she still started to give him an abrasive answer when she felt some liquid running down her cheek. She thought it was blood and, for a second grew angry again. For the briefest of seconds, her impulse - born of habit - was to challenge. To characterize his use of violence as evidence of his inneffectiveness in otherwise presenting his position. It had always worked before. But she had never really been in physical danger before. Now - finally - she realized that she truly was in physical danger.

She answered. "Jane Reston. The student who was supposed to have the hearing last night. Apparently she's missing." Her voice was a whisper. 'Once he let her go,' she was thinking, 'she would have his ass in court and off the campus. He wouldn't get away with this.' Unfortunately for her, Al-Asif knew that was what she would be thinking.

"Jane Reston. Cann's student friend - or client?" He frowned. "What does she look like?"

"Average. She's an average, cute kid. Sandy hair, medium height, medium build, attractive. She's got kind of a baby face but the rest of her is grown up."

The description could fit any number of female students, Al-Asif knew. But he also knew - just somehow knew - that the girl at the house was this Jane Reston. 'In the name of Allah. How could this be? All his plans...'

"Thank you, Caroline. You should have told me this sooner. There was no need for this violence." Al-Asif's tone was condescending.

"Fuck you."

Al-Asif shook his head. She couldn't control her mouth even now. He wasn't really angry. But he knew she was out of control. And too many other things were starting to go wrong. He couldn't risk the attention she would surely bring and decisive action was appropriate. And besides, the months of insults and condescension had to have a price, after all.

Al-Asif took the point of the letter opener away from Klein's eye and inserted it straight into her jugular vein, giving it a slight twist to enlarge the hole in her neck so that the blood would flow more freely out of it. He quickly arranged Klein in a sitting position inside the kneehole of the desk and arranged her so that the blood ran out of her neck and onto her right shoulder and down her arm which he placed into the trash can under the desk. He watched for a second to make sure that the rivulet was flowing as desired and then adjusted Klein so that she would stay in the position until the flow stopped.

He put the letter opener directly into his pants pocket without wiping off the blood on anything. He picked up Klein's purse and dug out her keys. Then after a long look around the room, he left making sure the door was locked behind him.

*　*　*　*

As they left the White House, Cann and Matsen exchanged very few words. They knew each other's thoughts on what had just occurred and knew that their views were in agreement. They rode back to the offices of Loring Matsen in silence, each absorbed in his own thoughts.

Although it had been several months since Cann had been in the Loring Matsen office building, it didn't feel like it. His appearance caused a small stir as several people came up to say hello and tell him he'd been missed. He went out of his way to say hello to Milly in her office and then walked down the hall to his own. It was undisturbed despite his leave of absence and he was immediately comfortable as he sat in his own chair and reached for the phone.

He didn't need to look up the number before he placed a call to Tip-Top Temps, a temporary employment service located in Alexandria. He left the usual message that he was in need of some clerical help for a short period of time and that language skills - unspecified - were more important than typing abilities. The person at the temporary agency - perhaps new - tried to correct Cann, telling him that it sounded like he wanted a translator or interpreter, not clerical help. Cann insisted that the message was exactly as he had stated it and that it be given directly to Mister Goren. He had always dealt with Mr. Goren and he would understand. He left the number of his private direct outside line for a return call.

Cann knew that there was no certainty that Goren was around or even in the country and there was no certainty of an immediate return call even if he was, but he wanted to wait - for a while at least - before leaving his office. He leaned back in his chair and spun himself around and put his feet up on the sill of the window that looked out over the beltway. The position reminded him of the events of a Sunday night less than two weeks before.

*   *   *   *

Ramadan Al-Asif had gone directly from Klein's office to the Office of the University Registrar. As a faculty member, he had access to the student files which included application materials among the other records. He requested Janie Reston's packet and when it came he went straight to the application form itself with the small passport sized photograph stapled to it.

Damn it!

He forced himself to observe the campus speed limits as he drove back to the house. He turned right on Rasen Street and accelerated the short distance to the driveway and then turned hard right into it and slid to a halt on the dirt.

All five men were in the house. Massoud was in the study and jumped up and ran to the window when he heard the vehicle in the driveway. He knew from the facial expression and purposeful walk that the chief was displeased about something. He hurried to the door and opened it just as Al-Asif reached it and pushed his way in past Massoud asking, "Where is the girl?"

Massoud pointed to his right. "In the game room - with the others."

Al-Asif walked straight into the game room and looked around. Sami was seated in one of the easy chairs absently flipping through a magazine. Basheer was reading a book. Abdullah was stretched out on the couch apparently sleeping and Naji was seated on the rail of the pool table absently throwing the cue ball and watching it bounce from bank to bank to bank.

Janie was sitting up in another of the easy chairs in the room still naked and with her head tilted to the right side and down on her right shoulder. She looked as if she had been dropped into the chair and her arms dangled over either side of the chair. Her legs were out in front of her and bent with the knees pointing away from each other so that her thighs were wide open. Al-Asif noted with indifference the bruises on her face and body and a trickle of blood running out of her vagina.

Three of the men looked up as the chief walked over to the rack on the wall which held the pool cue sticks. Basheer didn't move on the couch. Al-Asif absently picked out one of the pool cues and twirled it in his fingers like a long narrow baton. Then he began to unscrew the two halves of the custom-made stick as he spoke. "We have work to do, gentlemen." His voice caused Basheer to jump up and look around blankly until his sleep-induced disorientation disappeared.

"An assignment?" Sami offered brightly.

"Unfortunately not," Al-Asif answered. "We must again do some cleaning up just to protect what we already have. It seems that Yousef continues to draw attention to us even in death."

The other five men said nothing and Al-Asif continued. "Yousef's little gift to us," he tossed his head at Janie, "comes with some complications. She is close to a man who I have long felt is a threat to our network - a man whom I suspect is not what he claims to be. I fear that this...girl's presence here may bring us unwanted attention. And anything...," his voice rose sharply, "anything that brings us to such attention is a threat to the cause. And this," he turned and viciously whipped the thick end of the pool cue into the left side of Janie's face leaving an impression of the carved design on its handle in her cheek, "brings attention to us."

He was working himself into a rage. "Unbelievably, gentlemen, this is the second incident today which forces me to deal with threats of exposure. But - make no mistake - I do not shrink from it." He walked over and stood next to the chair where Janie was sprawled. "I do not shrink from any of my responsibilities to the cause or anything required to protect the cause." This time he laid the handle of pool cue violently across Janie's thighs leaving a thick red welt running across each leg. No one noticed the slight grimace as Janie's mouth tightened almost imperceptibly as the pain penetrated her stupor.

Al-Asif walked back and forth between the pool table and Janie as he continued to rant. "I should have killed Yousef much sooner. But now, seeing the danger he saw fit to bring, I regret that he is already dead because I would do these things to him and more." He lashed Janie across the stomach leaving another welt as his voice grew in a crescendo of hate. "I will let nothing interfere with what I have built. Nothing." By this time he was screaming. He literally jumped off his feet as he turned and lashed the thin end of the pool cue across Janie's breasts. The skin broke and there was a wide red line of blood that ran all the way across her chest from armpit to armpit. No one saw the single tear that ran out of the corner of Janie's eye and on to her cheek.

Al-Asif tossed the two halves of the cue stick onto the pool table. He spoke more softly now but his anger was hardly suppressed. "This thing," he indicated Janie, "cannot stay here. There must be another accident - away from here." He picked up the cue ball and tossed it and caught it it his right hand over and over as he spoke. "A non-survivable accident with severe injuries gentlemen. Very severe." He spun again and smashed Janie's face with the cue ball. Then he did it again and then again a third time finally succeeding in crushing her cheek bone. Then he stopped and tossed the ball onto the table. "We will dispose of her after dark. In the meantime, have your fun with her," he looked down at the bloody mess and smirked, "if you can stand it." He strode out of the room tossing his head to signal Massoud to follow him.

When they were alone in the study, Al-Asif reached in his pocket and took out Klein's keys. "There is another item that must be cleaned up, Massoud." The second in command nodded.

Al-Asif explained to him what had occurred in Klein's office and directed him to clean up that scene and dispose of Klein body - separate from Janie's. Two distinct accidents. The chief was gaining control now but still angry at the series of events that was threatening his network. "How can this be. Just as I succeed in ridding us of Cann, this will bring him back. Kismet curses me, Massoud." He waved his hand dismissively. "But we can only deal with situations as they are."

Massoud expressed his disagreement with the chief's orders. "We must handle this differently than Yousef's death. We cannot continue to have these accidents occurring like this. This will be three in two days. That alone will raise suspicion - bring unwanted attention."

Al-Asif nodded. "What do you suggest?"

"I will make the bodies disappear. Let me take care of it. Nothing will be found. And if there is no evidence, there can be no connection."

"No, Massoud. If they disappear completely, the police - and Cann - will look everywhere, including at us." He repeated himself. "No. They must be found so that the cases can be closed."

He thought for a moment. "All right. Yousef is in the quarry and may never be found. Let there be a single accident this time - where both of these women are killed. The mystery of why Klein and the girl were together will even help to obscure our involvement. The authorities will expend much energy on trying to figure that part out. And," he brightened as he recalled the aborted disciplinary meeting of the night before, "Klein actually threatened the girl to Cann at the meeting. Yes. This is ideal. Dispose of them together. In Klein's vehicle. A fiery crash. Yes. Yes. That will do nicely." He flipped his hand at Massoud to dismiss him. "You still have a couple of hours before dark. Go. Go. Prepare."

* * * *

The phone on Cann's desk rang and the red button indicating his private line lit up. Rather than activate the speaker phone function, he picked up the receiver but said nothing.

A voice at the other end said, "I am returning a call to Mr. Black."

"This is John Cann, Zvi. Thank's for returning my call."

"Of course, John. And of course I knew whom I was calling. How have you been?"

The two men chatted amiably for just a couple of sentences before Goren got to business. "I'm happy to hear that you are well - and supportive of our recent election. Does your call have anything to do with that?"

"No. Not really. Though..." For a moment, Cann considered telling the Israeli agent about the White House meeting. He decided that it was out of order at this time. In fact, he hadn't decided what - if anything - he would do about it at all.

"No, Zvi. We need some information about a group here in the US that we thought you might have kept an eye on."

Goren said nothing at the other end of the line. Then he spoke. "Is this line secure, John?"

"Yes. And I can go on scrambler, too, if you like."

"Why don't we. Yes."

There was the usual minute of screeches and other high-pitched electronic noises as the respective devices activated. When the noises ended, it was Zvi Goren who spoke first. "All right, John, what group are we talking about? But please understand, while you are personally held in the highest regard, we are officially forbidden to reveal information considered vital to Israel. It is a shame. I miss the old days of cooperation."

"I know. A lot of people do. And I understand your position. But let's see what you're comfortable with. The group is CISP - the Committee for the International Support of Palestine."

There was only a brief moment of silence before Goren said, "We are aware of it." Cann knew this meant they were watching it. "A fund-raiser and a research operation." Another moment of hesitation. "Also a front."

"For whom."

"Does it matter?" It was an uncharacteristically flippant answer from the serious security man at the other end of the line and it caught Cann's attention.

"What does that mean, Zvi."

"Just that as far as we can tell, it's being set up as a network for any group that wants to use it. As far as we have determined, it is just now being organized. It is to be a - what was that thing in your history? An underground railroad. For operatives - terrorists. As far as we can tell, it hasn't been involved in any operations to date except for the..."

"What?"

A long pause. "I am growing less comfortable with this conversation, John." But he went on anyway. "We feel that they may have aided the escape of one of the operatives in the New York incident. As far as we know, they were not involved in the planning. And wouldn't be. Their role is anticipated to be in logistics - hiding and moving the tools of the trade."

"Do you have assets in there?" Cann had barely concluded the sentence when he shouted, "No. Forget I said that. Please forgive me, Zvi. I'm rusty. I don't want to know." Cann had asked the unaskable and, if it had been anyone else but Cann, Goren would have terminated the conversation without another word and never taken another call from the asker.

"Yes, you are rusty, John." That was all he said about it. "But perhaps we might count on you to be an asset of sorts for us?" It was a question. A recruitment question.

Cann was thoroughly confused by that. "What does that mean, Zvi. I'm always an ally. You know that. But I don't know anything about this CISP - other than what you're telling me now."

Goren was speaking slowly now. Leading up to something. The two men began to engage in a sort of tradecraft two-step.

"Are you saying you're not watching them yourselves, John?"

"No. I mean yes, that's what I'm saying. The first time I ever heard of them was this morning when Arthur asked me about them. No. I take that back, I'd heard of them. But that's it. Prior to today, as far as I knew, they were what they said they were. Except that nobody ever is."

Goren waited a few seconds before replying. "I didn't think I would ever say this, John, but I'm not sure I can believe you on this. You must be open with me. What was it that Arthur asked about."

Cann was too confused to be angry at the implication regarding his credibility. He explained in total detail his conversation of the morning and the investigation into Wagner's death. "...That's where CISP came in and I told Arthur that I would try to find out who they are."

This time Goren hesitated for a very long moment after Cann stopped speaking and Cann didn't interrupt his thoughts. Finally, Goren said, "Let me give you some detail on this, John. But it didn't come from me."

"Understood."

Mostly, he listened, but Cann took some notes as Goren explained how CISP was the creation of one Ali Hamahni - 'an interesting chap' was the way Goren put it.

"At the beginning, he was involved in the formation of the PFLP - even involved himself in his younger days with the planning - and reportedly on occasion - the execution of some terrorist operations. When Fatah and PFLP and DFLP and the other Palestinian groups decided to unite under the PLO umbrella, he stayed with the PFLP. As you know, Arafat assumed the leadership of the PLO and Hamahni started trying to curry favor with him - even claimed to have seen the light in regard to peace over terrorism. So when Arafat turned to his so-called peace initiatives, Hamahni followed him and for that was expelled from the PFLP which wanted no part of peace. Our own opinion is that Hamahni is an opportunist who likes the limelight and recognized Arafat as the wagon to hitch his star to. His present activities show that he never completely renounced terror.

Arafat used him - and not in a bad sense. He really listened to Hamanhi's counsel which seems to have been of genuine value to Arafat in the peace initiatives. Although not as much as Hamanhi himself would claim to have had. The man has some delusions of grandeur. But he contributed. No question.

In spite of that, the rest of the PLO Council didn't trust him - or resented his closeness to Arafat - and he was never officially accepted into the leadership of the PLO. That was a real disappointment to him. His dream was to be liaison with Washington when they recognized the PLO. But it didn't happen. Ever since he's been on the edges of the PLO which wouldn't take him in and with the PFLP which wouldn't take him back.

So he ended up playing the game at both ends. The action groups look at CISP as a player - a logistical support asset for their operations. At the same time, Hamanhi plays at the role of peacemaker. Believe it or not, there are some people who think that Hamanhi has successfully convinced Arafat that CISP is a genuine research organization that's just waiting for relations to be established at which time it will be in place to make a contribtuion. Most of us - and I know this includes you, John - figure Arafat knows what Hamanhi's doing but, of course, deniability is everything and everywhere.

What you may find most interesting - and this is the basis of my previous inquiry to you - is that the logistical support network that Hamahni is building is intended to be nationwide and involves the use of academic institutions - specifically Middle Eastern Studies Departments. The perfect cover, don't you think? Is this starting to mean something?"

It was. Cann frowned but didn't answer.

"They have begun several bases of operation around the country and have just completed setting up the first unit of the network at... Care to guess where, John?"

No response.

"Oh, yes. Charlestown University. Now do you see why we think you have been involved in this for some time. And could perhaps be of assistance to us?"

Cann spoke in measured tones. "Zvi, you may not believe this...I'm not sure I would if I were you...but my presence at Charlestown is coincidental. I didn't know and I wasn't looking for anything." He thought for a moment. "So this guy Al-Asif...?"

"Hamahni's second-in-command. His organizer and hatchet man. We know you have met him. What did you think of him?"

"Well, I only chatted with him briefly at the new faculty reception. I can tell you that nothing tipped me off about him. He comes across as a timid sort of academic. No big surprise there, I guess, if he's any good at what he does."

"Yes. He is a chameleon. But make no mistake, he is a textbook sociopath and capable of anything. There is no absolute right and wrong. Only what is good for him at the moment."

"Is there anything you can tell me about what they're up to now?"

Goren thought about his answer before he gave it. "They have just welcomed some faculty to the newly approved department. As far as we know, there are no operations in motion but..."

"But?"

Goren spoke even more slowly now. "John, I absolutely should not tell you what I am about to. It reveals more than the words say. If it was anyone else but you..."

Cann said nothing. It was up to Goren to decide.

314

"There has been some turmoil in their unit. We know..." He hesitated. "Last night they killed..........someone. Use this information as you will but it didn't come from me. There is a taxicab in a quarry eleven miles west of the campus. It contains two bodies. One is a civilian but the other is a player who is of interest to your authorities. And there is still tension in the house. They are having problems."

"How do you....?" Damn it! Cann caught himself again. That was the second time that he almost broke the unbreakable rule. By telling him such up to date and inside information, Goren had already implicitly revealed that the Mossad had an asset in the CISP organization. To reveal that to Cann was a sign of the utmost trust. For him to again ask...

Even though Cann wanted to know more, he knew it was time to terminate the conversation.

"Thank you, Zvi. For everything. One more thing. Do you have descriptions of the CISP people at Charlestown. I'd..."

Goren interrupted with irritation. "You really presume on our friendship, John. You know that don't you?"

"Yes, Zvi. I appreciate your position, believe me. But we've lost one of ours and the trail leads to these guys. Can you help?"

"I think that I need my head inspected - or examined I guess is the phrase." He expelled some air. "Plug your fax into your secure line and I will fax you photographs of the players." His anger was gone and Cann could tell that he was now only feigning irritation. "May I go now, before you ask me for my shoe size?"

"Of course, Zvi. Thank you again. I owe you."

"Indeed you do. I expect you to share whatever you learn with me. Do I have your word on that?"

"You do, my friend. You have my word."

Goren was satisfied with that.

Chapter Twenty-Four

It was almost 11:00 PM in Jerusalem as Benjamin Menahim slid
the copy of the diplomatic dispatch across the conference table in
his office. Lev Shelanu picked it up and read it carefully without
apparent reaction. When he was finished, he turned a superficially
expressionless gaze upon the soon to be former Prime Minister of
Israel and simply said, "Did you have any idea?"

"Of course not, Lev. This is betrayal of the worst kind. I would
never have..."

"I know." Shelanu shook his head at his own question. "I
shouldn't have even asked, Ben."

The two men sat in silence for a moment. Finally Shelanu said,
"Have you told the cabinet?"

"Not yet. I wanted you to see it first."

Shelanu was dumbfounded by the unthinkable nature of what
he had read. "We'll have to prepare the armed forces - and the
country - for the worst. We can't let this happen. If we accept this,
we no longer have a country."

Menahim looked across at Shelanu. "That is not precisely true.
We can negotiate..."

"If the United States - or anyone else - thinks and acts like they
can give away a portion of what we - as a sovereign nation -
consider part of our nation, we no longer have a say in our
destiny. That's the same as not having a country. Good god, Ben,
it's not even the Golan he thinks he can give away. This is

Jerusalem. We have been left with nothing to negotiate. Even if we wanted to do that." Shelanu's mind was racing from cause to effect to consequence, one after the other. "Just imagine. Israelis would need visas issued by the PLO just to visit our holy places. That is unthinkable."

"I must believe that any diplomatic recognition would be conditioned on guarantees against such things. I cannot..."

Shelanu tossed the dispatch onto the conference table where it slid across to Manahim. "Here is what guarantees mean, Ben. What good are guarantees except those we can enforce ourselves. We are alone."

The older man nodded. "Yes, I know. There aren't any alternatives now. There's no longer any need for the United States to worry about what the other side will do. In the old days, we were at least a chip in the big game, as the Americans were so fond of saying. But, I must tell you. This was something I feared might happen. One of the unpleasant - for us at least - consequences of the end of the cold war. Back then, it was the uncertainty alone that would have prevented this. Now we don't even have the Soviet Union to turn to. Not that I would. "

"Nor I, Ben. Nor I." They fell silent again. Then Shelanu shook his head. "Who do you think will stand with us? Anyone?"

"England? Germany, almost certainly. How ironic, heh?" Both men smiled sardonically. "Not France, that's for sure. Nor Italy. Maybe the rest of Europe - Western Europe, anyway. I don't know. Not Eastern Europe, for sure. Little if any of the Third World. Not South America. Canada maybe." Menahim shrugged. "In Asia? China? - no. India? - no. Japan? It depends on the economics. But any of the 'support' we get will not be of the kind that will deter Assad from the Golan - and our very heartland if he thinks he can take it. He'll see this as a blank check."

"Why not? That's what it is. And a stab in the back."

Shelanu looked across the table at the man some thirty years his senior with a mix of respect and affection. Notwithstanding the occasional acrimony of the just finished campaign, Shelanu knew the man before him as the patriot he was. Shelanu actually regretted the magnitude of his margin of victory in the election. That had to have hurt. He spoke gently to Menahim. "You were here at the beginning, Ben. Is this how it ends?"

Menahim simply couldn't speak for a long moment. Then he said. "I don't know, Lev. I don't know. Shame on me perhaps but this is a question I never allowed myself to ask. I never even wondered how long Israel would exist. It's my country. Our country. I never thought my own life span would exceed that of the country we love."

* * * *

Cann was leaning back in his chair studying the images that had just come in from Zvi Goren. Possessed of a near total recall, he would remember them and filed them in his mind with the information he had just received. He was mentally collating everything when the intercom buzzed and the girl on the desk said, "Mr. Matsen would like to know if you could join him in Conference Room B, Mr. Cann."

"Please tell him I'll be right there."

All the conference rooms in the Loring Matsen offices had the glass walls on the hallway side that allowed the passerby to see - but not hear - what was going on inside. The glass walls also had full length blinds that could be lowered for privacy but they were rarely used - most depositions and meetings look alike to those who can't hear what is being said. The same couldn't usually be said for the frequent divorce and property settlement confrontations that took place - the blinds were often closed for those.

The blinds were open as Cann approached and he could see Arthur Matsen sitting inside at the head of the table with papers strewn about in front of him. The thick glass door opened with a slight whoosh as Cann went in.

"Thanks for coming, John." Cann smiled inwardly. For as long as they had known each other - and given their relative positions in the hierarchy in both the firm and the world at large - Matsen was unfailingly polite and gracious.

Cann assumed that he had been called in to report what he had learned about CISP but before he could start to speak, Matsen turned in his chair and reached for the intercom on the table against the wall behind him. He pressed the button and said, "Please put the call through to Mr. Iverson, would you, Libby. Transfer it in here when it's ready." He turned back to Cann.

"Well, we know how Ted died, now." He was holding the latest report from Iverson received by fax within the half hour. "We still don't know why. But let's see what we can put together from all of this." He waved his hand at the papers on the table.

Both men had read all of the earlier reports from Iverson and were familiar with the details of the investigation. Now Cann was reading the direct evidence of specific occurrences received from a suddenly cooperative - and very frightened - Dr. Quefar who had been an eyewitness to Wagner's death.

"'An accident', he says. 'Unintentional'. 'It wasn't supposed to happen that way'. If I had a nickel..." Cann didn't know whether or not he even wanted to believe what he had just read.

"You don't buy it then?" Matsen asked.

"Oh, I don't know. It's plausible enough, I suppose." Cann looked almost absently out the huge window and said softly. "I guess that's another way of saying nothing surprises me anymore." He looked back at Matsen and straightened up in his chair. "But I think we both agree that if Brian says this is what happened, this is what happened."

As if on signal, the intercom buzzed. "Mr. Iverson on teleconference 3, Mr. Matsen."

"Thank you so much, Libby." He picked up the remote control and pushed the power button and then the number 3. Iverson's image appeared on the large screen televison at the opposite end of the conference room.

Matsen spoke. "Thank you so much for joining us, Brian. I know it's what," he looked at his watch, "going on 10:00 PM over there. You probably want to get home. As, you can see, John Cann is with me."

"Brian, nice to see you."

"Hi, John. Same here."

"Brian," it was Matsen, "we've read the report and we'd like to walk this through with you from the beginning so that we can get the continuity that you have. But we're interested in the end result and it seems this Dr. Quefar has given us that. Was he credible?"

"In my opinion, yes, Arthur. He knew a lot of the details we already had especially, the Rohypnol and another drug that hadn't even shown up in the tests. You don't make lucky guesses like that." Iverson shrugged. "And besides, he seemed quite scared."

"Of what," Matsen asked.

"Well, he appears to have gotten the impression that I was an Israeli agent."

Cann smiled. "Any idea why he would think that, Brian?"

"Well, I never said I was, that's for sure. That's against policy. Right, Arthur?"

"Right, Brian." The senior partner knew that his more active field men were having a little fun with him and he didn't mind a bit.

"But the important question is still the why of Ted's death. This Dr. Quefar says he didn't know?"

"No. And I don't believe he does, Arthur. He says he was only following orders." The phrase evoked a greater degree of solemnity among the men.

"Well let's take it from the top, then. See if there's something along the way."

Matsen nodded at Cann. "John, do the honors?" It was a tried and true device. Someone other than the lead investigator would recapitulate the facts and surmises of an investigation. The different perspective tended to break mindsets that had developed and frequently something as simple as a change in phrasing could lead to an alternative that hadn't been explored. The tactic often revealed a trail or an item or even a conclusion that the investigators had not seen or considered because of their closeness to the investigation.

Cann nodded and began. "Okay, it's Friday night, September 6, in Geneva and Ted needs to be in Frankfurt on Monday, September 9, for the IMF meeting. He's persuaded to detour to Lucerne and spend the night there because of this rare wine or this girl - probably a little of both. Not like Ted - at least as I knew him but..."

Matsen interrupted. "Query, Brian. It would appear from what Gunther Abel learned in Bad Durkheim that the bottle of rare wine - the trocken whatever - might have been a set-up. Why the detour all the way to Lucerne? I mean, why not just take him straight to Bad Durkheim if that's where the wine was supposed to be?"

"Because Lucerne's where the auction was. Plain and simple. It's an annual thing - very well known in wine collector circles. Keep in mind that Ted was a professional. If somebody had skulked out of an alley and gone, 'Psst. Hey buddy, want to buy a 1976 Trockenbeerenauslese?' every alarm in his head would have gone off. I suspect that he knew about the auction - talked about it at work - and might have already been planning to go. Or maybe he was thinking about it and the Trockenbeerenauslese - or the girl - was the frosting on the cake. The fact that he made a note about the wine - the TBA - on the top sheet of the note pad, is some evidence that he heard about it from an outside source. By phone. If he was indecisive or wavering about going, that would have gotten him. Or the girl. I understand that she's an absolute knockout. That part we may never know if we don't find this Lisa Harmony."

Matsen shuffled a few papers and picked one up. "We've got some information in that regard that I don't believe you've seen yet." He put on his bifocals and peered down at the sheet of paper. "EI kept on the trail of those credit card and telephone card numbers you gave them. It seems that at 5:30 AM yesterday - your time, Brian - Ms. Harmony rented a car in Geneva with her gold card. We know that she dropped off the car in Bern about two hours later. There's been no further use of the card and we now know it was cancelled right after she turned in the rental."

"Obviously she was tipped off and that was of the greatest concern to us. Leaks just can't be permitted. However, gentlemen, we had EI work backwards on this and it seems that many of the credit card companies have begun to offer a service of instant notification of inquiries to cardholders willing to pay for it. EI's questions were tracked and passed on to CISP. We'll make adjustments in our inquiries in that regard but it would seem that that is how Ms. Harmony - or CISP to be precise - learned of our interest - and cancelled the card. Once the card was cancelled, we might have run into a dead end in Bern - hopefully not - but you never know. Fortunately, we didn't. We ran the manifests of the airlines with flights out of Bern that morning and, lo and behold, we found a passenger booked on Syrian Air Flight 804 from Bern to Damascus by the name of one Lisa Hamanhi."

"Spelling, please, Arthur?" That was Cann.

"H-a-m-a-n-h-i."

"Hamanhi." Cann grunted and raised his eyebrows.

Matsen went right on. "Lisa Hamanhi. A homophone for Harmony perhaps? We sent a man to the airport and he had no trouble finding the ticket agent who remembered Ms. Hamanhi. Apparently her description is not exaggerated. We are told that the ticket agent practically hyperventilated just talking about her. And for the icing on the cake, Interpol has confirmed through the fingerprints Bucher lifted that our Ms. Harmony and Ms. Hamanhi are one and the same."

Cann interjected. "I know we want to go in sequence here but would anyone care to know the name of the head of CISP?"

Matsen and Iverson both said, "What?" at the same time.

"Hamanhi. Ali Hamanhi. Not an uncommon name in the Middle East to be sure but it's worth a look for a connection."

"Indeed it is," Matsen said, "but for the moment, Dr. Quefar has described Ms. Hamanhi's role in this matter. Getting to her in Damascus would be difficult - not impossible - but at this point, further efforts in that regard would be directed at the 'why' of all of this. And closure. So, let's continue with the 'what' for the moment. Brian?"

"It seems pretty clear that Lisa Harmony set up the call about dealing directly for the bottle of Trockenbeerenauslese to get Ted to Bad Durkheim. Gunther Abel of the Federal Police here has been - once again, Arthur - of invaluable assistance. I can tell you that we would be no where near what we have without him. He cut days or more off this investigation. Anything you can do..."

"The highest praise will be passed up the line, Brian. You have my word on that."

"Thanks, Arthur. Anyway, Gunther found the abandoned vineyard where Ted was supposed to be held and he also came up with an invoice which led to a medical supplies company that delivered a long list of hospital equipment to the house there - hospital beds, intravenous set-ups, the works. Now keep in mind that Gunther had already established a connection by phone between Quefar and Harmony and then, when he got to Kaiserslautern, he got his connection between Quefar and the medical supplies company in Ludwigshafen. Everything fit.

"By this time, I was back in Germany and Gunther had me meet him at the base above the village where Ted was killed and he had Quefar in custody. At first, he wouldn't talk but..."

"Something scared him." That was Cann.

"Yeah I suppose." Iverson smiled. "Anyway, Dr. Quefar told us that the orders came from CISP to hold Ted in the vineyard in Bad Durkhein until further notice. There was never any order to kill him. They were just supposed to keep him sedated until they received word to let him go. Quefar was adamant about that. You know, for what it's worth I think Quefar was actually professionally embarassed by the mistake. Deep down, he didn't give a rat's ass about Ted's life. But I don't think he was part of an attempt to kill him. Ted was supposed to be freed at some point. After something happened. And Quefar really didn't seem to know what the triggering event was supposed to be."

"Anyway, according to Dr. Quefar, they had no problem with keeping Ted at the vineyard Saturday night. They apparently went through a lot of German wine. I don't know if Ted ever got his Trockenbeerenauslese. But they all supposedly drank a lot of wine."

"Our surmise is that Ted got up with a nice hangover on Sunday and took some of his Migramol to help it. He may have even taken more as the day went on. Who knows?"

"Then later on Sunday, when Ted made noises about getting on the road for Frankfurt, they popped him with the Rohypnol - first by slipping a 'roofie' in some water, and then setting him up with an automatically maintained dosage with the equipment they had brought in."

"That's when things started to go wrong. As they were attempting to adjust the dosage of the Rohypnol in the drip, Ted came out of it enough to complain of a severe headache - that can be one of the side effects of Rohypnol, coincidentally enough. Well, this Lisa Harmony didn't really know what it was that Ted had been taking for his migraines, so she slipped him some of the Migramol he'd picked up in Lucerne. We don't know how much but whatever the amount was, it coincided with an increase of the flow of the Rohypnol in the IV drip. The combined effect of the Rohypnol and the Migramol started the shut down of Ted's entire system."

Matsen interrupted. "Brian, why couldn't Dimsen tell that right away. Didn't he say that the combination of Rohypnol and Migramol by itself shouldn't have been enough to kill Ted?"

"Yes, he did, Arthur. That's the kicker here. The printout that Dimsen received from his own toxicological tests gave him the brand name of the drug that was in Ted's system - not the components of the drug. Dimsen manually looked up Migramol in the PDR and that's where he got the ingredients ergotamine and caffeine. That's what he based his opinion on. The problem is that the European version on the same drug - Migramol - differs from the version sold in the United States in that it has belladonna alkaloids in it in addition to the other two ingredients and the Migramol sold in America doesn't. Don't forget that Ted had taken the prescription he got in America to a pharmacy in Europe.

And that's what went wrong. The combination of Rohypnol with the ergotamine was potentially bad enough. The belladonna pushed it over the edge and shut Ted down."

"Shouldn't the pharmacist in Lucerne have known that?" Matsen asked sadly."

They could see Iverson shrug. "Maybe. I suppose. But even with the belladonna alkaloids in the medication, Ted would still have been alright except for getting hit with this powerful central nervous system depressant. I don't think you can blame the druggist for that. And a lawsuit won't bring Ted back now."

Iverson stopped for a moment and then went on in a slightly quieter voice. "And that wasn't all. They called Quefar in Kaiserslautern from Bad Durkheim when it became obvious that something was terribly wrong. They described what was happening to Ted but Quefar didn't know about the Migramol so he couldn't tell them what to do. That's why he had them rush Ted over to his office in Kaiserslautern. He tried to reverse the effects of the Rohypnol by giving Ted a drug called flumazenil - which is supposed to reverse the effects of a benzodiazapine which is the class of drugs Rohypnol belongs to. The problem with that is that one of the effects of flumazenil is to supress respiration - and Ted's system was already shutting down. The instant that drug hit Ted's system, it made things that much worse. Quefar stopped injecting it immediately - that's why there wasn't even enough of that to show up in the toxicology printout. He couldn't save him and once Ted was dead, the good doctor," he was being sarcastic, "reverted to form. He wanted Ted out of his office and had his people take him to the base in Sembach. They put the whole accident scenario together and just went ahead and did it. Boom, boom, boom."

Iverson looked like he was finished but then spoke up again. "One thing that really pissed me off about this guy Quefar, though. After he finished telling me the story, he wanted to know how we figured out it wasn't an accident. When I told him that it was the gangrene that first caught our attention, his reaction was 'so our plan was good. It was just a foolish mistake.' That's all he said."

All three men sat immersed in their silent thoughts on the fragility of life. Finally Matsen said, "Well, that's the what. We still have the 'why' to consider. And the connection that runs from the United States to Germany through CISP - and maybe back again." That was Matsen who turned to Cann and said, "Your earlier reference indicates you've learned something about this CISP. Let's look at that."

Cann related what he had learned from Goren. Even though he would not hesitate to trust his own life to the two men he was talking to, he didn't reveal the source of his information. And they would not ask. That's how it was done.

When he was finished, Iverson spoke first. "So we have the trail leading from Geneva to Lucerne to Bad Durkheim to Sembach then across the Atlantic to Virginia - DC actually - and then down to Charlestown University." Iverson had a somber and at the same time quizzical expression on his face. "Are you two thinking what I'm thinking?"

Matsen had removed his glasses and was pinching the bridge of his nose bewtween his thumb and index finger. Cann sat in his chair with his hands folded across his stomach but he said nothing. He had indeed deduced the 'why' of Ted Wagner's death during his conversation with Zvi Goren.

"It certainly seems plausible that Ted died just because John's presence made this guy Al-Asif nervous." Matsen spoke very quietly. "More than plausible. Even likely."

"What a waste." Iverson repeated himself. "What a waste. But it fits. They keep Ted out of sight and he has to be replaced - and John is the likely replacement. The only one really."

Cann felt yet another twinge of guilt over Wagner's death as Iverson continued his analysis. "So Ted just disappears and has to be replaced. Their hope is that John gets pulled off campus and sent to Geneva. Or Frankfurt. Or wherever. If he does, Ted turns up with no explanation of where he's been. He's certainly not going to be put back on the job right away - if ever. So John stays.

And in a very short time, too much of the academic year has passed and John can't go back. It fits."

Matsen asked a question. "But how does Al-Asif know who John is? Why would he figure John - and not someone else - would be sent to replace Ted. As it turned out, it didn't happen that way anyway."

"But as soon as things heated up - it probably would have." That was Cann.

Matsen kept on. "But the question remains, how would Al-Asif know about your areas of expertise and the interrelationships within the firm?"

Iverson offered an answer. "A lot of it's public knowledge, Arthur. The Middle East expertise. Even some of the history." He paused for only a second before going on. "Then there's Lisa Harmony. As a Legal Assistant, she wouldn't have access to anything confidential but John's areas of interest and expertise are no secret within the firm."

Cann interjected. "And Roger Walder waxed pretty eloquent at the new faculty reception when he introduced me. He went into a few details. Nothing that isn't public knowledge but he allowed some inferences to hang in the air. I remember that Al-Asif was there. I didn't think anything of it at the time but..." He shook his head for a long moment. "That alone could have done it. Damn."

Matsen put his glasses back on and sat up straight. "The question now is what are we going to do from here." He looked at Cann. "John, how much of what you've told us about CISP can we give to the people on our side."

"None, Arthur. Anything my source told me has to remain here until I can verify it independently. We can't take any chance that any of this might be traced back to...my...this source. I have the advantage of knowing the conclusions. I just need to corroborate or develop the information from other sources we can attribute it to."

"Understood. I agree." Matsen started to absently gather the papers on the table together. "When will you go back to Charlestown - tonight?"

"Yeah. I don't feel like sleeping in a hotel and I sub-let my condo to a couple of flight attendants for the academic year. There's nothing in the lease that let's me drop in whenever I'm in town - though it might be fun."

Matsen smiled in agreement.

"Anyway, there's an 8:30 PM Flight out of National. That way I won't miss any more classes." He stood up and adjusted his clothes. "I'll get right on this as soon as I get back, Arthur. And I'll keep you posted."

"Yes. Indeed. Do that." Matsen looked up at the screen as Iverson spoke.

"I'd like to know where this all ends up myself, if you don't mind."

"Of course, Brian. And, as always, marvelous job."

"Thank you, Arthur. A lot of the credit goes to Gunther. And, John," Iverson continued, "first chance you get, come on over for a visit. I found a new place with an oxenschwanzezuppe that surpasses the Gasthaus Rinnert - if you can believe it."

"Love to, Brian. Take care."

Iverson waved and punched the button on his console causing the screen to go blank.

*　　*　　*　　*

Massoud knew he couldn't go to the salvage yard for the second day in a row to purchase another barely functional wreck. The odds were too great that one or more of the workers would recognize him. Instead, he provided Sami with one of the many fake identities they had available and sent him over to obtain the vehicle they would use to dispose of Janie and Klein.

At about 5:00 PM Sami returned with a crumpled mustard colored something or other that he pulled directly into the garage that was attached to the house. Massoud went into the game room where only Abdullah had had the stomach to use Janie one last time and lifted her with ease over his shoulder. He took her out through the kitchen and into the garage where he dropped her

328

roughly into the trunk. He slammed down the lid and went back into the house to gather his things.

Around 5:45, he left for the campus. With sunset occurring at around 7:23 PM, he figured that by the time he was done cleaning Klein's office and packing her up, it would be dark enough for him to get her out to the car.

The campus was not totally deserted but it was less active than during the day. Massoud pulled into the lot outside the Sanger building and parked very carefully indeed. It did not pay to attract attention when one was on such a mission. He got out of the heap and scanned the parking lot noting the several cars scattered around in different slots. All were empty except for the one directly opposite the slot he had parked in which contained a couple much too busily involved in amorous pursuits to pay any attention to him.

He reached in through the opening where a window had once been and took the large folding suit bag from the rear seat of the junk car and walked up the steps of the building. No one was about.

The outer doors of the Sanger Building were still unlocked. He followed Al-Asif's directions which took him straight to Klein's office without incident. The keys he had been given fit as they should and he went in and immediately set about his work.

Klein was where the chief had said she would be. Jammed in a seated position inside the kneehole of the desk, feet on the floor, knees up, and upper body leaned to the right against the wastebasket into which her right arm dangled. It had been several hours since the incident and he noted that her face and head were peculiarly pale in comparison to the rest of her body - or what he could see of it. There was a fair amount of blood in the wastebasket. Since Al-Asif had punctured a vein, which carries the blood back to the heart from the rest of the body, Klein's heart had continued to pump until the blood supply was sufficiently depleted to impair its performance. The remaining blood had settled to the lowest points of her body and, had Massoud been inclined to look, which he was not, he would have seen that her buttocks were unusually dark because that was where the rest of the blood had pooled in the hours after her death. The same was true to a lesser extent with regard to her feet where the blood which had been in her lower legs had settled. Massoud checked the puncture wound in her neck to see that it was no longer bleeding.

Because Al-Asif had left Klein's body in such a sharply bent position, it would make this part of Massoud's job a little easier. Just as Yousef had done with the much smaller Janie, Massoud would place Klein into the folding garment bag and bend her at the waist and simply carry her out. It would not be a light load but Masssoud was a powerful man.

Getting her into the bag would not be significantly more difficult than usual. Bending her over at such an acute angle could have been a problem, however, except for the way that Al-Asif had left her. Six hours had passed since Klein had expired and the process of rigor mortis had begun. If the chief had laid her out flat, Massoud would have been put to extraordinary measures to conform Klein's body to the bag. The spine is fragile by some standards but it is not that easily snapped. The fact that she was bent so severely at the waist meant she was already in the correct position. Her legs, however, would need to be straightened. Massoud set about his work without thought.

Ensuing events showed how timing is everything.

If Massoud had come down to the front door of the Sanger Building with his grisly baggage perhaps three minutes earlier than he did, he would have seen the couple in the car disentangling themselves from each other and straightening their clothes. He would have seen the man who was in the passenger seat get out of his car and walk to the far side of the parking lot and get into his own car. He would then have seen the woman start up her own car and put it into reverse to back out of the slot opposite the wreck that held Janie in the trunk. Because of the approaching darkness, he probably wouldn't have seen that, as she was backing out, the woman was looking in the rear view mirror at the state of her hair and not directly behind her where her car was going. But it was fairly certain that he would have watched with some apprehension as the woman backed her car directly into the wreck he was driving. And it was even more certain that the apprehension would have turned to horror or perhaps rage when he saw the impact cause the trunk lid of the old car to pop up and remain open.

For a moment - just a moment - he would have felt the exhilaration of relief as the woman glanced back, put her car in drive, and started to drive away, no doubt thinking that she couldn't possibly have done any damage to the car that anyone would care about.

But the horror would have returned when Massoud saw the brake lights come on and then watched as the woman get out of the car to close the trunk lid and then recoil with her hands over her mouth as she looked down into the trunk. For some reason founded in her reaction to the horror of what she was seeing, the woman reached up and slammed the trunk lid down before she turned and ran. She was back in her car within five seconds of her first view of Janie.

Massoud would in all likelihood by then have put down the bag and been out the door and perhaps even running trying to reach the woman before she got back into the car - a third body would have complicated things but it would be better than being discovered - but he wouldn't have had enough time to reach her.

But even if he hadn't tried to reach the woman or had tried and failed, he would have at least been alerted to the fact of the discovery and could have taken steps to accelerate his activities or construct alternatives.

But as it was, he had trouble breaking Klein's left leg so that she would fit more neatly in the garment bag and it delayed him just long enough that he reached the front door of the Sanger Building just as the brake lights of the woman's car disappeared as she turned right out of the parking lot.

He calmly walked out of the building struggling slightly with the 150 pound load and looking to his left and right as he walked. He was about halfway to the old wreck when the frightened woman was pulling up behind a police car whose two occupants were eating Big Macs for supper.

Massoud opened the trunk and actually noticed as he did so that it didn't appear as if he even would have needed to use the key. But no matter. With two hands he lifted and threw the garment bag into the trunk where it landed heavily on top of Janie. He walked to the side of the car to get in and was just putting the key in the ignition when the police car screeched to a halt directly behind him preventing any escape.

Chapter Twenty-Five

Cann's plane left Washington National almost precisely on time at 8:33 PM en route to a scheduled change in Atlanta at 9:46 and a final arrival just after 11:00. This was not to be. Severe thunderstorms closed Atlanta's Hartsfield International so Cann's plane was diverted to Columbia, South Carolina landing there about 9:30 PM. Cann and the rest of the passengers were asked to remain seated until the flight was cleared to continue on to Hartsfield. The passengers complied with varying degrees of pleasantness.

Cann leaned his head back in the seat and closed his eyes. What was supposed to have been a quiet year in academia was now a mission to see what - if anything - Al-Asif and his crew - and by extension Cann himself - had to do with Wagner's death. In his own mind, Cann was certain that Ted Wagner had died so that Cann would leave Charlestown. It didn't seem like much of a reason but Cann had seen many people - and knew of many more - who had died - been killed - for lesser reasons than that. It didn't make it any more acceptable, but it happened. A lot.

Then his thoughts turned to Janie Reston and especially to why she hadn't called him since the hearing. It wasn't that he expected her to feel like she owed him her life. A thank you would have been nice, though. But something more nagged at him. In the short time he had known her, she pretty much always did the right thing. It was that simple. She wasn't a robot or a slave to convention. She just seemed to be one who would always say please or thank you or write the thank you note because she agreed that it was the right thing to do. Her failure to call was out of character.

Even now, though, Cann still hadn't entertained a thought of anything being wrong. Never having been a parent, he didn't have the highly tuned sense of foreboding that comes with uncertainty when it applies to one's flesh and blood. So he still thought that she was just living her life preoccupied with one thing or another. He pretty much expected that there would be a message from her when he got home.

If he ever got out of this damned airport.

He sat in the plane for a while longer and then began to consider that he could make the drive from Columbia to his condo in about two hours. Even if his temporarily grounded flight was cleared to fly to Atlanta at that very moment, by the time they flew there, landed, he changed planes, and flew out again, it would be well over the time it would take him to make the drive. He advised the flight attendant of his wish to deplane and, was told that if he did that, his checked baggage would still have to go on to Atlanta with the plane, and be delivered the next day or as soon thereafter as possible. Like most seasoned travelers, Cann had the things he most needed in his carry-on anyway and there was nothing in the checked bag that he couldn't do without. So he deplaned, rented a car, and drove. His bags would arrive when they arrived.

He arrived at his condo a little before 1:00 AM, went in, flipped on the living room light, and walked to the bedroom, hoping to get at least four or five hours sleep before he had to get up for his first class. Just before laying back, he picked up the telephone by the bed and heard the chattering dial tone that indicated he had messages on his personal secretary. He dialed the retrieval number then his code and was told he had one message. He hit '1' to hear it and was a little surprised at the twinge he felt in his gut when it wasn't Janie's voice.

It was Roger Walder sounding extremely subdued - even somber. In the message, Walder told Cann that he had 'called Loring Matsen in DC and been told that Cann was on his way back. That was good. It was very important for Cann to call Roger as soon as possible.' Walder had hesitated in the message then said that it was 'imperative that he and Cann talk. If Cann didn't get the message till morning, he should know that Walder had already arranged for - and paid - a substitute for Cann's first class. There was no need to go the 8:00 o'clock class so please come straight to the Dean's office in the morning'.

Cann considered for a moment if he should call right then remembering the message that Matsen had left for him with the intention that Cann call any time of day or night. But that was Matsen and that call involved global issues. This was Roger and it was after 1 o'clock in the morning. It could wait.

*   *   *   *

By Al-Asif's reckoning, Massoud should have been finished with his work and back at the house by 9:00 or 9:30 PM, if all went as planned. When he still hadn't gotten back by 11:00 PM, Al-Asif turned on the television to watch the local news.

It was the lead, of course.

"Local police are investigating the discovery of two female bodies found in the trunk of a car parked outside the Sanger Building on the campus of Charlestown University. Sources tell us that the body of a young woman - possibly a student at Charlestown - was found naked in the trunk of the car and another body - a woman reportedly in her thirties or forties - was found stuffed inside a garment bag which was laying on top of the younger woman. An unidentified male who was apparently about to drive away in the car when police stopped him has been taken into custody. Stay tuned and we will keep you abreast of this breaking story as we learn more about it. In national news...."

'Perhaps it was not meant to be,' thought Al-Asif after he watched Massoud being placed in the back seat of the police car.

Al-Asif had noted approvingly that at no time did Massoud allow his face to be clearly photographed even though his hands were cuffed behind his back. He sat at his desk and thought for several minutes.

After more than a year's worth of time and effort - and the expenditure of huge sums of money - the mission was in danger of ending with no concrete benefit to him or the cause. Of course, the expenditure of the money was of little concern. The funding was as deep as the oil fields that were its source.

But the complete lack of results was a matter of great distress to Al-Asif. Even the transport and concealment of Yousef - which, as far as it went, had proven the effectiveness of the network - had had a negative and unanticipated conclusion. A necessary one, however, to be sure. As before, Al-Asif only regretted Yousef's death in the context of his own regret that he could not kill him again.

He blamed Yousef for much of the difficulties they now found themselves facing. If he had stayed in concealment, most of the current circumstances would not be present. That was not, of course, entirely true - but who was there to contradict him.

He also blamed Cann whom he was convinced had come to Charlestown to monitor their efforts. But he thought he had dealt with that. Indeed, he had found that Cann was not on campus all that day - perhaps that part of his plans was showing results. But this business with the girl - damn that Yousef! - that could bring Cann back.

He was still not prepared to concede that his carefully planned development of the network had been fatally compromised. Damaged - to be sure - but perhaps only temporarily and not beyond repair. He knew that, if it were, he would simply move on to the next project. This was his life's work and there would always be another mission. And he knew that it was most important that he ensure that he be around to accept it. He was not happy with the turn of events but...

He sat up and went through the desk and took out the important papers that he needed to have with him. There was little in the desk that did not support and verify that the man and the house and the others were all what Al-Asif had said they were. What may have indicated otherwise, he placed into his briefcase. He walked to the door of the study, turned back to see that the desk was clean, turned off the lights and closed the door.

He put the briefcase on the small table by the front door and turned and went up the stairs to the sleeping quarters of the guests. He had long ago decided that, in the absence of Massoud, of the four guests, Sami was the most accomplished and the one Al-Asif would look to for the most competent assistance. He didn't knock on the room where Sami was asleep but opened the door and walked across to the bed where Sami was sleeping. When he called the other man's name, Sami opened his eyes and looked up at the chief but didn't otherwise move.

"You should not take the term 'safe house' too literally my friend" Al-Asif said with a wry expression. "I could have been anyone."

"But you would have been a dead anyone," Sami answered with a smile as he reached across his body with his left hand and peeled back the sheet revealing the 9mm pistol in his right hand pointed directly at Al-Asif's stomach.

Al-Asif was pleased. He saw that his choice was a good one. "Very good, Sami. Now listen. Massoud has been detained."

Sami raised up onto his elbows. The choice of words was significant.

"As you know, in the last two days, we have had to respond to occurrences that may have placed our mission in jeopardy." Sami nodded. "Well it has gotten worse." Al-Asif filled Sami in on the latest occurrences including the failed body disposal and Massoud's arrest. "More than ever, we must be discreet. In the morning, you should call campus security and advise them that the entire staff has been called to a one day conference in - oh, say, Atlanta. Request that they lock and secure our building and post a notice for the students that all will be back to normal in the morning. I hope that proves to be true. In the meantime, I feel it is vital that you make sure the men stay in the house. Until we know what is going on, any interaction could lead to further trouble. The others do not need to know about Massoud or my absence. I will consult with my superiors and determine our course. I hope that our operation can be salvaged but I doubt that it will survive any more exposure. Be very, very careful, Sami. Do you understand?"

"Completely."

"However, there is one exception to the order to remain in the house. I entrust this to you." Sami nodded again, pleased with the honor. "This man Cann. I am now certain that he bears much of the responsibility for our difficulties. My plan was to divert him away from the campus entirely. Now, just as it may have worked, this thing with the girl could bring him back. If we are to have any hope of preserving," he waved his arm in a circle about him, "all of this, he cannot be allowed to remain. I want you to carefully - very, very carefully - see if he is still here. If so, it will mean we are under further and greater surveillance. Make him disappear. Leave no trace, Sami. There must be nothing that can lead back to us."

"I understand, ray-yis."

*   *   *   *

Cann's expectation of getting something resembling a night's sleep was thwarted by the phone ringing at 6:30 AM. His brain was deep below the REM level of dreams at the place where true rest occurs which made the intrusion all the more jarring. Still, he was instantly awake.

He rolled onto his left side and reached for the phone on the table by the bed. This time, his mind made no predictions as to who was on the other end. He just said, "Hello?"

"John." A familiar if not often heard voice. "It's Lev." Cann sat up against the headboard.

"Lev. Good to hear from you. And congratulations."

"Thanks, John. Though the celebration may be very short-lived, I'm afraid." He paused only for a beat and then got right to the point. "John, for god's sake, what's happening. I'm told you were consulted on this decision. Is that true?"

"No."

"But, you were at the meeting..."

"Lev, please. You can't believe that I signed on to this thing. This President and I hate each other's guts. I was only at that meeting so that the President could tell me the decision had been made and..."

"Why? You're not an adviser."

Cann got angry. "Lev, we've known each other for too long for you not to give me the benefit of the doubt. I know this is an intense situation, to say the least, but where's the trust of the last twenty years?"

Shelanu was quiet but only for a moment. "Yes, I know. But I was told that you were at the meeting and that you did agree that this was a good thing."

"Wrong. Think about this for a second, Lev. You're asking why the President would advise me of this decision. Ask yourself why he made it a point for you to know that I was there. The answer is the same."

Shelanu thought for a long time. " Ok, John, I give up. I can't come up with an answer."

"That's because you don't know this President, Lev. And you're a statesman. You probably won't understand this even after I explain it to you. It's ball-busting pure and simple. It's...."

"No, John. I can't accept that. I cannot accept that anyone - even this man - would play with so many lives for such a superficial reason."

"Like I said, you don't know him." Cann was speaking more calmly now. Both men were. "During that meeting in the White House, at one point he said to me, 'When he calls, and he will, tell Shelanu, this is personal'."

"Personal? We've never met. This is...."

"Insane? My word exactly. I caught myself saying that several times to him. All it did was piss him off more."

"But, why?"

"For me, it's because I don't hide my contempt for him. If you want my ten cent psychoanalysis, he's one of these guys who's overwhelmed by his own inadequacies but the trappings of power let him ignore them. When the power's gone, he'll revert to the horny little weenie who entered politics thirty years ago just to get laid."

"Fine, John. But every leader in the world has inadequacies. They don't set the Middle East on fire over them."

"This one does. Look, I don't know if he doesn't see things or if he really doesn't care. I'm prepared to believe either about the man. But the question is - what's going to happen, Lev? As wrong as he is, he's succeeded in putting your backs to the wall."

"They've been there before and we've survived. There's nothing that unites Israelis more than a threat to their country's survival."

"Have you gotten any sense of a move against you?"

"Nothing concrete. And," Shelanu hesitated before going on, "you won't believe this - I'm not sure I do - but we've gotten feelers fron both Iran and Iraq that they might be willing to stand with us if Syria and Jordan and Egypt and the rest decide to make a move. Do you believe that? Talk about strange bedfellows."

"You wouldn't accept, would you," Cann asked knowing what the answer must be.

"We'd hold our noses but we'd accept if we had to, John. Believe me, I liked it better when we could actually count on the United States but... Did you ever think it would come to this?"

Cann remembered a conversation from long ago. "Yes. Danny brought it up once. That's what we were talking about when he died." Cann went deep into reminiscence for a while then brought himself back. "Anyway, can you tell me any of what's being done," he asked?

"Menahim's on point. I don't get sworn in for two weeks anyway so it's still his call. Of course we're in the closest consultation but he'll be out front for now." He huffed a sort of dry laugh. "Probably just as well. Given the rhetoric of the campaign, he's in a better position to sit down with them anyway."

"And you said you wouldn't."

"Wouldn't what?"

"Sit down with Arafat."

Shelanu corrected him. "What I said was I wouldn't sit down with him unless the security of Israel demanded it. I would think that applies to this situation." He was silent then said, "I'm a practical man, John. So is Arafat. He knows that we cannot - will not - allow an unfriendly nation to be forcibly placed in the heart of Israel. This proposed state would be within fifty miles striking distance of every strategic location in Israel. I believe that Arafat realizes that even though this is his dearest goal - this is not the way to achieve it. To force this on Israel from the outside will be suicide - probably for Israel as well. Someday it may happen - but only if the parties themselves evolve towards it. And contrary to all the rhetoric - especially from your government - I won't be the one to stand in the way." Cann sensed the smile through the phone. "But keep that between us for now, please, John. We need to keep the 'good guy, bad guy' option alive. For now, Ben can be the good guy and leave unspoken the possibilities of what the bad guy can do. That's me. The bad guy. What's the world coming to, heh?"

*   *   *   *

Cann arrived on campus at about 8:30 Thursday morning and went into the Page Building and, as Roger had said in the message, straight to Walder's office. When he walked in the outer door, Beverly looked up and when she saw who it was gave him one of those grimace-like smiles that says 'hello' and 'isn't it awful' at the same time. The door to Walder's inner office was open and he saw Cann come in and shouted, "Come right in, John," even before Beverly could say a word.

Cann walked into Walder's office still looking back at Beverly and her expression. He was about to ask Walder if she'd had a death in her family or something when he saw, through the window in Walder's office that overlooked the quad, that, as early as it was, the quad was crowded with people - some carrying signs - most milling about.

"What's that all about?" he said tossing his head forward at the scene outside.

"A protest against campus violence. We've had a little, I'm afraid. Most of those people out there are protesting Klein's murder."

Even though he raised his eyebrows, Cann accepted the news of Klein's death with the equanimity of one familiar with sudden and unexpected death. He was surprised but not upset. He didn't like Caroline Klein but he didn't wish her dead either. Maybe. Still, he felt no loss nor did he feel any obligation to feign one. He spoke evenly. "Caroline Klein was murdered?"

"In her office. Yesterday afternoon. But that's..."

Cann was curious, though. "Any suspects?"

"Besides you, you mean?"

"Me?" Cann was genuinely surprised at that. "Why?"

"You've got a few people mad at you. Klein I can understand. But Sara Furden named you to the police. Said you were 'involved' with Janie and had made threats against Klein. A lot of people backed her up on that. And you've got Buffinton ready to let the wolves in the door at you because of the business about Klein making the initial report on Janie. She doesn't like being lied to. What was that about anyway?"

Cann shruggeed. "You kept telling me how these people play hardball. I wanted them to see that they weren't the only ones who could be good at it."

"But how did you get the security sergeant to back you up."

Cann smiled crookedly. "She knew she was finished here. I promised her an inteview with security at Loring Matsen."

"You'd foist that woman off on your firm?"

"Nope. I promised her an interview - nothing more. And I'd be sure to tell Matsen what a sleaze she was before that."

Walder clucked his tongue. "Isn't that sinking to their level, John?"

"Sure it is. Sometimes you have to. If you're not willing to meet someone on their turf and their terms, they have the advantage. And they know it." He got back to the matter at hand. "But I had nothing to do with Klein's death." He held up a finger. "You said it happened yesterday afternoon?"

Walder nodded.

"For almost the entire day yesterday, I was sitting in the White House including the early afternoon when I was in the Oval Office with the President of the United States and a number of others. I wasn't alone at any time for the rest of the day - well a little in my office. But I was still in DC. It's totally verifiable. My regrets to the constabulary, Roger, but they're going to have to leave me out of this one."

"That's the first good news I've heard in the last twenty-four hours, anyway. The police were very serious about you. They've been told by a whole lot of people that you threatened Klein at the hearing Tuesday night?"

"I did."

Walder's look at Cann became more intense and quizzical and Cann held up his hand and said, "Mostly for effect, Roger. That's all." He turned to sit on the arm of the easy chair opposite Walder's desk. "And anyway, it was only a provisional threat - contingent on something happening to Janie Reston."

"I know." Walder was somber again.

"So, my threat against Klein would only be...." A knot formed in Cann's stomach and he found that he had to force himself to ask the question. "Did something happen to Janie?" He was amazed at the fear he felt for her at that moment. "Did Klein do something to her?" Cann had never imagined that Klein even meant her threats let alone would act on them. "Tell me, Roger."

"It doesn't appear that Klein did anything. Except get herself killed. But her body was found with Janie and..."

"Is..." Cann was a man who always faced everything head on. But he didn't want to face this. It took all his will to ask the question. "Is Janie dead?"

343

Walder shook his head very slowly. "No," he said. The pain he felt turned his face into a tragic drama mask. "But it might be better if she was. She was treated pretty brutally. Raped - repeatedly - and beaten savagely. Over and over. Her skull's crushed in several places. She probably won't make it. And it might be just as well. "

Cann's head burned. He couldn't believe the pain he was feeling. He said nothing for the moment but inside he cursed himself for ever coming to this place.

For all those years, he had existed in another world - a world that - like every other world - required certain accommodations. He had grown over the years to make those accommodations to his chosen world and one of them was not to feel. One did what one did. 'It was business - just business', they often told one another. 'Nothing personal'. If it ever got personal, it got out of control. And control was everything. 'Controlled action comes from controlled feelings'.

He'd always thought that made him stronger - the acquired ability to not feel. Now he realized that it hadn't made him any stronger - it had only made him safer. It kept out the pain.

But his citadel of strength and safety had been infiltrated by the truth and beauty of this young woman who was barely more than a child. How corny, he thought to himself. He hadn't even known her that long. But it was true. Janie hadn't conducted a frontal assault on his defenses. That kind of attack was easy to repel. Janie had just not acknowledged that the defenses existed. As a result, they didn't as far as she was concerned and she'd acted accordingly. Honest - warm - open - give no rejection and expect none. Those were the weapons that had disarmed John Cann. Without realizing it, Cann had let her inside. And now...Damn it - this hurt!

Cann had dealt with pain before - many, many times. But that was physical pain imposed by an external force. The kind that's dealt with by resisting and repelling it. This pain he now felt was on the inside and was based on things that had been allowed - even invited - in. The time to resist and repel had long since passed. This pain - Cann remembered from long ago - had to be accepted. To reject the pain would be to reject Janie and Cann couldn't - wouldn't - do that.

Walder was watching Cann closely and could see the emotion in Cann's eyes. He felt it too. This little girl - that's how he thought of her - had captured both their hearts. The horror of what had been done to her was almost overwhelming. He didn't even know the details. And didn't want to. There was no need for him to know all the lurid details. There was nothing they could do.

That was the difference between Walder and Cann. A part of Walder's pain - a part that Cann didn't feel - came from the Dean's knowledge that there was nothing they could do about the terrible things that had been done to Janie. Whatever they might do now - if anything - would not undo the damage. So the wisdom of Walder's world was that they would therefore do nothing. Turning the other cheek had become the end in itself.

Not so for Cann. As Walder watched there was a glacierization occurring in Cann's face. The pain wasn't disappearing - it was withdrawing behind a slowly falling curtain. 'What's going on inside,' Walder wondered as every visible aspect of emotion on Cann's face seemed to retreat to a spot somewhere behind Cann's eyes. It was like watching one of those 'morphing' scenes in the techno-thrillers. Walder had an idea of what Cann was capable of - maybe. But he still wondered, 'What's he thinking? What does he think he can do?'

Cann really didn't want to know the details of Janie's ordeal either. But unlike Walder, he knew that he needed to. Maybe in Walder's world - it would never have been Cann's - no matter what - there was nothing to be done. But Cann's world - the 'real world' - wasn't this fairyland where actions frequently had no consequences. Or if they did, they were artificial. In Cann's 'real world', retribution wasn't a dirty word.

Would retribution undo the damage to Janie?

No.

Would it ensure that no one else ever got hurt in the same way?

No.

Would it ensure that whomever had done it to Janie would never do it again?

Oh, yes.

That would be enough. It would have to be.

And it was the right thing to do.

In Cann's world, retribution was a simple function of 'cause and effect'. Every cause had an effect. Good or evil. Action 'a' led to response 'b' - or 'c' or 'd'. For better or for worse. And it was a given. If you do 'a' you get 'b' and you shall not be allowed to avoid 'b' if you have done 'a'. It was clean and it was moral.

So Cann needed to know the 'what' of 'what happened'. That knowledge would help lead him to the 'who'.

He didn't care about the 'why'. There was no valid or acceptable 'why'.

Neither did he care about the 'where' or even the 'when' unless it helped to discover the 'who'.

But god help the 'who' when Cann got the information.

* * * *

Al-Asif had instructed Sami to be very guarded with the others with information about the events of the night before and Massoud's detention. And even of the chief's morning flight to Virginia. There was no need for them to know. If Sami needed assistance in something, he could advise Basheer but Al-Asif was adamant that Sami say nothing of the situation to Abdullah or Naji. Those two reminded the chief of Yousef - that was not a good thing.

Sami rose early and took his coffee into the study. He felt great pride at sitting in the chief's chair at the desk and he gloried in the feeling of being in charge. Of course, the exultation was minimized by the fact that no one else knew of his appointment. But the chief had said that he could share information with Basheer. He would do so. And he would delegate some of the responsibilities to Basheer. All great generals delegated responsibilities, he thought. He would assign Basheer the task of following - and taking care of - Cann.

Sami called Basheer into the study and briefed him on the situation. He showed Basheer the photograph of Cann that the chief had provided and told him that his assignment was to see if the man was on campus. They were still unfamiliar with much of the campus, so they went over the college locater map in detail seeking to determine the areas where Cann was most likely to be - if he was around. Before leaving for the campus, Basheer got on the computer and using the national directory software, found Cann's address. He also accessed the DMV computer to find what kind of car Cann drove and its tag number.

Sami made it very clear that although ultimately they were to see that the man disappeared, Basheer was to do nothing on this reconnaissance mission unless the perfect situation arose. "Remember, he is merely a professor and you are trained in these things. So seize the opportunity if it arises. But only if no one can see you with him, no one can see you kill him, and no one can observe you conceal or dispose of him. Unless those circumstances exist, do nothing more than locate him and return here. We will devise a suitable plan after that."

*   *   *   *

With the information he had, Basheer found Cann without much effort. To be precise, he found the Corvette in the parking lot of the Page Building. He maneuvered the Land Rover into a parking spot right next to another sports recreational type vehicle which was across the lot from the Corvette. From where he was, Basheer could look through the windows of the other vehicle and see the Corvette quite clearly. At the same time, Basheer calculated, the sun would reflect off the other vehicles windows and hamper Cann's view of the Land Rover. The fact was he wasn't overly concerned about that since Cann didn't know him but why not use what was there. He settled in and waited.

Cann felt an obligation to meet with three remaining classes but after barely going through the motions with his 11:00 AM Contracts class, he knew that he was doing the students no service to require their attention. They would be better off with an assigned study period and he arranged for Sylvia to leave notes to that effect on the doors to the respective classrooms.

He left the Page Building and strode to his car. From where Basheer sat, he could clearly see Cann come into the parking area. By comparing him to the photo he had on the seat beside him, Basheer was able to recognize him by the time he was barely halfway to his car.

So Cann was still here. That was it. It was now his duty to report that to Sami. The first part of the mission had been accomplished quickly.

Too quickly.

Basheer was an excellent soldier who followed orders and completed tasks. But, like most men of intelligence, he prided himself on having initiative as well. Sami had told him that if the opportunity arose, he should take the man out. Basheer would not be content to just wait and hope for opportunity. He would see what he could do to help it along.

Cann wheeled the Corvette out of the space and through the parking lot to the street where he turned left and headed for the hospital. The Land Rover followed unnoticed a short distance behind.

Chapter Twenty-Six

The experienced operative can often sense - actually usually knows - when the subject being followed suspects something. They will make an unusual move or take unnecessarily circuitous routes designed to induce the follower to duplicate a contrived or superfluous action.

Cann did none of those things. He drove directly to the hospital by the shortest route following all traffic signs and signals on the way, which didn't surprise Basheer. The quarry was, after all, only a 'civilian', a school teacher - a college professor, to be sure, and worthy of respect in that regard - but a non-professional in the ways of the world that Basheer had inhabited for many years.

Cann turned into the main driveway of the city hospital and drove through several parking lots to the one closest to the main entrance. When he reached it, he noted that it was reserved for administrators and doctors and select others who possessed the plastic access card which would raise the gate protecting its entrances. He worked his way back past several other parking areas until he found one which was open and accessible to the public where he pulled the Corvette into the first empty space. He turned off the ignition and set out for the front entrance - a good quarter of a mile away.

Basheer had watched Cann turn into the hospital grounds and continued down the road to the next entrance into the parking areas. From the opposite end of the main parking areas, he watched Cann's advance and then his retreat and then his final surrender to the distance requirements of the hospital heirarchy. When he saw Cann alight from the Corvette, Basheer pulled the utility vehicle as close to the curb as he could get it, placed a sign inside the windshield with the word 'Delivery' written on it, and got out.

Basheer was sure that Cann was not aware he was being followed. Still, there was no reason to alert the man to the possibility so Basheer utilized the device of circling ahead and anticipating the subject's move so that he was not approached from behind. As Cann walked through the parking lots and then turned slightly to his left to climb the stairs at the front of the hospital building, Basheer approached the same entrance from the opposite direction, holding back just enough so that he did not prominently cross Cann's line of vision. Basheer made no attempts to hide himself from Cann and the result - as always - was that Cann paid no particular attention to him. The timing was perfect and Basheer reached the door just after Cann had gone in, to the point of catching the door before it had completely closed.

Cann walked straight to the large desk marked 'Patient Information" and Basheer maneuvered close enough to hear the conversation.

"I'm looking for a patient named Janie Reston?" It was stated as a declarative sentence but it was a question.

The receptionist punched the keyboard of her computer and after a moment said, "That would be the ICU - Intensive Care. Fourth Floor." She gave Cann the same pained smile that Beverly had exhibited earlier in Roger's office and Cann nodded brusquely in acceptance of the silent condolence and moved off to the elevators.

Basheer watched the light go off in the green triangle above the elevator doors and the red one go on indicating that Cann had begun his ascent. Then he walked back to the front doors, ignoring the receptionist's polite, 'May I help you, sir?', and stepped out onto the front steps in deep thought.

"Res-tohn? Jah-nee Res-tohn?" He mentally chewed on the name.

Basheer's motive in following Cann into the hospital had been twofold. He would have quickly and decisively seized any opportunity that would have presented itself to dispose of Cann as Sami had directed. But he hadn't seriously expected that such an opportunity would have arisen in this place. His other reason was to simply find out why Cann had come to the hospital. Any knowledge - and any addition to present knowledge - always afforded increased opportunity and increased advantage in an operation.

But he had not expected to recognize a name - or did he? Why was that name familiar?

Then he remembered. Sami had said it that morning in their discussion of this Professor Cann. 'A friend of this Jahnee Restohn girl,' he had said.

But that made no sense. Sami had been referring to the girl they had all used at the house over the last couple of days. And that girl was dead. She had been beaten far beyond what many strong men had survived. She could not possibly be alive.

But - stranger things had happened. Basheer had seen them. ICU. Intensive Care. Yes it fit. It could be. He must call Sami.

The elevator doors opened on the fourth floor and Cann stepped out into a surprisingly colorful hallway dominated by a blue carpeted and heavily flowered sitting area on his immediate left opposite the receiving desk which was to his right.

In the farthest corner of the sitting area was a man and a woman who both appeared to be just entering early middle age. The woman was sitting half slumped in one of the chairs against the wall just staring down at her own clasped hands. The man was sitting a little more upright in the cornermost chair with his right arm across the woman's shoulders. But he had the same blank expression on his face.

The only other person in the waiting area was a large man in a rumpled suit seated in a chair against the adjoining wall directly next to the man and perpendicular to the couple. He was leaning forward looking down but his facial movement and expression showed he was talking to - maybe at - the couple.

Cann approached the desk on his right and asked about Janie Reston.

"Are you a relative?" he was asked.

"No. A friend."

The attendant smiled halfheartedly. "I'm sorry, sir. We can only give information on patients to close relatives. Or those with the permission of the next of kin." She smiled again. "Those are Ms. Reston's parents over there. If they want to give us permission to talk to you......"

"Thank you." Cann had no desire to interfere in their grief but he wanted intensely to know Janie's condition and prognosis. He also knew that often those in grief could receive some degree of solace from knowing that others cared about their loved one too.

As he approached the rear of the sitting area, he could hear the conversation that was going on. The man in the rumpled suit was saying, "Look, I know this is difficult but if there's anything at all that you can tell me ..."

The woman didn't look up but turned her head from side to side as she said, "But we don't know anything about what happened. We live 180 miles away. The last time we saw her was only two weeks ago when we dropped her off before the first day of classes and now...." She emitted a muffled wail. The rumpled suit sat back in his chair with a pained expression of his own.

Cann approached the threesome but spoke to the man in the middle - Janie's father - a dark-haired pleasant looking man with slavic features. Cann could see Janie's slightly rounded face and pronounced cheekbones in her father. "Excuse me. My name is John Cann. I knew your daughter at the University and I just..."

Janie's mother glanced up for a brief second and then looked back down at her hands.

The rumpled man stared hard at Cann.

Janie's father answered. "Yes. Professor Cann. Janie told us about you a couple of times. She liked you very much."

"The feeling was mutual, believe me," Cann smiled slightly.

"Was it?" The rumpled man was still staring hard at Cann.

Cann glanced at the man on his right and let his eyes rest stonily on the man's face for a moment without saying a word before turning back to Janie's father.

"Can you tell me how she's doing?" he asked.

"Not so good." His voice broke just the slightest bit. "The doctors say there's brain damage and..." He couldn't continue.

The pain Cann was feeling for Janie magnified a hundredfold. 'Oh, that mind. That joyous wonderful happy creative playful penetrating glorious mind' was all that Cann could think. The phrase 'what a waste', didn't even come close. The promise of ... Before she'd ever had a chance ...

Cann was still trying to re-build walls that had come down in the last couple of weeks but all that was accomplishing now was to enclose Janie within them.

"I'm so sorry." What a stupid ineffectual thing to say. But what else was there to say. He paused then asked, "Mr. Reston, would you mind if the hospital people discussed Janie's condition with me?"

Janie's father shook his head.

Cann turned back to the reception desk and waved a hand to get the attendant's attention. When she looked up, he pointed at Reston who nodded his assent from across the room. Cann walked over to the desk and asked again about Janie.

"She is listed in extremely critical condition, sir. Her entire body is covered in abrasions and contusions which are mostly the result of numerous blunt trauma injuries that appear to have been inflicted on her by hands and feet as well as other kinds of objects. She has enormous welts across her legs, stomach, and chest from being struck by some kind of thin instrument that actually cut right into the skin." The attendant was speaking in her best clinical tone but it was obvious that even her years of experience had not exposed her to any previous horror that compared to this. "She has a broken jaw and her left cheekbone is crushed. Both her right arm and hand are broken as are several of the fingers on her left hand. The tarsus of her left foot is cracked and she also shows a hairline fracture of the left tibia." The attendant moved on to the next sheet on her clipboard. "She has three separate skull fractures ... Are you at all familiar with shrapnel-type wounds?"

Cann nodded.

"Well, she has numerous pieces of her skull in sizes varying from tiny slivers to pea size chunks imbedded at the sites of all three skull fractures. The most serious of the fractures - they're all serious - separated a 3 inch square of skull which embedded itself in the tissue of the brain on that side causing a severe compression of the left temporal lobe."

The attendant stopped speaking for a moment and took a deep breath before going on. "A complete physical examination has been given and it indicates that she has been sexually assaulted by several different individuals more than," the attendant hesitated, "- more than twenty times in a thirty-six hour period." The attendant suddenly spoke more rapidly as though she were rushing to finish. "There is also further evidence of sexual mistreatment indicated by abrasions, lacerations, and other trauma to the breasts, thighs, groin, anus, and the exterior and interior of the vagina. Her uterus has also been torn by ... " She looked at Cann and he could see the grief in the eyes of the attendant. "Someone actually shoved something so sharp into her that they punctured her uterus." Finally it got to be too much and her voice broke. She emitted a quiet sob. "That poor child. I have never seen ... If I ever see anything like this again, I won't be able to do this work. I..."

Cann eyes were fixed and the rest of his body was rigid. His teeth were clenched so tightly they hurt and his fingernails dug into his palms inside the closed fists that hung stiffly by his side. He had to take several deep breaths before he was able to ask for the prognosis.

"I'm afraid it's much too early for anything like that. We believe she'll live. Her vital organs are intact and she seems to have the strongest heart that any of us have ever seen. She's on a monitor but that's just to keep us apprised of how she's doing. She's breathing and pumping well on her own. The head injuries are most severe. Areas of her brain have been badly damaged but the hindbrain where the cerebral cortex regulates her automatic functions is intact. The temporal area was badly injured and even in the best case scenario, she'll have speech, hearing, and balance problems and a lot of cognitive disorders."

Cann was a study in fire and ice. His sorrow was genuine and his pain was intense. And yet, he knew that, given the opportunity - and he would use every resource at his disposal to ensure that he did in fact get the opportunity - he would inflict similar injury on those who had done this to Janie.

He was aware of the dichotomy. How is it possible - is it possible? - for a man to feel such compassion and grief and yet be capable and willing to inflict the same pain on others.

He knew that the Kleins of the world would have gloried and delighted in what they perceived as his hypocrisy. They would have taken pleasure in the pain he was feeling over Janie and reveled in their presentations to him that this was retribution for his own evil deeds. They would conveniently overlook what Janie had suffered in their elation at making a point.

But they would get no satisfaction from Cann. He had long ago stopped trying to explain or feeling the need to do so. He had examined the same question many times for many years in regard to things that happened in many different places.

And the answer was context.

He had rejected the elaborate and abstract theories that sought to remove human nature from the examination of human experience. He had decided that what we do, we do because it seems right at the time and place we are in. At least the good ones do it in the hope that it's the right thing to do. And we judge the others, by whether or not what they have done is right - by a subjective standard defined by our own experience and relationships.

On the other hand, he had also rejected the theory embodied in the tatoo he still carried on his right shoulder. The death's head with a banner underneath containing the initials K-E-A-L-G-S-E-0. The letters stood for, "Kill-em all. Let god sort 'em out." It was a twentieth century bragadoccio that the special forces and others liked to pretend to live by. But as individuals, few did.

In the pitched battles - in the heat of the firefight - one did what was necessary and without thought. Later, when the killing was conscious and with forethought - with or without malice - it became of necessity a matter of context.

Rationalization?

Possibly.

Probably.

But Cann knew that if it were not for accidents of time and place - if not for some genetic variance of a thousand generations ago - if not for taking a right turn instead of a left - if not for the millions and millions of seemingly insignificant choices that are made over a lifetime - the person with the gun and the person receiving the bullet could easily have their positions reversed - or be friends. So you go with what you have and what you are and hope for the best. But when push comes to shove, you make choices the best way you know how. And you make them in the context of who has been hurt and whether they are with your side - or your gang - or your clan - or your tribe - or your country. It's all the same.

No excuses. No regrets. 'A' causes 'B'.

His focus returned to the attendant who had been watching him think. "Can I see her?"

"It's not pretty." She showed him a tight non-smile with her lips and nodded to her right.

"I understand." He went down the hall and into the second door on the right.

The room was, as is usual in an ICU, a jumble of machines and wires and IV's amid a cacophony of hums and beeps and whirrs. In the middle of it all, small and far beyond vulnerable was Janie.

Cann crossed over and looked down at her. She was a broken

doll. Every part was broken. If she had really been a toy, she would have been thrown away.

Her torso was covered by the hospital gown so, except for the ones on her face and arms and from just above her knees on down, the cuts and welts and bruises were not visible. But he knew they were there. Her left foot was taped up and her left leg had a brace anchored by a thick steel pin drilled through her knee to immobilize the tibia. She had a cast on her right forearm that ran to the base of the fingers on her right hand and small splints on many of the fingers on both hands.

But it was her face that actually brought tears to Cann's eyes. He couldn't remember the last time he'd cried and the sob that escaped came as a shock to him.

That lovely, child-like face with all its life and laughter and affection wasn't a face anymore.

The pale blue eyes that seemed to have looked at everything with a smile were buried somewhere underneath two slotted purple domes that were her bruised and swollen eyelids. The cartilage of what had been a small cute nose was destroyed - completely gone - and where the nose used to be were two flat holes in her face like a snout. Her lips were five times their normal size and the swelling caused them to peel back from her mouth revealing a cavity devoid of teeth. Her right cheek was swollen and rounded looking like an object the size of a softball was inside. The other side of her face was caved in, the bone underneath crushed to pieces. And just above and to the front of her left ear was a perfectly round depression where the cue ball had imprinted its exact shape on her beautiful young head.

Cann closed his eyes. Not to shut out what Janie had become. He was in no way disgusted or sickened by her appearance. What he had come to know of Janie was in there and always would be.

But he wanted to recall what she had looked like - and remember her that way, too. Two images - side by side in his memory. And he would not allow himself to think of her only as she used to be until he had settled accounts with those who had done this.

He walked out to the desk and asked the attendant, "How is she fixed for insurance?"

The attendant made a crooked face and said, "Not so great, really. It only covers the basics and maybe not all of those."

"Not any more," Cann said as he took a small plastic card out of his own wallet and handed it across to the woman behind the desk.

"As of now, she is covered by the best care in the world. You verify that with the people at my firm - here's the number. And from this moment on, anything she needs - anything - she gets it. Understood?"

"Absolutely." The attendant cast an appreciative and admiring smile at Cann's back as he walked over to the Restons.

He squatted down in front of them and said, "I wish there was more I could do but I did want you to know that Janie was helping me with some legal research which made her technically an employee of my firm. That means she's covered by our medical insurance plan which is pretty good." He patted Mrs. Reston's hand. "So you don't have to worry about that at least."

Janie's mother smiled at Cann and squeezed his hand. Her father just kept nodding over and over with tears in his eyes.

"And we're going to find out who did this to her, believe me."

The man in the rumpled suit was no longer seated next to the couple but he was still only a few feet away from them in the waiting area and heard what Cann said.

"We, cowboy?"

Cann turned and glared at the man. He was not in the mood for any cruelty towards these people, intentional or otherwise. He had pegged the man as a police detective from his demeanor if not his clothes and, while his instinct was to afford the police officer all the professional and other courtesies unless and until persuaded otherwise, at that moment, it wouldn't have taken much persuading.

"If you want to talk to me, let's go over here," Cann said indicating the hallway with his head. The man followed.

Cann walked around the corner into the hallway and stopped. He extended his hand. "John Cann."

"Detective Pen Avery, Mr. Cann." He took the offered hand in a firm grip that actually swallowed Cann's slightly larger than normal-sized hand. The term ham-fisted is usually just a figure of speech but... The detective was a large man – about 6'3"- and easily over 250 pounds - but even so, Cann was astounded at the size of Avery's hands which really were the size of small hams.

"I'm in charge of the investigation of the Klein murder and this assault."

"I figured that out." Cann bore right in. "Do you have a problem with me, detective?"

Avery tried unsuccessfully to hitch the waist of his pants over the belly blocking the way. "You were the chief suspect for a while, did you know that?"

"So I hear."

"What does this Furden woman have against you anyway? She was pushing pretty hard for you to be picked up."

Cann wanted to be generous. "All I know is she's known Janie all her life. This can't be easy for her. I think maybe she felt a little threatened by my relationship with Janie."

"Which was?"

Cann tensed the muscles in his arms and hands and looked hard into the detective's eyes. He was mollified when he didn't find the expected leer.

"Counselor. Adviser. Lawyer in a way. And friend. Don't read any more into it, detective."

Avery saw the intensity and felt the power of the man and what he had just said.

"Okay. Your alibi checks out anyway."

"It should. At the time of Klein's murder - all of yesterday for that matter - I really was sitting in the White House. Some of the time with the President of the United States."

"The ultimate character witness, hmm?" Avery commented.

Cann shrugged. "Maybe to you. But it is conclusive evidence of where I was." He squinted at the detective who still had a cynical look on his face. "Is that what this attitude is all about? You thought you were going to have a suspect handed to you on a silver platter and now you're pissed because you'll have to do some work? Because you might have to find evidence that leads you to a suspect instead of tailoring what you do find to one you already have?"

The detective turned his head and made a threatening face at Cann and jabbed a forefinger into Cann's shoulder.

"Listen up. You keep..."

Cann made a flicking motion of his hand that Avery didn't really see and barely felt but an instant after the detective had poked Cann, he realized that his hand was hanging loosely at his side, fingertips tingling slightly, and he frankly didn't know how it got there.

Cann felt strongly that this was neither the time nor the place for a confrontation, however. "Detective, listen. I'm not going to give you a lot of melodramatics about how sweet that kid in there was....is. But ... have you seen her?"

The question made the detective pause. "Just when she was wheeled by," he said. He was suddenly speaking more softly and Cann could see by the look on his face that the detective was stricken by Janie's condition in spite of his demeanor. That revelation changed Cann's attitude toward the detective.

"Did you see what she looked like before?" he asked in a softer tone of his own.

Avery nodded. "The mother showed me a picture." He blinked and turned away for a second. "Look, I've got three daughters of my own. All grown now but..."

Cann continued the truce. "Listen, I apologize for the 'suspect' remark I just made. It was out of line."

Avery brushed the back of his hand through the air as if to say, 'Forget it'.

Cann decided to see if he could get some information to start with. "Has Janie spoken at all? Has she been conscious at all since she came in?"

"No. Aside from the injuries, she's still got so much of that drug in her that the doctors feel she probably hasn't been conscious for the last forty-eight hours. Considering what's been done to her, I suppose that's good."

"What drug?"

"The one they call 'roofies'. I don't remember how to say the exact name.

"Rohypnol."

"Yeah. That's the one."

Cann's eyes narrowed. "Have you got any suspects - besides me, of course?"

Avery began to look a little irritated again but he answered. "Just the guy in the car with them."

No one - Roger included - had told Cann about Massoud.

"What guy?"

Avery in turn was puzzled by Cann's obvious surprise. "It was all over the papers about the guy driving the car with the two women in it. How come you didn't know?"

"I really was out of town, Detective. Who is this guy? What's he look like?"

Avery looked askance at Cann for a moment trying to make a decision. Then he reached inside his suit jacket and took a mug shot out of the pocket. He handed it over to Cann.

Cann recognized the face in the photo instantly from the ones that Goren had faxed over to him.

But it made no sense. Those guys were involved in Ted Wagner's death. Or at least with the group they had connected to Ted's death. What possible connection could there be between Ted's death and Janie's attack? And what the hell did this guy in the picture have to do with Janie?

It wasn't easy for Cann to conceal from the detective all of the thoughts and questions running through his head.

But he did.

He could have shared what he knew with the detective and let the law handle it.

But he didn't.

Because he knew that if he told Avery that this man in the photograph was living at a house rented by the Chair of the Middle East Studies Department, and that there was a potential connection between the people living there and Middle East terrorist groups, the detective would take no immediate and direct action. He couldn't. He would be required to start a process that would begin with a conference with his superiors who would then check with a prosecutor who would in all likelihood decide that there was insufficient probable cause to support a search warrant or any other immediate action. A decision might be made to seek authorization for a wire tap but that, like an application for a search warrant, required an affidavit from someone who had personal knowledge of sufficient facts to support the request. And that would be Cann whose only source of the information was Goren and he couldn't reveal that.

Another reason that Cann wouldn't give Avery the information he had was that it would go into the detective's report which would end up in files that were public record and therefore accessible to the police reporter who sanctimoniously placed his determination of what was important and what was not ahead of every other consideration including privacy and public safety. Notwithstanding national security or Janie's safety or even the simple concept of justice, this reporter would smell 'his Pulitzer' in the revelation of this putative worldwide conspiracy and, in the exercise of the 'people's right to know', - unconstrained by any concomitant duty to inform - he would reveal to the perpetrators all they needed to know to allow them to use their network and resources to be long gone before any repercussions befell them.

And Cann intended to see that there were repercussions. That was the biggest reason Cann had for keeping the information to himself. He wanted to. This was his to take care of. And he would. No apologies. No excuses. In an instant, he had been handed the information he thought he would spend days gathering. He had a very good start at the 'who' of Janie's horror. 'A' begets 'B'. Bravo. How appropriate. It wasn't that he would derive pleasure from what he was about to do. But he would get satisfaction. That would do.

*   *   *   *

Basheer had gone back out to the Land Rover after calling Sami from the hospital lobby.

"What do you mean - alive?" Sami had said impatiently. "How can that be? Why do you say it?"

Basheer told him what he had done and seen and overheard. Sami was not yet comfortable enough with leadership to question Basheer for taking the assignment beyond the parameters of what Sami, and by extension, what Al-Asif had dictated. And, in any case, he felt the beginnings of resentment toward the responsibilities of leadership.

Al-Asif was the leader. But he was away. And because of the cell organizational structure of the network, he couldn't be reached. Sami knew that the chief was outside Washington somewhere - in Virginia actually but that was all he knew. He had no telephone number and wouldn't have used it if he did.

So Sami knew that it was upon his shoulders to analyze the situation and decide upon a course of action and then see that proper action was implemented.

He was silent on his end of the phone for a long time as he considered the possibility that Basheer was simply wrong. But based on what he had been told - and that was all he had - and Basheer was known to be reliable, he concluded that the girl whom they had mistreated so badly and whom they all thought was certainly dead, was not.

In addition, this man Cann who posed some kind of threat to the mission in his own right had now gone to visit the girl. By itself, the information the girl could impart would destroy the men and the house and the mission and perhaps lead up the network and back to the source. That could not be allowed to happen. It was possible that she had already communicated with Cann and he already knew about the mission.

Sami had decided. He told Basheer. "Stay with Cann. Follow him and find the opportunity to take him out. Create the opportunity if you must. But remember the chief's orders. It must be done unobserved - invisible. Be patient. You have time with you as long as you do not let him out of your sight. The opportunity will come. Go with Allah."

"What about the girl?"

"I will take care of the girl," Sami replied. "Don't concern yourself with that. You take care of the professor."

Basheer waited for a half hour before Cann came out of the hospital and walked to the Corvette, got in without looking around, started the engine, and drove to where the driveway exited onto the street. Basheer, still confident in his anonymity, pulled up right behind Cann.

Except that Cann was back to business now. He first felt and then saw the vehicle pull-up behind him and, while he knew it could be the most innocent of actions, he was in his business mode.

In a Corvette, the side view mirrors are controlled by levers that sit in a recess in the console to the right of the driver and down on the floor. They can be moved up or down, right or left, either side, with one finger of the right hand. Cann maneuvered the mirrors to focus on the driver's side of the passenger compartment of the Land Rover behind him and was able to do so without any movement discernible to its driver.

Yes. Another face from Goren's faxes.

Cann put the Corvette into first gear and turned right out of the parking lot with the Land Rover following close behind. "Time to rock and roll, my friend," he muttered without moving his lips and began to accelerate.

Cann felt a mild sense of professional irritation at the way he was being followed. Basher was making no effort to conceal his actions as if Cann was a rank amateur. Then Cann reflected on his own unconcern for the basics of tradecraft that should have been automatic on the way to the hospital and realized that he had probably lulled his follower into a false sense of security.

"Score one for the good guys," he thought. "Let's keep it that way."

He came to a stoplight at the intersection just a few hundred yards from the hospital. The light was red and as he came to a halt he instinctively scanned the area - and the people - around him.

His eyes fell on and passed over the driver of the blue sedan which was facing in the opposite direction across the intersection from Cann waiting for the same light to turn green so he could continue down the road toward the hospital. The tiniest spark of recognition clicked in Cann's brain and he looked back at the man who at that moment was surreptitiously finishing a nod to the driver of the Land Rover behind Cann.

"When it rains, it pours, doesn't it?" Cann mused as the light turned green. "Okay. The more the merrier." Without looking over, he mentally jibed, "See ya," as the other car passed by on his left.

But his flippancy evaporated as he comprehended the full meaning of his observation. The man in the blue sedan was one of the same group as the driver of the Land Rover and the man who was arrested with Klein and Janie. And he was headed to the hospital. Cann completed the scenario and knew that Janie was in danger - again. If it was possible for a thought to hiss out of clenched teeth, one did. "You will not lay another finger on that girl!"

Suddenly suffocating under the weight of the urgency he felt, Cann dialed information on the car phone to get the number of the desk in the ICU at the hospital. He agreed to pay the charge to have it dialed automatically. The attendant answered on the second ring.

"ICU."

"Hello. This is John Cann. I was just there visiting Janie Reston?"

"Yes, Mr. Cann. What can I do for you?"

Cann made sure to keep his body language loose so as to look relaxed and unconcerned to the driver behind him.

"Are the Restons and Detective Avery still there?"

"The Restons went down to the cafeteria but the detective is still here. Well, actually, he went out to have a cigarette but he said he'd be right back."

Cann looked into the rear view mirror at the man who was now the quarry but didn't know it.

"Please listen," he said. "When Detective Avery gets back, tell him that I called. Advise him that one of the men who did this to Janie is on his way to the hospital."

The attendant gasped.

"Please. Just tell him that." Cann described Sami more from the fax than the sighting and told the attendant to give the description to Avery.

"And listen, if Avery wonders how I know or anything just tell him I'll explain later. But he's got nothing to lose by being on alert anyway."

Cann still had some concerns that the detective's cynicism would attempt to reassert itself.

"Here's my cell phone number. Give it to him if he wants to call. But whatever you do - convince him."

The attendant was already looking around with eyes that reflected the fear of a cornered animal.

"I will," she breathed.

As soon as the connection was broken, Cann got his bearings and turned right onto a two lane county road that had little traffic and no buildings.

A couple of miles down the road, Cann made the car start to buck by hitting the gas pedal over and over. When he reached a stretch of road where nothing was around, he put the car in neutral and let it coast to a stop. He pulled on the hood release under the dashboard to his left and popped the hood. He got out and lifted the heavy fiberglass hood until the catch snapped into place on the metal slide that became a prop. His follower had pulled up behind him and gotten out of the car.

"Having trouble?" The voice was heavily accented. The man appeared quite smug and arrogant. As if he knew he was in complete control of the situation.

'Good', thought Cann. 'My advantage there'.

Cann answered in his most naive voice. "It just started bucking. You know anything about these things?"

"A little," said Basheer. Actually, he really did. "Such problems are usually electrical these days - you will need to check your computer."

"Where's that?" Cann knew that the diagnostic readout for the Corvette's computer was inside the car under the dash but he asked the question anyway.

"Right there." Basheer pointed to what Cann knew to be the fuel pump relay. "Do you have a screwdriver?"

Cann was fully alert now as it became obvious that Basheer wanted him to turn his back. Cann complied, grateful for the gleaming chrome valve covers that sat atop the two manifolds of the huge 5.0 Litre V-8 engine. Basheer's reflection was clear and detailed in the one closest to Cann as he leaned over the engine. He saw Basheer take what looked like an ice pick from his coat and slowly - meticulously - line the instrument up with the base of Cann's skull. 'Quiet. Efficient. I would approve the method', thought Cann – 'if it were somebody else'.

Timing really is everything. Just before he thrust the pick into the back of Cann's head, Basheer took a breath - a universal anticipatory action - and pulled back the hand slightly that held the pick. At that moment, Cann moved to his right and turned his body in a counter clockwise motion raising his own left hand and grasping the back of Basheer's right wrist. By this time, Basheer had started what was intended to be his deadly act and Cann was able to use Basheer's forward momentum to guide the ice pick - and hand - into the side of the several hundred degree aluminum block of the corvette engine.

The ice pick broke and the flesh was seared but Basheer remained calm. He knew he would complete his mission. He was a trained killer and this man was a school teacher. Basheer had the advantage.

He knew that it was not size or strength that was the biggest advantage in a confrontation such as this. Nor was it training and skill, or even injury. Although all of those were factors. No. Basheer knew that the difference between a killer and another was simply that the killer would kill. Someone who had not killed would in all likelihood not be able to kill. It was almost a certainty. So that this man before him, who had caused him pain – yes - and avoided the first deadly attempt was still going to die because, unlike Basheer, he would not be prepared to kill.

Cann let go of the burned hand and, in a single motion, stiffened the three center fingers of his right hand and thrust them - arm rigid - into the cartilage at the front of the throat which protects the esophagus. The Adam's Apple. Even a light blow to that cartilage will jam it into the esophageal passageway causing a choking sensation that will debilitate the strongest attacker. A stronger blow will collapse the cartilage into the esophagus and block the airway causing a painful choking death.

The force of Cann's thrust was such that he felt the upper vertebrae of Basheer's spinal cord at the back of his neck with his fingertips as he completed the blow. Basheer fell to the ground and writhed around making gurgling sounds for several seconds before he stopped. Cann closed the hood of the Corvette and got Basheer back into his vehicle which he then pushed down the embankment on the side of the road and into the cornfield where it came to rest hidden from whatever traffic might come by. It wouldn't remain hidden forever. But it would be long enough.

He jumped back into the Corvette and turned the car 180 degrees by hitting the accelerator and turning the steering wheel hard to the left. As he sped down the country road, the cell phone rang. It was the attendant speaking in a hushed whisper as she crouched behind the desk in the ICU.

"Mr. Cann. Detective Avery never came back. And that man is here. He went into Ms. Reston's room. What should I do?"

Cann tried to hide his fury at the stupidity of calling him on the phone instead of doing something there. "Call security! Find Avery! Just do something! I'm on my way."

Chapter Twenty-Seven

Sami stepped through the doors of the elevator after it came to a stop on the fourth floor and looked to his left at the sitting area and to his right at the desk of the ICU.

Nothing. No one.

His initial surprise that it was completely empty was immediately overridden by his own conception of the United States as so technologically advanced that computers handled everything. It shouldn't be the least bit unusual for there to be no humans about. That also meant, however, that the area might be monitored by video cameras but he had minimized that risk by appropriating a set of doctor's greens from an untended storage closet.

He walked past the ICU attendant's desk on his right and went straight on into the hallway stopping at the first door on the right. He opened it and saw that it was empty so he crossed the hall and looked into the first door on the left. That room was occupied by an elderly man who didn't even notice the intrusion. He went back across the hall one more time and opened the second door on the right.

"Ah, there you are," he whispered to himself. He stepped inside pausing for a moment to make sure that he closed the door behind him.

He looked around the room and then walked over to the bed and stood looking down at Janie.

"That's funny," he said aloud, "but I remembered you as being more attractive." He laughed out loud at his own humor and then caught himself. He gave an initial cursory glance around the room. Then he looked down and travelled his gaze slowly along the length of Janie's body which was mostly covered by the off-white dressing gown. He reached out with his right hand and lifted the hem of the dressing gown exposing Janie from the waist down. "Ah, now I recognize you," he chuckled to himself. Then he put on a false pout. "But I'm sorry. I have no time." Another chuckle. Finally, tiring of his little game, he turned away from Janie making no move to cover her with the gown.

He began a more complete survey of the machines and devices around the room. 'Perhaps I should have let Basheer take care of this,' he thought to himself. Basheer knew computers and electronics. Sami was a historian by education and knew less of such devices.

His attention fell onto on the greenish-hued screen with the straight horizontal line moving across it punctuated regularly by the periodic beep accompanied by a spike shooting upwards to form a brief sharp peak. He knew of but had never seen life support systems and, knowing first hand the injuries Janie had received, assumed she was being kept alive artificially. He further assumed that the machine made Janie's heart beat, not the other way around.

'Not for much longer,' he thought as he traced the leads from the monitor to the bed and on to Janie where they picked up the electrical signals of her pulse. Without thought or care, he tore the patches from her and immediately the intermittent beeps elongated into one constant tone indicating to Sami that Janie's heart was no longer beating. His task was done.

With one more glance at Janie, he moved to the door, opened it just a little and started to peek his head out to see if the hallway and the rest of the ICU remained empty. As soon as enough of his face was showing through the space, one of Avery's five pound fists crashed straight into Sami's face sending him reeling back into the room and down into a sitting position on the floor.

Avery crossed the room to where Sami was and grabbed him by the front of the tunic he was wearing to pull him up to a standing position and place him in handcuffs. The detective's mouth was already beginning to form the words of the Miranda warning when he caught sight of Janie and the way her clothing was arranged.

He looked down at Sami who had followed his glance and who was now looking up into Avery's eyes which were no longer the eyes of a professional. Sami saw that they had become the eyes of a madman.

"You bastard! You little cocksucker! You haven't done enough to this kid? You had to..." Avery drew his right hand back and crashed it into the face of the terrified terrorist. Sami started to fall but the detective held onto the tunic with his left hand and supported Sami's weight to keep him standing. Again, the huge fist came back and again it crashed into Sami's face. Blood and cartilage were starting to stick to Avery's knuckles.

At about the time Avery was administering the third blow, Cann exited the elevator, dashed down the hall, and slid the last few feet to the door of Janie's room. He halted in the doorway with both hands braced on the frame of the door.

Avery didn't see him and Cann said nothing. By now, Sami was again in a sitting position and Avery had gone down on one knee still supporting the insensate Sami by the front of his shirt. For a fourth time, and then a fifth Avery methodically drew back his massive fist and slammed it into the increasingly unrecognizable face of his target. He had no thought of stopping of his own accord but as he drew his arm back again for a sixth blow, his positioning turned enough so that he caught sight of Cann standing in the doorway. It brought him part of the way back to reality and he lowered his fist.

"Don't stop on my account," Cann said calmly and meaning it.

But Avery had regained some of his control. He looked into Sami's face, then he looked at his own fist, and then he looked back at Sami.

"I shouldn't have done this. I just lost it when I saw..." He nodded toward Janie and Cann looked over. He crossed quickly to the bed and pulled Janie's gown down and gently smoothed it over her legs. Then he turned to Avery.

"In case you haven't guessed, it makes no difference to me if this guy's dead. As far as I'm concerned he is already. And if he isn't, he will be." Cann bent over the prone Sami and pressed his index and middle fingers against the jugular. "Okay. No need for anything else." He nodded to Avery. "You've done a service."

Avery shook his head in the negative. "No. It's not right. I have to report this. I was six months from retirement. And now this."

"And now what?" Cann asked. "Listen to me, Avery. Right now you're trying to apply frames of reference in a world where they don't fit. Understand something. This guy was a terrorist. A real live terrorist." Cann nodded at Janie and Avery followed his look. "You've seen what he was capable of. And terrorists don't give Miranda rights to their victims." Cann scored a point with that one. "What's done is done. And in a lot of people's books, you really have done a service. Like they say in the westerns," he pointed at Sami, "he was a man who needed killing." He spoke earnestly to the detective. "We're the only people who know what went on here. If you don't tell, I don't tell."

"I have to report it. It's my job."

Cann gave a short humph. "This? Your job? Maybe it should be but no one will see it that way. You'll be a bum and this pig'll be a hero - or a victim. There doesn't seem to be a lot of difference to some people these days." Cann looked hard into Avery's eyes to see if he was focused and listening. He was.

Avery was unsure of one thing. "This leaves you with something on me. I don't like that."

"All I can say is that won't be a problem for you. I know you don't know me but you'll have to trust me on that." Avery still looked a bit skeptical. Cann added. "If it helps, I'll tell you right now that I've already killed one of his pals. You'll find him inside a Land Rover in a cornfield a couple of miles down Highway 64 off the main roads." He stared at Avery with a questioning expression on his face and Avery stared back. Cann asked him, "Is that good enough? Are we even?"

Avery understood the deal and accepted with a nod before asking, "So what do we do with this guy. The receptionist could be back any time. I told her to wait downstairs but that won't last forever."

"Well, we've got to get him out of here, that's for sure," Cann said. "I'd keep him with me but I don't have a trunk in my car. This is your turf, Avery. You'll have to keep him for a while."

"How long's a while?"

"A few hours tops. And then I'll want you to bring him to the house these guys live in." He gave Avery the address.

"That's right off the campus," Avery said.

Cann replied, "Yup." He looked like he was considering something - trying to decide whether to do something or not. Then he reached his conclusion. He spoke to Avery. "Listen, if you want to spend some productive time in the months until your retirement, you might try to figure out what these guys - and that includes the one in your jail - had planned that involved more than teaching Middle East Studies."

Avery stared at Cann but not blankly. He was too astute a detective not to know that he was being handed the beginnings of a major case on a silver platter. And ending his career with an investigative coup wouldn't hurt his retirement - or a future as a security consultant or private investigator. He was also astute enough to know that under the circumstances, Cann couldn't and wouldn't give him any sources. He would have to develop his own leads.

But Cann surprised him by giving him one. "You might even want to start at a quarry 11 miles west of here," Cann continued. "I'm really not even sure of what you'll find. A cab - and a couple of bodies but I don't know whose. These guys killed him. That's all I know and don't ask me how I know."

"I didn't intend to." Avery knew where the quarry was and he knew of a snitch he could ascribe the tip to. But first things first. "Let's just get this guy out of here."

"Any ideas?"

"Same way they got Klein out of her office."

Cann didn't know what that meant until after Avery had been gone a few minutes and then came back with a large garment bag. Avery explained the plan as they packaged Sami for the trip.

As they worked, Avery kept looking at Cann. Finally, he asked. "Who the hell are you anyway, Cann."

"Don't worry, Avery, I'm one of the good guys."

"I believe you are, Cann. I wouldn't be doing this if I didn't."

Before they left, Cann reattached the leads from the heart monitor and the device immediately began to beep and spike in a regular cadence that indicated to Cann that he had done so correctly and Janie's heart was still going strong.

Cann looked fondly at her for a moment and then asked Avery if there was any way to put a guard on the door. "There are still some others who might want to hurt her."

"I'll see to it," Avery said gently.

"It won't be for long," Cann said quietly. "Just a few hours more.

*   *   *   *

On the way back to his condo, Cann stopped at a convenience store to pick up a newspaper. He scanned the banner headline which read

MIDDLE EAST PEACE!
President's Diplomatic Stroke of
Genius Breaks 50 Year Logjam

———————————

Arafat Names Ambassador Designate
Israel Frantically Maneuvers

Cann could see that he wouldn't have to read the articles to get the slant the press would be putting on what they were calling this 'diplomatic stroke of genius' on the part of their golden boy president.

He would eventually read the whole thing. Just not now.

He flipped to the Almanac information on the last page of the first section of the paper. Sunset: 7:21 PM. Dark about a half hour later. 8:00 o'clock would be just about right. He looked at his own watch. 3:52 PM. T-minus four hours and counting.

His bags from the previous night's flight were sitting outside the front door of the condo when he arrived. He brought them inside with him and threw them unpacked on the bed.

He stripped down to his underwear and got down on the floor to do some stretching exercises followed by a mild set of calesthenics. He exercised every morning and had done so this day but he wanted to be a little looser and would repeat the movements yet again a little later - before he went out.

He strode into the bathroom off the master bedroom glancing at himself in the mirror as he went by. His eye caught the tattoo on his shoulder and he remarked to himself that this time it just might apply.

He showered for a long time and then, still dripping, he went to the closet in the bedroom and took out a large boxy old-fashioned suitcase which he unlocked with a key he took from a small slot in an obscure pocket of his wallet. From the case, he withdrew the almost new Sig-Sauer P229 semi-automatic pistol which he had chosen to replace the damaged - well, destroyed actually - Beretta 92-F which had served him so well for all those years.

He field stripped the P229 and gave it a thorough cleaning before reassembling it. He also examined and cleaned the silencer that had been custom-made for the pistol. Then he took two empty clips from the suitcase and compressed 9 .40 SW ACP cartridges into each of the magazines. He gently placed the weapon, silencer, and ammunition on one of the night tables by the bed.

He went through the same process with the Colt Mustang Powerlite 380 pistol - minus a silencer - that fit neatly into the molded compact ankle holster which he placed on the table next to the Sig.

Then he pulled out the foot long black-bladed Muelay knife with its 5" handle and 7" blade. He felt the oil still on the blade from when it had been last put away. He gave the blade a gentle swipe with the cloth and placed it back into the scabbard which would itself fit snugly into the sheath sewn into the small of the back of the black coveralls which were the next thing he took out of the suitcase. Cann unfolded the coveralls and snapped them like a washed sheet in front of him and then hung them over the back of the chair by the dresser. The last item he pulled out was a pair of black slipper-like foot coverings with very tacky soles which he placed on the seat of the same chair.

He sat down on the bed, his back against the headboard, and picked up the phone and dialed.

Tip-Top Temps answered on the second ring.

"Mr. Goren, please."

"Who's calling, please?"

"John C. Black."

"Thank you."

Less than ten seconds passed before Goren picked up his extension.

"You're pressing both our lucks, aren't you, John?" No greeting.

"You asked me to advise you of what I learn about our friends. Remember?"

"I do. What have you got?"

Cann relayed the matter of Massoud's arrest which Goren indicated he already knew. He did not, however, know about the deaths of Basheer and Sami and whistled softly when Cann told him that.

"You're cutting quite a swath through their operation, John. What do you expect to accomplish with all of this?"

"This isn't an operation, Zvi. Not a sanctioned one, anyway. It's personal." He explained in general about Janie and what he intended to do in response to it.

Goren listened without emotion. He was a spymaster. A handler and existed in a world where the innocent got hurt all the time. He tried to get a vicarious sense of what Cann was feeling by imagining he had a daughter and she had been treated as this girl had been. But he had no family and couldn't really conjure up the feelings within himself to empathize. "So, what do you want from me, then," he finally asked.

"Two things. First, I want to know if it creates any problems for you or your people if this group is taken out."

"It's a fine time for you to ask, now," Goren chuckled. "There's just the two left by my account - this Naji and this Abdullah."

"Four, you're not counting Massoud or Al-Asif," Cann responded.

"Well, I don't know what you think you can do about Massoud while he's in jail but there's something I can tell you that you apparently don't know about Al-Asif. He left the house very early this morning for Virginia. You've only got two in the house now."

That was useful information for Cann and he thanked the Israeli agent. "But I'd still like to know if they'll be missed, Zvi?"

Goren's tone was completely indifferent and utterly conversational.

"Not by us. Obviously the operation is totally blown anyway. We're ... we have other ... what's that phrase – 'fish to fry'? Let's just say they won't be missed. What's the second thing?"

"Cleaners. About 9:00 PM. At their house. Tonight."

Goren weighed the negatives of becoming that closely involved in Cann's unsanctioned operation and decided they were negligible. Cann was known to be the consummate professional so it was highly unlikely that he would place them in a bad situation. Also, Goren had known Cann for a very long time and wanted to do this for him. You never know when he might need something from Cann in the future.

And Goren's cleaners were very good. These inhabitants of the nether world of evidence removal and body disposal made people and things disappear without a trace. Goren knew that the other side would be disturbed - some even intimidated - more by a mysterious disappearance than by a massacre. Helping Cann would be good for business.

"Okay. How many people will be travelling?"

"Three at the house - Naji, Abdullah, and we'll be bringing Sami to join them. There'll be a fourth outside of town." Cann described the location of Basheer's body. "Thanks, Zvi. I owe you."

"Not at all, John."

They both knew otherwise.

Cann hung up the phone and stretched himself out on the bed and went to sleep.

*　*　*　*

At least Cann had made one of his four classes that day. Sara Furden hadn't made any of hers. She'd intended to. She'd tried to. But she was out of the office in the morning and, after she'd returned, as the time for each class approached, she was unable to leave her office and face the students.

The young faces.

So, since three PM, she'd been sitting in a booth in the university Rathskeller in a sort of trance that was partially alcohol induced and the rest was the result of what had happened to Janie.

She'd been furious that the police hadn't called her until this morning about Janie even though they had found her last night. She was the one who reported the disappearance and they knew that here at Charlestown, she was closest to her of anyone. She hoped.

The police had said that they needed to be sure of the identification and then they had to notify Janie's parents first.

Still, Furden thought, they waited until 9:00 this morning.....

When they'd finally called, she'd rushed over to see Janie right away. Despite the nurse's warnings, there was no way she could have been prepared for what she saw. And she wasn't. Her experiences with injury were limited to the arena of athletic competition. Probably the worst thing she had ever seen - prior to this - was a compound fracture where the ulna of a volleyball player had protruded four inches through the skin of her forearm after a collision on the court.

But that was an accident. This.....And this was Janie. Her Janie. She was supposed to take care of her.

And Maria - Janie's mother - hadn't said a word to Furden. 'She blames me'. She knew it. When Furden was at the hospital, Maria just sat and stared and didn't answer Furden when she tried to talk to her.

And the police said it couldn't have been John Cann. He was in Washington. With the President, they said.

How convenient.

Well, then who was it?

She reached for the glass of deep red wine in front of her and took a sip. She wasn't really drunk. This was her fourth glass in about four hours and while she wasn't completely metabolizing the alcohol as she sat in the booth, the mere passage of time was dissipating some of the effects of the alcohol even as she took more in.

It had to be Cann. Who else could she blame? Only herself.

Janie had come to Charlestown because of Furden. Ever since there had been talk of college, it was assumed that Janie would come to Charlestown and Furden would take care of her. And look at her now. The agony was physically painful for Furden. Intolerable.

It had to have something to do with Cann.

But even that was Furden's fault. Janie wouldn't have known Cann if it wasn't for the nude dancing thing in the gym. Furden gave her the key. Furden didn't tell her about the alarm. Once again, she went through the jumbled analysis about why security showed up in the first place. She still didn't have a good answer to that. The knot in her stomach drew even tighter as she remembered that she had actually chuckled at first when Janie told her about the incident. 'Really funny, Sara!,' she thought with a vicious sarcasm directed at herself. This *IS* all your fault.' But whenever that thought tried to settle itself in her consciousness, her psychic self-defense thrust it violently out. Furden's head actually snapped when that happened.

'No! It can't be my fault! It has to be Cann! Who else could it be?'

And as it had throughout the day as Furden alternated between blaming herself or Cann - or an unnamed someone else, the tide of self-loathing ebbed temporarily. After four glasses of wine and four hours of continuous sitting, the need to urinate finally overcame her obsessive and repetitive dissection of events.

She went into the ladies room which was in the rear of the Rathskeller in the southwest corner of the building. The Rathskeller itself sat just inside the south entrance of the Charlestown campus facing east onto the campus extension of the north-south State Road 53. On the west side of the building and behind it, was the parking lot where Furden had left her car when she came in. She wasn't sure if she was going to try to drive herself home when - or if - she left the Rathskeller.

But there in the ladies room - for no good reason - she decided to open the window to check on her car. Break-ins weren't all that infrequent although, right now, she really didn't care.

She pushed open the small window which was hinged at the top and looked out into the semi-lighted parking lot. The cool air felt good on her face which - she now realized - had been flushed for most of the day.

Then to the left, just out of the corner of her eye at the far end of the parking lot some 30 or 40 feet away, she saw some movement. Probably some guy taking a leak in the parking lot. She would never understand why men seemed to prefer to relieve themselves outside even though they had just left a place with a perfectly good and certainly more private facility available.

But the man wasn't relieving himself. Furden watched as the dark-clad figure went up to the six-foot wooden fence that bounded the parking lot on three sides and, on the south, separated the lot from the large residence on the other side which Furden knew was the house where many of the faculty and staff of the Middle East Studies Department lived.

At that moment, her brain suddenly switched from its repetitive abstract wanderings to information retrieval and analysis. The police had arrested a middle easterner - as far as they knew since he wasn't talking - who was with Janie when she was found. Middle East? Was there ... ?

The man in the parking lot was standing right at the fence facing toward it and then reached both hands up and grasped the top of two of the wooden planks. He looked to his right - away from Furden - and then back to his left to see if he was being observed. There was just enough illumination from one of the half-useful security lights for Furden to see his face. And recognize it.

Cann!

Furden watched as he jumped and pulled with his hands at the same time and effortlessly cleared the high fence almost seeming to float over it and down on the other side.

Cann! And a Middle Easterner was with Janie when they found her! And he's going into the Middle East studies house. There *is* a connection. It *is* Cann's fault! She knew it! It had to be!

It didn't occur to her to wonder why Cann was sneaking over the back fence if he was acting in concert with them. For the first time all day she felt - just a little - vindicated.

Chapter Twenty-Eight

Cann dropped soundlessly on the other side of the fence and remained motionless for a while in a squatting position. While he watched and listened for any signs of activity, he completed some preparations.

From the modified fanny pack he wore in front of him, he took out the small round canister and blackened his face with the contents. It is a common misconception that a person who is outside in the dark and looking into a lighted structure will not be visible to a person inside. To the contrary, the light spilling from the structure will readily be caught and reflected by the skin of the person in the dark. Cann corrected that and rubbed the excess into his hands and then put the black latex gloves on over it. Then he extended his right leg out in front of him and reached down into the large rectangular right front thigh pocket of his coveralls where he carried the Sig-Sauer P229 semi-automatic pistol. He took the silencer out of the fanny-pack on his belt and carefully lined-up its threads with those in the barrel of the P229. He screwed the noise suppressor on tightly and slid the assembly back into the thigh pocket.

When none of his senses indicated any movement or other activity between him and the house, he moved forward. Much of his movement was cloaked by the large oak trees dripping with enormous tendrils of spanish moss which formed a ghostly curtain between him and the house.

The back of the house loomed large in the darkness. To Cann's left was the rear of the one story windowless garage whose weathered shingles melded into those of the house proper. Visually surveying to the right he saw nine windows lined up across the second story. The first floor had eight windows, each one directly under one on the second floor except for the center one, which had a glass paned wooden door which probably led directly into a kitchen. Running along the entire length of the rear of the house was a porch raised a foot off the ground and with no railings but which held the base of eight narrow columns supporting an overhanging roof which itself ran the length of the house just under the second floor windows.

There were two lit windows on the side of the house facing Cann as he approached. One on the second floor near the westernmost corner - Cann's right - and one on the first floor immediately to the right of the door in the center. The pane of glass in the kitchen door was also lighted. Cann knew that that didn't mean those were the only potentially occupied rooms in the house or even that they were occupied at all so his eyes continuously scanned the back of the house and the surrounding area for movement. Scanning instead of staring also afforded him greater night vision in general since the rod shaped cells of the retina have much greater acuity in lowlight situations than the cones which are designed to pick up and discern specific shapes but need more light to do so. From training and experience, Cann knew that it was always easier to see something in the dark if you are not looking directly at it.

Cann began to move forward. His advance on the house would take as long as it had to take. Survival is the antithesis of impatience. Every step he took was measured and silent and coordinated with every component of a full set of integrated parts. A symphony of stealth in which a solo can be deadly - each piece operating independently but ineffective if isolated. In that way did Cann conduct his approach to the house, moving his feet and body while observing everything around him with every sense he had.

He reached the porch at the first column to the right of center and stopped yet again, senses attuned to every possible stimulus.

Sight and sound reported in at once. What appeared to be the muffled thump of a refrigerator door closing was followed a microsecond later by a glimpse of movement in the kitchen. Cann was by now seated on the ground against the porch with his right shoulder perpendicular to and pressed against the column which was between him and the house. His eye peripherally caught movement in the kitchen and he turned full face in that direction. Through the lighted window, he could see the upper back and head of an obviously large man. Cann couldn't see his face. He knew from his own process of elimination in combination with the information from Goren that it should be either Abdullah or Naji.

The man in the house walked away from Cann toward the entrance to the kitchen and out. Cann waited before moving closer to the house. Suddenly, the man returned, standing in the inner kitchen doorway with his face toward Cann who could now recognize Naji from the photo. Naji stood in the doorway with a cigarette dangling from his lip and a plate of food in his right hand and a glass of something in his left. As Cann watched motionless, Naji lowered his left shoulder and reached out with his left elbow to flip the light switch down. The kitchen went dark.

Cann waited for his eyes to adjust to the diminished light and then crept across the porch to a spot under the kitchen window on the right of the outer door. Stretching his neck carefully up he confirmed the prior perception that he had been able to hear the refrigerator door slam because the window was open - about four inches. A good sign that the alarm system - if they had one - was not active.

The light in the kitchen came back on. Cann scrunched down under the open window. He heard heavy footsteps pound on the floor of the kitchen and then the muffled clink of plates being placed on the table. Then the footsteps continued on toward the outside door of the kitchen. It opened.

Cann tensed where he knelt in anticipation of the man inside coming out onto the porch, his left hand reaching down and around into the small of his back for the Meulay knife. He could see Naji's shadow fall and grow across the threshold but the man inside didn't follow. Cann stayed crouched and pressed against the outside of the house, his attention riveted on the opening through which the light seemed to blaze. Then Naji's hand flicked the remains of a lit cigarette out into the yard behind the house and disappeared back into the house. The door closed behind him and Cann heard the footsteps recede.

The kitchen went dark again. Cann allowed his muscles to untense just a little, and, still crouched, leaned his back against the wall and rolled his head to the left until he could see into the window. Because of the darkness, he also searched the kitchen with senses other than sight to satisfy himself that the room was empty. Then he removed the silenced Sig from the thigh pocket.

He had also noted that Naji's casual manner in opening the door was further evidence to Cann that the entrances to the house were not alarmed or, if they were, the system was not set at the moment.

He twisted on the balls of his feet, still crouched, until he was facing the door. He turned the knob with his left hand and, muscles once again tensed and poised to propel himself away from the house and back into the shroud of spanish moss if an alarm went off despite the contrary indications, he pushed the door open.

No alarm. No audible one anyway.

Of course, if the house had a silent alarm, it wouldn't take long to evoke a response - some movement should become apparent within seconds. So Cann waited and watched and listened for several minutes.

When nothing happened, he half hopped, half-duck walked inside and slid to the right of the doorframe with his back now against the inside of the outer wall. He closed the door with his left hand and stopped and listened some more. The only sound -

if it even was that - seemed to be very subdued and muffled voices coming from somewhere else in the house.

He remained quiet and used his available senses to examine the kitchen in the darkness making sure he knew where everything was before he made any move. Then he slowly made his way across the kitchen to the doorway he had seen Naji exit through a short time before.

Only then did he stand up and put his back against the interior wall of the kitchen. Once again he tilted his head back until it touched the wall behind him and rolled it, this time to the right, to peer out. He saw that on the other side of the wall was a hallway that ran the entire length of the house.

He slowly extended his head further into the hall and swept his vision to the left and right. He saw no light or other evidence of first floor activity in either direction.

Then he looked straight across the hallway into the front half of the house. He could see all the way through to the inside of the front door of the house. About eight feet back and to the left of the front door, Cann could see the baluster of the handrail of the steps that apparently led to the second floor but any further view to the left was blocked by the stairway itself.

To the right of the front door from where Cann stood, shimmering dully on the wall, Cann saw splashes of light that seemed to change randomly in intensity from second to second. The light exhibited a non-pattern like the flickering of a candle but lacked the warm reds of candlelight. This light's existence was defined in shades of gray like the light seen from outside a dark room where a television is on.

Cann crossed the hallway in one large step and positioned himself with his back against the right wall of the foyer opposite the staircase. He sidled along the wall until he was opposite and beyond the baluster he had observed and just to the left of the door from which the gray light emanated.

He looked up the staircase and saw a miniscule amount of light in the second floor hallway which was likely to be coming from the lighted room at the far western end of the house.

First things first.

One more time, Cann rolled his head along the wall until he was able to see into the room to the right of the door. He saw that the light was indeed coming from a television set and it enabled Cann to observe a second large man apparently asleep in an easy chair opposite the television.

Cann recognized the man as Abdullah.

He slid his back down the wall until he was in a squatting position again and rolled his back around the frame of the door to his right and into the room where Abdullah sat sleeping.

Cann surveyed the room which was dominated by the huge pool table running lengthwise to his right and left in the center of the room. The wall he was leaning against had a couch against it and next to that a small desk at the corner. The wall that ran away from Cann on his right was all floor to ceiling bookcases. The wall opposite him also consisted of floor to ceiling built-in bookcases with two easy chairs angled in front of them. The wall that ran along the front of the house - to Cann's left - had a small writing table at the point farthest from Cann, then the chair, angled toward Cann, in which Abdullah was laying with his head bent forward at the neck, and then a floor lamp with a tiffany-type shade on it. It wasn't on.

The only light in the room came from the television which was on a wheeled wooden portable stand in front of the bookcases on Cann's right. It was turned slightly away from Cann so that it would face the chair Abdullah was in. As a result, Cann couldn't see what was playing on the television.

He really didn't care. He was here to do a job.

If this had been strictly business, Cann would have been out of the room already. Within seconds of his entry, he would have taken careful aim from where he was and put a bullet into the head of the sleeping Abdullah. It was an easy, elementary shot with a 0% chance of error on Cann's part.

But this was personal. And so he hesitated. It wasn't a matter of savoring the moment - or was it? All Cann knew was that it would be too easy for Abdullah to be allowed to check out without knowing he was going. This man had to experience at least a fraction of the fear that Janie must have felt at his hands. And even if he felt no fear, Cann would at least make sure that he experienced the moment when he knew - without a doubt - that he was about to die.

Cann checked quickly back over his left shoulder into the foyer for any movement and, seeing and sensing none, slid up into a standing position. He walked slowly toward Abdullah, passing between the front wall of the house and the pool table on his right. When he reached the corner of the pool table, he placed his rump on the rail and slid along it until the side pocket of the pool table was just below the small of his back. He looked over at the sleeping Abdullah whose chin was on his chest and whose right hand was stuck down inside the front of his pants.

Cann looked around for something to prod the sleeping Abdullah with from a distance and saw a pool cue leaning against the corner where the two walls of built-in bookcases met. He lifted his weight from the side of the pool table and took a few steps forward and to his right to reach and grab the cue stick. As he turned to step back to the pool table, his eye caught the activity on the television screen.

In all his years of field work - on all the missions and assignments he had undertaken - Cann had been renowned as the quintessential professional. Business-like and emotionless. Nothing had ever shaken him or thrown him off his plan.

But on the screen he saw Janie being held from behind in a sitting position on the pool table by Naji while Abdullah and Basheer each held one leg out to her side almost perpendicular to her torso while Sami shot the cue ball - hard - into her groin - over and over. And each time the cue ball struck, all four of the men cheered obscenely.

In the hospital, Cann had cried. Now he choked. A brief rattling noise escaped from his throat as the bile and venom in him grew to a point where he was on the verge of losing control.

If Abdullah had awakened at that moment, he would have had an edge on Cann who - most uncharacteristically - was immobilized by shock and rage. It only lasted a few seconds before training which had long ago become reflex regained control.

Cann pulled his eyes away from the image of Sami poking at Janie's groin with a cue stick and looked down again at Abdullah. Then he took the cue stick he was holding in his left hand and tapped the small end twice on Abdullah's cheek. The large man stirred and scratched himself with his left hand before opening his eyes. When he saw Cann standing over him, he didn't jump or start or make any sudden move of any kind. His eyes went from Cann's face to the silenced pistol and then back up to Cann's face again. He started to withdraw his right hand from his pants and then stopped and with a tiny motion of the fingers on his left hand indicated to Cann that he wasn't about to try anything - he just wanted to remove his hand.

Cann flipped the muzzle of the P229 up and down twice to signal that he could remove his hand - but slowly! Abdullah already knew that. He pulled his hand out from under his belt and placed it carefully on the right arm of the easy chair matching the position of his left hand.

Abdullah began to speak. "What do..."

Cann quieted him by waggling his left index finger in the air and lifting the P229 slightly for effect. Abdullah stopped talking.

Cann shifted the pistol into his left hand but kept it pointed at Abdullah. It occurred to Cann that Abdullah might see this as an opening for him to move against Cann on the assumption that he was less effective from the left side than the right. Abdullah would have been fatally wrong.

With his right hand, Cann reached out and grabbed the upper front corner of the television set and turned it on its casters so that it still faced mostly toward Abdullah but where Cann could see the lighted surface of the screen from the side.

Abdullah looked at the activity on the screen and looked back at Cann with no discernible emotion on his face. Then he looked back at the screen again and again looked back at Cann. He raised his eyebrows in a questioning manner and slowly turned his hands over onto their backs where they rested on the arms of the chair. What? He didn't understand. What is the problem?

Cann spoke very very softly. And very calmly. And very coldly.

"That girl was a friend of mine." He shifted the P229 back into his right hand.

Abdullah continued to stare blankly at Cann for a moment then a small degree of understanding started to evidence itself on his face. With the backs of his palms still resting on the arms of the chair, Abdullah splayed his fingers questioningly. His eyes widened and his upper lip curled in a look that could have been fear or could have been arrogance.

"But ... these things happen," he said in a tone that was equally ambiguous.

"So do these," Cann said as he lowered his aim and squeezed the trigger and fired one very accurate and effective round into Abdullah's groin.

Silenced pistols are not really silent. It's all relative. But the muffled popping sound was over in an instant. Abdullah's grunt as the bullet struck him also passed quickly but then the slow realization of what had happened to him grew and, finally, Cann saw fear.

Abdullah looked down into his lap and seemed fascinated with the spreading red stain that seeped through the crotch of his pants. After a moment, he looked up at Cann, turned his hands over to a palms down position, and gripped the ends of the arms of the chair. Cann saw his forearms tense as the wounded man tried to transfer his weight forward and pull himself out of the chair. He only got part way up before falling back. Not because the injury was that close to draining the life out of Abdullah - it was actually a quite survivable wound and would take a very long time to cause death through loss of blood - if at all. But it was not an easily repaired wound and the realization that even if he lived he would do so without his manhood was what momentarily deflated Abdullah's resolve.

Cann was not ordinarily a cruel man and even taking into account what this beast and the others had done to Janie, he took no visceral pleasure of his own in what he was doing. This was for Janie.

Once again, Abdullah sought to heave himself from the chair and this time managed to get shakily to his feet.

Cann shot him once in the stomach and Abdullah fell back into the chair. Unlike the groin shot, the stomach hit was a life threatening injury. Left untreated, Abdullah would die. That was precisely what Cann intended. And dying from a gunshot wound to the stomach was a slow and painful death. That part wasn't something that Cann required but - make no mistake - if he had the time, he would have let Abdullah linger.

But there were other things to do. And it was time. Cann had seen the look he needed to see and knew that Abdullah understood his condition and knew with certainty that he was going to die. The brutal terrorist's face underwent a perverse transfiguration as he looked up from his stomach, his eyes widened, the rest of his face twisted into a mask of lines and wrinkles, and a sob burst through his contorted lips.

Cann raised the P229 and pointed the barrel directly at the forehead of the sobbing terrorist whose eyes - for a brief second showed a flicker of disbelief, a suspicion or a hope, perhaps, that this man really wouldn't kill him. Then the realization of imminent death returned and Cann squeezed the trigger gently until the Sig-Sauer popped again and a small, clean, initially bloodless hole appeared instantly just above the exact mid point between Abdullah's eyes.

'Dead center', was the concept that crossed Cann's mind as he watched the terrorist slump the rest of the way back into the chair ending with his head back, eyes shut, mouth wide open.

Cann pushed himself off the rail of the pool table and stepped across to where he could see the television screen and what was playing on it. He picked up the remote control and hit rewind and waited. He didn't want to see what was on the tape but he was determined to know if there were others involved that he didn't know about. He turned the television set so it faced in the direction of the pool table and sat back against the rail.

He watched the numbers on the tape counter run backwards until they reached zero at which time the VCR didn't stop but went automatically into the play mode and the scenes of horror began. It was intensely and physically painful for Cann to watch and he accelerated the speed to get through it quickly. At least the herky-jerky fast-forward play gave the events some small degree of unreality. But nothing could minimize the magnitude of what Janie had endured. With teeth clenched so hard his head ached, Cann watched to the end past the point of Al-Asif's savage beating and Abdullah's final act of degradation. Cann saw enough to identify all the perpetrators of the torture and confirm for himself the integrity of his course of action.

When the tape ended, he dropped the remote behind him onto the green felt of the pool table and, using the snowy gray light of the screen to help him see, he re-filled the magazine of the P-229 with three more shells he took from the front fanny pack. He smacked the replenished magazine back into the pistol with the heel of his left hand, pulled the slide back and then forward as quietly as he could to ready the weapon for use, and then moved out into the foyer.

He crossed to the foot of the stairway and again stopped and listened. He heard nothing. Then, back pressed against the wall to avoid the centers of the stair treads - it was an old house and if they were going to creak it was likely they would creak in the middle - he sidled up the stairs slowly - one at a time - testing each step. He reached the landing at the top without making a sound and rolled his head around the corner so he could see down the hall.

In addition to the door directly opposite him, there were four more running down the hall on the far side. The last door on the left was partly open and a dim shaft of light spilled into the hallway. It enabled Cann the advantage of seeing dimly but well enough all the way down the hall. More importantly, it would allow Cann to see a shadow moving inside the room before it ever emerged into the hall.

Cann sidled around the corner, pistol held against his right thigh pointing downward. Still keeping to the wall, he made his way down the hall toward the lighted room. He reached the first of the four doors on his way to what he presumed was Naji's room and noted that each door on the opposite wall had a counterpart on his side of the hall. To see if they were generally locked and for future reference if needed, Cann tried the knob. It turned and the door opened a crack. Cann pulled it closed and moved on to the next set of doors.

Just before he reached the second door, two melodic tones reverberated incongruously throughout the house. Cann's first thought was a grandfather clock of some sort? If it were that, it was likely that Naji would not react to it. He focused all his attention on the light coming from Naji's room and waited. No movement. No apparent activity. Then the tones rang out for a second time and the sound sorted itself out in Cann's cognition - the door bell!

He reached for the knob to the second hall door. Unlike the previous one, this one was locked. Never taking his eye off the entry to Naji's room, Cann slid quickly back along the wall to the first door he had passed and opened that door with his left hand just as he saw movement in the lighted room. Naji actually came into the hall an instant before Cann was able to duck inside but because of the change in the lighting and Naji's own inattention, he didn't see Cann.

Naji pounded down the hall shouting in Arabic at Abdullah, questioning him with obvious irritation as to 'why he cannot answer the door'? Cann heard the terrorist stomp past the door of the room and listened as he turned left and went down the stairs. A second or so later, Cann cracked the door open and exited, stationing himself at the corner where he was well positioned to observe whatever happened in the foyer.

Naji reached the bottom of the stairs and glanced over into the room on the right as he reached for the front door handle. If the pool table hadn't been between them, he might have seen the red wetness over Abdullah's front but, as it was, what he could see of the position Abdullah was in was not unusual and Naji assumed he was asleep. Mumbling a proverb about the rewards of the lazy, Naji opened the door and stared indifferently down at the woman standing there.

"I want to see John Cann." Sara Furden drew herself up straight and slurred her words only a little bit.

Naji's English was excellent but like almost everyone in an alien culture, he was insecure about it and assumed he hadn't understood.

"I beg your pardon," he said almost totally without an accent.

"John Cann. I know he's here," Furden insisted. She moved forward slighlty but Naji didn't move and their relative positions remained unchanged. Naji squinted down at Furden. He was beginning to sense something was wrong. He didn't know what but his nerve endings were starting to tingle.

Cann heard Furden ask for him twice and, while he hated the man at the foot of the stairs, he didn't underestimate him. It was an absolute certainty that the terrorist was already on alert. Cann regretted that he wouldn't be able to require Naji to experience the moment of awareness of death, but it was time to act. He had a clear shot at the back of Najils head and raised the Sig to eye level and started the steady pull on the trigger.

Furden's eye caught the slight movement as Cann raised the pistol to fire and on instinct alone shoved Naji back, shouting, "Watch it."

The bullet traveled between Naji and Furden and thumped into the thick mahogany door frame. In an instant, Naji grabbed Furden by the arm and pulled her along with him into the room where Abdullah lay dead.

Cann knew that there would be at least a brief interval while Naji collected his thoughts before attempting to look out of the room or otherwise locate Cann. He also knew that the worse place for him to be was the last place he had been seen. Silently but swiftly he slid his back down the wall of the stairway and turned himself quickly into the study opposite the game room into which Naji and Furden had disappeared.

Naji was not one for inaction. Seconds after falling into the room, he crossed around the pool table and past the television which was still emitting its snowy illumination. He glanced down at Abdullah and assessed his condition and the situation in an instant. Without hesitation, he continued across the room and reached behind several books in the case against the wall and took out a gun - a standard mildly antiquated army issue Colt .45. He popped the magazine out of the handle and checked to make sure it was loaded. Then he slammed it back into the pistol, charged a round into the chamber, and crossed back across the room to where Furden was standing. Without hesitation or a word of any kind, he grabbed her and turned her so her back was to him, threw his left arm around the front of her neck, and walked her to the door of the foyer.

Cann had moved to the back wall of the study and then crawled all the way around the walls of the room until he was positioned at the doorway with his back toward the front wall of the house. Once again he had the advantage of looking into a room with illumination but in this case, the flickering television kept giving out false alarms.

Suddenly, Naji was in the doorway facing out at an angle but with his back to the same wall as Cann's and with Furden held in front of him. He was looking up the stairs to where Cann had been when he fired the shot.

Cann was amazed at how much of himself the big man was able to hide behind the much smaller Furden, leaving Cann no clear lethal shot at the terrorist, who shouted, "Throw down your weapon and come out or I'll shoot the girl." Naji was certain that the American would foolishly comply with this demand. To Furden, he whispered, "Don't worry, I won't. But this will get him to come out." Furden nodded slightly, believing the lie.

Cann said nothing and examined the scene across the foyer from him. Naji was scrunched down behind Furden so that none of his head or torso was exposed to Cann. The only parts visible were his legs and his right elbow which was pointed directly across toward Cann - though Naji didn't know it. In his right hand, Naji held the gun to Furden's head. Cann could easily have shot Naji in either knee which would have made the terrorist go down but such a shot wouldn't have impaired his ability to execute Furden.

One thing was clear. Cann was not throwing down his gun and was not 'coming out'. He knew that for him to refuse to do so meant that Furden might be killed. He knew with greater certainty that for him to comply with Naji's demand meant that Furden would definitely be killed and so would he. It was only in the movies that such saccharine stupidity had a happy ending. He would prefer to see Furden survive this episode - he wasn't sure why - but giving up his gun was the best way to ensure that she - and he - would not.

The longer Cann waited, the more likely it should have been that Naji would move - even slightly - giving Cann a head shot or some other debilitating target. That was the theory. But Naji was like a rock. The time element was starting to turn against Cann. The longer the silent impasse continued, the more likely it was that Naji would start to figure that maybe Cann wasn't where he thought he was and look around. Who knows what would happen then. A fire fight perhaps with everybody dead.

Cann decided to go with what he had. With the Sig-Sauer P229, Cann knew that he had sufficient power to fire straight through Furden and - with proper aim and no deflection - kill the terrorist. That, he decided, would be his last resort. A direct hit to the elbow should disable the terrorist's arm to the extent that he couldn't fire into Furden's head - but maybe not. It was also possible that the bullet could deflect off bone and make its way through tissue into Furden anyway. Oh, well.

Cann made a quick, mostly sincere, wish for Furden's safety and squeezed the trigger.

The bullet shattered the humerus in Naji's arm and caused the nerves to jerk the muscles in a motion like a patient's reaction to the doctor's reflex hammer on the knee. Naji's right arm extended outward and his fingers splayed so that the gun was flipped unfired away from and in front of him.

Furden didn't escape completely unscathed, however. The bullet from Cann's pistol was deflected by the bone in Najils upper arm and traveled slightly downward and roughly along the underside of the terrorist's forearm until it exited near his wrist and entered Furden's shoulder tearing the deltoid muscle but missing the clavicle before it exited out her front. To Naji and Cann, the wound to Furden would have been relatively unnoticeable. But all she knew was that she had been shot by John Cann. More from shock than injury, she fell forward onto her knees – and found her right hand resting on top of Naji's gun.

Naji staggered back from the impact of the bullet as Cann leaped across the foyer. He stopped in the doorway and drew up the P229 and pointed it straight into Naji's face who stared defiantly. Cann recognized the look of a man who knew he was in danger of dying but was not going to stand still and let it happen. Both men knew that the terrorist would act in accordance with the premise that the best defense is a good offense and attack and try to get to Cann before the final hit. He had nothing to lose. He charged. Cann fired.

In the briefest micro-instant before the firing pin in Cann's P229 struck the charge in the bullet casing, Furden fired Naji's gun from a sitting position up at the side of Cann's head. Cann caught the movement in the corner of his eye and the distraction caused him to jerk the Sig just a hair.

When a shot is missed through inexperience or movement on the part of the shooter, it is almost always missed high and to the right of the point aimed at. Cann and Naji both knew this so that, as Furden fired, Cann jerked his head back and away from the trajectory of her bullet. Even so, the missile created a hairline scratch across Cann's forehead.

At the same instant, Naji dropped and pushed to his right and the bullet fired by Cann went just above the terrorist's left shoulder. Naji wasn't done yet, however. After pushing to the right off his left foot, he planted his right foot, changed direction, and came crashing at Cann.

Cann's weight had been shifted back as a result of his own evasive move and, as Naji came forward, Cann extended his right foot a distance behind himself and caught the charging terrorist coming in. Cann used a part of Naji's own momentum to turn him to the right and shove him into Furden knocking her back down and further away. The impact also caused both Cann and Furden to lose their grasps on the guns they were holding.

After striking Furden, Naji turned back to Cann and prepared to charge again. Cann was still in a crouched position and took advantage of that by using the strength in his legs to add force to the upward strike to Naji's face with the heel of his hand. It was a crushing blow and stunned Naji almost to the point of unconsciousness. The terrorist staggered back into the pool table and then, after teetering on the side rail for a brief moment, fell all the way back, his head striking the slate much like Janie's had just two very long days ago.

Even with that, Naji was still not unconscious and he stirred slightly moving his back on the VCR remote which protruded slightly from under his left shoulder. Unnoticed on the VCR front panel, the numbers on the tape display began counting backwards from 2680, at first slowly and then with increasing speed.

Cann's own momentum carried him forward and he ended up face down on the green felt bent over the side rail at the waist. Furden had been scrambling around on the floor trying to find Naji's gun which had been dislodged from her hand in the collision. Instead she spied Cann's silenced weapon under the small desk beside the couch and reached out and grabbed it. She stood up and turned around and aimed the gun directly at the center of Cann's back as he turned toward her and started to straighten up. Cann looked at Furden and put his hands up in front of him. The tape counter was at 1750.

"Hold it, Sara. You don't want to do that."

"Don't I?" Furden said coldly. "You hurt Janie."

"No, that's not true. These guys here are the ones who hurt Janie, Sara. Not me." The numbers flew past 1200.

Furden shook her head back and forth in exaggerated movements. "No. No. I can see what kind of man you are." She waved her left hand around the room. "You shot at this guy and you killed that man," she said nodding at Abdullah, "and you shot me and you hurt Janie." She straightened her arms pushing the gun closer to Cann's chest. "And I'm going to shoot you."

The counter on the VCR reached 400. Naji sat up groggily and rubbed one hand across his head. Then he looked up and saw Furden with the gun pointed at Cann and a small smile creased his face. He moved a bit to his right to add a little distance between himself and Cann just in case.

200

Furden glanced at Naji who nodded to her and then nodded at Cann. "Shoot him. He is the bad man here." Furden looked back at Cann and began to squeeze the trigger.

100

Naji rubbed the blood and cartilage that used to be in his nose off his upper lip and looked at Furden again. "If you don't want to do it, I will be happy to," the terrorist said.

Furden hesitated and then said, "Maybe that would be better."

0

She started to lower the gun to hand it over to Naji when the television screen behind the two men changed from snow to clear action. Furden made an involuntary grunt as the picture came on showing Naji behind Janie with his hands over her breasts and then taking her nipples between his fingers and pulling them – stretching them far out in front of her. And laughing. As the other men on the screen were laughing.

Naji saw her expression change and turned to look back over his shoulder to see what she was looking at. By the time he turned his head back to face Furden, she had put the gun not twelve inches from his face and was already squeezing the trigger. Naji knew he was about to die and he was right. The hand that he willed to grab the gun got no further than an inch from the surface of the table when the bullet blew a small hole in the front of his face and a much larger one out of the back of his head. Once again, his head slammed into the pool table surface - this time it would be the last time.

Furden threw the gun down onto the pool table where Cann gathered it up before she could change her mind.

"I still hate you," Furden spat at him.

"You have no reason to, Sara," Cann said with a gentleness he didn't completely feel. But she didn't care. She turned and walked out of the room and toward the front door where she bumped into Detective Avery who was coming in with the body of Sami draped over his shoulder.

It was all completely beyond Furden's normal frames of reference. She looked at the detective and at the body and sank to the floor in a near trance of helpless incomprehension.

Cann studied Furden for a moment. If this was another time or another place, the solution - the action to be taken - would be clear. Not nice. Not clean. But clear. But this wasn't another time and another place. This was here and now and the decision had to be made in this context. Cann looked at Furden some more. He still didn't know why she hadn't mentioned the silent alarm to Janie. But, for now at least, he knew that she wouldn't have wanted to hurt her. For now that was enough. Maybe someday he would ask. And - regardless of how she felt about Cann and what she wanted to do about it - Furden meant a lot to Janie. Cann hoped that someday, somehow he would be able to visit with Janie and have her know that he was her friend - and had been her friend's friend, too.

Cann came over to the detective and gestured for him to drop Sami on the pool table next to Naji. Then, he told the detective, pointing at Furden, "This one's a loose end. I don't know where she's going to come down on all of this or what she's going to do when - if - she sorts it all out."

Avery looked around the foyer and the room where Abdullah and Naji lay. "She saw you do this?"

"No. She wasn't here when I killed the one in the chair. And believe it or not - I didn't kill the other one." Cann paused for effect as Avery looked at him quizzically before the light dawned.

"She killed the one on the pool table?" he asked incredulously.

Cann nodded. "Shot him point blank in the face - as I assume you can see."

Avery nodded over and over for several moments then said, "So I guess she's in the same boat as me, huh?"

"We all are," said Cann.

Avery nodded some more and then told Cann, "Leave her with me. Maybe this'll be okay."

He walked over to where Furden was still sitting against the wall and gently lifted her by the elbow until she was standing. Then, with his hand still on her elbow, he walked her out of the house. As they went out the door, Cann could hear Avery saying, "Now, don't worry, Ms. Furden, but I have to do this. You have the right to remain silent. Anything you say ..."

Cann looked around the foyer before going back into the game room. He barely glanced at Abdullah, Naji, and Sami as he crossed over to the VCR and removed the vicious offensive tape. He paused in the doorway one more time and then turned and exited the house. As he walked down the front steps, he held up three fingers to the dark car that was sitting on the road a little way down from the house to the west. The figure in the passenger seat nodded to Cann and held up a hand in acknowledgement. Cann nodded back and turned left to walk around behind the house and return to his car the way he'd come.

Chapter Twenty-Nine

The first thing Cann did when he got back to the condo - before he changed or showered or anything else - was destroy the tape. It was a task that could easily have been accomplished by tossing the offending plastic and whatever else videotape was made out of into the trash compactor and letting the appliance crush it beyond repair. Or he could have thrown it on a fire of any size and the heat would have rendered it unviewable even before the flames consumed it.

But in an almost ritualistic attempt at catharsis, Cann pried apart the plastic case that held the tape and then, using the Meulay knife, he cut it down-the center for its entire length and then snipped the two halves into random lengths until he had a small pile of snippets which he burned in a large metal ashtray. For no rational reason whatsoever, he crushed the black plastic case into smaller and smaller pieces before throwing it into the compactor and pressing the button.

He stripped off his clothes and showered. Then - for the second time that day - he field stripped and cleaned the weapons in his personal arsenal and checked the other items of defense and offense he carried with him. It was a task that could have waited but it kept his mind attuned to the matter at hand. Not that his attention was wavering. It wasn't. But he wanted to keep the edge. He wasn't done yet.

403

Cann's plan was to go to Washington the next day. He had considered leaving that night - immediately - but concluded that there was no operational reason for him to rush to the capital. Under the circumstances, there was little reason to think that Al-Asif would come back to Charlestown. He had to have seen that too many things were already starting to point to him and the Middle East Studies Department at the university. Cann assumed that was at least part of why the terrorist had gone to Washington. Cann also believed that there was at least a 50-50 chance that Al-Asif had left with no intention of returning at all - that he had abandoned his erstwhile cohorts to be diversions while he moved on to the next project.

Despite the fact that it was 10:00 PM. Cann placed yet another call to Goren. He would thank him again for his assistance and see if there was more definitive information on Al-Asif's whereabouts and plans. Given the time of day, Cann wasn't surprised that Goren wasn't in. Cann left the phone number of the condo and a message for the Israeli to please call as soon as he received the message.

Cann next dialed a number in Cheverly, Maryland, where the phone was picked up by Marge Cortez.

"Hi, Marge. John Cann here."

There was clear delight in the voice at the other end of the phone. "John, how nice to hear from you. It's been too long." The sincerity in the greeting warmed Cann.

"Yes, it has Marge. I'll be back in DC soon and we'll get together. Dinner. My treat. That's a promise."

"Sounds great, John. We do miss you."

"Thanks. I miss you guys, too."

Marge Cortez was the perfect navy wife and knew when to get to the point. "May I assume you're looking for Jay?"

"Well, not that it's not a pleasure to talk to you but, yeah, I am. Is he there?"

"Just a minute." The line went quiet for barely a second before Marge came back and quickly added, "and don't forget your promise." She went off the line again before Cann had a chance to respond but she left him smiling.

He spent the next several moments picturing the classicly beautiful Marge Cortez locating the movie star handsome Commander Jaime Cortez and getting him to the phone.

A deep baritone came on the line.

"John! Buddy. What's up?" There was pleasure in Cortez's voice that matched that of his wife. Cann was warmed again but the warmth was tempered by Cann's awareness of the perverse contradictions and inequities of life. This couple - and so many others - happy and successful while five hundred or so miles away from them someone else lay destroyed. Cortez. Reston. Beverly Hills - Appalachia. Monaco - Bangladesh. No rhyme or reason. No connections. Just incredible disparity. Cann didn't begrudge them their happiness. To the contrary, he wouldn't have it any other way and if he could make it even better, he would. But at this moment he was struck by an angry realization of the disjointedness of the world. Cann had often mused that John Donne was wrong. At one time or another - maybe most of the time - we are all islands, entire of ourselves ultimately on our own.

Cann lurched out of his acid analysis and tried to match his friend's pleasantry.

"Hi, Jay. How's it going?"

"Good. Good. You?"

"Okay," he lied. But Cann needed to make his plans, so he got right to the point.

"Jay, listen. I need a favor."

"Name it."

"I need to get to Washington tomorrow and, for reasons that shall remain unsaid, I don't want to go commercial and I don't want to drive."

Cortez didn't hesitate. "You're in the Charleston area, right?"

"Right."

"Okay, let me make a call. I - or someone down there - will get back to you ASAP. Give me a number." The two men chatted briefly and hung up.

Cann crossed over to the computer on his desk and modemed up to the secure access computer at Loring Matsen in Washington. He inputted all the codes and passwords to gain entry and then downloaded all the information on CISP that EI had in its files. As far as he was concerned, that was to be the full extent of Loring Matsen involvement in this action. There was no reason for anyone in the firm - including Arthur - to know about any of this.

The downloaded information consisted mostly of what Cann himself had learned from Goren but there were some additions to the database including what he was looking for - the actual physical locations of the office of CISP and other addresses where he might look for Al-Asif. He printed it out and was reviewing the data when the phone rang. It was Cortez.

"Hey, John. It's Jay. Okay, a couple of Cobra's are being shuttled from Charleston NAS up to Quantico at 0930 hours tomorrow. Will that do?"

"Sounds perfect, Jay. Thanks."

"You'll need to check in with a guy named Chubb Maskery who'll be the lead pilot on the mission. He's a good guy and won't ask any questions."

"I don't know if I want to go up in the air with a guy named, Chubb, Jay," Cann joked. "Will there be a problem with overweight?"

Cortez joined in with a chuckle. "The guy collects specialty cars and the name refers to an insurance company. But listen, John, he's a stickler for the regs - no civilians allowed - so you'll have to be in uniform and show your reserve ID to catch the ride."

"No problem."

Cortez paused, then spoke. "John, I don't know what's up and I know if you wanted me to know, you'd tell me. But you do know if you need help - any kind - I'm here."

It was a tempting offer. Cann and Cortez had operated together several times and he was a good man to have along. One of the best. But Cann was determined to involve no one else in this operation. Only his ass would be on this line. This was unauthorized. Unsanctioned. Totally free-lance. It was more than free-lance. It was personal.

Cann knew his friend meant every word. "Thanks, Jay. I do know that. But no. This is a solo. From here on out, forget I called. Marge, too. You haven't heard from me since the last time. Okay?"

"Got it." Another pause. "Except for the part about dinner, of course."

Cann laughed at that. "Right. I'll call soon. And thanks again, Jay."

Cann fell asleep waiting for Goren to return his call but not before he had packed what he would need into a small overnight bag and settled onto the bed with the newspaper he had bought earlier in the day. Almost against his better judgment he read the pieces about the President's decision regarding recognition of a Palestinian State and the frantic Israeli-Palestinian discussions it had engendered. He was truly angered by this President's treatment of Israel. But he had to admit that one of the things that angered him the most was that what the President had said about public perceptions and media manipulations was coming true. The press was trumpeting that this courageous president had forced Israel's hand and dragged them to the bargaining table against their will. As if that country - under siege for fifty years - didn't want peace.

Of course, no mention was made of treaties, and defense pacts, nor of promises or integrity or of the pedestrian concept of friendship. Those things had all apparently become alien concepts in this context. Cann noted that nowhere in any of the articles or news service compilations did the word betrayal or back-stabbing come up. It was as if this were an unqualifiedly good idea that somebody should have thought of long ago to get this recalcitrant school child of a country to stop holding its breath till it turned blue.

Cann also had to give grudging credit – on an intellectual level – to Arafat who had mitigated the disater by suggesting a more graduated approach to full diplomatic recognition starting with an enhanced mission status to the United States. Such status would, however, enjoy the unusual prestige of being represented at the full ambassadorial level with all its diplomatic privileges and immunities.

Cann was jarred away from his global irritations and back to the matter at hand when he read that President Yasir Arafat had named renowned Palestinian advocate and the head of the Center for the International Support of Palestine, Ali Hamanhi, as Ambassador Designate of the State of Palestine to the United States of America.

Cann tossed the paper aside on the bed in disgust and willed his mind to clear itself of the torrent of conjectures and conclusions that caromed about inside his head.

Cann was awakened at 6:00 AM by Goren's call. He lifted the receiver, fully awake. "Cann here."

"John? Zvi Goren." The Israeli seemed in an almost jovial mood even at the early morning hour. "You called me for the third time in two days? Have you made more messes for me to help clean up, my friend?" he joked.

"No. Not yet, anyway. Listen, Zvi. I really wanted to thank you for everything. Did things go smoothly for your people?"

"Yes. No problems. It is clean. There will be questions but there are always questions. No?"

"Yes. And I have one more for you."

"You are insatiable." Goren chuckled. "But go ahead. What is it now?"

"Is Al-Asif still in Washington - at CISP?" Cann asked directly.

Goren was equally direct. "Yes. And to anticipate your next question, he will not be going back to Charlestown. Our information is that he knows the whole operation is blown although he doesn't yet know the fate of his comrades. If we have done our part correctly, he may never know that. Rest assured,

John, that this chapter is closed. My sympathies to your young friend - and you. Thank god, it's over."

Cann's mind involuntarily replayed the tape of Al-Asif's savage beating of Janie. He thought.....but did not say aloud, "No, Zvi. Not yet. It's not over yet. Not quite."

*   *   *   *

Cann's military ID and the two silver eagles on the shoulders of his fatigues - all quite genuine and valid issue to an Army Reserve bird colonel - got him into the Charleston Naval Air Station without difficulty where he was met just inside the gate by Lt. Commander Chubb Maskery. Cann noted that the nickname really must refer to the insurance company Jay had mentioned because Maskery certainly didn't have the bulk to justify it on the basis of his weight.

The slender helicopter pilot leaned over and pulled up the lock on the passenger side of the motor pool vehicle and said through the open window, "Good morning, Colonel. Nice day for a ride, sir."

"Morning, Lt. Commander. " Cann shook his head and smiled. "These ranks could get a little unwieldy. If you'll call me John, I'll call you Chubb." With a two grade difference in their ranks, it was Cann's call.

"It's a deal, sir." Maskery said. "I mean, John."

The flight took just about three hours and was uneventful. On landing, Chubb Maskery offered to check out a motor pool vehicle for Cann but he declined. He would involve no one else in his actions - no one. Instead, he made his way through reception and check-in area and, when he was alone, ducked into a rest room and took off the shirt with the name Cann over the pocket and put on one with the name Billsen on it. He fished the matching full - and fake - set of identifications from his bag with which he would rent a car under the name of someone who had died very young, long ago, and very far away.

Following the route laid out on the triptik he had pulled from the computer the night before, Cann drove up US 95 north until he reached the Capital Beltway where he took 495 west which soon turned itself from a westerly direction to the north. He continued north until he exited the Beltway onto Interstate 66 which he took almost all the way to Arlington. A couple of secondary roads into the McLean area of Virginia and then, just a couple of miles after county road 695 crosses state highway 309, Cann pulled into a Burger King just across the road from a small suburban professional/industrial complex of two and three story red brick buildings. Cann needed to find out as much as he could about where he was going inside the complex and he needed to do so in the most unobtrusive manner possible. It was vital that he get his bearings before approaching the building where CISP had it's offices but that couldn't - well, shouldn't - be done by driving into the complex more than once if it could be avoided. Few things can wreck a surveillance faster than the surveiller blundering around in full view of the surveillee while trying to find what he is looking for. Cann knew that under normal circumstances a single, unremarkable car wouldn't usually be noticed. But these weren't normal circumstances and Cann assumed that, given its nature - and recent events - there was a very good chance that CISP had implemented much more active and ongoing interest in its passerby than your usual friendly insurance agency or other tenant of the complex.

Cann was hungry anyway so he went through the drive-through of the Burger King and then parked in the front of the lot facing across the road to examine the complex while he ate. He knew that CISP was in the "C" Building and was gratified to note that the identifying letters were big and white and readily visible from where he sat. For now, Cann just wanted to observe. He didn't know if Al-Asif was inside the "C" building. He hoped so but he knew that sooner or later he would find him. For now, Cann was going to watch the building and see who came in and out. If he saw Al-Asif, so much the better. If he could take him right away, even better still.

Cann ate slowly concentrating his attention on the relationship between the "C" Building and the "A" Building which fronted on the highway and was the first structure as one entered the complex. It's right rear corner pointed at the front left corner of the "C" building across the main road of the complex, a distance of perhaps only 50 yards. Cann noted that a large number of vehicles drove behind the "A" building which faced him directly from across the road. He also noted that all the vehicles didn't necessarily drive right out again.

At the same time, several cars that Cann hadn't seen go behind the "A" building did come out from there. Cann concluded there was a good sized parking lot behind the "A" building and, since the "C" building was diagonally across from and to the rear of the "A" building, the lot would be a closer and better vantage point.

Cann repackaged the trash from his meal and dropped the bag over the rear of the front seat onto the floor behind. Then he took a right turn out of the Burger King and drove down the road for a short distance as if going back from where he came. When he was well beyond the sight of the "C" Building, he made a u-turn and drove back up the same road to the complex where - looking for all intents and purposes like someone who had business to attend to and knew exactly where he was going - he made a right turn into the complex and then a left into the parking lot behind the "A" Building. He was pleased to see that the lot was indeed large and busy. He was also pleased to see an empty slot in the corner facing the "C" Building with a tree strategically located between his observation point and the building he wanted to watch. He slouched down just a bit in the front seat as much to get comfortable as to lower his profile. He was prepared to be there for a while. Then he leaned over to his right placing the tree directly in front of his line of view. With a slight move of his head to the right or left, he could see the whole front and side of the "C" Building while, thanks to perspective, he remained mostly concealed from any eyes searching from the inside. He adjusted both side view mirrors in and down so that he could see the sides of the car and the ground running alongside. The better to spot a surreptitious approach. He also adjusted the rearview mirror so that he could see any direct approach from the rear of the car. He had no reason to believe anyone knew he was here or what he was doing but ...

While the traffic into and out of the lot he was sitting in remained fairly constant, there was little activity in and out of the "C" Building. In an hour of watching, Cann had seen two people go in and three come out - none of whom were familiar to him by either sight or description. But the inactivity did not lull him into inattention. He was aware of what was going on around him – including the multi-colored delivery van which halted momentarily behind him. Cann saw it come into the lot and watched closely as it pulled up behind and perpendicular to him and then stopped as the driver - who never looked over at Cann - picked up a parcel next to him and checked it for the address and moved on. The van wasn't stopped behind Cann for more than five seconds, if that. Cann checked the side view mirrors, saw nothing, and returned his attention to the "C" Building.

What he didn't see - couldn't see - because virtually every vantage point has a blind spot, was the man who lowered himself from underneath the van where he had been suspended as the delivery vehicle had approached Cann's rental car. It took barely a couple of seconds for the man to drop himself perpendicular to Cann's rear bumper and then propel himself by his elbows, heels, and rear end straight under Cann's vehicle where he stopped and lay completely still for several seconds after the van had pulled away.

The man lay on his back and slowly opened the front of the jacket he was wearing. It had the kind of closure mechanism found in Zip-Lock food bags. Buttons can be clumsy and snaps, zippers, and velcro all make noise. From inside the jacket he took out a foot-long canister with a gauge and valve on top much like an oxygen or propane tank. But this one contained natural gas - without the additive that gives it its telltale odor. As a result, it was odorless and would be undetectable to the human senses.

The man also took out a device that looked more like a cordless toothbrush than the drill it was. On one end, it had a very fine bit where the bristles should be. He calculated where the carpeted floorboard behind the passenger seat would be and engaged the entirely soundless electric motor which rotated the bit until it had made a miniscule hole into the floorboard of the rental vehicle.

Cann had an opportunity - however remote - to discover the intrusion when the bit caught briefly on the tissue like wrapping of the hamburger Cann had eaten. But instead of investigating the almost imperceptible rustle of the paper, he just glanced back and made the uncharacteristically dismissive assumption that the paper had merely settled of its own accord.

The last thing the man under the car took from his jacket was a piece of hose, one end of which screwed onto the valve at the top of the tank and the other end of which was fitted with a pin sized nozzle similar to the kind used to inflate basketballs and other sports equipment but even smaller. That end he inserted neatly into the hole in the floorboard made by the tiny drill. After checking that the fittings at both ends snugged tightly into their prescribed connections, he turned the petcock that allowed the tank's contents to flow into the car. Cann lost consciousness without ever knowing anything was wrong.

*   *   *   *

If Cann were susceptible to nightmares - he couldn't ever recall having one - one he might have at this point in time would involve his waking up and finding himself staring into the wickedly grinning face of Ramadan Al-Asif in a situation where he - Cann - wasn't in control.

That's what he woke up to.

But it was no dream.

Once he started to regain consciousness, Cann came out of the stupor fairly rapidly but he would make no sudden moves until he had checked his surroundings and situation thoroughly. He looked around the room slowly.

Cann had no idea where he was. It might be Building "C". It might be anywhere else in the world for all he knew at that point. He couldn't even be sure how long he'd been out.

He was sitting against one of the walls of a windowless medium sized room - about 15' x 15' - slouched in one of two overstuffed easy chairs covered in green vinyl. He noted that there were two doors into the room - one in the wall to his right and one in the wall to his left - each directly opposite the other. Across the room from where he sat, Al-Asif occupied the chair behind an executive sized desk. The terrorist chief was leaning forward, wicked grin and all, with his elbows on the otherwise empty surface of the desk. The only other piece of furniture in the room was the other green vinyl easy chair which sat angled into the far corner of the room to Cann's right. It was occupied by a man Cann didn't recognize who sat - also slouched - with what appeared to be Cann's P229 dangling loosely in his right hand over the tufted arm of the chair. He was also grinning.

The man in the easy chair casually lifted the pistol and pointed it in Cann's general direction as he spoke in unaccented English.

"Mr. Al-Asif has something important to say to you, Mr. Cann, so please give him your undivided attention, if you will." When he finished speaking, he re-pasted the superficial grin back onto his face.

Cann looked back to Al-Asif with stone-hard eyes. For a moment the two men stared at each other until Al-Asif began to feel a chill. He blinked. Several times. Then he spoke.

"I understand that you would like to kill me, Mr. Cann," Al-Asif said. "Is that true?"

"Yes."

No elaboration was needed. Both men knew that the look had said it all.

"May I ask why, sir?"

Cann didn't answer right away. None of this was making any sense to him. 'What the hell is this?', he was thinking. 'Why are they asking me questions? Hell, why was I even allowed to regain consciousness? These guys have no qualms against killing people. Why were they orchestrating this stupid conversation?'

Finally he responded to Al-Asif.

"I think you know why, Al-Asif, but why are you even asking? Why haven't you killed me already?"

The chief opened his eyes wide and shrugged his shoulders. "Because you are an important man with high connections, Mr. Cann." Al-Asif looked like the snake oil salesman he was trying to be at the moment. "Your death - or even disappearance - would be noticed and a cause of concern."

"Unlike the girl in your house at the university?" Cann monotoned. If it were possible for an iceberg to smolder, that was the emotion that Cann projected at the man opposite. He was like the volcano inside the glacier in Iceland.

Al-Asif tried not to sound dismissive as he said, "That was an unfortunate incident - which I regret." He didn't even look like he meant it.

"Regret doesn't make it. Not even fucking close." Cann knew that under the circumstances it was futile - perhaps folly - to be overly assertive. But there was that - something - about the situation. If he wasn't already dead, they mustn't want him dead. Or he would already be.

He furtively flexed the ankle and calf muscles in his right leg trying to see if he still had the Colt in the ankle holster. Sitting across the room from the other two men, he was visible from head to foot so only the most stealthy moves could be attempted. He couldn't be entirely sure. Sometimes muscle memory played tricks but ... it seemed like he could feel the muzzle of the .380 compact resting on his ankle bone.

Even that raised questions. 'Why? Why did he still even have it? It was inconceivable that they wouldn't have searched him thoroughly while he was unconscious. Unless ...'

"You must understand, Mr. Cann. I didn't know the - shall we say the particulars - of the way your young friend was being mistreated. I certainly took no part in it and I..."

The enormity of the lie yanked Cann back to the present.

"You're a fucking liar, Al-Asif."

"Mr. Cann," the terrorist was almost pleading, "by the time I found out what my men had been doing, it was too late. It was I who directed my associate to take her to the hospital. He shouldn't have put her in the trunk to do so. I agree, but ... my intentions were good. You must..."

As contemptuous of the man across from him as he was, Cann still couldn't believe his ears. "Who do you think you're kidding, you lying....." Cann's voice was choking on the acid that rose from his stomach. His voice was raspy as the realization hit him.

"You didn't know it was being taped, did you?" He spat. "You stupid bastard, you didn't even know."

Al-Asif's eyes widened. "Taped?"

"I saw you beat her almost to death - on tape - all of it. You didn't succeed - but not for lack of trying."

Al-Asif looked cornered. "I don't believe you. I must see that tape."

The idea of this leering monster watching Janie's torture and degradation as if it were a sitcom disrupted the practiced restraint Cann had developed over the years. With no thought to the man across the room holding his P229, Cann reached down for the Colt at his ankle.

It wasn't there. His nerve endings had deceived him.

He looked at the man holding his gun who was watching Cann closely but without any tension. When Cann had reached for the Colt, the man had pointed the Sig at Cann but - what? - casually. Not a sharp move - nor a hard stare. The man hadn't even sat up. He remained casually slouched in the green vinyl chair. Of course, he knew Cann didn't have the Colt – but Cann was used to being a bit more feared – perhaps these people ...

Cann decided to test the issue. He took a step toward Al-Asif.

The man in the chair started to sit up and then all three of the men in the room looked to the door on Cann's right as it opened - and Zvi Goren walked in.

Suddenly some of what was going on made some sense to Cann.

Well, it didn't make sense but he thought he understood.

He looked at Goren who was looking back at him with a sheepish sort of half-smile on his face. "I didn't know what else to do, John. Any suggestions?"

Cann stared sadly.

"He's one of yours."

"For many years," Goren replied. He walked over to the desk and flipped his head at Al-Asif who obsequiously surrendered the desk chair to Goren and walked over and stood in the corner of the room. "The usual sad story," Goren said with mock sympathy. "Our friend here had a cousin on the West Bank who needed a work permit and I got it for him. Then I had him do a few minor things for me - really quite innocent things but things that could be made to look bad - which, of course, I documented. Then I asked for bigger things and when our friend here resisted, I told him that I would spread rumors that he was collaborating with the Israelis - had already collaborated with the Israelils. I had the documentation to support it. And it doesn't take much to convince other Palestinians to do rather nasty things to alleged collaborators. He's been an asset ever since."

It was a familiar story to Cann of how most intelligence assets don't work for ideological reasons at all. Nor for money - although once begun, many figure it's foolish not to accept it. It's frequently a sad story of manipulation and betrayal.

But he felt no sympathy for Al-Asif. Or Goren.

"You let these things happen, Zvi."

Having said that, Cann knew what was coming.

"As you have in the past, John. There's no difference. And now we're on the verge of the biggest coup possible. Al-Asif is second in command to Ali Hamanhi. Frankly, I'm sorry now that I gave you all the information I did. But Hamanhi is about to become Palestinian Ambassador to the United States and we'll have - I'll have - his deputy in my pocket. Can you imagine?"

Cann looked over at Al-Asif who looked worried in general but didn't react to Goren's references to him at all. The terrorist had long ago learned that his humanity didn't exist for his handler.

Goren talked about him the way people talk about furniture or the dead at a wake - they know they're there but they're no longer relevant.

Goren was pressing his point earnestly. "Let him be, John, please. Leave him alone. Imagine the pipeline we'll have." He bore in on what he thought would interest Cann the most. "And I'll share it, John. I don't care what the heads say in Israel. You'll have access to what I get."

"You didn't see that little girl, Zvi. You didn't..."

"But I've seen a thousand like her, John," Goren snapped. He saw the venomous look Cann threw at him and waved his hands in the air.

"No, John, no. I don't want to hear this. I'm sorry. I know you knew her. She obviously meant a lot to you. But the bottom line is that this shit happens a thousand times a year all over the world." He pointed his index finger at Cann. "And you've been involved in it, too." Again Cann reacted but Goren charged on. "Ok. I know. Not rape. Not this kind of treatment. Not torture. I know all that. But dead is dead. Injured is injured. And you've inflicted your share. What makes this different?"

"You already said it. I knew her. I'm not going to lay some deep profound philosophical argument on you. She was a good kid. A friend. Or maybe would have been. I didn't know her very long but I guess I even loved her. I would like to have protected her anyway. That's what makes the difference." Cann nodded toward Al-Asif. "Listen to yourself - the way you talk about this guy. Consider the way you think about him - and treat him. And then tell me a story - I know you'd have lots of them - about how pissed off you are when the Syrians or the Iraquis or the Iranians do the same thing to somebody you know. What's the difference? Some people are on your side and some are on the other side. And we choose. And we identify. And we protect. Or try to. We have to, Zvi. It's called loyalty."

Goren saw his opening. "And you're as loyal to Israel as almost any Israeli, John. Think about what this would mean to our security."

That was a telling argument to Cann. It made sense. Except in the context of what Al-Asif had done to Janie. Once again, it was a matter of choosing sides.

Janie's face flashed in front of him in a macabre before and after scenario.

But then, so did Danny's.

Is this what it came down to? A choice between love and honor?

Cann knew he wouldn't betray Janie. Not if he could help it, anyway.

But for twenty years he had remembered his pledge to Danny Shelanu, "...to rid the world of this curse."

Must he choose?

Suddenly the answer was clear.

There was no choice. When Danny spoke of ridding the world of the curse of terrorism, he didn't mean by surrendering to it. He didn't mean by rewarding it with legitimacy and position. He didn't mean by betraying the hundreds and thousands who had died trying - as best they knew how - to protect the world from it.

And Danny would never have walked away from Janie and what had been done to her - and neither would Cann.

Suddenly it was all too clear to Cann that to fail to avenge Janie would also betray his pledge to Danny - and Danny's honor as well as his own.

Goren watched Cann for a long time and finally concluded that his continued silence was acquiescence. He jerked his head at Al-Asif for him to come across the room and leave with him.

To do so, the terrorist had to cross between Cann and the desk. Within reach. As he passed in front of Cann, Al-Asif looked at him with an evil gloating grin of victory - an openmouthed smile with his lips drawn back over his teeth that made his mouth looked empty in an evil and unpardonable final mockery.

Cann's right hand reached out and grabbed Al-Asif by the throat and pulled the terrorist to him and up against him. The move took Goren by complete surprise but he recovered quickly and with a flick of his right forefinger indicated to the man on his right to aim the Sig at Cann. Cann paid just enough attention to the series of movements opposite him so that he didn't feel Al-Asif raise his right foot off the floor. If he had, Cann would have simply pulled his own foot back away from the terrorist. But he didn't and Al-Asif crushed his heel down into Cann's right instep causing an involuntary lurch which enabled Al-Asif to free himself and bolt across the room. But instead of trying to simply attain the protection of Goren, he went at the man who had been standing there pointing Cann's own gun at him. Al-Asif's intention was to get the P229 in his own possession and resolve this matter once and for all.

Al Asif struck the other man with enough force to propel the other man back against the wall. But just before his head slammed into the wall behind him, rendering him unconscious, he made a split-second decision and flipped the P229 forward - away from Al-Asif and toward Cann.

The terrorist saw the prize sliding into his enemy's grasp and desperately grabbed at the fallen man's coat - and found Cann's other gun, the Colt Mustang Powerlite 380.

Just as Cann was picking up the P229 and Al-Asif was retrieving the Colt, Goren was pulling his own 9mm pistol out of the holster in the small of his back. At the same exact instant, all three men raised their respective weapons and aimed them. Cann pointed his at Al-Asif and Al-Asif pointed his at Cann.

So did Goren.

In an instant, chaos turned to suffocating silence.

"John. Please don't." Goren asked quietly and politely.

"There's no other choice, Zvi. You know that. I'm sorry for depriving you of this professional coup but there's no reason to think that this scum would be of any benefit to Israel no matter what position he holds. You have no reason to trust anything he does. And, in the final analysis, there's no benefit he can give you or Israel that won't immediately be undone by your counterpart on the other side."

"It's the achievement of a lifetime for me, John. Just to get him." Goren was plaintive.

Cann sympathized, but..."I know you think it's corny and don't understand it, Zvi, but there's a kid in a hospital who's not going to get to achieve very much at all."

Cann continued to stare at Al-Asif as the two men stood facing each other with their guns pointed at each other's heads. Cann spoke to the terrorist almost conversationally.

"You know there was a movie several years ago where there was a situation like this and the hero asked the other guy if he was feeling lucky today. Are you feeling lucky today, Ramadan?"

Al-Asif knew how good Cann was. He wasn't sure he was as good and the sweat started to form on his upper lip as he saw the calm professionalism taking over in Cann's eyes. Without looking away from Cann, the terrorist hissed at Goren, "Shoot him, you fool. Shoot him."

Goren was watching Cann's finger. "I will shoot you, John. It will make me sorry, but I will do it."

"Before or after I shoot this bastard, Zvi?" Cann never took his eyes off the precise center spot of Al-Asif's forehead where he knew the bullet would go.

Goren had no answer to the question but it told him that Cann had decided to do this thing even if he died in the same instant that he did it. The Israeli answered softly. "Does it matter?"

Cann nodded ever so slightly and said, "So let's let god sort it out."

The terrorist suddenly swung his aim to his left and pointed the Colt at Goren's head instead of Cann"s. "Shoot him, you idiot, shoot him now or I will shoot you."

Goren didn't even look over at Al-Asif but continued to watch Cann, his eyes growing sadder by the second.

Al-Asif glanced back at Cann out of the corner of his eye and then shifted his eyes back to Goren. For a long moment, the only movement in the room was that of the terrorist's eyes as they darted back and forth from Cann to Goren and back to Cann again.

"He knew about your colleague in Germany, Cann. Did you know that?" Al-Asif tried to shift some of the blame to Goren.

In actuality, Cann had already made that assumption.

Cann said nothing but Goren felt the need to explain - at least a little. "I am truly sorry about that, John. He wasn't supposed to die. We're still not sure why he did. But I am sorry."

Cann just stared at Al-Asif who saw that he hadn't risen to the bait.

Al-Asif's eyes roamed about the room now, not seeing the walls but searching for a way to get through to Cann.

"Goren knew about the girl. He knew what they were doing to her all along." Cann didn't say anything. "He really did. He approved it. He suggested it."

Cann just stared and kept the Sig pointed at Al-Asif's head.

Again, Goren responded to the terrorist's accusation, this time in the negative. "That, John, I promise you is totally untrue." He still had his own gun-pointed at Cann but the pressure he had on the trigger lessened imperceptibly.

Al-Asif's eyes now seemed to be blank - or looking inward searching his memory for something - anything that would make this American spare him.

For his part, Cann wasn't exactly toying with his target. In no way was this a game to Cann. But he knew that every time Al-Asif came up with another ploy - another attempt to save himself - the terrorist revived hope for himself.

And as anticipated - inevitable - as this man's death was, Cann would insist that it be preceded and accompanied by the utter absence of hope. The retribution would not be complete until Cann took that away before he took his life.

Al-Asif's eyes came back to Cann's. He could think of nothing else to say. Except, "I have done nothing that the two of you have not also done." He lowered his gun and opened his hands towards Cann having decided to plead for his life. "What can I do to stop you from killing me?"

"Nothing." Cann answered simply. No explanations. No qualifications.

Al-Asif opened his mouth to speak but nothing came out. There was nothing to say. Then he began to cry. Not quietly but in fearful wracking sobs. And finally - hope departed. Al-Asif knew.

And Cann knew he knew. And fired.

Dead center.

Cann waited for the shot from Goren. But it never came.

Goren continued to hold his gun pointed at the side of Cann's head for a while - but he didn't shoot. He looked down at Al-Asif and then he looked back at Cann. Then he lowered the 9mm in defeat. Goren looked down again at his dead asset like a baseball player looking at a broken bat - as if in it's destruction it had betrayed him.

Goren put the 9mm back into the holster behind him and bent over the other man who was starting to regain consciousness. When he'd satisfied himself that he would recover, he stood up and said to Cann,

"Get your Colt, John, and get out of here. I'll call the men to clean this up."

Cann started to say something but Goren held up his hand. "No, John. Just go. Get out. There's nothing to say."

Cann pried the compact from Al-Asif's fingers and turned to leave.

"And John," Goren spoke one more time, "don't ever call me again. I won't be in."

Cann nodded and left.

EPILOGUE

The peace process in the Middle East continued to progress as both sides continued their forced focus on results instead of procedure and the President of the United States won re-election that year based in large part on his perceived contribution to the breaking of the logjam. Many pundits, however, attributed his re-election more to the opposition party's insistence on nominating a candidate on the basis of party loyalty instead of what was good for the country or even his chances of winning.

The sudden disappearance of the entire Middle East Studies Department at Charlestown University became the instantaneous stuff of legends, taking its place alongside the disappearances of Jimmy Hoffa and Judge Crater. The case remains unsolved. Matters only got worse when Massoud was found hanged in his jail cell, an incident which also remains unsolved. For his part, Cann knew that he had nothing to do with it and didn't know who had. He speculated that Avery may have taken it upon himself to tie up the last loose end but didn't really think the detective would be that cold-blooded. Cann knew it could have been any of the parties involved. Goren for reasons unknown or just in a fit of pique. Other elements of Israeli intelligence perhaps. Even the Palestinians themselves who wouldn't want their new found legitimacy to be tainted by revelations that Massoud could have made. Indeed, it could even really have been a suicide. Who knows?

The largest segment of Charlestown University assumed it was all a nefarious conspiracy of the university administration and beyond that was, of course, racially motivated. The individuals who were actually injured were quickly forgotten as the various factions vied for the mantle of vicarious victimhood and all of the benefits that entailed. Although – or perhaps because - there were rumors that he had some sort of involvement in the matter, Cann was not bothered by the protestors.

To Cann's great surprise, he was not asked to forego the remainder of his year at Charlestown as the Visiting Johnson Scholar in spite of Elizabeth Buffinton's unceasing antipathy towards him for lying to her.

No surprise whatsoever to Cann, however, was Arthur Matsen's immediate and enthusiastic endorsement of Cann's actions with regard to medical care for Janie Reston. Indeed, after hearing the details, Matsen visited Janie in the hospital after which he very unofficially adopted her, overseeing her move to a rehabilitation unit not far from where she grew up and where she endears herself to every staff member for the will she shows in her treatment. Plastic surgeons recruited by Matsen have managed to restore Janie's appearance to very close to what it was before and he makes frequent calls to world renowned specialists he knows or knows of in an effort to find ways to restore or at least improve her ability to hear and speak. He continues to monitor her progress, however slow, and revel in her improvements, however small.

Cann visits her often.